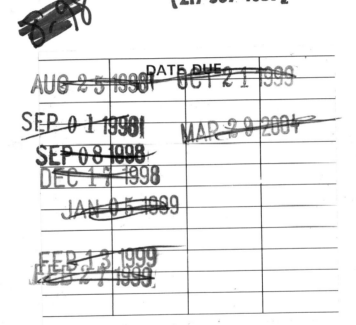

Gaff Topsails

Gaff Topsails

A NOVEL

PATRICK KAVANAGH

VIKING

VIKING
Published by the Penguin Group
Penguin Putnam Inc., 375 Hudson Street,
New York, New York 10014, U.S.A.
Penguin Books Ltd, 27 Wrights Lane,
London W8 5TZ, England
Penguin Books Australia Ltd, Ringwood,
Victoria, Australia
Penguin Books Canada Ltd, 10 Alcorn Avenue,
Toronto, Ontario, Canada M4V 3B2
Penguin Books (N.Z.) Ltd, 182–190 Wairau Road,
Auckland 10, New Zealand

Penguin Books Ltd, Registered Offices:
Harmondsworth, Middlesex, England

First American edition
Published in 1998 by Viking Penguin,
a member of Penguin Putnam Inc.

1   3   5   7   9   10   8   6   4   2

Portions of this novel in somewhat different form have appeared in *Descant*,
The Malahat Review, *Quarry*, *TickleAce*, and *Waves*.

The author gratefully acknowledges the assistance of the Canada Council and
the Ontario Arts Council.

PUBLISHER'S NOTE
This is a work of fiction. Names, characters, places, and incidents either
are the product of the author's imagination or are used fictitiously, and any
resemblance to actual persons, living or dead, events, or locales is entirely
coincidental.

LIBRARY OF CONGRESS CATALOGING-IN-PUBLICATION DATA
Kavanagh, Patrick, 1950–
Gaff topsails / Patrick Kavanagh.
p. cm.
ISBN 0-670-87766-2 (alk. paper)
1. Fishing villages—Newfoundland—History—20th century—Fiction.
I. Title.
PR9199.3.K388G34   1998
813'.54—dc21   97-22192

This book is printed on acid-free paper.

∞

Printed in the United States of America
Set in Cochin
Designed by Kathryn Parise

For Sarah

We are as near to heaven
by sea as by land.

—*Sir Humphrey Gilbert*

Contents

Contents

Gaff Topsails

I

Locomotive

Michael Barron takes hold of the moon.

Gibbous and bone-white, it hangs just above his head. He reaches into the sky and takes the moon in his hand. He grips it in the lazy way that a baseball ought to be held.

He pictures himself standing in the middle of the diamond. The pads of his fingers fall gently across the threads. The batter, the catcher, the fielders, the other team, the umpire, the crowd—everyone is watching him, waiting. Yet until he makes up his mind to throw the ball, nothing is going to happen. It is a grand feeling—being silent, yet being heard—and he wishes that he could stay here in this place and keep hold of the moon for ever.

He yawns and extends his long legs the width of the stern. His shoulders can feel the languorous ocean lifting him up: that is the moon again, working the tides. The closeness of the satellite gives texture to the surrounding sky. Michael Barron can see the real dimensions of the heavens. He can measure the spaces separating the stars. The notion shoots a tingle along the spine of his neck. Without warning the heavens turn bottom-up.

Michael Barron falls.

Spiralling he falls into the sky. The starred canopy is

ripped away, the pit that yawns behind it betrayed. Cold and alone he tumbles, towards the farthest reaches of space.

He tumbles and his brain reels with vertigo. This must be, his mind is thinking, what happens when you die.

In panic his hands grope the dark. His fingers clutch the handle of the widowed oar the lads are using for a rudder. Michael Barron heaves himself bolt upright in the boat.

Sweat drenches his body. His heart thumps against the walls of his chest. His lungs heave.

The night is steady again, and familiar.

He digs from under his oilskins matches and a ready-made, and he lights a smoke. The sweat cools against his skin. Terrors ebb. His roaring heartbeat, his panting subside. Yet he remains vaguely troubled: danger is out there in this night, somewhere.

Pop said to him one time: If you wants a man to believe in God, get him to spend a night in an open punt, off a good ways, off in the deeps beyond the ledge, way out where anything can happen. But Michael Barron already knows well enough the face of God. And whatever is this thing in the dark, it is not God. It is something other—something menacing.

He thinks of when, not many years ago, Pop took him one hot evening up onto the Brow. The old man ordered him to listen. Michael listened, and he felt the ground purring under his feet. The purring did not come out of the land at all: it came from the sea. The child thought it was some monster, some large cat, asleep at the bottom of the ocean, but Pop said it was only a German submarine prowling the coves.

The danger he feels now is more certain. It is inescapable, like that other time, last summer, when he hiked miles across the barrens, alone, just to have a look at the tracks. He stood on a sleeper, between the rails, and although his ears heard nothing, he could feel the vibrations roaring down the steel and across the wood and up into his chest: the train was surely coming. If he stood in this place, sooner or later the locomotive would round the corner and it would kill him. The queer thing was, the deadly faith, the inevitability promised by that narrow band of creosote and shale, gave him a sinful pleasure.

Michael Barron pulls off his glasses and rubs his eyes awake. He puts his glasses back on and tries to make sense of the dark.

The embers of two cigarettes glow from the fore-rooms of the boat: that is only his mates. Like himself, they cannot sleep, and each one is dreaming inside his own mind.

A mile westward, farther than Michael Barron could ever swim, a shaft of light rakes the surface of the calm: that is the lighthouse. Its beam swings hypnotically, the sad watch of a cyclops. It comes round and pierces straight into Michael's eyes and leaves him momentarily blinded. The beam carries on to brush the pinnacle of the iceberg, to illuminate the ice just the way a photoflash might do. Beyond the lighthouse, in the place where the parish is, at the bottom of the cove, Michael sees only blackness.

From deep up in the country, from somewhere in the region of the Gaff Topsails, comes an eerie, mournful wail: there it is now, the inevitable locomotive. You can hear the train only on nights like this, nights when the air is dead still. The sound it makes is that of some great lonely beast, crying out for a mate.

As if in reply, Brimstone Cape, miles down the coast, moans: that is the foghorn. Its echo catapults among the headlands, and slowly dies. And then comes faintly to Michael Barron's ear a hiss and a long-drawn sigh: that is the vast indolence of the North Atlantic—the dozing of the swell against the beaches. In the distance he can see the shoreline softly burning. A salt smell stings the boy's nostrils, and for an instant he reckons it is the odour of his own sperm. But it is only the smell of the sea.

II

Sunflowers

The eastern sky burns.

Reaching hands streak and mount the night, and push aside the black. The bands of silver stop for a time. They brood.

Advancing again, they fill the greys and bestow a texture on the morning. The sky flushes pink, as if echoing the flames of some remote sea-battle.

Shoreward, silhouettes lift. Like loaves of bread rising, full purple contours of hills take shape. Points of land sail boldly at the dawn. Spruce-stands and bogs and beaches appear.

The sea-horizon flashes with green, then bubbles up red. The sunshine leaps and flares, and like a shout from God it spills out at last on top of the broad water.

The face of the calm, which beneath the stars was a dark terrible pool, now slumbers a bountiful blue-green. Blankets of fog hiding in the inlets and hollows evaporate under the sun. The granite air melts. The sun ignites the shelf of sea. The bolt of light torpedoes across the falling tide.

The bubble-eye in the windowpane smoulders.

The curtains whisper. They net the sunshine and billow. A

spider threading down from the ceiling is betrayed by the light. Within the walls, mice scratch. Kitchen shapes arise out of the dim.

The crucified Christ, on vigil, blesses the iron tabernacle of the Waterloo, fluted and whorled and dormant. He blesses the cracked canvas floor, the splits and chunks and the scuttle of dusty coal behind the firebox, the poker, the mitts drying on the line above, the bone and ash within, the teapot and squat black kettle snoozing on the damper, the nursing rocker drawn up to the oven, the sad-iron. He blesses the wellingtons, the new broom, the galvanized gully, the sooty kerosene lamp, the bare lightbulb, the radio gaunt and brown, the rickety whatnot in the corner, the barometer, the embroidered "God Bless Our Home", the Doyle's calendar June 1947, the yellow teeth drowned in the yellow mug, the sailcloth couch and its cushions in repose, the Dodd's almanac hanging by the nail, on the sideboard shelf the missals and harmonica, the sunflowers blazing from the wallpaper. He blesses the table snuggling the window, the birch chairs pushed to the dropleaf, the crumbs of 'lassy bread, the biscuit box, the jamjar, the cups and saucers bottoms-up, the three loaves rising, the knitting half done, the ace of hearts on the checkered oilcloth.

He blesses even the tomcat arching and curling across the oven door.

The eight-day grandfather tick-tocks.

III

The Crows and Gulls Hour

I spiral up. I swirl on the hot wind, up to mid-heaven.

*Here is a snowpeak, just below me. I wheel about, and I glide down.
I slide down the face of the mountain.*

*And then the mountain is no more a mountain. It is a schooner,
and in the sunshine the sails are white.*

The sails burst into fire.

A breath of light touches Michael Barron's face. He shakes
away the ragged edges of a dream. He fixes his glasses in
place on his nose and his eyes open to the dawn.

Gus Gallant bestraddles the standing-room. His hand, gingerly gripping the taut line, is drawn towards the gunnel,
hovers a moment there in suspense, then jerks away with a
rasp and a trailing spray of brine, as if teasing the jaws of
some deep-sea monster. With practised cadence he repeats
the motion. The boat rocks gently like a cradle.

Gus scratches at the crotch of his oilskins. Gravely, mock-
ingly, his dark pitted face peers down upon Michael. He
turns towards Wish Butt, and grins.

Lazily Wish leans his elbows upon the roof of the cuddy.
The roll of his stocking cap conceals his walleye, and his
lobster-red face reveals nothing. He hawks and spits over
the side.

Michael watches the spittle fall upon the face of the North Atlantic and dissolve into the swells of all the oceans.

Like a calm brushed by cat's-paws, the surface of Michael's spirit is barely moved by the things he sees. The figures of his mates, the new colours of the land and the sea and the sky, the pott-pott of a motorboat echoing so dimly he cannot be sure it is even real—all this comes to him from a far dimension. Only the rhythmic swish of water against the hull is close to his ear, and true. Michael Barron looks out upon the world from the start of all things.

He curls up on his side like an infant. He closes his eyes and enjoys the roll and swing of the boat upon the undulating sea. His mind surrenders and falls away from itself. Head over heels he tumbles, back into his eternity of sleep.

An echo startles Michael Barron awake. The sound comes from beneath him, from within the belly of the sea. It may have been a drumroll, or a thundercrack, except that he didn't so much hear it as feel it, inside his chest, like a tiny earthquake.

Of course: it is only the ice.

Around midnight the boys noticed a smell, musty yet at the same time pure, like the air in a vault that has gone undisturbed for centuries. Out of the gloom the white cliff reared up with a ghostly luminescence.

Despite the calm, the berg drifted serenely down the coast. It sailed south, in front of the warning beacon and just past their berth. Michael remembered the story Pop told him once, about the squid-jiggers.

The year 1902 it was. A dozen punts were moored together on the ground. The squid were running fast when someone whispered, "My God." The men glanced up to see a fantastic white schooner. The helm was unattended, but on the deck a lovely young woman, bare-breasted, waved to them. Like a mirage the vessel sailed on and disappeared around the point. But that wasn't the strange thing. The strange thing was that ever afterwards, not one of the men spoke a word of the sight that each one of them had witnessed.

Last night, while the ice mountain sailed past—so slowly you would think it was the berg that was stationary and the boat that was moving—Michael looked for the bare-breasted woman. He heard only the crying of seals. And then the ice was swallowed up by the dark.

Now in the dawn here it wallows, moaning, forlorn in dis-integration, abandoned on the ebb tide just off from the Foot, the southern bill of the cove, where it has grounded on the ledge.

Michael recalls the Mary atop his dresser—the Mary who glows in the dark. He remembers another of Pop's stories, about the berg he sighted on the Banks, June 1905 that was. It bore the precise form of the Virgin, so perfect it must have been carved out by God Himself. Star of the Sea, Pop called it. But here in the dayshine this common thing—a mere basilica—throbs a benign baby blue, while below the wa-ter's surface its greater part slowly falls to pieces.

Gus, slack-jawed, sleeps face down across the middle thwart. The line is still wrapped around his fallen hand and it runs unattended over the side. In the foresheets Wish is slumped like a man sitting in a barrow. His hands are folded before him as in prayer. His cap has fallen off, and his face bears the same emptiness asleep as it does awake.

The pott-pott of the invisible motorboat drums against the sky. The sound might be coming from any bearing, from any of the little recesses that line the shore, from behind any of the island-rocks that rip the surface like teeth. In Michael's ear, pressed to the wood of the punt, the motor throbs like a great pulse, like a heartbeat pounding out of the breast of the earth itself.

The horizontal light falls upon the iceberg squarely and fills the shadows in the jagged pinnacle. Michael Barron studies the ice, trying to decipher its contours, when suddenly the prism sends to his eye a spark, a glance of dark blue. And off there on the North Atlantic, the boy's head fills with the smell of incense. At the same time, under his fingers the rough pine of the rowboat becomes the smooth varnished mahogany of the church pew, and before him blazes not the iceberg at all, but eyes blue behind a veil.

Eastward, a vapour shades the horizon. The mist fuses into aquamarine the greens of the sea and the blues of the sky, so that if a vessel were to come out of that quarter it might seem to drift down from the heavens. The cat's-paws have vanished and once more the water is as clear as a looking glass. Westward, the calm reflects the ochre bluffs that fortify the shoreline, capsizing them, making the cliffs appear twice as high and twice as formidable. At the Head, the northern point of the cove, the beacon that measured the night so languidly is smothered now under the brilliant dawn, and even the lighthouse itself is lost, like a particular stone in a cemetery, amid the cluster of houses that squat behind it.

The night-sky was bottomless and terrifying. The new morning with its vague horizons, its silences and distant sounds, its faraway hills taking shape, even the mass of water below, has its own feeling of space, its hint of eternity. The boys and their little boat, it seems to Michael Barron, are small and infinitely remote. He can see, high where the stars were, wheeling in circles, a solitary gull — a speck. In the bird's eyes the boat must be nothing more than a red speck, stark and vulnerable in the middle of a blue-green void. He thinks of the iceberg, its most deadly portion submerged, yet so massive that, when you drift above it, the deep cobalt seems to pull you down.

Even though surpliced and soutaned, little Kevin Barron shivers.

The frayed rope threads down out of the slot in the belfry ceiling and dangles before the child's face. He reaches forth his priestly fingers and grasps the hemp, and breathes. His feet leave the floor and the boy swings, Tarzan-fashion. But the rope fails to yield. He jumps higher and again he pulls, and this time the rope gives slightly. And yet again. And now, finally, from the steeple, the boom sounds down the well of the spine with the report of a cannon.

The great bell is awake.

Maria, the bell is christened: the nuns told him that. Although he has never seen the huge piece of cast iron, many times heavier than he is himself, he thinks of it as his friend. Again it peals, yet again. The boy clings to the rope and it bobs his flimsy body down and up and down. His surplice billows like a jellyfish. His neatly combed hair flies askew. Pulling on the bell, the boy decides, is like pulling a heavy anchor, not up from the depths of the sea, but down out of the nether regions of heaven—it is like bringing a little bit of heaven to sanctify this sinful earth.

The sounds roll abroad, tumbling over the parish in every direction, madly, like stupendous cartwheels.

The child imagines the cartwheels tumbling through heads—the heads of all the nuns, and the new priest, and brother Mikey and Gus Gallant and Wish Butt, who are out on the water, and Mother, and Pop asleep on the settle behind the stove, and Mr. Casey, and all the cats and dogs and goats and sheep and gulls and crows, and the Pothole Man and his horse, and Martha the witch, and the old pagan Johnny the Light, and many others, perhaps even through the heads of some people Kevin Barron does not know.

Little Kevin Barron would never dare to speak to so many people at one time. To the strangers he would not dare speak at all. But with Maria his voice, each morning he speaks to every one. Each morning he cartwheels through their waking dreams. Each morning he sanctifies their day.

Out of the hollow of the cove, a mere grotto in the fortress that runs fifty miles between the great capes, Fogo and Brimstone, a chime sounds. Across the calm the chime advances like a glass ripple. Then sounds another, another, another. The chimes overlap and grow in volume, and mingle with their own echoes coming off the cliffs so that by the time the sounds reach the boat they roll, and roll again, in light carillon, over the heads of the boys.

That is the voice of little brother Kevin. The chimes remind Michael Barron of the dorymen, the ones who were caught out in the fog and were drawn home by those very bells — through the night the people took turns pulling the rope. Or of the old schooner masters who could navigate the darkness by listening for the echo of the ship's own danger-bell bouncing back to them off the cliffs. Or of the disaster of 1914, when the freezing sealers, miles from their home vessel, gained hope after hearing the ship's gong. Whenever a bell rings, Michael holds his breath and listens.

Now he hears, from over the marshes, the faint squawk of a crow.

It is the crows and gulls hour. It is the lonely stillness in every morning, the lull between dawn and life.

But except for the cairn known as the Naked Man, which outspreads its stubby arms like a blessing over the low-lying Foot, on the whole of the land — that is, westward to the cascade at Freshwater Room, then past the blowhole Barnaby's Gun, around the horseshoe escarpment to the crescent of Admiral's Beach, then up-country to the far peaks of the Gaff Topsails, and again back down this way, miles and miles, to the lookout, the great boulder that stands like a nipple against the sky, down again the long spine of the ridge, along the gravel road that threads among the houses and the sheds and the fishflakes and withers at the grave-yard, then across the trackless waste to the lighthouse on top of the Head—Michael can see not a single figure, not even an animal.

The houses seem farther apart than they really are, the roadway less hilly, the landscape elongated by some perverse prism. He cannot tell the buildings one from another. He remembers how, when he was a child on the water for the first time, his own birthplace appeared to him strange and foreign. Pop noticed his terror, and the old man said: Look out for the cross, boy. As long as the crucifix is plain to the eye, a fisherman can always get home.

Michael locates the spire with ease, and instantly the landscape retreats into familiarity. It is as if God is assembling the world piece by piece in a jigsaw puzzle: there's the school, and Casey's octagon, and here on the rise the palace with its great birch trees, and Academy Hall, and Gallant's house, and Butt's, and the little bridge at the brook.

And there.

Under the low light, the saltbox glows a robin's-egg blue. A wisp of white smoke lifts straight up out of the chimney: the house is awake.

The windows of the house reflect to him, to him alone, the early morning sun. Young Michael Barron must bring up his hand to shade his eyes against the splendour.

The church bell reaches over the rooftops and taps on the window, rattling the glass.

Mary pushes her face into the warmth of the pillow. The girl tries to cling to her dream, but it slips out of her grasp. She can hold on to nothing more than a dim notion of flying. Each toll of the bell rouses her and brings her, dizzy, back down to the solid real earth.

She is vexed. An unremembered dream can aggravate you all day, like a stone in the shoe. She pulls aside the blankets and slides her feet onto the cold canvas. From under the valance she draws out the johnny-pot, and she drops her pyjama bottoms and squats. When she is done she kneels and stares up at the headboard, at the Paternoster that Father carved there. As quickly as she can she whispers her morning prayer.

The ribs of the house groan and crack. The woman is down in the kitchen, poking the stove, stirring the embers awake. Through the louvre in the floor Mary can hear the voice. The woman is talking to the baby. Mary does not particularly want to hear whatever it is she says, so the girl climbs back into bed and pulls the covers around her ears, like a nun's cowl.

She wiggles about in the cool flannels until she finds the body warmth she left behind. Shivering, she places her hands inside her pyjama shirt and presses a palm lightly over the cone of each of her new breasts and hugs herself warm. Within the folds of the bedclothes she can smell her woman's smell, new and sweet and thick.

Her eye scans the burst of sunflowers that paper her walls. It falls upon the statue of Jesus and upon the white candles that flank it on her chest of drawers. The statue is awash in the horizontal morning light. Suddenly Mary remembers: this is it! This is Sweethearts' Day. This is the day that it will happen.

Glory be!

Raw as the tomb down in this. Catch your shivering death. Here, you just lay your little paw on that stove, will you, my love: a bloody block of ice, isn't it? I confess, that man is the trial.

Get away, you bloody cat.

Lord have mercy, yes, your daddy he's the torment. Tore off and forgot the fire, again. But not to worry, my duck. A few junks of wood and a nugget of coal and we'll have the kettle humming right quick.

So how's Doctor John Thomas Mullock this fine morning? Does he know he was laughing in his sleep? Yes he was. Smiling away his dreams he was. But your poor old mother, she had no happy dreams. Stricken with the hag she was, she'll have you know, yet again. Awake all night long, trying to heave off the monster. So, you be a good boy now and give your poor old mother a grand hug, a big kiss, a great squeeze.

Directly we'll go up and roust them sleepyheads. We'll tell them all to say their prayers, or Mommy she'll take the broom to the herd of them. Or Mommy she gives all them snotty-nosed ones the fine tanning.

But first you and me we'll have a gander out the window, try to find your daddy. Upsy-daisy!

Look there — not a cloud in the sky, not a breath on the water. A wonderful grand day is bestowed upon us, thank God. Can you feel the sunshine, my love? The sun is for you. Now you see why the Lord made you, don't you? He made you so the sun would have somebody to warm.

Yes, your daddy, he's out there on the water some place, out there in the back of beyond, Lord be with him. Other side of that big iceberg. Gone in the dory, gone to kill a fat fish for us. Fish for tomorrow. Fish for Friday.

While the bell is still ringing now you and me we'll say a prayer that God He brings your daddy home safe to us. Kneel down here quick and bless yourself, that's a good boy: In the name of the Father. . . .

Sweethearts' Day! She throws back the covers and leaps from the bed and scurries to the window. Against the sharp light Mary brings her hand to her brow. She studies the glass tumbler that rests upon the sill.

Taking care not to jostle it, she examines the egg-white suspended in the water. She searches the swirling threads and strands of coagulum. At first she makes out nothing in particular. But then she sees it: an outline of hull and masts and sails. No mistake. It is the shape of a fishing schooner.

Side by side with the woman's voice, which she tries to push from her head, the lovely smell of the warming stove wafts up through the louvre. Abroad in the morning, the church bell rolls on. The girl sits on the windowsill. She thinks about the word that suddenly means so much.

Fisherman.

Fisherman: it is such a plain everyday word.

Mary presses her face to the window and the sunshine feels like the palm of a hand against her cheek. Everything outdoors seems fresh and new. Even Father's old fishflake, rickety and splayed atop a thicket of knotted posts, from this angle looks like a living crab. She half expects to see the frame pick itself up and scrabble across the landwash. Not a stain of weather inhabits the sky — only the bright moon and the clear blue, the very thing. The lighthouse down on the point stands stark and bleached, a pillar gleaming. A red punt far outside, off the ledge, drifts underneath the belly of the sun and slides into the bolt of flame on the sea — maybe it is the same boat she heard last night, in the dark. The water is just as calm as it was then.

And the berg is still where it was then, stranded just off the Foot. With the low sun shining through it the ice is translucent, like the dull flickering glass of a vigil candle. The peak of the berg shoots a spark to Mary's eye. It is winking. It is saying to her: Yes, this is the day.

Unmindful of the cool air, she opens the window to the morning. Instantly it comes to her nose: the scent of new lilacs blooming from the back garden. For a moment she fancies that she smells, too, the salty tang of spawning capelin. She surveys the beaches for tell-tale signs of the little fish, but the gulls are roosting and untroubled.

She holds her breath and listens.

Between the peals of the bell, her room fills with the surge and fall of water against the landwash. The sound is hypnotic, and she thinks again of the capelin. Tonight, surely, thousands, tens of thousands, will cast themselves up on the beach. Tonight the tide will caress their seed. She listens to the sound of the sea stroking the earth, tenderly, at the narrow band between the tides, the ever-moist zone, the special place where the land and the wash are one.

A crow settles on the church spire. That means that nobody is about on the road. There is no one who might see her. Mary unbuttons her top and spreads it open to the sun and allows the light to warm her new body.

Gelid porcelain jolts his flesh. In the shadows of the privy his breath steams. The austere grille gives the enclosure the gloom of a confessional. Patches of sunshine sift through the screen, or else the light enters in slivers by way of the chinks and the knotholes in the walls. It reveals the cobwebs and the rusty nails, the weeds growing out of the floor.

The church bell rings near and loud. *Vox Dei,* the priest says to himself—and chuckles feebly at the notion. The notes resonate within the sounding-box of the outhouse, crowding close, relentless, one upon the next, loud and near, taking possession of the enclosure. Yet he hears nothing but hollowness. It is the same hollowness he used to hear in the *kundu* drums. The young men would shuffle up and down the football pitch, and pound away, hour after hour, day after day, monotonously, for no reason that he could fathom. Now, as then, he cannot tell if the hollowness inhabits the sound itself, or if his soul has merely painted it so, in the way the face of a stranger, casually encountered, is sometimes infused with one's own emotion, one's particular feeling of the instant.

In the lull between the reverberations, the cell magnifies the buzz of a fly. A hard foul coldness wafts upwards and engulfs him. He remembers how, when he was a child, he believed that the Devil betrayed himself by the chill of a room. He remembers how he would suffer the terror of dying in his sleep. His nostrils could smell the raw sulphurous ash, the stink of the ash-pit of eternity, and in the darkness of his bed he would fear that some awful being was about to reach up and drag him down. . . .

In dread he kicks open the door. Belting his trousers as he runs, his shirt-tail billowing rearward like a cope, he hurtles from the foetid enclosure and into the bright morning. He steps round to the side of the outhouse and, perspiring, collapses against the clapboard. As he recovers his breath, he smiles weakly at the ridiculous image he surely would make — if anyone were about to see him.

The sunshine presses his forehead. The door of the privy, half-hinged, totters drunkenly from the sash. The low light reflects off the gloss of the crescent and sharply stabs his retina. He shuts his eyes, wearily.

His mind sees a lingering shadow.

Something is there, on the water. Something odd.

He opens his eyes and shading them with his hand he squints oceanward. Yes indeed. A new iceberg.

This one is late, the last for this season, probably. Yesterday it was nowhere in sight. You would think that it had ascended out of the sea, like a volcano. The priest finds the shape of it faintly disturbing. He frowns.

He pulls out a cigarette and lights it.

Not a breath stirs the ocean. Even though he is far from

the shoreline, still he can hear the sound the sea makes rubbing against the land: it is like a long train moving very slowly. The only life out on the calm is a red rowboat, a mere chip of wood drowning in the glare, far off. Among the houses and stages and fishflakes that ring the cove the priest spies no movement. The road is empty. In all of the parish he can spy but one smoke—the chimney with the chair.

Years ago—the memory is painful—he used to overlook Dublin in just this way. He would arise early, and cast his eye along range upon range of shuttered windows. She is there, somewhere, behind one of those, he would say to himself. Whoever she is.

An awful sadness takes hold of him. He drops the cigarette unsmoked and sets out determined to find Jackman.

Moving delicately, like a brittle puppet afraid of unhinging his limbs, he crosses the yard and comes to a halt near the carriage house. He bends and parts a bramble of alders, still dew-damp, and pricks his hand against a splinter. He searches under the branches. A lambent smile, faint as moonshine, brightens his pallor. He raises himself upright and inhales deeply and he breaks out, uncertainly, in tenor:

> *When ʃun rayʃ crown . . . thy pine-glaɔ hillʃ,*
> *Anɔ ʃummer . . . ʃpreaɔʃ her hanɔ . . .*

Out of the bush lopes a large black dog, tongue lolling, tail wagging, stinking. The priest greets the animal with a slap on the haunch.

"Aye, Jackman."

The dog bounds away and ambles towards the outhouse. Against the corner of the structure the animal cocks a leg. Vapour rises from the stream of piss. Then, snout to the sod like a warthog, the dog ignores the man and snuffles off again to disappear under the bushes.

Deeply the priest sighs. He turns and enters the back porch of the old mansion that the people here call the palace.

Soon he emerges, bespectacled and collared and cassocked and hatted. In his right hand he wields the cane of stout blackthorn that he discovered only this week, dusty in the top loft. In his left hand he dangles by the tail a raw tomcod.

He whistles into the alders. The dog does not show.

Daintily the priest tosses the fish towards the thicket. Instantly the dog bursts forth and with a low growl it pounces. Crouching like a sphinx, the animal traps the fish underneath its forepaws and gnaws at it unpleasantly.

The man advances and stoops and pats the dog benignly upon the shoulder.

"Aye, Jackman, you old hero!"

The dog snarls from the side of its jaw. Glowering back over its shoulder, it retreats with the fish into the bush.

Prista Wetman, yumi wantok—Father White Man, you-me one-talk. You me one family. How the priest would love to hear those sounds, just now.

He peers down the incline of the white-pebbled land that the people in this place exalt by calling it the avenue. Somewhere beyond the birch grove, in the vicinity of the church, a crow caws. Beyond that, in the far distance, the gravestones gleam under the sun like rotting teeth.

Within his abdomen the knife begins its morning work. To and fro it rips, hacking and shredding, hollowing out his insides, the way a sago trunk is devoured. He bends slightly and leans upon the cane and waits. The blade, which has been part of him for decades, never breaks the skin, and no one but himself knows it is there. While he waits for the spasm to pass, he thinks: of the holy trinity of cures— marriage, alcohol, suicide—only two are left to him. In his feeble way he smiles again, as if he had told himself a joke.

The pain eases. He straightens and gathers his body and, joining his hands at his back, he sets off down the lane, down the tunnel formed by the overhanging birches. Behind him in the pebbles his cane drags like a dead branch.

A miracle! . . . Sister, come quickly!
What do you want, Sister? It's late. The bell is ringing.
God help us! A miracle! . . . Could this be the work of the Lord?

Johnny the Light rises fully clad from his pallet. Sleepy, tormented by fractured dreams, he ascends out of the cellar-gloom of his lighthouse.

Wheezing and coughing, the old man hobbles his bent form round to the sun-warmed face of the beacon. The sudden brilliance blinds him. Towards the dawn he shakes his fist and in his rasping voice he stutters:

"H-H-Hushta!"

His lighthouse garrisons the beetling Head. He steps to the brink of the precipice, and clumsily his maimed fingers unbind the length of rope sustaining his trousers. He drops them to his ankles and squats behind a nettle-bush and urinates, in the manner of a woman, over the edge of the cliff.

Johnny the Light sniffles and spits. After arranging his clothing he leans against the lighthouse's weather edge. He inhales a piece of the morning. He rolls the cool air over his tongue like blueberry wine, smacking his lips, tasting. Behind, distant, the ringing of the Mass bell echoes in the bowl of the cove and comes to him from odd directions. He turns his head to bring about his left ear, the good one. His eyes, through the film that veils whatever he looks upon, perceive hazily the triangular form of the new iceberg, white and gleaming across the water.

A quizzical expression grips the old man's face, as if he

does not believe what he sees. Stock-still he stares. With sudden agility, he lurches round to the landward side of the lighthouse and ducks under the ladder and is swallowed by the low dark door. Instantly he reappears, bearing in clasped hands before his eyes, excitedly, as if it were a monstrance, a bottle of navy rum, uncorked and half empty. He raises it high and draws a long gurgling draft.

"G-G-Glory be to God!" he shouts. "There's our ship! Come along, lads! We're s-s-saved!"

After he has rung the great bell for fully five minutes, little Kevin Barron releases his hold on the rope, but the rope, ghost-fashion, continues to rise and to fall, and the bell, as if it has a mind of its own, rolls on and on, and thunders three times more.

In the stern of the red rowboat offshore, Michael Barron hears the chimes stop. The echoes come following behind, bouncing this way and that way off the cliffs. But before long the echoes too fall silent.

IV

The Landlocked Archipelago

In the beginning God says: Let there be light.

In the beginning God creates the heavens and the earth. He makes the world according to the beauty of His divine plan, and He blesses the world with living things. He blesses the earth with the birds that fly in the skies, with the fish that swim in the sea, with the trees that yield seed and fruit across the land, and with woman together with man.

For six days God works. At the end of the sixth day, He tosses the refuse of His labours into a rubbish heap. The debris falls in the north salt seas, far from the remainder of His creation.

On the seventh day, God rests.

Time passes.

God's rough pile of scraps and leavings, cast away at the edge of nothing, abandoned beyond all horizons, suffers the gentle erosion of wind and rain and tide. The mass of debris sorts and settles itself until it comes to adopt the softly rounded contours of a single territory—an island.

A hundred thousand years ago, for reasons that are still unknown, smoke and ash gather in the air. The dust dims the skies above the earth, leaving the sun a pale disk that shines down only gloom. Winds blow from the polar regions and all latitudes are chilled.

Blankets of frost smother the island. The frost wedges itself into every fissure in the bedrock. It sets about shattering the surface granite to flint and rubblestone. Echoes of booming detonations fill the air, but no ears hear these sounds.

On the higher levels snow falls, for centuries without pause. The snow grows heavy upon the land. It collects until the strata underneath crystallize into an ice that is pressed harder than the hardest rock. Inch by inch, the rock-ice fills the basins and cavities and hollows of the island. It levels the interior to a grey plain. Across this plain, which glows eerily under the moonlight, nothing moves but the wind and the driven snow.

The snow falls and the surface of the ice-plain piles higher. Eventually, a strange kind of life appears: the ice stirs awake. Frozen waterfalls spill out and with infinite slowness they stream down off the plateau.

Tendrils of the marbled cascades flow in every direction from the central plain. At first the glaciers occupy the valleys. They give the appearance of a spiderweb snaring the land. In time the ice swells and spreads and, like a ponderous quilt miles thick, contains the island completely.

It might appear, were there a bird high enough to see, that the island is entombed—is dead. In fact, underneath the surface of the quilt the ice continues to advance. It moves with small sudden pulses, each one the breadth of a hair. Under its own weight the ice groans, shudders. At every tiny surge in its tortured course the earth shakes.

The ice wields embedded at its underbelly the wreckage of rock-crumble that it has collected. These fragments rip channels into the bedrock, or else themselves become faceted and grooved by the scoring action. Afterwards, sand and silt and meltwater polish the bedrock to smoothness. The ice strips bare the terrain. It even plucks massive boulders and carries them off, in the way a child might gather pebbles.

With relentless malice, the ice hammers and tears at the face of the island.

Each of the ice-rivers bears down upon the salt water. Like a crystal dragon it presses across the foreshore and beyond the strand and for some distance along the seabed. It moves forward until its tongue is buoyed by the water. The ice groans and buckles, makes a rumble and a crack and a roar, and at last, after so many immensely slow years of confinement, a titanic calf is born.

The new berg wallows in its own waves. Behind it, another colossus breaks free prematurely and plunges into the deep. This one reappears in a tumult, and only after a display of bobs and rolls does it settle into equilibrium. Next, an underwater spur cuts loose and without warning launches itself to the surface, waterfalls of foam glistening down its blue sides.

One by one the icebergs drift seaward, moving boldly in the face of the wind. Together they form a crystallized world, complete unto itself, silent. Among their shapes are fluted statues, serrated and turreted castles, pinnacled basilicas, even entire islets bearing caverns and tunnels and ridges and rolling hills and crested mountains. They sail through a smoky gloom and over the horizon, southward, with all the majesty of a doomed armada.

After thousands of years have passed, after measureless leagues of glaciers have formed and migrated to the sea and given birth to countless icebergs, the atmosphere thaws.

Bright light fills the skies. The sunshine penetrates the glaciers and they glow and start to melt. The ice wilts and re-

treats. With the rearward slink of a cat each glacier withdraws, twisting and shrivelling back up the same valleys
down which it earlier spilled. In the amphitheatres that for
so long were their womb, the glaciers dissolve into neat circular lakes, and so die.

As though the smoke has lifted in the aftermath of some
dreadful battle, the melting ice lays bare a disfigured terrain.

The ice-claws have corrugated the earth and left it grotesque and frightful. They have deepened and widened the
valleys and out of the bedrock have gashed massive new
trenches, elongated V-channels gouged in the parallel lines
of open graves. The land is covered with hideous veins of a
greenish sea-blue, the colour of the gelid water that fills the
new troughs and craters. This water bears not the sweet
smell of fresh rainfall but the acid suggestion of slush, infused as it is with a turquoise powder, the gritty rock flour
from centuries of grinding. The number of new lakes and
ponds and pools is so great that a panorama of the island's
interior yields more water than dry terrain. The mangled
hinterland has become, in fact, a kind of island-studded sea,
a landlocked archipelago. Where the earth shows itself here
and there among the waters it is usually in shades of grey.

In dropping its load of rock debris the receding ice has
moulded gruesome relief forms. Serpentine eskers of sand
and gravel with steeply sloping sides and sharp crested
ridges curl now in cicatrices towards the horizons. Oval
hills, laid down in the direction of the ice movement, give the
terrain a blistered complexion. Combinations of drift deposits such as drumlinized till-ridges and ribbed and fluted
ground moraines only embroider these scars. In many places
the flesh of the earth is slashed by ragged outcroppings that
resemble raw sores. All of these serve as dams to confound
the pattern of the lakes and streams, so that a landscape that

might have been filigreed like a Celtic jewel is instead left ghastly and repulsive.

The outcroppings ascend towards the interior to become bony ridges that themselves climb to meet a long range of bleak hills. In these fields of barren rock the chiselling action of the ice has been vicious. Glacial tributaries, slicing less deeply than the main river, have formed hanging valleys at the intersections, and down each of the vertical cliffsides now tumbles a pale and lonely cataract. Against the sky stand silhouetted the horns, the grim saddleback passes, the cols and glens cleaved in ridges where the ice-rivers have leaked, the freakish paps of upstanding bedrock atop a rounded summit. At the innermost recesses of the island, sawtooth mountains command the sky like the spires of a lost windjammer.

The wasteland is strewn with boulders. Scores lie scattered across the barrens with the abandon of spent cannonshot. In other areas, the stones were released in orderly fashion, in far-flung trains of erratics, as if the ice carefully marked the path of its retreat. Often, too, a solitary megalith crops out atop a bare, isolated knoll, where it sits like an anchorite, aloof and holy.

So it is, after the ice has finished its tormented ploughing and gnawing and etching, that the grim and austere and grandly remote island is left utterly different. The granite is monochromatic, grey and obstinate, a haggard stone. It is the dull hard edge of the earth. All nakedness and wind-blown barrens, reeling crags, raw peaks, it is a barebones of a territory—a penitential place.

On every land's-end, monstrous capes jut into the sea and soar skyward. They loom out of the fogs like forlorn sentinels. They are watching for God, waiting for Him to return to bless the land He has so long deserted.

V

Consecration

One morning, suddenly, the winds collapse.

Sickly yellow haloes ring the sun. A swell lumbers under the sea. Deep in the submarine trenches, whirlpools eddy and flare. Vapours gather above, and from out of these mists waterspouts reach down, hover a moment, then brush at the ocean's grey face. Across the calm a few gusts skitter in panic. Restlessness stirs at every quarter.

Around midday the salt winds return, in earnest.

The sky darkens in the east. A hideous black cloud appears above the horizon. It towers in the air like a volcano born of the sea. Composed seemingly of some solid material, it rolls upon itself, flinging pitch-black streamers far in front.

The winds mount. The ripples become a chop. Scud races aloft. Offshore, foam flecks the slate sea. Whitecaps topple forward upon themselves, advancing at full gallop in perfect battalions. The air bears an electric charge.

Led by the rabble of wild tumbling cloud, the black roller sweeps overhead. The air turns dark and cold. The cloud hurls down crackles of lightning. Every colour drains from the earth. With a simple fury the storm bursts upon the island.

The blast howls and whines and keens. The winds shred the snowflakes into crystal thorns. A blizzard of needles cuts the dark. The winds overrun the coastal ramparts and trample beyond. They rake the barrens. They pierce the rocks. They strip the land of every particle too feeble to resist. Nothing remains but the skeleton of the earth.

Meanwhile, the sea is a monster. The water gathers itself, growling, falling back to such depth that the trough exposes the ocean floor. The liquid mass lifts and heaves ponderously and rears up, at its high point stops and then, roaring, tumbles forward, gaining momentum as it collapses, the wind whistling and whipping the spume from the brow of the avalanche, a scream made visible, until the wall of ocean thunders in a joyful rage against the cliffs.

Bluffs crack apart with nauseating crump-sounds. The breaker submerges gaunt outlooks that normally dominate the sea. Jets of water spew out of niches and chasms and blowholes. Whooshing geysers erupt up the perpendicular face of the rock and discharge shards of granite to crash back to earth far beyond the reach of the wave itself. Salt-spray catapults into the upper reaches of the wind and is carried far across the territory. Even while airborne, the sea drizzle freezes solid. The sleet glazes blue the bare bedrock and the newly fallen snowdrifts. The air tastes of brine.

Stunned by the concussion, the sea staggers backwards. Black pyramids reel about aimlessly, colliding one against another. But soon the water growls again, and again the winds scream for vengeance and the stumbling sea coils itself for another charge. From the shore all the way back to the horizon there is no lull, no truce.

Into the next morning and the next and beyond, the storm shrieks. Both the daylight and the darkness are shrouded with blinding chthonic shapes, madly churning, all deranged, all a moaning terror.

After nine days and nine nights of this horror, the weather breaks.

The sun lifts in a blue sky, cloudless and cleansed and drenched in light. The air is spacious and the atmosphere strangely dazed. Out of the east now comes a soft lime breeze that warms the shores of the island. At the horizon a speck of white appears.

It is a sail.

VI

The Paradise Stone

Wish Butt makes the sign of the cross.

The boy mounts the bow of the punt, bends, grips the grapelin by shank and crown, hoists it above his cap, staggers, inhales deeply, and in his shrill voice bellows across the water towards the detail of houses roosting on the cliffside:

"DEPART FROM ME, YE CURSED, INTO THE EVERLASTING FIRE!"

With that, in the style of a harpooner, he launches the grapelin.

The iron claw punctures the ripple with a great roil of bubble. The trailing hemp, bearded with kelp, uncoils snakelike from the roof of the cuddy, spirals madly over the gunnel and runs vertically—fast, faster, ever ever faster—until, just when it seems the loose tail will hurtle over the side and be lost, it expires, limp. In two vicious motions Wish tightens a clove hitch on the stem, as if strangling the throat of the punt. Under the light westerly idling off the land the rowboat with a soft jolt comes about, hard and fast. Placidly it swings on the rhode.

Around his head, lasso-fashion, Gus Gallant whirls the jigger, a leaden fish sprouting from its maw a pair of evil flukes, like a tomcod trying to swallow a tiny anchor. Coolly

Gus plops it into the sea. He studies the steeply arching line, feels it slide across his fingers until it slackens and, satisfied that the hook has reached the bottom, stretches wide his arms in the manner of the crucified Christ to measure the fathom of drawback. He wraps the line twice around his palm and commences his teasing, sawing motion.

Gently the boat rocks.

"Yes by the Jesus. More goddamn fish out here than you can shake a stick at. . . ."

It is Wish who speaks. He perches astride the bow, like a gargoyle in the saddle, wellingtons outboard, toes brushing the ripple. He has picked up the shotgun and he aims it this way and that upon the sea surface, pretending. He sits back-on to his mates, and his voice comes to them in a faraway drawl.

". . . It's the truth. Johnny the Light, he's after telling me."

Gus responds by ripping thrice upon the jiggerline. Each rasp scores a fresh notch in the wood and arches a geyser into the midship-room. It appears that the boy is trying to saw the punt in half.

"Johnny the Light! Huh!" he snickers. "However much he knows about fish, the left cheek of my arse knows more."

Gus turns to Michael Barron, who is curled in the stern, and nods scornfully back in the direction of Wish. Somehow Wish senses the mockery that is directed at him, because without looking he jerks his thumb at Gus, violently, obscenely. But Michael is oblivious to this exchange, for his soul is lost in the west.

Lazy clouds like jellyfish drift down on the wind. From the Gaff Topsails their bright shadows cartwheel across the land. The shadows brush the lookout, and slide suddenly fast down the slope of the ridge, and wiggle spookily through the parish lanes. They pass over the houses, the barns and woodsheds and privies, the lilacs blooming purple everyplace, the clotheslines where flannel sheets, pink and white and green, wave like flags. They pass over men boiling pitch and hammering lobster pots and caulking dories, over women weeding gardens and picking eggs and laying fish on the flakes. They pass over the Pothole Man and his nag and dray inching down the road. They pass over the cross on the spire of the church, the school where scattered dabs of colour converge from both directions on the gate, the convent, Casey's sprawling octagon and the palace and Academy Hall, the forge and the graveyard and the lighthouse.

The shadows touch reverently the saltbox of robin's-egg blue. They touch the chair that sits on the roof. They touch the smoke that curls like incense from the chimney and spirals seaward, in Michael's direction, on the soft west wind.

"God's truth. Over that way," Wish aims the gun, "you marks off your cross-bearings by the church and the titrock, and over this way by the south one of the Gaff Topsails and the waterfall in Freshwater Room. And there you are: right aboard of her. Smack on top of her." Wish tears a splinter from the cuddy roof and he picks at his teeth. "Johnny the Light, he's after telling me: There's more fucking fish on this ground than you can shake a stick at."

"I suppose," says Gus, "he's after telling you to line up by that junk of ice too."

Still aground just off the Foot, perhaps a half-mile from their berth, the berg soars boldly out of its own leeward calm. Michael watches the mirror pool of sea. At any moment a block of ice as big as a house may hurtle up and shatter the glass.

To allow for his walleye Wish skews his head, and this gives him the appearance of trying at once to watch the ice and to listen for any sound it might make.

"Tell us, Butt, you whelk," says Gus to Wish's back. "When you are ever after seeing that old boo out on the water? I never seen that aboard a boat. Not the once in my life."

Wish spits something into the sea. "Well, he must have been aboard a ship once. How do you suppose he got to the Front? You think he walked on the water?"

"Everyone knows he was aboard a ship. And sure, he was a tallyman on the Banks too. But was he ever aboard a *boat?* Butt, my son, that loon is only pulling your leg about the fish. Johnny the Light, sure," Gus speaks matter-of-factly, "he's cracked."

For a long time Gus draws upon the codline in surly silence, then abruptly he drops the line and stands bolt erect.

"Look! There's nary the goddamn fish way to Christ out here. We listen to that old drunk and by God we'll be the highliners of sweet fuck-all. Pretty shitty show spending the whole night on the water and not hauling one Jesus tomcod."

"Well, no wonder," says Wish, straight-voiced. "You're the jinker, you are, for talking about how much you're after catching."

Giggling softly, Wish rests the gun across his lap. He brings forth from different pockets underneath his oilclothes matches, papers, a pouch of Target, and a dirty handkerchief. He spreads the handkerchief over the stem as a priest might the veil over the chalice. He plucks a paper and holds it aloft in his right hand, as a priest might the Host, then sets it on top of the stem. With similar gestures he withdraws two more papers and lines them up side by side. They look like little white dories, moored side by side in back of the wharf. He unwraps the pouch and pinches three miniature haycocks of tobacco and drops one into the middle of each paper. With one eye on his task and the other vaguely on the iceberg, he speaks with indifference.

"Guess what Johnny the Light says to me . . ." Wish picks up a paper and with his forefingers he pokes and prods and

presses the tobacco to a reasonable uniformity. Tentatively
he folds one edge, tests the affair between forefinger and
thumbs, gently, as though measuring the texture of silk, then
sets it on his thigh and rolls it against his trousers until it
forms a cylinder. ". . . He says the fish is what makes the
waves on top of the water . . ." He runs it like a little harmonica along the wetness of his tongue, seals it, nips its
straggle-ends and drops them into the pouch, and places the
cigarette in the corner of his mouth. ". . . Millions of goddamn fish wagging their tails."

With a theatrical gesture of his free arm Gus indicates the
well-rippled sea. He snorts, and viciously he yanks upon the
line.

"And you know what else?" Wish speaks from the side of
his mouth. Deftly he rolls a second cigarette. "Won't eat fish,
Johnny won't. No sir." He places the cigarette in his mouth
alongside the first. "Says you don't know what in Christ's
name the little bastards get on with down there in the dark."
He rolls the third, and this too he places in his lips. "Chewing on God knows what. Breathing their own piss."

Gathering up the handkerchief he shakes the fallings into
the pouch. He strokes a match along the stem and ignites
two of the cigarettes. The flame, still robust, he tosses into
the sea, which it scalds with a hiss. He strikes a fresh match
and lights the third cigarette. Momentarily he is headless in
a fog. "Johnny says you can't trust a goddamn fish as far as
you can throw him." Wish hands two smokes to Gus, who
passes one forward to Michael. "No sir, Johnny won't lay
fork to any fucking fish. Not so much as a capelin." Then,
Wish speaks with false seriousness. "Yes, by God, Gallant,
you're right! Now that I thinks of it myself, I allow it: the old
boo is cracked."

"Hushta Johnny!" Gus mutters fiercely, eyes bulging,
mocking. "Hushta! Divil haul ye!"

The three boys smoke.

Gus falls into a listless rhythm.

Wish yawns and gazes towards the pott-pott sound of a motorboat hiding somewhere in the cove.

Michael leans over the transom and shades his eyeglasses against the glare coming off the sea. The triangle of calm just astern forms a window in the ripple so that the ground far below is visible to him.

He sees a corrugated landscape, a panorama of dark caverns and trenches and crevasses broad and deep enough to swallow a church, of reefs and sinkers bristling up on fractured gleaming light and seemingly threatening the hull of the tiny punt. The bland sea-shelf, before this moment sustaining the boat as would a cushion, in Michael's eyes has collapsed underneath the keel. In its place rears up a terrain of jagged fearful aspect: the raw bones of the earth.

"Hey, Professor!" Gus in his heavy voice bawls sternward. "Catch sight of a fin?"

The punt wheels on its mooring and instantly Michael fancies himself up in the sky, clinging madly to a kite, a kite soaring high above the corrugated ridges and valleys of the Gaff Topsails. Tightly his fingers grip the woodwork of the stern. But just as suddenly, with the motion of the boat, his window is swirled, opaque, the calm broken, the fearful ground far below lost now to his sight. Again the three boys are nestled safe atop the pillow of the sea.

"By the Lord, they put the right name onto it when they called it cod," Gus speaks to no one in particular. "It's all a goddamn cod."

"The fish they are lazy," says Wish. "Anyhow, a bad start is sign of a good finish."

"Shut up, Butt, you stupid slug. Or I'll fucking finish you . . ."

With a heavy grinding scream the line stops.

"By the Jesus!" Gus howls, grinning. "By the Lord Jesus!"

Briskly he brings up the jigger, hand over hand delivering the line coiling around his ankles. The rasp rises towards crescendo until the hook clunks against the side of the boat and—there!—a small codfish flops into the midship-room.

Gus seizes the fish at the gills and rips the hook from its gut, eviscerating the beast. With one hand he flings the creature at Wish and with the other he launches the naked hook again unto the waters.

"Jamaica slop," Wish mutters, scornful of the undersized catch. He spins about on the cuddy and kicks the fish to the boards.

Michael watches the creature writhe against the planking. It slaps its tail madly, squirming for the salvation of the ocean so close beneath. He remembers Pop's warning, to brother Kevin: Watch your mouth, lad. Look at all them codfish. It's by the mouth they dies.

But not this codfish. This one was hooked through the heart. It makes a furious spasm and its body knots and stiffens. The gills huff, the mouth gasps, the eyes stare. The beast, Michael knows, wants to speak.

One morning last summer, himself and Pop were out pulling lobster pots. Aboard this very punt they were. It was Michael himself who noticed the birds, dozens of them, shrieking in circles above an empty dory.

Them gulls is the eyes of God, Pop declared. They misses nothing.

The dory was the buff colour of Lukey Dwyer's. They paddled along to it and sure enough, there he was, a fathom below the surface, arse up. Somehow he had got himself tangled in his own trawl and pitched over the side. Pop gaffed up the trawl and Lukey rolled over in the water and a bubble ballooned out of his jaws like a scream.

He was bloated just like a dotard seal. His cap sat firmly on his head. They hoisted him into the punt, drained him a bit, and settled him snug and cozy against the thwart. Then Pop allowed that the only proper thing was to proceed and pick the trawl—for the benefit of Mrs. Dwyer. No sense leaving a line of fish to rot. So they got to work and piled a quintal of cod on top of Lukey's long rubbers.

Lukey's face was bleached as white as the fish-bellies that blanketed him. His mouth gaped, his bare gums showed pink. The eyes were wide open, the expression in the face that of a man who wished to speak, who had something to say, something so desperately important that at last Pop asked casually, half expecting an answer: Well, Lukey, tell us: What's so strange and startling? What are you after seeing down there?

Even though last summer Michael was a mere child, a boy without thoughts, it was then that he noticed a very queer thing. Each of the cod bore that same expression, as if Lukey and the fish nodded among themselves in commiserative horror: Yes yes, I know. I know all about it.

The line rasps.

Gus grins like a cat. "By the Jesus! We'll put this god-damn old tub down to the gunnels!"

He pulls until he drags a goat-sculpin over the side. The fat fish does not trash about at all, but lies calmly in the well of the boat, a blob of aspic, huge eyes bulging, horned gills puffing. Both its wide blubber lips are impaled by the hook. Wish intones:

Jumpin' Jesus, what a job,
Catching sculpins by the gob.

Wish stows the gun and climbs down from the cuddy. He steadies the creature under his boot and tears the hook from the lips, shredding them. Taking care to avoid the spines, he grips the sculpin by the tail and proceeds to whip at the

underbelly with a loop of the fishing line. Spasmodically the
fish swallows the bright morning air and inflates like a bal-
loon. Wish drones:

Nelly Pelly,
With the swelly belly.

Wish dangles the swollen sculpin before his face and
speaks to it. "Now, my son. You got your Jesus-boots on, you
can fucking well get out and *walk!*" He slings the heavy beast
in a towering arc, oceanward. It splats down atop the calm,
where it bobs like a cork, paddling clumsily to and fro, bewildered, a bottom-fish stranded high and dry on the surface.

Sea-scorpions, Pop calls them. Toadfish. Horny whores.
He swears they never die. Michael watches the mutilated
fish drift in the direction of Ireland. He imagines it wandering the Atlantic currents for all eternity, for ever lost, friend-
less, homeless.

Bluntly the line whines and stalls and cuts deep into the
wood. Gus is jolted. He staggers and nearly tumbles over
the side.

"A very monster," Wish remarks.

Gus recovers and leans out and holds the line free of the
boat. He dips the fibre, needle-taut, testing it against his
forefinger. He pulls, gingerly, but the line does not yield. The
punt lists under the strain.

Michael wants to look down into the water, but he fears
what he might see. Across his brain one by one swim the
monsters of the deep.

He imagines, tugging the nether end of the line, an enormous ray like the one Pop hooked as a youngster on the
Banks, and about which the old man often boasts — broad as
an altar it was, and so tough that to kill the flapping of its
wings he had to muckle it between the eyes with the back of
a hatchet. Michael imagines a giant squid with fifteen-foot

tentacles, like the greasy brute Joan snapped on the Admiral's Beach shingle back in 1927—that was before Michael was even born. He thinks of the beast that swallowed Casey's grapelin—just four or five years ago this was—and towed his motorboat beyond sight of land before it surfaced and showed itself to be, not the biggest greediest shark in the world, as Casey half hoped, but only a German submarine. He tries to imagine even the mermaid that Johnny the Light says he spotted sunning her tits on Gallows Beach. Michael remembers with horror the blackfish, a full ton if it was an ounce, that lumbered underneath this very punt—its dorsal brushing the keel and leaving him nauseated with fear—and then breached at the stern in a white surge, spewing foul steam like the Devil ascending out of hell.

Yes, by God, when you drop your line down into the dark you never know what might answer your call, what awful thing you might bestir and bring to the light.

Gus draws hard on the string. The punt careens almost on its beam-ends, pivoting wildly on the thread, coming full about. Michael recoils from the brink.

Just when it seems the boat will capsize, the hull shudders and rocks back on the keel—the line is broken.

Gus brings it up in a fury. Over the side the rag-end slithers like a muskrat's tail, dripping a few cold drops of the North Atlantic, limp, jiggerless.

Mute and surly, like the victim of a prank, Gus glares down into the sea. He studies the water all around, as if the thing—whatever it was—might yet surface. Wish giggles.

Gus scowls in a way that suggests he might kick Wish in the face. "Come on," he spits. "We're hauling to Jesus clear of this shithole."

Wish does not argue. He clambers atop the cuddy, and takes a grip on the rhode and drags the grapelin free of its mooring and grunts and heaves, until the spider of an anchor, stinking with seaweed, dripping, clanks across the bow. Into the aft tholepins Gus levers a set of sweeps. He braces his feet against the risings and wields the oarbutts cocked and ready. Wish takes his post, behind Gus, at the fore rowlocks. The paddles shovel awkwardly at the water, but soon the strokes are synchronized and the pins creak in harmony and the blades, feathered, pausing after each stroke as though to admire their own work, knife neat little eddies curling in the bow wave. The gunnels lurch and the punt canters away.

"Cox!" Wish bellows to Michael. "Launch her out for the shoals."

Michael grips the makeshift tiller. He leans athwart the stern and observes his mates.

Wish and Gus wear the same faces they did years ago, when the trinity of them were altar boys together (they were all three born the same spring—sons of the fire, Pop jokes). Michael pictures them working the oars in red soutanes and lace surplices. In his mind his mates have always been children. But in the middle of each paddle-stroke the fists gripping the oarbutts screen the faces for a brief moment. The fingers are gnarled and weatherbeaten, the nails dirty, the knuckles swollen and callused—these are the hands of fishermen. With each stroke Wish and Gus grow old, and Michael fancies that sooner or later the fists will come down and his mates will appear wearing the faces of their fathers.

Although Michael steers the boat southward, along the line of the ledge towards the berg, his eye leans to starboard, towards the parish.

It is a scene of glorious peace. He sees no movement other than the smoke spiralling from the chimney of the blue saltbox. As the boat crosses the mouth of the cove he watches the landscape on either side of the dwelling stretch and distort. Oddly, the house itself—as though occupying some exalted realm—seems not to change. The structure brings to the boy's mind the shape of a tabernacle.

Swiftly the punt bears down upon the ice. The edge of the spire cuts sharp and keen into the sky. Within the pocket of stillness in back of the berg the air hums with a galvanic chill. Michael hugs his oilcoat tight against his shoulders. How strange, he thinks, how frightening, to approach at close range something so large that you have known only from afar.

A clutch of barrels and corks roosts in the pool leeward. The trap is moored by way of a long leader to a rusty spike driven into the rocks at the toe of the Foot. The stone scarecrow of the Naked Man stands watch.

"That cunny Casey," Gus spits into the sea. "No flies on him. That hawk can smell where the fish is at."

"Yes, them buggers," says Wish, "they likes the cold water all right."

The keel slides between the corks. The suspended netting fades into the depths. The walls and corners give the trap the appearance of a submerged house, yet the netting undulates eerily on the current—it could be a living membrane. It could be beckoning him down. Gilled fish, tangled among the twines, loll lifeless.

In the middle of the corral Wish and Gus boat the oars. The vessel comes to, becalmed a gunshot's range short of the berg.

Wish busies himself rolling a fresh round of smokes.

"Come to the doctor," says Gus to the cod. He stabs thumb and forefinger in the eye sockets, pinching the brains, and slaps the fish down across the thwart. The creature twitches. With his free hand Gus roots about in the cuddy until he finds the cutthroat. He throats the fish and slices the belly cleanly all the way back to the tail.

"And may the Lord have mercy on your soul."

Using his fingers he scoops away the liver and what is left of the guts. When he peels out the soundbone it makes a noise like the ripping of cardboard. All of this gurry in one handful he tosses abroad on the water. He snaps off the head against the edge of the thwart.

Above, three gulls materialize from pockets in the air. Screaming the way children do, calling to one another, they circle and swoop and dive and gobble up the fish slop, and they flee, flapping pompously, the prizes in their beaks, towards the broad open sea, where magically they evaporate into the haze.

Gus opens the carcass like a prayerbook and rinses it over the side. He takes up the head and gouges out the tongue. From the cuddy he produces a length of chicken wire upon which he impales the tongue.

"Tally wire. After all," he winks to Michael, "we got to know how much we're after catching."

Gus hooks a finger under the teeth of the cod's head and he flips the head into the sea. The teeth put into Michael's mind the ghostly line of cod's jaws nailed above the lintel of the splitting shed. On moonlit nights they glow, seemingly from the sky.

Michael watches the head sink. From every direction, smaller shadows like tadpoles appear out of nowhere. They approach timidly and nuzzle the dead face. Michael can see white chunks of flesh torn away. The head jerks and tumbles. He watches the head and the little shadows ferociously kissing it until all of them fade into the murk.

Michael wants to leave this place. Lazily, so that his friends will not notice, he sculls the punt beyond the pale of barrels.

The boat creeps across the calm towards the mural wall of ice. Under the midmorning sun the ice is blinding, and its glare casts down upon the three boys a palpable warmth. Hard aground, Michael thinks. Now the moon and the tide will do their deadly work.

Above the summit, the clouds roar out of the western blue.

A faint jangle touches Michael's ear. Across the water he can make out the nun who is swinging the handbell. Kindergarten patches of colour funnel through the school gate, drawn by the summons as though on strings.

The bell stops.

Mass is just out: it must be nearly nine.

Father MacMurrough emerges from the church and his gaunt figure paces the landing. The hunched silhouette of Johnny the Light, unmistakable even at such a distance, lurches across the wilderness towards the cemetery. The Pothole Man with his nag and dray has made his way to a point on the road just this side of the blue house. On the roof of the house the chair is still empty.

Michael fixes his eye on the back door. At that moment, as if by some miracle—as if it knows he is watching—the door opens. But at the same moment, because of the motion of the punt, the house drifts behind the corner of the iceberg, and the house is lost.

Directly, the school and the church and the octagon and the forge and every one of the houses are gone from his sight. Beyond the edge of the ice-cliff, all that remains of the parish is the Head and the lighthouse that crowns it.

Now, the schoolbell clangs from the opposite direction—of course, it echoes off the face of the Freshwater bluffs. When the bell falls silent, Michael hears only the sound of slush grinding against the skirts of the berg.

His hand trails in the sea and the frigid water feels blood-warm. He looks down, again, upon an expanse of jagged ridges and perilous trenches sweeping away into the dark. At first he thinks that it is the ledge. But it cannot be, for this new landscape glows an eerie blue.

It is the ice. The blue light throbs, softly, with the kind of glim one might find in a midnight cathedral, under a single smouldering charcoal.

A simple longing takes hold of the boy. It is an urge to

abandon the safety of the boat, to slip gently over the side and to sink into the sea, into the fearful blue ground of love.

Mary stretches her bare arms wide in the sun. People walking up the road might think she is pretending to be Jesus on the Cross. They might think she is mocking the crucifix. But today, Mary doesn't care what anyone might think.

This morning the marshes are brilliant, with bakeapples and raspberries and blueberries, and the meadows too, with dandelions and day's eyes and bachelor buttons. If only she didn't have school, if only it was tomorrow, she would tramp over back and pick berries, or wild mint or fiddleheads. She would spend the day hopping the marshes, lightfooting it from one hummock to the next, the way a field of icepans is crossed. She would find herself a cozy bum-rock and she would sit and take off her shoes and stick her toes deep into the silky cool muck. If no one was around she would lift her skirt as high as her bloomers and let the sun warm her long legs. It would be so grand. This morning she is still a child, so all of that would be just the right thing for her to do.

She jumps and spins so that her pearly sundress billows and her thighs feel the heat. Her hair flies up too and brushes the lilacs. The blossoms hang heavy as cherries today, and they give the breeze a purple taste. She puts her nose to the flowers and they smell like the incense in the church. The smell puts a picture into her mind: the priest processing solemnly down the main aisle, his censer swaying like a pendulum, in slow time with the big bell overhead. Right away she pushes the picture out of her head—she will not allow gloom to shadow *this* of all days. For today is the day it will happen. Before the sun sets, she will know. And when she knows, she will be a grown-up at last.

In her bedroom this morning Mary dropped her pyjamas and stood before the big glass on the washstand. She studied herself from head to toe and she was able to make out, at one and the same instant, the departing child and the advancing woman both. The sight made her think of those trick sketches in the encyclopaedia: is it a vase, or is it two faces in silhouette? The notion addled her brain a little. It even made her wonder whether it was proper to put on such a grown-up dress. The dress came as a hand-me-down, from cousins in the Boston States. Ever since grade one, all Mary ever wore to school was some dreary grey frock of a uniform. Sister Valentine said the uniform gave the girls the air of postulants—as if that was a recommendation! Today being the last day, they are spared that gunnysack, thank God. Anyhow, when she buttoned up the dress and stood in front of the mirror, her first thought was that it made her look like a different person—like a stranger.

But then the woman came in the door and eyeballed Mary up and down, and promptly declared that the item was too good for her to wear. Mary should put it away for the grave. To this Mary said not a word. She didn't want a row, not this day. She only lifted down the glass and marched right out with it. Herself meanwhile babbled along behind her, the way the woman does: Listen now, girl, you scurry along, before it burns off. The bell is just after ringing. Be sure you don't miss out.

All of this Mary ignored. She carried the mirror outdoors into the back garden and propped it against the trunk of the ash. And now, here in the smell of the lilacs, here in the hot sun, Mary studies herself yet again. She wants the light as bright as it can be. She wants to see what she will look like for the rest of her life.

The light bounces off the mirror and sifts through the dress. Her top is bare behind the cotton, and the press of the sun is warm. So scarce a bulge she makes she hasn't got her corset yet. Alice started hers last year, in grade ten, and of course Moira, that big chest, has been into one since she turned thirteen. Everyone says that Mary is like the summer, a late bloomer. The sun strokes her skin with the feel of waves on the pond. It gives her the fancy she wouldn't mind being a mermaid. In the shop one day Moira overheard Johnny the Light whispering across the counter, telling Casey that he saw one — one of *them*. The creature was taking the sun, he said, naked, on Gallows Beach, below the lighthouse. According to Moira, Casey straightaway opened his spyglass and went to the window and had a gander, but he came back to the counter with a long face.

On the spur of bedrock the tomcat basks, smiling at the east. "Nice for you," Mary speaks aloud, as if the beast could understand. "Nice for you to sit on a steamy rock all day and soak the lovely sunshine. I wish I had time for that." A red monarch flutters by. The cat starts up and stalks after it, lion-like, slinking through the grass. The butterfly escapes into the alders. The animal decides to notice the girl and it comes bounding over. Purring, it rubs its black fur against her ankles.

Mary crouches and strokes the animal's neck and her fingers feel the dark heat. But when she caresses the cat's underbelly, her hand comes away cold and wet with dew.

Yes, plenty of time.

The cat catches sight of its reflection in the glass. It hisses, flattens its ears, and backs away.

Mary looks to where the cat looked, deep into the mirror, and she herself is startled. The glass is mesmerizing. It makes distant places near. On the crest of the ridge the lookout stands hard and stark as a teat — normally the boulder is lost in haze. The curve of the land looms so close that Mary is sure she could reach out and stroke it. Clouds float on a thin westerly and drift down from the chimneys of the Gaff Topsails. Mary fancies they are snowbanks on the wing. She takes hold of the frame and tilts it so that she can follow in the glass the path of the clouds across the sky. They sail above her head and slide over the parish and down the shore, past the lighthouse and on out into the North Atlantic. She imagines the clouds sailing all the way to Ireland.

Under the nine-o'clock sun, the sea ripples blue and green. The fresh new iceberg glints like a diamond. Across her mind drift images out of her dream.

Last night, Alice and Moira came over so that the three of them could bake up their dumb-cake. They waited until the youngsters were gone up to bed. For such an important job the girls wanted peace and quiet. And peace and quiet they got—that is, until the woman came down from tucking in the baby. She sat herself behind the kitchen table and there she perched all the while, playing patience—pendulum and bristol and rainbow—and cheating against herself the way she always does. Between tries she shouted at them about what pan to use and how much Cinderella to mix in and how many junks of wood to pile on the fire, and all the rest of it. And over and over she would call out: Not a word, mind you, nary a word.

Mary was surprised at her own self, because for the first time in God knows how long she paid some attention to the woman. Alice and Moira did too, and not a vowel did any one of the three utter until after the batter was mixed and the coal put on the fire and the cake baked and cooled and set on the table and sliced into three huge pieces and the last crumb devoured.

Now, the woman said, now you are allowed to talk. The girls had been so bottled up—it was like holding their breaths underwater—that of course they burst into hysterics. For five minutes it was nothing but shrieks and laughter. When they composed themselves the woman dealt out the cards and they started up a game of four-handed auction.

Well, they never even got to the first kitty before Alice and Moira fell to arguing. Each one had her own opinions, about dumb-cakes or dumbledores or scarves or eggs or God knows what. But by now Mary didn't really care what those two youngsters had to say. She ignored Alice and Moira altogether. Even though lately she can hardly bear the sound of the woman's voice, last night it was only herself that Mary paid any mind to. After all, Mary thought, she was the lone one of them that was ever after divining it out true. And Mary in the flesh and blood is the walking proof of that.

Anyway, the only trouble was, no matter what way was mentioned, the woman would only shout: There's the thing, yes, there's the proper thing for Midsummer Day. And so by the end of it, by the time Alice slapped down the ace of hearts and made her one-twenty and scooped up the pot of coppers and they all laughed and shouted and put away the cards and boiled the kettle for tea, Mary was not much the wiser.

She shades her eyes against the sun reflected in the mirror and watches in the mirror the clouds drift away over the iceberg. Her dream from out of the dumb-cake floats through the back of her memory. But just as quickly it fades and is gone. All the girl can cling to is hazy remnants — shadows of white mountains, notions of flying.

Over in the schoolyard the nun is hammering the bell against the air with the particular jangle that means: final call. Mary swivels the mirror on its corner and looks into it across the marsh. She can spy the dark figure framed in the school door. At such a distance the clang of the bell is out of kilter with the swing of the black arm, so that the sound and the sight are oddly disconnected. The tag-ends of the youngsters funnel through the gate and into the schoolyard, chittering and piping as they go. The priest paces his skinny form across the top of the landing. The door shuts upon the nun, and a second later a disembodied clank arrives at Mary's ear.

Her mind is getting addled by this mirror. Leaving it under the ash, she wanders down to the woodhorse and sits astride the frame. Deeply she inhales the cool green savour of the sawdust. The hex-sun that Father painted on the door of the henhouse, last year, glares sharply against her eye. The girl pictures the chickens roosting snug there in the dark. The thought gives her body a pleasant hum. Although it is getting late, she dismounts from the woodhorse and bends under the low lintel and steps inside the coop.

The hens scatter, clucking, rustling. The air in the pound is heavy and warm, and tastes faintly acidic. The feathers smell like her own pillow. She yawns. When her eyes have adjusted to the light, Mary reaches a hand underneath one of the birds and pulls out a fat brown egg. The egg is warm. She holds it awhile between her two hands as she might cradle a chick. The hen clucks with displeasure and carefully Mary returns the egg to its place.

By the time she steps squinting back into the light, only the priest remains in Church Square. The youngsters have been swallowed by the school. She had better hurry, else she will miss out.

Mary marches down the sloping ground to the road. Her long legs bear her body forward with an angular gait, in the style of a colt.

On the road, she is pleased to see that the potholes are fresh-filled. Against the canvas of grey gravel the damp clay makes orange-brown patches. She straddles the potholes the way she straddles the keeper in hopscotch. After today, there is nothing to stop her and Alice and Moira from playing all the morning, every morning. The musty odour of the clay smells to Mary vaguely familiar, and she sniffs at her fingertips. Beyond the sharp tang of Sunlight she can still draw traces of it—her own, her woman's grown-up smell.

Mary does a hop and a step and jumps high and spins fast so that her dress billows. She alights face-on to the west.

Just for the fun of it, she freezes in the attitude in which she lands. She will not move a muscle—not until her eye has traced the full long wiggle of the road.

From the cross, where the gravel leaves the paved highway—which leads in both directions God knows where—the road follows the power line and skirts the water, drops steeply into the gulches, scales the cliffy rocks, and darts pinched between the fences and the landwash, bypassing Moira's house and Alice's house and dozens of others, until it arrives here, beneath her feet, here in front of her own house.

She places one shoe into the fine soft clay that fills the hole and the shoe sinks deep. Out loud she says to herself, "This is where I am at."

Under the sun the blue shingles of the house stand clean and sharp, like the scales on some weird sea-beast. The chimney smoke draws above her head, spiralling seaward, and joins with the clouds sailing over the ocean. Easily Mary can hear the singsong of the woman's voice coming through the kitchen window, open to the day. She can guess the prattling words, but she does not want to hear them—not this particular morning.

On the sill of her own window the tumbler glints, framed like a photograph. She thinks of the schooner shape that the egg formed this morning, and aloud she says, "Which one is it to be?"

She leaps again and spins again and lands, and now her eye follows the road as it travels away from her, eastward.

The gravel chases the power line again and swings past the wharf and among the fishflakes, through the marsh and over the bridge and along the edge of the Brow and past Academy Hall and the palace on its little hill, and through Church Square past the school gate and the octagon stores and Admiral's Beach and the forge. A good ways farther on, the road achieves the graveyard, from which point it continues alone, minus the power line, into remote fenceless fields that never once in all her sixteen years has she visited. Somewhere down there, she has heard tell, the road shrivels to a lane, and then to a cowpath, and it expires, perhaps by way of sliding into the sea, in the wilderness near the lighthouse.

Whoever he is, he is *somewhere*. He must be.

Last night, the woman was dealing a hand of cards and her mouth as usual was going on like a river when she said one single hard thing. She said: Sure, the tumbler is fine—if all you wants is his station. But if you wants his initials, my children, you got to try the dew. I'll tell you that much for free. The morning dew.

Mary hates to bypass anyone without saying hello. That is the sort of bad-mannerly thing that strangers do. She waves hello to everyone: to the youngsters rompsing in the hay, to Mrs. Hanly turning saltfish on the flakes and Mrs. Coady weeding the potatoes and Mrs. Byrne and Mrs. Corbett taking a spell and gossiping over the fence, to old Captain Joy carrying water and Mr. Cleary ploughing his garden and Missus May hauling kelp for it, and Mr. Slatery chopping firewood. The chuck-sound of the hatchet splitting the block comes to her ear a full second after the sight of it. Her voice whispers out loud:

Chop your sticks on Sunday,
Hump your back on Monday.

That addles her mind, and she has to stop in the middle of the road and ask herself what day of the week it is.

Mary waves to the crowd of men putting up the pine frame of Casey's bungalow. The new thing on the land makes everything around it look fresh too. She has overheard Casey say that he aims to call the house "Jim", so she waves and calls out, "Hello, Jim!" She waves to the sparrows lined up on the telegraph wires. She waves even to the trigger-mitts drying on the picket-tops, and fancies them waving back to her.

She scans the low tide in the lee of the public wharf. She is looking for sign of the capelin scull. There! A sliver in the calm . . . but no, that is only a wind-ripple. On the wharf, gulls roost in such numbers that the jetty is alive and itself rippling in the sun. The birds seethe and stir, like children waiting to be fed. Mary knows that the gulls will spot the capelin ahead of the other birds. Father told her it was the gulls always showed him where to set his line. Eyes of God, he said.

Tonight, drawn by the grand bonfires, the capelin will surely make up their minds at last. The cocks will push the hens to shore, then press the eggs out of the hens' bodies, then squirt to start them off—yes, tonight the capelin will come spawning up on the sandy beaches, rolling and glistening, wetter than all the wetness of the sea.

The gulls put Mary in mind of the wedding. All spring long, the woman has been telling the story over and over, to anyone who will listen. Mary herself hears it practically every day.

It was a spring marriage they had. The snow was nearly melted. After the Mass, the church bells was ringing non-stop, and the full parish made a procession. They cheered the wedding party all the way to the wharf. The men and the boys fired off their guns into the air. At the head of the wharf the priest gave his blessing and the bride and groom went aboard a beautiful white schooner. *Happy Adventure* she was called, fresh-painted, triple-masted, ablaze in new canvas. The vessel cast off into a spanking westerly, and the wedded couple, still in their finest, sailed for the Labrador and a summer of good fishing. The best of it was, they were saluted out the cove and around the Head by seagulls, clouds of seagulls blowing about in the sunshine, just like confetti.

Yes my dear, the woman would declare, marry in white, you'll always be right. She would smile her long-ago smile and turn her face out the window and she would not speak again until spoken to.

The dirt road under Mary's feet, the stretch of gravel she has tramped at least, she reckons, ten thousand times in her child's life, in her mind now becomes the broad main aisle of the church. She takes Father's arm and together they advance upon the altar. At the marble rail she whispers softly the verse she has learned by heart:

> *For this cause shall a man*
> *leave father and mother,*
> *and shall cleave to his wife*
> *and they two shall be in one flesh.*

Father's fishflake is crimson with blasty boughs. It reeks of briny, decayed fish. Mary bends and stares, as though under a giant bed, between the legs of the structure.

When she was little, the space seemed as big as a house. All the youngsters played inside there. They would eat the fish-flavoured grass, and tell secrets, and show off their pee for one another, and dash about in hide-and-seek behind strouters fatter than they were themselves. Sometimes, when Father barked nets in the gigantic iron kettle that is there yet, he used to tease Mary and threaten to drop her into the cauldron and boil her for his dinner.

Beyond the kettle, the dory rots on the sod. Belly down it looks like a coffin. Please God, Mary says to herself, tomorrow we'll see there a yellowed patch of grass. Maybe that is what it will take to burn the hag.

A crow struts atop the hull. The bird does not flee when

Mary comes up but it turns its head and follows her with its bold eye as she moves away. She looks over her shoulder and the gaze of the beast is steady and fixed upon her.

Mary is vaguely aware of the shape of her own house. If she decided to look, she would see clearly, on top of the roof, the big chair that the woman sits in every day. She claims it came off a wreck. It was the captain's throne, she says. But Mary doesn't believe that. Bad enough she sits up there jabbering—even though she makes out she is talking to the baby, everyone knows she is talking to herself—but now that the weather is fine, God save us, she's taken to feeding the baby in full view of the parish.

Perhaps, Mary thinks, I should have a quiet word with them janney-thieves. The only trouble is, the woman took a hammer and big nails and she crucified the feet of it solid to the linney.

The road drifts inland. Aimlessly Mary kicks a stone until it escapes into the ditch. She picks up a stick and rattles it along Barrons' fresh-painted fence. For good luck she raps every third picket. The priest's smelly black dog scrambles out of the marsh and comes over and snuffles under the hem of her dress. She is afraid the animal will soil the hem, so she threatens the beast with the stick. The dog cowers away.

The marsh is ablaze with the little yellow suns that decorate the dandelion. The woman calls them buttercups. Piss-a-beds—that is what the boys call them, just for badness. But the girls call them what they are: faceclocks. Every day, Alice and Moira hold a faceclock under their chins and watch for the golden blush that means they've got a sweetheart. Mary wishes the pair of them wasn't in school already so they could all have a try.

Gus Gallant swears there is a treasure over back, somewhere beyond the bog, perhaps near the graveyard, a pirate's hoard of silver and jewels, with a curse on it. And the grown-ups tell stories, winter nights, about the Boo Darby that haunts the ridge, the Black Stranger who skulks behind the berry bushes with his deadly black bag. If you are a bad girl, the Darby will spring from the weeds and stuff you into his sack and make away with you, truly.

On the bridge Mary bypasses Mrs. Pelly, homeward bound from Mass. Although Mary says good morning, the woman steams forward without so much as a nod. Mary does not mind—Mrs. Pelly is intent on doing her beads. And for good reason. Yesterday in the schoolyard, Wish Butt pulled his shirtfront bulging out from his gut and he sang:

Nelly Pelly,
With the swelly belly!

Once upon a time, Alice used to say that babies come out of the cellar. Moira used to say that babies come in the satchel the doctor carries. Now, all three of the girls know the true facts, thanks to the woman. She told them the full of it, in the kitchen, by kerosene and candlelight after the power lines went down, one stormy night two winters ago. She was that way herself then, big with baby brother—that was what started them talking.

Mary studies the retreating stump of Mrs. Pelly. The girl marvels at how careful she has to be, how she can never raise her arms over her head for fear of cording the child, or smell anything nice for fear she won't be able to satisfy the craving, or mock a cripple for fear the child will suffer the same affliction. Johnny the Light comes into her mind—but then of course he was never a natural cripple.

The rotting rail of the bridge teeters above the brook. Mary leans her weight upon the wood. She is not afraid. She looks down into the stagnant water and sees the reflection of her own hair falling wild about her shoulders—the long dark mane. In back of her hair, the clouds race one another across the sky.

When she was four, Father took her by the hand and led her up the big aisle of the church. Midday it was, the nave cool and drenched in colours from the windows, and echoing of their footfall and smelling of God. At the altar rail, he hoisted her to his shoulders and he pointed to the statue. It was the Virgin with the Infant Jesus cradled at her breast. He said to her: There you are now, there's Mary herself.

At first she misunderstood. She thought it was the child he pointed to. He laughed and corrected her, but her mind stayed mixed up. For the rest of that day, that day so long ago when she was so little, she couldn't decide whether she was a child or a grown woman.

Looking below now into the brook, she pulls her dress full out at the belly and watches in the water as the child turns into a woman. She lets go the dress and the woman turns back into a child.

A fat black eel slithers through the weeds. Mary jumps up onto the rail and hurls the stick at the creature. The stick misses the target and disappears in the sludge. The mud swallows it with an ugly sucking sound, the sound of a deadman's bubble: guck.

From her stand in the pit of the marsh, out of the stir of the breeze, Mary can hear the pott-pott pott-pott of a motorboat. In the next instant, the sound echoes off a cliff somewhere and its tone shifts. The report taps her ear in an odd pitch, an octave higher than the raw sound itself, and it sends a tingle up the back of her neck. The echo reminds her of the lovely story she read in the book, about the nymph who pined away for Narcissus until nothing was left of her but a voice.

The delicious odour of fresh boiled tar drifts down from a roof. Mary's senses get tangled and her mind imagines it is the sound she smells, the smell she hears. In the pocket of still air, the light hums. She can hear the light as if it was music—harmonica music. She can hear it all over the parish, in the bleating of the lambs and kids across the meadows, the cock-a-doodling of the roosters, the barking of the pups, the calling of all the gulls and crows and song-birds and crickets and bees.

She arrives at the rusty old field-gun the lads prised out of the bog. Brushing away a beetle she straddles the iron. The metal is scalding hot against her thighs. She sights down the barrel—pure wickedness it was how the lads aimed it at the convent. She remembers the pictures in the history book, of d'Iberville's men who knocked down every house on the shore. She fancies that the handsome French soldiers are marching this very road, right now, perhaps at this very moment dragging their cannons round Parsley's Turn. She fancies the finest-looking of them picking her up in his strong arms and carrying her away.

A tiny aeroplane buzzes out of the muzzle of the gun and startles her from her daydream. Horse-stinger! The insect swoops at her face and circles her hair and threatens to become entangled. Devil's darning needles, says Alice, they sew you up. Moira calls them arse-stingers. The creature plunges towards Mary's feet and she dismounts and clutches the skirt of her dress and holds it closed shut at the knees until the insect flies off.

Mary overtakes the Pothole Man and his dirty white stallion. Both of them drone in clouds of fat bluebottles. Once a month he patches the line, but Mary does not know his name. She does not know whether he is old enough to have youngsters the age of herself—his cap shades his eyes from her sight. She does not know whether he has a wife or what house he sleeps in, only that it is up-country. Side-saddle the man perches his skinny frame on the shaft of his dray. He holds in his hand a tin cup. From time to time he brings the cup to his mouth and spits something black into it. You would think he did not want to dirty up his precious road. At each fault in the gravel he bawls out: Hor-rus! Hor-rus!

and the nag halts. Grudgingly the man sets down his cup
on the shaft and dismounts. With the same nodding walk as
the horse, he goes round to the tailgate, which hangs down
like the flap on a set of longjohns. The animal waits while
slowly the man takes out the shovel and spades the sticky
clay from the draybed into the hole, tamps it down, and
shuffles back to his post. He mounts and picks up the tin cup
and spits, and calls out: Hor-rus! and the beast plods on.
The animal's shoes ring against the stones embedded in the
road. The big wheels rumble and the red spokes flare like
rays of the sun.

When Mary comes up broadside of him the Pothole Man,
as usual, turns his face full away, towards the sea-horizon. It
is the horse that swings its great dinosaur head in her direction. It examines the girl with a huge unblinking eye. The
beast snorts and she feels its hot wet breath on her neck.

Mary hurries to leave them behind. She dares not look
back, but her mind imagines, bearing down upon her from
the rear, a Roman chariot, pulled by a snorting white stallion
galloping out of the sky to sweep her away to the clouds.

She draws opposite old Martha's shack. This is where she
must quit the road.

The shack is little more than a tilt, unpainted and tumbledown. No smoke lifts yet out of the chimney. Martha is still
asleep on her pallet.

How old she is now! When Mary was in grade one,
Martha was already a dry old witch. The crone would cower
behind her fence and watch the children pass by. The girl
often wonders what it was that left the woman so shrivelled
up, what happened that made Martha so tiny and wizened
deep within her black shawl. Some people says bad things
about her: that she was a ship salvager, or a grave robber, or
a midwife who collected the bodies of dead babies and cut
the hearts out of them. She sleeps this morning, but tomor-

row, enlaced in the soft grey moss of her years, Martha will be up with the dew, poking and ferreting among the ashes.

The dew! Mary must hurry.

Smartly she turns right and heads down the spine of the Brow, straight forward on to the sea. Her feet rip through fields of faceclocks and she kicks at the little furry balls that the children call bully-boo. They fly up into the breeze and the breeze scatters them like confetti. She picks a yellow blossom and clutches it to her palm—for the luck that she is going to need.

The dandelions give way to stinger-nettles, and before long the sod is gone altogether. Her shoes slip on the bare clifftop.

Easily she finds the scar from last year's fire. The patch of rock is as sooty as the charcoal in the priest's censer. You would think it had been scorched by a million bolts of lightning. The blackness draws the sun and the granite smoulders warm underfoot.

Nearby, a crow struts—perhaps it is the same bird, stalking her. On any day but this, at any place but this, Mary would dodge away from the sullen creature, but this morning she shouts at the beast and waves her arms and she even picks up a stone to throw. The bird flaps its wings and flees across the water, cawing.

Mary searches for what she came to see, but she is gripped by panic—there is no sign of the thing. Maybe the crow stole it. Or maybe some person came by this morning and found it, and now that person will enjoy all the good of it. All the joy.

Her feet are at the very cliff-edge.

One hundred feet below, giant swells churn. The sight makes the land shift under her. It makes her head spin. She backs away from the rim, and turns around—and nearly steps upon it. There it was, all along. A second later she realizes a terrible thing, and it makes her dizzy all over again: how very close to the edge she must have gone, last night in the dark.

The hour was late when Alice and Moira finally went out the door. The house was left dead quiet. The woman said: Do it, girl, go. She gave Mary her own best scarf, the blue woollen cloud with the whorls and spirals and filigrees, and she pushed the girl into the dark.

Never had Mary been abroad at such a time of night. Every window in the parish was black. Yet the world was awash in a peculiar purple light. A swollen half-moon hung just above her head. The stars blinked like church candles. The gates and the fences and such things near enough to lay hands upon were lost in the pitch. On the bridge, a shadow walked right by her, but Mary could not make out who it was. Although she said hello, the figure gave no answer. It made Mary feel that she was no longer in the parish where she had lived her whole life, but that she had stepped through a magic mirror and passed into a foreign land, into a place where everyone was a stranger.

But the oddest thing was, objects too far off to touch she could see almost as clear as day. The wide bowl of the cove had a queer glim on it. The lighthouse beam brushed the water over and over, hypnotically, and after every sweep it left behind a kind of shimmer on the calm, like the shine on the tomcat's fur when you stroke it. The beaches hissed with the swell. An electric odour came to her, and she heard a groan echoing under the water—she squinted her eyes and she saw, beyond the cove, grounded, glowing in the moonlight, the new iceberg. It must have only just drifted in, but already it was dying.

She groped her way blindly to the edge of the Brow. She waited for the swell to swing against the cliff and for the detonations. The booming sounds came finally, from one, two, three sides of her—and then she knew she was in the right spot. When the sea fell away and relaxed, the night became so still she could hear the hollow sound of paddles working somewhere on the water. She could hear the train crossing the barrens, miles up-country. She could hear even the sad moan of the foghorn, from God knows how far away.

At last Mary did what the woman said for her to do. She spread abroad on the rock the good scarf, and she walked away from it and left it behind in the night. She left it there to wait for the dawn and for the dew that would tell her.

Mary stands before the scarf in the attitude of a communicant. She will not look upon the cloth until her soul is prepared. She shuts her eyes and she makes the sign of the cross and she whispers the Our Father. Now she is ready. She speaks in a firm voice:

Drop down dew, ye heavens, from above.

The sea booms around her. She smells inside her head the colours of the church windows. The time is come: she will look now.

She opens her eyes.

A cloud starts its passage in front of the eastern sun.

The wind gusts. A flurry of bully-boo hurtles out of the west like a thin snowsquall. Mary shivers and wraps her arms around her shoulders—she has heard people say that pockets of spring snow still survive up in the Gaff Topsails.

The cloth is dry.

Mary's nostrils fill with the stale odour of last year's ash. The shadow of the cloud covers the iceberg, and, if she were to look in that direction, she would see the ice shade momentarily a darker blue.

She bends and picks up the scarf from the rock and holds the cloth near her nose. She inhales the night-smell that rises from it. She presses the scarf full against her face. But it is useless. The cloth is mute.

Mary makes her way back to the road. When she reaches the field of dandelions she tosses down the blossom, crushed now, that she has been carrying. She ignores the fresh blooms still rooted in the earth. Instead she selects a wide blade of grass. Gently she joins her hands, as if she is cradling an egg, and she presses the grass between the cheeks of flesh at the base of her thumbs. She takes a breath, and blows through the reed a long, high-pitched note. Aloud she mutters: "It is not *my* fault. It is the sun's fault."

When she arrives at the road she wraps the scarf around her hair and ties a rough knot—after all, it is only an old scarf now. Out of the corner of her eye she senses the silhouette of her house, and the chair on the roof, and, sitting in the chair, a human figure. Mary turns her head away so she will not see. Whatever I am to be, she vows, it will not be that.

She makes straight for school. Her feet scuff at the gravel. She bypasses Academy Hall and the avenue leading up the little slope to the palace, and then, for no reason whatsoever, she breaks into a run. Down the dusty road she runs until she reaches the holy ground of Church Square. There she slows to a walk, a processional pace. She is winded.

As she passes by Casey's shop she notices something in the window, and she stops. She ignores the wealth of goods and stores on display within. It is the reflection that draws her attention.

Beyond the glass hovers a thin figure. The face, shadowed deep within the borders of a shawl, is unrecognizable. And suddenly Mary understands: she knows what it was happened to old Martha. She knows now what made the old woman so dry and withered and barren.

In raw terror the girl rips off the scarf. Fiercely she glares into the mirror and she shakes her long hair wildly about her head. She shakes her hair so that it flies up among the clouds that tumble through the sky.

She bolts away from the window. Her breath comes quick and hard.

The church's snow-white front dazzles her and she can feel the heat it casts down. The rose window blazes in the sun. A small delirium spins her head.

The doorway of the church gapes ajar. In the dimness beyond the threshold, the red pinpoint of the sanctuary lamp illuminates faintly the outline of the tabernacle. Mary knows that God is present here. The smell of incense wafts like prayer into the morning. On top of the landing the priest leans on his cane. He has been expecting her.

Therefore now they are not two,
but one flesh.

What therefore God hath joined together,
let no man put asunder.

The great rose window blazes like a mirror to the sun. Radiant in her white dress, Mary takes Father's arm and they advance into the light. Within the church her bridegroom, her lover, waits for her.

The spire soars. The cross reels against the blue sky like the masthead of a schooner. In her mind the land shifts under her feet and she is soaring aboard the deck of the lovely white vessel, soaring smartly across the waters, onward to the Labrador Sea, and a thousand gulls blow about in the wind, like confetti.

Please God she's not after missing out. There she goes, lollygagging. Tail of the pig as usual. If the last they shall be first, the girl is far in front. You're too young to feel it, my son, but I tell you—it's a melancholy display, that one disappearing through the school gate. Before you knows it, the girl will be claimed and gone out of our sight for good.

Mind you, I got the one big consolation, don't I? When her and all the rest of this brood is departed from this house, I will still have you to keep me company.

But wasn't it a ructions this morning! Getting the lot of them scrubbed and their faces fed and putting the rags on their backs and shoving the arse-end of them along. All that carrying on and bawling and screeching and nose-picking. Had me tormented. Poisoned. Hopped up about their holidays, that's all it was.

But I suppose it's not many years gone since I had the same upheavals in myself. It seems like yesterday, don't it? Now, thanks be to God, you and me we can take a spell up here and chew the rag a bit, just the two of us, and have a gander out the water for your daddy. Yes, off goes your daddy this morning without his mug-up. And he left his longjohns in the bin. The smell of his feet in his old wellies. Didn't even light the fire—his only piece of housework and damned if ever he does it. I loves your daddy but sometimes I tell you he gives me the heavenly vapours.

Dear me. This is my comfort, darling. The first time I'm after sitting down since the last time. So nice to give the bunions a rest. By God, the old Pegasus is scalding on the bum this sunshiny morning. My mercy seat. But you would think the Devil himself just got up out of it. The roof tar, it smells so grand bubbling in the heat.

Yes, and did you notice? After all the wisdom I give that one and them two streels of hers last night, not a word did she mutter to me. Nary a word about her dreams, nor what the tumbler told her. This morning she wouldn't haul her arse from the bed to save her soul. Lost to the world. The dead arose, I says to her, the dead arose and appeared to many. She dawdled so much, Lord knows, by now she might be after missing out on the best chance of them all.

But I suppose I shouldn't be talking her down. After all,

the poor thing she was up till all hours, stomping the roads. Her soul is going through the same old storm every soul suffers sooner or later. I knows by God I did—I sweated a squall when I tokened out your daddy. All a panic. Hag-rid night after night.

But in the end, your daddy and me, such a grand wedding we had! Dad I ever tell you? It was a sunny morning just like this, Monday of the Rogation days. A dandy westerly was blowing, too. The whole parish paraded us to the wharf. Every man jack. Every bloody old mongrel too. Monsignor Conroy—Father Fran, God rest his soul—he stood on a grump and gave us his blessing and then your daddy and me we went aboard of the *Happy Adventure*. So lovely and white she was in the sunshine. The bells were ringing, and off we sailed to the Labrador for a summer of floating: my first time. A million gulls flew over the schooner and saw us round the Head. It was white everyplace you looked.

Speaking of hag-rid, I was rid again last night. A fright of a dream, my child. Dreadful. Cats and claws and crabs. Paralysed to the bed I was. Paralysed. But you don't want to be hearing about my nightmares, do you, my love? I knows what it is you really wants. Yes, Dudley Lovelace, I *do*. And here you are.

My, my, my, the light is lovely and warm on the chest. Hardly the stain of weather in the sky. We'll set you here snug and cozy in my arms so you can enjoy a taste of the sun too. Our dear father who art in heaven. As for your own daddy, I allow he's somewhere in back of that piece of ice. He says to me every spring when the ice comes down: the fish they follows the cold water, and the fishermen they follows the fish. He got salt in his blood, your daddy. But no fear, my love, up here by the chimney we got such a grand lookout, we're like gulls on the wing. We can spy all the way to the falloff of the sea, all the way beyond the back of the

land, and every mortal thing in between. You and me, we'll
beacon your daddy home safe and sound to us, just as true
as the holy cross.

With that smile shining in your little eyes you thinks you're
in heaven already, don't you, my darling. Yes, you noddy. All
your cares looked after. Now myself, I got one long dayful
of work before me. Very first thing is catch the blessings of
this fine sun and turn a yaffle of fish on the flake: I hates to
see a sun like this go to waste. And while the tide is down I'll
pull some kelp and lay it out on the rocks to dry. Then I got
to bake the bread for dinner for them rapscallions coming
home at noon. And I'll start on knitting them cuffs: bad luck
to launch out on a Friday. And I'll haul some water and chop
a backload of junks and wash the sheets and string them out
on the line while we got the wind, and do the ironing. This
is pot day and so I'll have to put on the fishfaces and brewis
and duff and colcannon for their supper. And maybe haul
a few stalks of rhubarb out of the marsh. As Nell says, one
bloody drop of sweat pushing against the next.

When it comes time for a spell from all that I'll pull a weed
or two out of the farm. And if them capelin spraugs I'll
spread a bucketful on the drills. Carrots and cabbage and
turnips and spuds—God, but you know I gets tired of the
same old chaw-and-glutch. Some days I thinks I'll plough it
all under and spread some loam and put in plum trees, or apple, or gooseberry bushes. Or a flower patch. Now there's
the thing. I just loves the smell of lilies and daisies and roses
and tansies and sweet rockets and the like of that. And
butterflies all around. The nuns they're after planting their
own little Garden of Eden there in back of the convent,
so lovely it is I swear the angels lays their eggs in it. The
trouble is, we got hardly enough ground to grow a plateful
of spuds. Well, at least we can enjoy our blessed lilac bush.
Lilacs is what makes the wind blow, did you know that, my
love? Of course it is: you can smell them on the breeze. See

them lilac trees scattered around the cove? They're all flapping their leaves and waving their blossoms.

Just look there: down the road. It's himself, staggering up out of the wilderness. The Janney Boo. The Darby. When you're a bad boy, the Darby he'll come and carry you away and lock you down in his black cellar. Indeed he will. Santa in winter, the Black Stranger in summer, he'll carry you away in his big bag, drop you down in the dark. But don't mind me, child: it's only old Black Johnny. Johnny the Light. And well-lighted he is, too. On the rocks already, even at this hour. Delirium tremendous. What a hard-looking skeet he's getting to be. Face on him like a boiled boot. His bones decked out like the bloody flag, high-water pants and all, every piece of his clothes inside out: and they calls that a token of luck. My dear, and don't he smell goatish. Something terrible. Stinks of his own pee. Once a man, twice a child. And him with a fine government situation too, down there at the light.

I suppose I shouldn't talk him down, poor devil, he's after having such a hard life. I thinks I got troubles till I sees the likes of that man. All his pain and suffering, and defilement, turning his mind and everything. And on top of it all, a hero besides—would you believe that? Them amadahns of youngsters, either they teases him sinful, or they is frightened to death of the man. They says his tongue has a beard on it. But do you know something? Johnny hasn't got an ounce of harm in him. I remembers when I was a ripe one like your big sister, I was over on the berry-brooks, the feast of Mary Magdalen, and out of nowhere along staggers himself, with his bottle, and I says to myself, he's going to rapture me. Of course I wants to scurry out of there but what with the moss underfoot I couldn't make a mile in a long hour, but all he says to me is: Do you want a glutch, miss? Up rises the hair on the back of my neck. I says: No sir thank you sir. Then he turns around and shakes hands with a spruce tree and offers it a glutch too. Off he goes along the ridge, tree to tree to tree. Tame as a pussycat. The poor devil.

Over here, now, here's another sad case—His Skinniness himself. Such a miserable sight, every morning pacing himself back and forth in front of the church. Black as the stranger with his black Irish stick. Face on him sour as a barrel of pickles. So lonesome he must be, nobody to talk to in the big old palace but that ugly mongrel. Hearing nothing from people but their dirty sins. Every morning rain or shine he's churching Nell—there she goes now, waddling along with her barrel up. With her Irish toothache. I'll catch her later, squeeze the day's dirt out of her. Yes, bornings all around him and not one for himself. I wonder in his whole life was he ever so close to a woman as to get a proper decent sniff at her.

Let me whisper, child, between you and me and the cat— and God forgive me for saying it—but even a priest needs a woman near to him. Every man does. And it goes the other way too. Every woman needs a man. Isn't that the truth, my darling? Of course it is. That's what we were put into this world for, nothing more. It's the same with them nuns. They got one another for company, but a crowd of women is not the same as a husband, now is it. The way they treats the youngsters, you know deep down they wants to have their own. It's a wonder they haven't got one or two hid away inside the convent. I tell you there's no denying nature. All the religion in the world can't stand in the way of nature.

There now, I've said it. And God forgive me if I'm after sinning.

Bless us, child, look at that: a crow on the church cross. In the name of the Father and of the Son and of the Holy Ghost. May God in heaven save us.

Time to climb down out of this, my darling. Time to make

the day. Time to make some life. Time to see to them loafs rising on the sill. Get dinner on the stove for them sleveens. Time for this, time for that—oh, there's always plenty of it. Please God there's time for the breeze to swing round and bring your daddy safe home to us.

My sweet, let me whisper something else, between you and me and the cat: sometimes I hates the sea. Dirty sweat of the planet, that's all it is. I pray to God when I gets to heaven there will be no sea in it.

In his lamb-like tread, little Kevin Barron ascends the three steps to the altar. He bears the candlesnuffer hoisted aloft before him, yet he pretends that he is the priest carrying the crucifix in procession. The child's thin arms quiver under the weight of the brass. He stations the bonnet in halo above the flame, then lowers it carefully, wary of touching the melted wax. He holds the bonnet suspended and waits for the grey wisp of death to seep from under the cone.

The child senses behind him the rustle of soft prayer. The weeping is so diffuse it seems to issue out of the very woodwork, out of every arch and niche and pillar. Yet he knows that the church is nearly empty. Only a few elderly worshippers remain.

The scattering of men kneel or sit in the pews. The women meanwhile, doing the Way of the Cross, tiptoe up and down the aisles, leapfrogging over one another like checkers. Little Kevin Barron does not know their names—these people were old before he was even born. In the transept, a woman prays transfixed before the statue of the Blessed Virgin Mary. Behind, in the sacristy, Father MacMurrough disrobes—chasuble, stole, maniple, cincture, alb, amice. The child can hear, outside in the yard, the ruckus from his schoolmates. The small sounds that manage to seep through the west windows only amplify the quiet of the nave.

By now, any one of the other boys would have thrown down his surplice and soutane and run along, run to enjoy the few moments of freedom before school starts. But Kevin Barron feels no such urge: the big boys who rule the yard only torment the likes of him. Besides, the period just after Mass, awash still in the sanctity of the Sacrifice, is a holy time—almost as holy as the Mass itself. The child breathes with pleasure the lovely lingering traces of frankincense. Little Kevin Barron will abide here until the nun rings the handbell.

In leisurely fashion he smothers the other candles on the Epistle side, then he sets the snuffer leaning against the altar and genuflects before the tabernacle. As he drops to his knee he brings his hands around in a wide embracing arch, fervently, the way the priest does during the Mass. As his palms come together, a thick sweet smell inflates the child's nostril.

Kevin Barron has watched, mortified, some of the older boys sneak a mouthful of the altar wine. He himself would never commit such a sacrilege. But before Mass this morning, when he topped up the cruet, he allowed a few drops to fall over his fingertips—the way the priest does at the Ablutions. Lovingly the boy sniffs at his hands. They smell like the molasses that Mother slathers over his morning bread. But the dark liquid glowing there within the crystal looks nothing like molasses. It looks like the real blood that it will become.

The boy rises to his feet.

Sunlight falls square upon the conopaeum. The light paints patches of green and pink against the whiteness of the veil. The colours are blurred and filmy, as though they have been cast adrift from a rainbow and have found shore here upon the tabernacle. Little Kevin Barron turns and follows the trail of light back through the dusty air—back towards the stained glass.

A spark of fear, a small sudden terror, ignites the boy's soul.

Oddly, it is the stained glass that frightens him. The tall window illuminates like a tapestry the east wall of the church. For some reason its holy form strikes the child as sinister and dangerous.

Kevin Barron studies the brilliant detail of the picture, yet he can find no evil in the image. Saint John the Baptist, clad in animal hides, gestures towards the Lamb that he shelters in his arms. It is a holy scene, full of colour and brightness — a vision of love, of protection.

Above the saint's head the sun flares precisely within his halo and produces a theatrical bolt of light. To soothe his fears, the child steps forward into the shaft. The light falls against his soutane and warms his chest. The boy says to himself: God the Father is here in this place.

The Lord is here, watching over little Kevin Barron, keeping the child safe from all harm. His strange terror subsides.

He picks up the snuffer and turns and carries on towards the Gospel side of the altar, where the candles are waiting to be extinguished.

"Our ship!" Johnny the Light bellows to all quarters. "Lads, she come to b-b-bring us home! Hurry on!"

With quaking hands the old man raises the bottle on high. His eyes, which anyway are weak, fail to notice the moon that lingers above the spire of the beacon. They are dazzled by the brilliance that reflects off the sea, that ripples through the tan liquid as splendidly as though through stained glass.

Down his gullet cascade the dregs of the rum. The raw liquor burns his throat. He doubles over and coughs and spits. With effort he gathers himself, rubs his eyes, and squints towards the ice. Broadly he smiles.

"Aye, me boys!" his voice calls out. "H-H-Here she be! And still more smokes again, right in back of her. 'Tis over!"

Joyfully he hurls the empty bottle towards the sea, but it slips from his maimed fingers and explodes against the scree slope.

Johnny tumbles into his cellar-quarters and fetches his greatcoat. He brings with him another bottle, nearly empty like the last. Snug he nestles it down the deepest cavity of the coat. He pulls shut the door behind him, and with an excited urgency he sets out westward.

The old man's figure is slight and bent. His coat hangs below the knees. This garment, combined with his gait—a sequence of painful lunges and limps, head bowed, hands clasped at the back—gives him the air of a monk in cloister. The laces of his decayed logans are hopelessly knotted, and the tongues dangle in a kind of dementia, exposing his calves.

The snarled undergrowth is dewy-damp with cobwebs. Soon the boots are wetted. Despite his damaged sight Johnny is confident of his footfall. Few animals travel the purgatorial wasteland near the lighthouse, and so in this region the faery paths are of his own making and are familiar to him. This morning he enjoys the pleasure of a slight breeze warming his cheeks.

He wears a dirty salt-and-pepper cap under which his head is bald. His earlobes are scarred and disfigured. Above his nose, leprous also, black brows converge and give his eyes the shade of death-sockets. A pingo of a mole sprouts great black hairs from his chin.

The old man hugs the edge of the bluffs until he comes to Gallows Beach. He stops here and gapes down the cliffside and surveys, as best his eyes permit, the yellow strand, the rocks, the glistening shallows. Finding nothing, he turns and strikes out overland, across the barrens. From time to time he glances back at the berg, its summit just visible above the scrub.

While he walks, Johnny speaks, in a voice coarse and stony yet so light that, were anyone strolling by his side, the person would barely hear. The old man seems to be speaking to the boulders and to the trees and to the wind.

"Come along, lads. Catch up. 'Tis over! Here's the *S-S-Stephano*, and the *Florizel*, and the *Bell*, and more besides. They're bringing t-t-tea!"

Johnny skirts the pond. Stagnant and nearly dry in this season, it smells of the colour brown. The surface is broken by dead branches like drowning hands clutching at the air. He makes his way across the wild field of pagan boulders. The stones are strewn across the landscape like some ravaged megalith. From the shade of a big rock a clutch of sheep scatters stupidly at his coming. Johnny gathers up a white lamb branded with a blue collar. The creature is too feeble to bolt, and he embraces the animal as if it were an infant. Smiling, he whispers to the beast.

"Aye, 'tis true! And here's our own steamer!"

Gently he sets down the animal and it runs bleating to its mother.

Johnny carries on. The boulders diminish and the terrain levels to bog. He stops to inspect the wide marsh and, while he weighs his chances of crossing dry-footed, he pulls the bottle from his coat and drinks.

Lightly, not daring to settle his weight lest it sink, he jumps from one hummock to the next, and so picks his way zigzagging to the far side. At each footfall his eyes grimace with pain. Secure on the far side, on firm sod, he wheezes and bends to catch his breath.

Steam rises from his heaving shoulders. He brushes away the clouds of mosquitoes and black flies that beset him. Nearby, in a shaded hollow, a pine rears up out of a mist-capped knoll. In the leaden calm of this place the solitary tree quivers before his face. His good ear picks up a sound that might be fiddle music. An unyoked goat stares down upon him from the summit of a scrape.

"Hushta!" Johnny hisses at the filthy animal. "Divil haul

ye!" The beast flees a short distance, then turns and glares back over its shoulder.

The old man follows a dry streambed and advances up the slope that is the ridge beginning to take shape. He passes through a bramble of blueberry bushes and lonely, squat spruce. The path is littered with boo-man's hats, sprouted overnight. The early sunlight grazes the curve of the land and bestows elongated shadows upon the trees. Johnny's own shade slides well before him, announcing his approach. In the higher branches, seagulls sleep like angels.

He flounders until he finds his handy network of rabbit-tracks. Each morning his passage through this area flushes out a fox, or a partridge, or a hare, or sometimes creatures that he cannot identify or that may not be there at all. Today he stirs up from the thicket three crows that were feeding on carrion. They fly in circles, cawing angrily, and Johnny shakes his fist.

"Hushta! *Hushta!*"

The landscape smooths to open meadowland with firm sod. Johnny climbs a set of drystone stiles. Soon he achieves the sequence of well-travelled paths that gradually widen to become the gravel road. Although the going is easier now, the old man is weary.

Opposite the graveyard he rests. Here the telegraph poles begin their westward march. His eye traces from one to the next—the way, he remembers, a trawl is pulled. Vaguely he makes out the cluster of colours in the distance: the parish. His eyes are too weak to sort one building from another. Normally he would hurry past the cemetery. Late evenings, making his way back to the beacon, often he is mortified to see sparks among the headstones. He leans against the covered platform at the base of the lane and pulls out his rum and drinks.

As the alcohol surges through his blood, the distant white form that he knows is the berg becomes more plainly triangular. It pleases Johnny to look upon such a simple shape. Meanwhile, the tinkling of the schoolbell floats down on the wind. Johnny turns his head and he listens intently to this sound.

He listens to the bell, and he smiles, then out loud he laughs. From head to toe his body quivers with jubilation. A chill wetness tightens in his groin. Great tears of mad joy roll down his skull face.

"Lads! 'Tis true. They come to save us! We's delivered!"

Father Gersam MacMurrough uplifts his eyes to the broken body.

Blood streams like red tears from the crown of thorns and across the brow and between the parted lips. The head is tilted back slightly, so that one might suspect the eyes are fixed on something out the window, the iceberg on the water perhaps. But in fact the eyes are downcast, the lids only half open, the pupils unfocused. The face of the crucified Christ wears a fathomless sorrow, an expression of such sadness it appears to Father MacMurrough that the plaster image may be alive—that it may even have something to say to him, something important.

The priest pauses at the gate. The muteness that confronts him recalls to his mind Denis the Carthusian, who wrote, nearing the end, *Ad securae taciturnitatis portum me transferre intendo*—"I am now going to enter the haven of secure taciturnity." The priest makes a small smile.

Yet, despite the smile, he continues to wait. *Christe eleison*, his soul implores.

But the Savior remains silent.

Sighing, supporting his thin frame with his blackthorn, Father MacMurrough genuflects in front of the tabernacle, turns, and steps onto the floor of the nave. He grips his hat and his cane behind his back, and makes his way slowly down the aisle.

Spectra of hanging motes slant diagonally from the high windows and lace the sanctuary with colour. His South Pacific flock enjoyed no such indulgence as stained glass. Of course none of them ever saw any, and he wonders how he might have explained the phenomenon to them. A filter that captures light — captures heaven? *Antap lait:* heavenly shine? *Antap fai ya?* Bernard of Clairvaux likened stained glass to the Virgin Birth—the light penetrates without breaking. On the other hand, Father MacMurrough has read somewhere that stained glass is enhanced by imperfections, by bubbles and scars and coarse violations. In other words, original sin is its very virtue.

The church is nearly drained of this morning's congregation. Women, shapeless and ageless under heavy woollen shawls, murmur into missals and worry prayerbeads and stare up at the Stations: Jesus Is Scourged, Jesus Falls the Third Time, Jesus Is Nailed to the Cross. A few old men, mildewed and wild-eyed, kneel in the pews and move their lips painfully against webs of dry sticky spittle. The priest nods as he passes them by. With tight smiles the people nod in return, then warily watch him from the corners of their eyes.

Here I am: the Black Stranger. He remembers that Protestant from Enniscorthy, the man who turned—he must have felt this way. Thirty years after he took the sacraments he was known, in whispers, as "the convert."

Here I am, Father MacMurrough smiles inwardly. Have yourselves a good look. But don't forget that I can see out the back of my head.

He in his turn distrusts the smiles he sees here. Like his own Irish, these Irish use courtesy as a weapon, to ward off the enemy foreigner. The ferocity of Celtic generosity, anywhere, is a wonder to behold.

From the recesses on the Epistle side comes the scrape of

a match, then the clank of metal on metal as a coin falls into the tin box. That can only be Mrs. Pelly.

The voteen is transfixed before the shrine. The veiled face of the Virgin flushes above the shifting colours of the vigil candles.

If you please, Father, Mrs. Pelly whispered across the rail, as she does every morning after Mass, I wants to get churched. He stood above the kneeling woman and pressed his hands upon her skull and sprinkled holy water and intoned the blessing, and he could not help but inhale the warm milky air that wafted from her. This morning he tasted it and it brought to his mind the warm smell of his own mother.

Halfway down the aisle the priest stops and rests his hat and his cane in a pew. He removes his glasses and rubs his eyes. He pulls his handkerchief from his pocket and wearily he wipes the lenses clean.

Outside in the schoolyard the nun rings the bell. The priest can hear behind him the boy, the pathetic child—an old man really—hurry out the back door of the sacristy.

The front entrance of the church bangs open. The crash echoes through the space and rattles the windows. Brief silhouettes, auras flaming, of a pair of schoolgirls bolt across the rectangle of white light flooding the doorway. Pressing upon their crowns one a handkerchief and the other the palm of a bare hand, they hurry through the vestibule, kneel in the back pew, make the Sign of the Cross, whisper a rapid Hail Mary, leap up, and run out, leaving the door ajar—all of it seemingly in the space of a breath.

From the cool interior Father MacMurrough steps over the threshold and into the sun. The hot breeze jolts him. He dons his hat to shade his eyes from the glare.

Drawn by the bell, droves of children converge upon the gate. They are in colours rather than in uniforms, and they squeal and skylark more exuberantly than usual. Of course, he forgot: today they get their holidays. At noon he must visit with them, speak to them, say important things. One after another they sing out: "Good morning, Father!" He knows none of the children by name, but he nods, and his face makes a tight smile.

Behind him Mrs. Pelly steps forth. The woman is wrapped in prayer and mercifully oblivious of him standing there. She descends the concrete stair heavily and sets off up the road, telling her beads as she walks.

The nun rings the bell again and the sound pulls the last of the children into the school.

The morning is empty.

The black slab that is the roof of the palace is barely visible above the birches. Low-browed like an aged boxer, the mansion has been battered into greyness by winds and neglect. Most of the musty rooms are barred. Only echoes pass in the hallways. The toilet is broken, awaiting a piece to come from Canada. The priest misses, more than the convenience of it, the warm noises that the plumbing makes, clanking like some troll in the bowels of the great house. As it is, no sound at all relieves the deadly silence of the nighttime.

The aftertaste of the wine lingers over Father MacMurrough's tongue. He is hungry and he would enjoy his breakfast. But after all the bustle and life of the Mass, and the passage of the children, the rectory will be a dismal place. In any case, nowadays his food often fails to fill him. He will pace here for a spell and take in the sun. Perhaps someone will want confession.

"Konfessio," he says, aloud.

He takes out a cigarette and strikes a match and smokes.

Deep in the sky, a gull hovers on the roof of the wind. White clouds billow in the blue vault. The breeze ruffles his cassock.

The press of the fabric makes him conscious of the frailty of his body. He is only in his forty-ninth year, but already his flesh is loosening from the bone. His face reflects the grey texture of faded wood. The broken nose gives his profile an expression of collapse. Only his eyes, which are a bright emerald, remain keen.

He tries to hum:

When ∂um-mer
Spread∂ her hand . . .

A figure lurches up the road from the vicinity of the cemetery. It's that ancient leper, what's his name? Johnny Delight? Funny there are not more like him in this place. Years ago, in some villages in Ireland, midwives strangled defective, newborns on the spot, so that today . . .

Why, he's staggering! At this hour. *Yu longlong long wiski,* the Goroka children would howl at the drunks.

It was only yesterday that the priest heard the youngsters in this place teasing the old man. Hushta Johnny! they squealed in his bewildered face. It gave the priest pleasure to see this happen. It gave him pleasure, and he was ashamed.

All too well he knows why he cultivates such un-Christian meanness in himself: it gives him reasons for his solitude. He can endure any retreat if it has a logic. So it is that he always seeks fault — drunkenness or weakness or deformity, or excessive piety. And where he cannot discover fault, he invents it. Of himself meanwhile he brandishes the worst side, and so he gives other people good reasons to retreat from him. All of this he well understands.

Disgusted with himself, he turns from the old man and faces west.

A horse and cart advance slowly. A young girl, a child really, runs down the road, late for school. *Pikkinini meri.*

On top of the house over the way, the woman has emerged to sit in her chair. Every morning, wind or rain or shine, she clutches to her breast the bundle of her infant and she watches the sea. There you have it, the very image of Christian hope: a woman waiting for her husband to come home. What, the priest wonders, would be the very image of despair — of *morosos?*

Out of curiosity he turns in the direction the woman faces.

A frown shadows his face.

Soon after he landed in the country, this spring, Father MacMurrough heard bizarre stories about icebergs. They take every size and shape you can imagine, the people said to him. They moan and cry like widows. They die spectacular deaths. When they break up, large swells can appear from nowhere on a glass-calm sea.

He suspected his leg was being pulled. But before long he had watched the flotillas sail around the cape and down the shore, and run aground, and commence to die, and he had seen that every story was true. At night in the palace, unable to sleep, he would lie wide-eyed listening to the hideous snapping and rumbling. During the daytime he would stand on the heights and watch the ice-mountains turn bottom-up, or else crack in two, or simply collapse and disintegrate into little cubes of slush and melt away to seawater.

The very whiteness of this berg deepens the tones of the sea and the sky. He is reminded of an old family portrait: someone overlaid a cutout image of a deceased child in an attempt to make her appear part of the living group, but instead, the effect was the opposite, and the child was fixed apart, ghostlike, already in eternity. In the same way, this piece of ice seems to belong to some weird dimension removed from the everyday world.

Its silhouette is honed and bristling, with the steep sides

and sharp peak of a tall ship. The notion troubles him, as it did earlier, outside the rectory, that this shape has touched him once already in his life.

Anyone watching the priest at that moment would see him raise his walking stick and point it seaward, then stagger slightly, as if struck by a pain in his midsection, finally plant the stick well in front of his feet and grip it with both hands, and so steady himself.

A young man, dressed in black, is busy fitting out the sails of a skiff. A young woman, all in white and wearing a straw hat, stands on the pier with her back to the young man. She is watching the break of day.

The light swells grey and then purple above the Kerry mountains and unveils a cloudless sky. It spills down and probes the texture of damp rooftops and chimneys and dank cobbled alleyways of Cahirciveen. The air tastes of the salt sea. Nobody else is moving in the town, and the only sound is the faint cry of birds. It is the crows and gulls hour.

When he has made things ready the young man reaches up and takes a basket from her hand. He steadies the boat and helps her down the ladder. He sees to it that she is settled in the bow and snugly wrapped against the cool air, and then he unties the painter. Gently he paddles out into the stream. As soon as he feels the breath of a cat's-paw he ships the oars and draws up the sail. The breeze bellies out the canvas and the boat surges forward, alive. He leans back at the tiller and smiles to the young woman.

The skiff glides up the corridor of the harbour, so quietly it seems to him it is the landscape itself and not the boat that is in motion. They slip past dinghies tethered and lazily swinging and past pebble beaches and patchwork green meadows bearing greystone walls and farmhouses still asleep. He extends a forefinger towards the old telegraph station, and he tells her about the undersea cable that runs all the way across the Atlantic to a place called Heart's Content.

The young woman, heavy-eyed, is observing a flock of gulls roosting on the berm. She smothers a yawn and draws the shawl tight against her shoulders.

The sun has climbed above the rim of the mountains and it shines down directly now. After rounding the headland the boat suddenly is naked on the open sea, lifting and sinking upon a long transatlantic swell. The young man steers southwest, towards a mighty rock bristling out of the horizon.

Skellig Michael, he tells her. It always reminds him of a clipper ship, a majestic tea-clipper, outward-bound with every shred of canvas set.

A scant breeze strays down from the pastures and brings the smell of new-mown hay. Lulled by the hollow slap of waves against the hull, the young man and the young woman fade into languor. Slivers of sunshine glance off the mirrors in the waves and the air tinkles with light. Against the glare she peers eastward towards Dursey Island. The beacon high on the cape blinks torpidly — once, twice — and suddenly it is extinguished, as if drowned under the flood of sunshine. As the boat moves offshore the ironbound coast northward to Slea Head melds into one grey palisade, so that the two people can no longer detect the narrows through which they have just passed. Neither the sweep of the land astern, nor the rock ahead, nor the unchanging hue of the sky gives any hint of movement, and it appears the boat is becalmed inside a sea of sunlight.

The ocean breathes like a great beast slumbering underneath a blanket. The young woman closes her eyes. Her head nods, and she drifts into a half-sleep.

Listlessly, the young man gives himself over to watching the outline of Skellig Michael as it swells before him. Jagged leaden corrugations appear within the darkness of the silhouette. The island takes on a three-dimensional texture. Soon the looming spires dwarf the vessel nestling in their lee, and it seems to his eye that the rock has weighed anchor and is itself bearing down, ponderously, upon the skiff.

Just then, his spirit is touched by a long plaintive note coming to him from the direction of the island. It is a dolorous cry, a lamentation such as might issue from all the suffering souls in purgatory. He listens and again the sound echoes off the face of the cliff and carries across the water. For an instant he fancies it is the great rock itself, sighing. He scans the waterline and against the background of a grey boulder he can barely make it out—a solitary grey seal. The animal makes its call a third time and then, wearily, it slips into the sea.

At Blind Man's Cove the young man helps the young woman onto the landing. He hands up the basket and then he moors the boat. Briskly they strike out along the path that snakes just above the landwash. Even before they round the corner at Cross Cove they can hear the shrieking of the birds.

The two people stop and take in the noisy chaos that bars their way. Perched upon narrow ledges on the sea-cliffs, or wheeling overhead, or spiralling and splashing head-first into the cove, are fulmars and razorbills and shearwaters, choughs and rock pipits and skuas by the thousands. As the pair are about to plunge through the hurricane suddenly she is alarmed, and she reaches out and grasps for his arm. He laughs, and shouting above the din he jokes with her. The birds are harmless, he says. They are only the spirits of the dead monks.

The two follow the track until they find the steps that have been chiselled from the rock face. The stairway, steep and eroded, zigzags up the cliffside and out of sight towards the sky. He offers his hand to her, and she takes it.

Soon they have ascended high above the birds and the screeching fades. Once again the air is transparent. The naked bedrock gives way to patches of sod spotted here and there with the white blossoms of sea spurrey and campion. Near the summit they come upon a level area which he tells her is known as Christ's Saddle. The going is easier now, and she surrenders his hand.

They follow the ridge towards the northern peak and pass through the tunnel in the retaining wall. The fullness of the enclosure comes into view.

At first sight, even to the acquainted eye of the young man, the compound contains nothing but haphazard mounds of rubble. But soon the scattered piles of rock take form and are seen to be a huddled gathering of beehive-shaped, drystone huts. At the fringes squat several tiny stone oratories, each one resembling in contour the hull of an upturned punt. The ruin of a window—all that survives of a larger chapel—gazes from its freestanding wall like a forlorn cyclops. Beyond, the ocean stretches away grey and empty. Outlined against the backdrop can barely be deciphered a crude slab of a crucifix. Its arms are extended seaward in the manner of a forsaken shepherd howling mutely.

The two people make their way down a winding path overgrown with sea pink. He speaks in an undertone, as though they are in church, telling her about the sixth-century monks who started this hermitage. Saint Michael was their patron, but the hermits remained so isolated that they fell out of step with the Christian calendar, eventually with Christianity itself. By the end of the first millennium, Viking raiders had driven them away for ever.

While he is still talking she leaves his side and wanders off the path. Her attention has been drawn by a row of coarse weather-scarred stones. He comes up beside her. The monks' graveyard, he whispers. The two people stand in the bright sunshine and make the sign of the cross and pray in silence.

He is about to speak but she hushes him with a motion of her hand.

Underneath their feet the ground is humming.

It is a soft whirr, like the purring of a cat. The sound seems to come from no particular place but from every quarter at once.

Off to the side there is a stir and a flutter. Out of a hole in the sod a puffin has emerged. The bird points its beak and glares indignantly at the intruders and then launches itself on clumsy wings over the edge of the mountain and into the abyss. From a second burrow comes another one, and another, and then as if by magic a small flock arises out of the ground and scatters downhill to the sea. After the last of the creatures has disappeared under the waves, the earth is silent once again.

Mutely the two people carry on towards the cluster of buildings. As they approach the first of the cells the young man begins to talk. He points out to her the clever corbelling of the stonework, and explains how it has kept the interiors snug and dry even after a thousand years of Atlantic storms. They bend under the short narrow doorway and enter the hut.

The chamber is windowless, and they must wait for their eyes to adjust to the dim light. They stand side by side in the middle of the cavity and listen to the sound of their own breathing. Gradually the hollow reveals itself. The low ceiling and the walls are of the same raw stone as the exterior. The floor is bare clay. There is no furniture of any kind, not even the vestige of a hearth. The cell is nothing more than an empty vault, a man-made cave. Yet the young man can sense something more. After the hazy ambiguities of the morning, after the vague distances of sea and sky, the interior surrounds him at last with close and solid boundaries. He can reach out and touch with his hands the steadfastness of the walls. Underfoot he can feel the firmness of the earth. The borders are palpable ones. A dreamy coziness embraces him, and he thinks: the sanctum of his mother's womb might have been something like this. He turns to the young woman, and he is about to ask if she shares in this feeling when he sees that she is no longer by his side but has already gone out through the doorway.

He follows her and emerges squinting into the bright open noon. Monks prayed in dark cells, he whispers, regaining her side, so that when they came out into the light they saw the glory of God.

After they have explored the oratories and the chapel and the other huts they move off to the crest of the peak. From this vantage it almost seems they can survey every corner of the universe. On a level patch of grass he sets down the basket, and he lifts from it a white tablecloth which he unfolds carefully. At diagonal corners of the cloth the two people recline.

He smiles as he brings forth a Waterford decanter. It brims with a wine so clear and lustrous it could be bottled sunshine. He sets the decanter in the glare of the linen, where the crystal scatters the light abroad in a rose window of watery colour. He produces a pair of silver goblets, fills each, with a flourish passes one into her hand, then raises his own heavenward in a toast to the sun.

They sip.

He reaches again into the basket for cutlery and china, bread and cheese and grapes. He arranges these items upon the cloth and then he slices the food. The two people bless themselves and say grace.

After the long journey and the climb up the mountain they are hungry, and they eat in silence.

When they have taken their fill they lean back on their elbows. Indifferently they pluck at the grapes and surrender to the heat of midday. The sun by this hour is directly overhead. The light is infused with a soft white texture, almost tangible, and it bathes the two people in a luminous wash.

The young man scans the sweep of the horizon. A veil of mist hides the line where sea meets sky. The surface of the ocean is calm now, and utterly barren. Vainly his eye searches for a break in the monotony of water.

He turns back towards the young woman. In her white dress and hat she seems to him draped in a film of gauze. He sees that she is smiling slightly at some thought of her own. Pulling the brim of her hat down to shade her eyes she avoids his stare, and now it is she who gazes out over the water.

While she is looking away the young man studies her face. He explores the line of her brow, the unblinking lash, the pale green of the iris. He cannot tell whether she is focusing on some point she has managed to find out on the ocean, whether her mind is far away, whether she is even aware of his presence.

So closely does he watch her that a curious notion takes hold of him: in his mind, everything beyond their little circle has evaporated. He imagines that the world, the expanse of sky and sea and sand, has perished, and all that remains is the two people and the radiant piece of linen and the dome of light they occupy. Nothing has survived, he fancies, but this lambent womb.

He leans towards the young woman and he whispers her name.

Upon his own ear the sound falls strangely, and he realizes that it is the first time today he has spoken it.

The young woman does not answer him but turns her face towards the ground. Although the brim of her hat conceals her eyes, he can see the nostrils flaring now, the lips no longer smiling but pressed firm and still moist from the grape she has just burst. Somewhere in the reaches of his spirit he hears the approach of the words he has waited all day to speak, as if the words already bore a reality of their own.

In a kind of slow motion, her head begins to turn. Her eyes come up as if to meet his, but instead they pass by and look beyond him. She is frowning. She is looking up towards the sky.

Just above their heads a bird hovers. Wings spread, stationary in the air, the bird seems to be suspended on a thread from heaven. It makes no sound. The plumage is pure white, the wings grey with black tips. Its dark hypnotic eye stares down and fixes upon the young man, and as the bird banks away he feels a twist of vertigo, the mountain dizzy and uncertain beneath him. Indolently the creature glides oceanward and dissolves into the haze at the horizon.

The bubble of light that the young man imagined is burst. Once again the world is remote, its borders veiled and precarious. He can hear, coming from some awful distance, the sorrowful murmur of the sea.

The two people watch the place where the bird vanished.

Finally she turns to face him. Her eyebrows are raised: What was it you were about to say to me?

He looks beyond her towards the western ocean. He sees a grey void all the way to America, all the way to Heart's Content, and he tries to recall something of Newman's he once read, something about going out on the open sea.

He shakes his head: It was nothing.

They sit a while longer and watch the shadow of Skellig Michael stretch across the sea towards the coast of Kerry. Tall bright clouds advance from the west and bring a cool breeze. The two people gather up the picnic and climb down the stairway and cast off for the main-

land. Before they have sailed out of the shadow of Skellig the young man hears once again the call of the seal.

Father MacMurrough draws forth from his vest his ancient Waltham. His grandfather presented it to him at ordination, and since that day it has spoken in the voice of a friend. He holds the timepiece to his ear and with pleasure he listens to the solid warm tik-tik tik-tik that it delivers.

The hands say nine o'clock.

A gust of wind cools his brow. He descends the steps and walks down the gentle incline of Church Square. He is making for the jerry-built sprawl of stores and lofts and warehouses that the people call the octagon. The trellis is padlocked—the shopgirls are late. The priest peers in at the window. The four-faced clock on the pillar says half-past nine.

Father MacMurrough is about to reset the hands of his timepiece when he notices the reflection in the windowglass. He steps back for a better look.

There it is.

Morosos.

He pockets the watch. Wearily, aimlessly, he wanders round to the back of the octagon.

The beach is there. The tide is low and the sand is wide. At the far end of the strand, Jackman shambles along the waterline. The beast snuffles among the tin cans and the rotting kelp and driftwood. The dog ignores the man.

The priest has nothing better to do. He strolls all the way down to the water.

His shoes sink in the damp sand. Landwash—that is what the people here call this: sometimes land, sometimes wash. Years ago, he heard someone argue that littoral dwellers are natural fundamentalists, that the apposition of land and sea informs all their choices with a plain clarity, a hardness. But now he can see that the issue is not so simple. At this moment, for example, the narrow strip of beach where he stands is land, whereas six hours hence it will be water.

He yearns for plain hardness, for simple decision. For a clear path.

Pebbles mutter under the swell. The beach sifts the sea. The priest pokes among the stones until he discovers a wide flat one. He tosses it high into the sea and it comes down and stabs the water with an ugly sound: guck. The children here have a good name for that: deadman's bubble.

His stick finds a pale blue rock. It is about the diameter of a fifty-cent piece, but rounded and purple and smooth—a fat marble. He digs it out of the sand and picks it up and rolls it in his fingers until the wet grains have fallen away, until the stone is dry. He squeezes the thing, admiring its plain . . .

And then, just then, with a sudden logic he could never put into words, he sees the clear path.

He smiles in surprise—flabbergasted, there is no better word—at the beauty of what he has discovered, of what he has achieved, at the sheer splendour of it. Such sureness and clarity. Such hardness. And all in so tiny a moment!

The priest lingers within the ribbon of his landwash. So charmed he is that he almost laughs aloud. This is his sublime moment, the moment between the decision and the act. Had he but known this territory would bear such enchantment—would be so painless!—he might well have visited it years before.

He gives the stone a final squeeze and lovingly slips it into his pocket.

He hurries back up the slope to the road. Looking neither left nor right, he bypasses the shop window and its four-faced clock and he makes straight for the palace. The stone will join the others, eventually, and already he has decided what name he will give to this one. He does not want to meet a single soul, for he cannot help the absurd smile that clings to his face.

VII

The Kingdom of God

Pushed by a warm eastern breeze, a tiny sailboat appears at the horizon. The storm has cleansed the air, the sky is splendid.

The sail threads among the icebergs that litter the water. A fiery cross illuminates its one small canvas. The arms of the crucifix bear the halo of the pagan sun. The sail propels a hull of mere ox-hide. Within this eggshell huddle eighteen Irish monks.

Timidly the vessel approaches the shoals.

It is five centuries since the torture and execution of the Nazarene.

A green flash at sunset lured the monks to abandon their Kerry hermitage and venture westward on the sea. They have come in quest of an enchanted island, a land of purity and grace where sins of the flesh have never been committed. The chronicles call this place the Isle of the Undying, the Promised Land of the Saints. For seven years in an open coracle the holy men have suffered the stormy winds and waves.

The monks have navigated by faith. Their crossing has been filled with the wonder of God.

They have fixed heading upon crystal basilicas that receded into the horizon before their advance. They have seen in the north night sky hues flickering like candles behind glass. They have passed through the Sea of Death and beheld the very maw of hell, where devils belched fire and smoke and brimstone that burned the nostrils of the holy men. Becalmed one bright midnight in fields of snow atop the sea, a limbo of neither light nor darkness, the monks wept to hear an eternity of unbaptized infants cry out for the salvation of heaven.

The coracle fell within the teeth of the hideous storm. For nine days and nine nights the blizzard roared. When the air cleared, the monks found themselves floating close among the very crystal cathedrals that had guided them from afar. In prayer they gave thanks for their lives, because their survival was a miracle, proof of God's blessing on their mission.

So it is they have come safely to the island.

Shouting *Terra!* the monks alight and explore. They find only desolation. Spying on the naked rock neither plant nor animal nor — despite the penitential terrain — any saint, they decide this is not after all the Promised Land. It is the Land God Gave to Cain.

Lacking trees to burn, they chop an oar and ignite a fire, in homage both to Saint John the Baptist and to the midsummer sun. They make the sign of the cross over the wasteland and they bless it: a land which the Lord thy God careth for, for the eyes of the Lord are always upon it, from the beginning of the year even unto the end of the year.

The monks steer southward. Behind them, the great rock sinks under the horizon. Unseen by human eye, a white bird flutters across the barrens.

Beyond the seas, the empire falls to the Ostrogoths. Saint Columba founds his mission at Iona. The first church bells ring out, in Rome. Persians sack Jerusalem and steal the True Cross. The Chinese invent tea and gunpowder. Moors invade Iberia and invent the astrolabe and coffee. Indians discover the zero. Anglo-Saxons conquer the Britons. The millennium approaches, and Christians everywhere fear the Last Judgement.

All the while, waves wash the shore of the island and etch their mark in its bedrock. The millennium is fulfilled before another vessel comes down upon the coast.

The hull is of stout oaken planks, clinker-built. Like a swan it sits lightly on the face of the water, yet it moves boldly. The single mast bears a single sail of coarse wool. From the prow glares a dragon's head, its tongue lolling. The boat is manned by squat warriors, dark-haired, armed with broad-axes and hatchets and swords and spears and clubs.

Hearing the boasts of Irish missionaries that their monasteries safeguard the treasures of Christendom, the northmen have sacked and laid waste all the holy houses of Ireland. In the last remote hermitage at the very rim of the known world, they found among the spoils an illuminated manuscript. The pictures told of an ancient voyage, a venture far westward in search of a blessed land. The northmen hacked the monks to pieces and sailed off in pursuit of the new prize.

Being poor navigators, the marauders discovered many lands. They chased towering crystal castles that retreated before their advance. At night their way was lit by the glow from the shields of the Valkyrie. Narrowly they escaped the lumps of fiery slag hurled by monsters from a black thundering fortress. They happened upon battlefields of snow where grazed herds of mermen, and although the mermen whined for quarter, mercilessly the seafarers clubbed their skulls and sliced them to ribbons and left the snow red with their blood.

Now, after years of wandering the northern seas, the raiders bear down upon the land of rocks.

The warriors take to the sweeps and run the keel high up

the shingle. They find the bedrock muffled in coarse shrubbery. The higher ground immediately they put to the torch, as a warning to enemies who might be about. The fires stir from the underbrush scores of rabbits and birds, and these the northmen kill. The shrubbery yields as well blue grapes in profusion. From these the northmen extract a crude wine, and so they name the place Wineland.

For weeks they prowl the land, but rabbits and birds and grapes are all they can capture. One dawn, on Thor's Day, bored from want of pillage, insane from a night of drinking, they brandish their broad-axes and run howling into the teeth of the storm-surf. Hacking madly at the winds and the waves, to the last man they are lost.

Taurus explodes. Halley's Comet lights the sky. Normans take England. Lady Godiva rides naked through Coventry. Jerusalem falls to the Crusaders. Walcher of Malvern invents latitude and longitude. Canon Fulbert of Paris castrates Peter Abelard. The First Lateran Council forbids marriage of priests. The Abbé Suger introduces the rose window. Ye Olde Bell pub opens near London. Normans take Ireland at the invitation of Dermot MacMurrough. Hats come into fashion. A meteor strikes the moon. King John signs the Magna Carta. Marco Polo travels to China. Roger Bacon predicts the discovery of the Western hemisphere. Glass mirrors appear. The peasantry suffer the Hundred Years War. The Black Death kills most of Europe. Gypsies bring playing cards from Arabia. King Philip the Fair cures scrofulites with his touch. Chaucer writes *The Canterbury Tales*. English archers rout French knights at Agincourt. Berbers take Timbuktu. Lisbon markets sell African slaves. Denis the Carthusian defines beauty as light. Turks take Constantinople. The peasantry suffer the War of the Roses. English and French conspire to burn Joan of Arc. Gutenberg prints the Bible. Vlad Dracula dies in battle. Prince Ferdinand marries Infanta Isabella. And the Inquisition tortures heretics for the greater glory of God.

Swells roll against the western island. The sea grinds the dead bones of the northmen to sand. The curves and whorls of the waves etch deeply into the granite. Five centuries pass before another European sets foot on these shores.

This crossing takes place a decade before the voyage of the Genoan, and begins in Ireland.

Famine ravages the Irish countryside. Horses feed on one another's tails, sheep on one another's wool. From remote parishes come rumours of cannibalism. The people, suffering every disease and misery, reckon they are living the Final Days.

In a Carlow vale, a mob begs for food at the monastery gate. The monks flee the horrors of the hunger—all, that is, but one. He surrenders his meagre pantry to the crowd. Guilt-ridden at watching the children devour scraps, the monk pledges to God that he himself will forswear food. He gives away every morsel, his only sustenance being the Host, until one morning as he elevates the chalice in the Consecration he collapses and perishes.

The monk leaves a son. The boy is of an age between childhood and youth. The mother is unknown to the child. The child goes by the name of Tomas Croft.

The monk has shaved the child's head and raised him in the austerities of the Rule. He has confined the boy to the cloisters and sanctuaries of the public church. He has allowed him only the freedom to climb the bell tower, whence the child has surveyed the landscape and smelled the salty breezes that come over the Blackstairs. He has taught the boy Latin and made him his acolyte. Thus, in the entirety of his life, young Tomas Croft has known only the ways of the holy men. He has spoken in earnest to none but his own father and God. While his spiritual learning is great, so narrow has been the range of his worldly experience that, as manhood approaches, the fantasies that excite him, that stir his body beyond his control and take fierce command of him, are provoked by such things as coloured glass, or the smell of incense in the church.

After burying his father's corpse, its fingers still clutching the chalice, the boy tolls out the knell. Never before has he been alone, and for three days he cowers in the confessional. A terrific hunger grips him, and he opens the gate and ventures forth. He steps for the first time beyond the walls of the monastery, into strangeness. He takes to the roads.

He scrabbles barefoot across the deserted bogs, down the empty glens, through villages corpse-strewn and silent. For countless leagues he travels. He eats grass and thistle. He devours the carcasses of sparrows and rats that contaminate the miracle wells. He chews upon discarded shoes. He eats even the cauls of unborn calves that the people use instead of windowglass. He smells the stench of a million deaths.

In the dark he sees no light. He hears only whimpering and mewling everywhere. He sleeps in cold pews in sepulchral churches. Sometimes the sky roars with the clash of demons fighting over the diseased corpses, and the boy fears that he has stumbled upon Slieve-nan-Or, the place where the last great battle is to be fought, where the end of the world begins.

One day, he comes into a town. The place, he overhears, is called Ferns. In the church he shrinks from a horrible image—a statue of a dwarf with his manhood slashed away, leering, pulling apart the gaping wound. Nearby, the shrivelled body of a dead sexton sits bolt upright in a pew. While Tomas Croft gnaws at the feet, the corpse's eyes, half open, stare mutely at him. Tomas Croft is reminded of the monastery, of the Jesus on the cross whose eyes stared down on the boy whenever he took Communion.

The corpse clutches a blackthorn cudgel. Tomas Croft

breaks the fingers and takes away the stick. With this fierce weapon he clubs rabbits and crows, cats and dogs. He eats their flesh raw and drinks their blood. His hunger only sharpens his skills, and he is able to defend himself against the desperate people he begins to meet, the walking skeletons who crave the food his enterprise has killed, or crave to eat his own living flesh.

Hordes of wraithlike beggars straggle south in procession towards the warming air. Stalking them, Tomas Croft comes after some days into a seaport. It is Wexford Town, of which his father often spoke.

The aroma of fish draws him directly to the quays. Never in his landlocked life has Tomas Croft seen so much as a rowboat. Now, weak and despairing, he takes the crucifix-forest of masts and spars before his eyes to be a vast cemetery.

The boy rests on a wharf-grump. He watches a rat waddle up the gangplank of a stinking balinger. Tomas Croft recognizes the holy word painted on the bow: *Trinitie*. Gripping his cudgel, trembling with hunger, he follows after the fat creature and climbs the gangplank. As he crosses the gunnel, the horrible stench of the vessel staggers him. In his exhaustion he faints, and he topples down the hatch — safely into a puncheon of raw capelin. When he comes to his senses he devours the little fish by the fistful until he has gorged himself.

Upon this mattress of scales the boy sleeps.

A thundering rouses him awake. The crew of the balinger have discovered Tomas Croft, and they are hammering on the walls of the cask. The boy raises his stick to defend himself, but at that moment he retches a gutful of fish, and the fishermen overpower him easily.

The *Trinitie* hails from Bristol. Every man is all for heaving the foreigner to the sharks. But the master is superstitious. He declares that the stowaway is a lucky omen and ought to be spared. But in return the boy must work. Because he is a bog-Irishman and good for nothing else, Tomas Croft will serve as the fish-banger.

The *Trinitie* casts off and sails out onto the swells. The anchor finds holding ground in sight of the Scillies. The crew climb into drums lashed outboard and proceed to work the handlines.

Tomas Croft is terrified of the ocean. He is frightened by the strange shifting sensation that floating is, by the sheer volume of the water underneath him, by the violence of even the mildest winds and waves. His job is to club the fish as soon as they are pulled in over the side, and he is fearful of the great thrashing beasts. But what frighten him most are his own mates. The monks who raised him always treated him with kindness, but here, all hands take turns at persecuting him.

His mates scoff at his blazing red hair. *Bonfire!* they cry, when from the rigging they piss on his crown. They scoff at his piety. They themselves pray not from faith but only for want of some divine favour, and every morning when the boy kneels they baptize him with buckets of cold seawater. They scoff at his innocence, and try to provoke his chastity with lascivious stories of full-breasted mermaids. They scoff at his ignorance of the sea, and petrify him with descriptions of the monsters that dwell below. They scoff at his tongue. Whenever he speaks, the crew make oinking sounds, for his Gaelic offends them. In their English eyes he is less than human, and they appeal to the master that he is not a lucky stowaway at all, but a jinxing swine, and that he should be tossed overboard.

Tomas Croft retreats into silence. The only sound he makes is when, on the captain's signal, he bangs his cudgel against the ship's bell and tolls out the watches. If his blackthorn is not needed he hides himself safely within the coziness of the ship's cuddy and watches the crew go about their business.

The boy's pleasure is cod tongues. After the fish are split, the master obliges Tomas Croft to gather the heads and slice out the tongues and string them on a wire, in decades like the rosary. In this way the captain—who believes it very bad luck for the crew to know how much they have pulled in and who consequently is content with the boy's muteness—keeps tally of the catch. After the master counts the tongues Tomas Croft greedily eats every last one, raw.

In this manner Tomas Croft survives.

The *Trinitie* enjoys a fortnight of profitable fishing. Suddenly, one fair morning, the hooks come to the surface bearing only the untouched bait. The cod have abandoned the waters.

The captain orders the anchor shipped and the vessel shifted to another ground. But just as the rising anchor breaks the surface, the winds fade. Strange tides swirl under the keel. An unknown current draws the vessel westward in a dead calm, sails adroop. The captain casts a wood-chip over the bow and makes for the stern, but instead of floating the length of the boat, as it usually does, the stick drifts forward and out of sight. The anchor is launched again and although the rhode is surrendered to its limit the flukes grab no mooring. Stern-first the *Trinitie* glides, the dark silhouette of Land's End sinking strangely before the bow.

The fishermen glare at Tomas Croft. The boy withdraws to the cuddy.

Within the hour, a dome of fog descends and smothers the balinger. It is a cloud fallen to earth. So thick is the mist that the clang of the bell echoes back, from above and from all quarters, as if the ship itself is snared inside a great carillon. The very wetness of the atmosphere quenches lanterns. There is no shadow, only greyness at every turn. From the stem, the crew cannot make out the tiller, nor from the deck can they make out the barrel. The air seems thicker even than the sea itself, for the only direction the fishermen can spy to any distance is downward. Their world is turned bottom-up.

Late that day, a dark presence, like the ghost of a gigantic galleon, passes slowly larboard. The sailors hear the thin cries of puffins coming down from on high.

Skellig Michael, the master declares in a trembling voice.

At this news, the fishermen shudder. Skellig! Where the souls of drowned sailors fly about in the air, weeping.

Christe eleison, they pray. The Bristol boat has drifted beyond the western edge of the Christian world. For all the sailors know, it is hellbound.

Day after day the fog holds. Tomas Croft is careful to keep himself out of sight. Sternwise the boat drifts. Week after week, the fishermen see neither sun nor moon nor stars. All that changes is the grey of day surrendering to the black of night. In hopes of buying a wind the fishermen cry out to malevolent spirits. For food they consume their capelin-bait. For drinking water they inhale the fog itself. None of the usual sea-things breaks the monotony—neither sound nor breeze, nor swells by which they might dead reckon their course, nor even birds or fish. The crew take to spending the daytime hours leaning over the rails and peering into the congealed ocean. Nothing is visible to them but cod-lines fading hopelessly into the murk. The fishermen are lost within eternity.

Once, in the distance, thunder rolls. The fog darkens and then glows like live coals. Nervous darts ripple the calm. The mist tastes of soot and ash. Abruptly, fiery rocks fall hissing all around. Stones splash and sputter, steaming, into the sea, or crash, still smouldering, upon the deck of the ship.

The fishermen drop to their knees and beg for deliverance

from this devil's sea. Fervently, to Saint Elmo, they pray, and at once the rumbling ceases and the rock no longer falls. Soon the atmosphere resumes its familiar pallor.

Later that week, the air chills. The fog freezes into needles of rime. Frost-smoke swirls off the sea surface. Every breath stings. Bones shiver. Decks and mast and rigging become encased in glitter so thick the boat teeters under the weight of it. The ice magnifies everything in a faint blue tint. The ice swells, like a living membrane, faster than the crew can hack it away.

The fishermen hear the crack of a monstrous whip. They hear terrible splashing sounds, like the roar of mountains tumbling into the sea. Swells uplift the hull, and the vessel threatens to founder.

Cliffs of ice sail out of the fog. From all quarters they bear down upon the balinger. They converge like the jaws of a titanic vise conspiring to crush the vessel. Immense collisions boom deep underneath the keel. The ocean boils. Blocks of blue ice charge to the surface and crash against the dealboard. The vessel shakes and careens. The mountains close tight upon the hull. The beams groan.

The sailors pray now to Saint Peter Gonzalez. Their prayers are answered, for they are still on their knees when the thundering and the groaning abruptly stop. The ice then grips the hull strangely, cradling the vessel plumb and safe in the water.

For three days the bergs tower, their peaks lost in the grey above the masthead. The sailors judge that the shafts must soar even beyond the roof of the fogbank, for fresh sunshine comes down within the prisms of crystal and surrounds the boat with curtains of colour.

On the third day the fishermen hear music. Sweet voices fill the ice canyons, sounding like the choir of some heavenly basilica.

Mermaids! the master whispers.

Sirens! cries a sailor.

Angels! cries another.

The crew scatter to larboard and starboard, stem and stern. They scramble into the drums outboard. They clamber up the rigging. Motionless as statues they listen, enraptured, to the voices singing from every quarter, singing seemingly out of the undulating colours of the ice itself.

The fishermen one and all hear the same thing—the eternal call of lonely women.

Each man hears a plea for his return. Each husband or father or son or lover hears the summons from across the sea. Unblinking, unspeaking, each man peers into the ice and seeks in the shifting textures of colour the shapes of love, seeks in the cadences of the voices the sound of his own name.

The master himself cries out to the mists: *Wife!* The word echoes around the corners of the ice canyons and fades.

The men call to their beloved women, to the wives and mothers and daughters and mistresses they left behind. They call to all the women they ever loved, to all the women who ever loved them. They cry even to imaginary women, ideal women, and some of the men caress soft shapes in the chill air. The pining of the fishermen mingles with the eerie chorus and with the interweaving echoes until the air fairly bleeds with longing.

Twilight settles. The choir fades. The fishermen fall silent.

The bergs throb with a faint residue of dayshine. In the darkness the ice casts a pale glow upon the vessel. The fishermen abandon their outposts and straggle one by one to their berths. Some weep.

From his sanctuary within the cuddy, young Tomas Croft watches all this in bewilderment. Never has he seen such strange and tender passion in these rough men, and he wonders at the reason for it. Never has his cloistered life given him the chance to so much as touch a woman. The closest he came was during Communion, when he would hold the paten under female chins and smell the women's warm smells. Now, after hearing the voices of the invisible choir, after witnessing his mates cry out with such feeling, after seeing the gentle silhouettes they cast in the air, he senses vague recollections stirring beyond the boundaries of his own memory.

Tomas Croft takes up his blackthorn and barefooted he scales the mast to the barrel—a place he is forbidden to go. He stares out into the night, but he can see nothing more than the ice-cliffs pulsating in the mist. Like an infant he curls up on the floor of the barrel. He sleeps, and he dreams.

He dreams of a woodland so real he can taste even in his sleep the colour green. It is a fabulous realm, warm, and peaceful. The trees sway in time with the sound of breathing.

Tomas Croft is awakened by ructions below.

It is light. The fog has thinned. The icebergs have moved off and the balinger floats free.

To a man the crew line the rail and gaze into the deep. From on high Tomas Croft can make out the object of their absorption, a faint stirring in the black water. It appears to be a surging mass of kelp. The seabed, the master says. But the tangle of weed is becoming ever more distinct to the eye. It looks as though the sea bottom is rising up to meet the keel.

Higher it rises, until Tomas Croft sees to his horror that the spectacle is not seaweed. It is a snarl of hideous serpents, a mass of hydra heads—a thousand Gorgons.

The crew flee screaming from the nightmare. In panic they bolt to and fro about the deck, or clamber up the rigging, or fall to their knees in prayer. The master himself is frozen to the rail, paralysed with fear.

The sea boils. The apparition of slimy bodies and gaping maws threatens the surface. The vessel heaves, its hull borne up sickeningly by the pulpy, slithering mass. At last, with a prolonged hiss and bubble, the creatures broach the calm.

The fishermen can hardly believe what they see, for now before them is a scene every bit as startling as the one that just terrified them. The ocean is alive not with lizards, or eels, or sea snakes, or octopi, or monitors, or dragons but with codfish.

The sailors abandon their prayers and climb down from their hiding places and crowd back to the rail. For a long time they remain so awe-struck they cannot move. Then the master collects himself and thinks to dangle a hook over the side.

Hundreds of fish leap from the water and fight among themselves for the privilege of swallowing the bare jigger. One great bull-cod pushes the others aside and is hooked and dragged onto the deck. Two of the crew hold the beast down while a third stretches forth his arms the length of the fish. The creature measures a full fathom from snout to tail.

Highliners! shouts the captain. He laughs and dances hysterically. Never has his keel sat upon such a ground. Never has he imagined such fat fish in such rich numbers, all so eager to be caught. The waters are blessed!

The master bids all hands launch forth their lines. Presently, a river of codfish comes pouring into the vessel. The crew in their haste and greed abandon the usual fish-saving business of heading and splitting and cleaning and salting. They simply fling the creatures thrashing down the hold.

From his perch aloft, Tomas Croft observes all this through a film. The grey mist envelops his mates still, but a shower of sunshine warms his own shoulders. The roof of the fogbank has settled now to the level of the barrel, and the swirling scene below his feet gives him the notion that he floats just above the clouds of paradise.

The mist burns off in airy vapours that are decorated here

and there with tiny fractured rainbows. It gives the boy pleasure to watch these. After weeks of greyness, here are light and colour. After weeks of confinement, here is space. A burst of orange-brown moths flutters before his face and just as abruptly is gone—a vision so sharp and clear that Tomas Croft imagines he is still asleep and dreaming.

The icebergs drift eastward, and beyond their summits he can spy all the way to the rising sun. Above his head, the dome of the sky is utterly blue. Westward, projecting out of the mist like one of the flyaway islands of which his mates often spoke, is visible a rounded contour of land.

As Tomas Croft beholds the curve of ground, he hears within his soul the voice of his dead father. The voice warns him that the sight is a forbidden thing, that here unveiled is a sacred and intimate and guarded secret—like the Blessed Sacrament in the monstrance—before which on pain of sin the eye must be lowered. But Tomas Croft cannot bring himself to bow his head. He stares unflinching at the horizon, for it reminds him of the soft woman-shapes his mates carved in the air.

The crew fill the hold and the hull settles deeper in the water. The deck is virtually at sea level, so they abandon the handlines and take up dipnets and simply lean over the side and shovel the fish out of the water and down the hatches.

The sun burns away the fog until only a thin mist obscures the surface of the sea. Meanwhile, the land to the west is slowly bared.

Tomas Croft is astounded to see that the *Trinitie* is becalmed not on a stretch of open coast, but inside the bowl of a small harbour, a womb of a cove, really, that is almost surrounded by rocky seaboard. To the east, two headlands— one beetling, one low—stand such close guard over the waterway that it must have been by the will of God that the boat drifted between them. The cliffs defining the horseshoe at first present to the boy's eye a seamless vertical mural, grey generally, but here and there streaked in dull red, the sweeping curtain broken only by an occasional waterfall. But as the fog lifts he perceives a bastion of minor points bolting seaward, each one wave-worn to the point of grotesque disfigurement. Between these points narrow inlets rut the land. It is a sea front of clefts and juttings.

The countryside behind the shoreline appears to be well wooded, with grey rocky projections breaking through the blanket. The rounded silhouette dominates the skyline, and to this forbidden vision the eye of Tomas Croft keeps returning.

Soon the mist has evaporated fully and the sea surface is uncovered. From his outlook the boy sees that the waters fairly swim. Although he does not know their names, he spots tomcod and connors, mackerel and herring and whole schools of pink salmon, singing seals and dancing dolphins, fat halibut lolling in the sun, tuna streaking like arrows, shoals of silver-sided capelin, and pilot whales breaching and boasting steam and then diving in lazy lumbering arches that leave not a ripple. Here is a city of life upon the sea.

His shipmates ignore these treasures, just as they ignore the strange land embracing them. Their attention is given wholly to the vicinity of the boat, and to filling it to the brim, and exclusively with the species cod. In their minds the cod is Neptune's sheep, the only real fish in the sea.

A wicker basket is produced, strung with ropes, ballasted and lowered. Directly it comes back bursting from cod. Intoxicated with avarice, the fishermen work insanely. To make room for more catch the captain tells his men to jettison whatever they can. Over the rails fly ballast, astrolabe, anchor and cordage, spare canvas, bait, ordnance, doors, hatch-covers, lanterns, mattresses, the stove, pots and pans, even the Scriptures. Bow to stern the *Trinitie* is scoured in search of sacrifice. Just when it seems the vessel has been stripped and every needless ounce has gone to the bottom, the captain himself calls out sweetly for his cod-banger.

Tomas Croft fails to answer. He is not found in his usual refuge in the cuddy, or anywhere else about the deck. Since no time can be wasted, they give the boy up for lost— perhaps already knocked overboard in the commotion, or else, as they first found him, smothered underneath the fish. They go back to their work and forget about him.

Speedily the hold is topped. Without a thought the fishermen set about stuffing their own sleeping quarters, and after that the captain's berth and the cuddy and the head and every last cavity big enough to hold even one runt of a rounder. Finally the fish are piled willy-nilly on the open deck.

With the catch flush to the risings, with mere inches of freeboard now, the master orders the culling of the satanic creatures swept up by mistake—the horned sculpins, the flatfish cursed with the migrating eye, the haddock marked by the Devil's thumbprint, the squid that reversed themselves like demons clear out of the sea and into the vessel. These infernal beasts are flung back onto the waters. The vicinity of the balinger is strewn with dead monsters, all bloated and belly-up.

As if sprung out of the very air, seabirds converge from every corner. They descend upon the vessel like starlings upon a church. Sleek gargling gannets, kittiwakes and shearwaters and petrels and jaegers, blackbirds and herring gulls as one galaxy wheel and soar overhead, dancing and laughing, then plummet crazily headfirst and gorge upon the litter of corpses.

Even when the boat is top-heavy and seemingly can bear not so much as a fin more, the fishermen work madly. In the end, they simply lean over the gunnel and reach hands into the sea and hook forefingers in gills and pull forth fish which are then launched clear across the hull to splash again on the far side. Starboard men cast to larboard, larboard men to starboard—all of it in a senseless delirium.

In the meantime, the sun crosses the sky and morning becomes afternoon, afternoon evening. The shadow of the mast stretches eastward. One after another the fishermen collapse, spent, atop the piles of fish.

With a flash of green the sun sinks precisely behind the rounded crest of land. Night silences all.

The surface of the cove is mirror-calm. From his station Tomas Croft sees the North Star reflected in the glass: before him sprawl not one but two night skies. The cod have retreated to the depths. Now it is an armada of glowing jellyfish that drifts just beneath the surface, placidly, like clouds fallen to earth. From off in the darkness a rhythmic slow sound touches the boy's ears, a broad respiration, like the breath the sea might make in its sleep.

Tomas Croft grips his blackthorn and descends to the deck. He wades over the fat mounds of fish-eyes glowing. In the dark he happens across the captain, snoring deeply. The boy looks upon the face and he imagines how, with one blow, he might easily bash the captain's brains like the brains of a fish. Tomas Croft raises his cudgel, but he cannot find within his soul the means to bring the stick crashing down.

Directly from the low stern he steps into the jolly-boat. He unties the tow-line and breaks out the oars and quietly pushes off. He rows, clumsily at first, then with a steady, loping canter. Soon the *Trinitie* is far behind him, merely the blackest part of a black night.

Tomas Croft pulls vaguely westward. He senses the land closing around him. The deeper he inches into the cove, the louder grows the night-breath of the sea.

He rests the oars. Immediately the skiff is drawn ocean-ward again, as though slipping downhill. He feels under-neath him a hesitation, a kind of gathering, a sucking back, and then an advance, a heavy uplifting of the surface. The boat is being propelled by an unseen hand. The noise be-comes a roar, the roar an explosion of spray. Tomas Croft is startled to witness a burst of nightshine at the crest of the breaking swell—in the darkness the water has become light.

The wash recedes. The radiance fades. But again the wa-ter advances. It rolls and bursts again, with a fresh lumi-nance. The light spreads until Tomas Croft finds himself floating in a lake of cool fire. Nearby, a fish, itself gilded, leaps and falls back with a plop that leaves behind shimmer-ing ripples. Tomas Croft can sense, just beyond the bounds of the strange light, solid land.

He awaits the crest of a swell and catches it and runs the skiff ashore. Tomas Croft steps off the sea and places his bare foot in the sand.

His footprints glow. The powder sinks softly under his toes like a feather mattress. Tingling with exhaustion, the boy lays his body down upon the beach. Sleepily he watches the exploding and fading of the luminous wash. He hears the movements of the tide, and the silences that fill the long mo-ments between the rise and fall of the swell. In the last in-stant before he passes out, hypnotized by the monotony of the sea, it seems that this glowing breath is nothing less than his own being, his own life and soul and spirit.

Tomas Croft awakens with the sun in his eyes. He feels rested and refreshed. A western breeze sweeps down over the land.

Already the wind has pushed the *Trinitie* far off shore. In the distance the vessel looks like a toy. The hull sits so deep in the water that it appears submerged. Somehow the balinger manages to negotiate the mouth of the cove and to stagger around the southern headland. The last thing the boy sees is the barrel, soaring disembodied above the low point. Then the barrel too is gone.

Unsteadily, unaccustomed to the firmness of land, Tomas Croft gathers himself to his feet. He goes down to the edge of the sea and peers into the shallows.

The boy marvels at the masses of seaweed, swaying and lifting like tentacles, and exposing to the light wonders such as whore's eggs and spiny-skins, slithering eels, hermit crabs and armour-plated lobsters, and periwinkles and barnacles and starfish. On the beach under his feet lie strewn treasures such as he has never before seen: desiccated kelp, and living crabs, and bleached driftwood, and mounds of purple mussel shells, every one cracked open.

He lifts his eyes to the countryside.

The beach is narrow and snug. A crossbow might easily shoot a level bolt the span of the crescent. On the one hand, southward, stands a raw grey cliff. Its face extends so steeply into the sea that a large vessel might come up and rub her sides against the wall without scraping bottom. Around the shoreline a ways, a cataract launches itself over a precipice and tumbles unimpeded to splash across a beach. The terrain to the north, meanwhile, lifts towards the rounded landform he observed from the balinger. Tomas Croft sees that the crest is topped by some sort of outcropping. It resembles nothing so much as the pap of his own breast.

He inhales deeply and he shouts: *Sláinte!*

From the cliff-face a voice answers: *Sláinte!*

Tomas Croft is so astonished he laughs aloud—and the sound of laughter comes straight back to him. He stands before the wall of granite and over and over he cries: *Sláinte! Sláinte! Sláinte!*

The boy remembers his mates talking about the rise and fall of the ocean. He notes on the beach the limits of the water and he drags the skiff safely above its reach. He takes up his muckle-stick and he leaves the sandy shore and walks across a cant of rolling shingle, then through a field of storm-boulders. Boldly he strikes out for the summit.

At the base of the ridge the land climbs so abruptly that the pap is lost to his sight. He finds that the hillside is clad in dwarf-spruce that mats close to the ground and is clotted further by vines and shrubs and mosses and ferns. This undergrowth is too thin to walk atop and too thick to walk through, so the boy picks his way uphill by following the rocky beds of trickling streams. Steam rises from his shoulders. The wind, which has swung all the way round and now comes boisterously out of the east, down the chute of the cove, pushes Tomas Croft up the slope like the hand of God. Soon he has conquered the brow of the ridge. The outcropping ascends into view before him.

He sees that it is a monstrous grey boulder, a stone every bit as long and broad and tall as the ship that brought him to this place.

Tomas Croft scales the great rock. Atop the crown the force of the wind whips away his breath. Backwards, down the hillside to the cove and to the skiff that is now but a speck on the beach, his eye traces the path he has just taken. Of the *Trinitie* he sees no sign.

From this lookout the wider shore presents the same sort of formidable face he saw from the ship's barrel—a bastion of grotesque headlands flanked by grey, ochre-pitted murals, and separated one from another by vaulted fiords rutting miles into the land. The cove is only one of countless notches, the ridge only one of countless elongated crests stretching back from the headlands. The coastline is a rough thing, thrusting and violent.

The wind surges, as if to nudge Tomas Croft about-face. The boy turns and looks now towards the interior of the land.

It seems to Tomas Croft as if all the robins of God's earth

have chosen to lay their pale eggs at the foot of this boulder, for the field before him reflects the absolute blue of the sky. Beyond the heath stretches a wide bog patched in red, and beyond that the land slopes easily up a green grassy incline spotted in bright yellow. In the distance, the terrain presents a marbled aspect. An array of parallel ridges are clad in undulating black forest, while down the valleys between them run sinuous lakes and ponds, with connecting watercourses all shining like beads in the sun.

Before him Tomas Croft sees the colours of stained glass. He smells in his head the aroma of incense. The boy's heart pounds.

The wind roars. He hears so many sounds that he can hear nothing at all. His blood flows madly. In a frenzy he tears open his breeches and he bursts out hard. With both fists he seizes himself and at once his whole body convulses and makes spasms. For the span of one breath, milky ribbons of his seed hang suspended before his eyes, and in the next instant are vaporized by the wind and scattered in a pearly steaming mist westward across the field of voluptuous blue.

Tomas Croft totters and buckles and falls back atop the stone. Languor eases his body in softly fading spirals. The beat of his heart slackens. The wind ebbs and perishes.

Atop the boulder the boy sleeps.

When he awakens he descends to the ground. He finds that the robins' eggs are blueberries, dripping from the shrubbery in succulent clusters. They grow in greater abundance than all the stars in the sky. He finds that the red of the bog is raspberries and strawberries and partridgeberries and chuckleypears, all of them ripe and fat and juicy. The berries are the first sweetness ever to touch the boy's palate.

Tomas Croft hops the peatland by way of hummocks choked with grasses and rushes and sedge. Around him, screaming ravens dive into the marsh and splash and surface with beaks berry-full. In the boy's path lies such a maze of lakes that he reckons half the countryside is submerged. The waterways are alive with marten and muskrat and otter and beaver and ermine and trout, and with the same kind of fat salmon he saw in the ocean, even with large black dogs that paddle as nimbly as any of these.

He discovers that the yellow is meadows of buttercups. By way of these meadows, easily traversed, his bearing is channelled naturally to the higher ground. Rupturing here and there through the stumpy spruce are crests of bedrock, richly clad in antlered lichen. The shrubbery gives way to grey-green alder, then to widely spaced pines and spruce and fir the size of Tomas Croft himself.

These trees on their east sides are naked, the branches withered to the bone, but on the opposite face they stream away full to the west, blasted askew by the storms. The world seems to be lopsided, everything hiding and clinging. Tomas Croft feels that a magical wind roars. Yet the air remains calm.

He comes then into tall thick stands, the sort of trunks of which masts are made — birch and tamarack and maple and poplar and ash and aspen. His breath tastes of sweet sap. The exalted trees, moss-bearded like bishops, stare down upon Tomas Croft, and in the Irish tongue he speaks up and addresses them reverently. The boy peers aloft and spots seagulls roosting in the upper chambers of the branches.

Later, he hears the song of the titmouse and of the chickadee. He hears the staccato of the woodpecker. He hears the voices of infinite numbers of fowls of the air — wild geese and ducks and ptarmigan and partridge and plover and curlew and hawk and soaring greep.

He finds that the barrens and the woodlands are populated with every sort of God's creature. Sleek wolves, giant hares, slinking silver foxes, black bears, lynx-leopards — all these animals are harmless to Tomas Croft. Even the deer follow and gaze boldly upon him. Majestic caribou climb the heights of land for no reason other than to observe him as he passes by.

He sees neither snake nor serpent nor any venomous or reptilian creature, and even though the air swarms with mosquitoes big enough to be called birds, they give him no annoyance.

Tomas Croft judges that this land is blessed, that God Almighty has smiled down upon it His fertility and His benevolence.

The boy's energy has been renewed by the berries. Desiring to learn the extent of the territory, he resolves to climb the burst of mountains that line the western sky. The farther he walks, the thicker grows the vegetation and the more difficult becomes his progress, so he surrenders and turns back. Along one of the land's serrated corridors he glimpses the green lick of the sea. He pursues a brook down its chasm to the waterline and hikes along the winding foreshore.

Every one of the little crannies in the rock face is crowned by a crescent of stone and pebble and sand. Tomas Croft listens to the sounds—the hiss of incoming froth and bubble, the retreating natter of rounded rolling shingle. Above the signature of the highest tide lies scattered a debris of storm-boulder and brash. Each shingle-strand displays its own fingerprint pattern of curves and whorls and stripes and ripples. Where the tide laps at bedrock it has licked the granite slippery smooth, has petrified an eternity of waves.

Tomas Croft makes his way back to the skiff. Although the sun is falling, he remains keen to explore. He launches the rowboat and paddles towards the mouth of the cove.

The sea-calm reflects the low sun and the light scorches his eyes. Avoiding the route of the *Trinitie*, the boy makes for the northern headland. Its overhang rears up like the granite prow of a granite ship. Brooding islets erupt from the swells churning around the point. An arsenal of submerged sinkers forces him to keep well away.

Tomas Croft passes from the shelter of the cove onto the wide-open sea. By now the sun has gone down. He steers the boat north. A great black cape, far more formidable than the mere headland, towers out of the dusk. Atop its vertical mural wall a rock formation like an armoured sentinel frowns upon him. He sees, beyond the cape, another just like it, waiting, and then another, and so on, seemingly without cease. The gargoyled coastline is a barbican of hostility, of death.

Deep into the darkness the boy rows, staying well off, always bearing on the North Star, until he falls asleep at the oars.

A hideous scream jolts him awake.

It is a bellow of pain and terror, not the sound of any earthly voice but a horror from the throat of some alien creature. Tomas Croft hears the barbarous ripping of flesh, the crush of bone and cartilage. He hears the thrashing of masses of water. Black waves rock his boat. A malodour like the stench of disease nauseates him. The boy hears one final rending scream, deep ugly sucking sounds, the bursting of an immense bubble, then silence.

Shaking with fear, he brandishes his blackthorn in both hands and climbs the thwart and stands watch. At first light he finds that his skiff floats in wide pools of oily blood. He paddles to get free of this, but his way is stopped, the prow impeded by flotsam — it is the severed tentacle of a sea-monster. The thing measures three times the length of the rowboat. It twitches even as Tomas Croft pulls madly away.

Later that day, a fish-shape streaks under the boat and broaches the surface nearby. The creature spreads stubby wings, lifts itself awkwardly just out of the water and flies. Tomas Croft sets to the oars and pursues. Skimming the wave-tops, the bird leads him to a bleak low-lying rock, a pancake so shallow that at flood tide a casual wave might easily submerge it. A louring maelstrom of a cloud circles above. From the distance the rock itself seems to be alive and moving. The air stinks with a dull roar.

Tomas Croft comes up and finds the rock aswarm, with auks—murres and guillemots and razorbills and dovekies, plus giant flightless creatures half the size of himself—and with gannets and puffins and kittiwakes and shearwaters and petrels. Here is more life than the boy has ever imagined. Like grains of sand on a beach, here are too many birds to be counted. Aloft, for want of space to alight, a thousand times as many darken the sky.

The boy manages to make a landing aboard the rock. The birds have no fear. They waddle down to greet him. He strolls among the beasts and calmly he gathers the fattest of them in his hands and wrings their necks. Aimlessly he swings his muckle in the air and kills whole flocks. He plucks up their eggs, which he drinks raw. Before long, the bedlam of the incessant croaking and shrill screaming mesmerizes him, and the stink of guano and stagnant waters sickens him. He flees to his skiff and to the peace and fresh air of the open sea.

In the boat he finds a splitting knife and he guts the birds and eats their flesh raw, and so sustains his strength. For many days he trends northward. The coast gives way to the northwest and he pursues it there. To pass the time he tallies his oar-strokes by reciting out loud the Litany. The winds return but by some miracle they always veer in favour of his course. The farther north he travels, the shorter become the nights. The water turns iron-cold.

One afternoon, he marvels to see a tall galleon of an iceberg bearing in the face of the breeze. Tomas Croft boards the berg and drinks the fresh water that cascades down its side. He chops cakes of ice to take away for his thirst. There is a cave, and barefooted he walks deep inside until the light is blue and dim. Birds nest there, and in the darkness they fly about his head like giant moths.

Another day, a large white bear, oblivious of him, swims calmly to the south. This he takes to be a favourable portent.

After safely doubling a cape that points like a huge finger to the North Star he rows for a long time southward, and then rounds another cape and coasts east along a castellated front. His course takes him deep into great bays, each as wild as the open sea and of such compass that from the vantage of either land's-end the bluffs on the far shore are lost below the horizon. He reckons that the bays radiate like cartwheels around the centre of the island, for at the head of each bay he is able to spy, in the interior, the range of sawtooth mountains that he failed to achieve overland.

One morning he recognizes the cut of the waves, and he fears that some devil is forcing him to live his life a second time. Then he spots the landmark he has been watching for, the great boulder atop the rounded ridge. He comes safely inside the cove, and soon he brings up in the same beach where he set out.

Tomas Croft has circumnavigated a vast triangular island—a new-world island.

He leaps ashore and in jubilation shouts to the cliff-face: *Sláinte!*

Joyfully the rock answers him: *Sláinte!*

Tomas Croft conceals the skiff behind the berm. He takes the knife and goes up-country, and painstakingly he chops down three spruce trees. One by one he drags them to a piece of sloping ground near the base of the ridge, out of sight but within sound of the sea. He strips the trees of their boughs and leans the trunks together, pyramid-fashion, and so erects a crude hut of wattle and daub.

Herein he lives his new life.

Each day, each week, each month follows the last. Tomas Croft names each morning according to the air that greets him: Fog-day, Rain-day, Snow-day, Wind-day, Storm-day. Sometimes in the course of an afternoon he experiences several weathers. The long-term climate is equally capricious and he pays no attention to the come and go of the seasons. He abandons all concern about the passage of time. He lives through entire winters without realizing it.

He enjoys the abundance of all things. He eats dandelion greens and the succulent berries. He mimics animal voices and so is able to lure fat creatures within range of his deadly blackthorn. He manufactures a hook from pieces of bone, and a line from lengths of moss, and so catches birds whose skulls he crushes with his teeth. He sharpens a stick of alder and in the shallows of the cove he spears fish and lobster and crabs and eels. He gathers periwinkles and mussels and clams and starfish and seaweed. Whenever he needs a cod he paddles out into the waves and the fish swim to the surface to accommodate him. Capelin and squid by the thousands sacrifice themselves to his beach. All these things he eats raw, for he has forgotten how to make fire. He is perfectly satisfied with this fare, for it is as plentiful and fine as anything his ascetic life has ever known.

When they make themselves apparent he stops up the leaks in his shelter with boughs and sod and mud and driftwood and kelp. In this way he fashions a cozy hut that harmonizes with the landscape so thoroughly that it deceives the eye and becomes invisible. Although it is little more than a cellar, it keeps him as warm and dry and comfortable as he has been anywhere else during his existence.

He is neither happy nor unhappy. The breezes blow away his thoughts so that he is seldom troubled by worry. His solitude does not drive him mad. He tames one of the bearlike

dogs, teaches it to haul wood, even rigs a driver sail to push
its dray, and with this beast he converses. In fact, every rock
and tree and wave has a personality of its own. He speaks to
all of these, and they reply to him, so that in his mind the island is as alive as he himself is alive. During the nights, the
sea comforts him with its steady breath of ebb and flow.
Whenever he feels the need he climbs the ridge and stands
atop the boulder. The land and he are as lovers, one together.

Thus the boy lives to become a man. His ruddy hair falls
beyond his shoulders and he grows a shaggy beard of the
same hue. He clads his body in coarse hides and bark and,
although he does not know it, he looks like an ancient Celtic
river god.

Once during all this time—just once—he sees another human being.

It happens on a sunny winter's day. A glitter-storm has
dropped a plate of ice and flattened the berry bushes coast
to coast. For once it is possible to walk over the dwarf-
spruce. Intoxicated with the sheer novelty of rapid movement, Tomas Croft rambles aimlessly overland, farther than
he has ever gone. In the middle of a wide barren he finds his
way blocked by a mysterious fence. It is made of pine poles,
and it stretches to the horizons north and south. Tomas
Croft follows the fence until he comes in sight of a creature
crouched behind it. The creature sees Tomas Croft and it
stands and waves a white skin.

It is a heathen, a man, clad in rough peltry, his flesh withered by the sun and painted ochre-red like the seacliffs. He
wears on his person the skulls of birds and the claws of
bears.

Neither one fearful of the other, Tomas Croft and the man
come together. The heathen smiles and gestures towards the
flaming red hair of the Christian, then reaches out his hand
and grips it. Tomas Croft is alarmed, and without thinking

he wheels his blackthorn swiftly and clubs the man until his brains spill out of his skull and onto the snow.

That night, afraid that more men will come and avenge their brother, Tomas Croft hides with the owls in the upper branches of a tall tree. Beneath him, a huge company of caribou files past, thousands, lowing and whispering, their eyes burning the darkness. In the morning he climbs down and gives the heathen a Christian burial like the one he gave his own father.

After that day, Tomas Croft begins to feel lonely. No longer is he one with his new world. Somehow, he is broken and incomplete.

He stands atop his great boulder and for hours he scans the interior, hoping to see more of the ochre people. He even climbs the headlands and searches the shore for signs of the *Trinitie* and his Bristol mates. But no one comes.

Years go by. Nothing happens to Tomas Croft but the routine of keeping himself alive. The memories of his monastic childhood fade from his mind. He takes it for granted that the *Trinitie* was lost and his mates were eaten by the sea, and that everyone in Ireland has starved. He comes to assume that he is the only soul alive in the entire world.

Early one airy morning, Tomas Croft is startled awake by the blast of a trumpet.

He runs to the beach and crouches behind a boulder. His eyes behold a wondrous sight.

A grand caravel, decorated with many-coloured streamers and banners and pennants, glides clockwise skirting the shore of the cove. The vessel passes so close to his hiding place that Tomas Croft can read the name carved under the up-cocked bowsprit: *Mathew*. Musicians, belled and beribboned like morris dancers, line the deck and play a concert to the cliffs. Tomas Croft hears, for the first time in his life, the pounding of drums, the whistle of fifes, the bold blare of cornets. The ship coasts towards the north head-land, and the breeze scatters the sweet sounds and soon they fade away.

So foreign to his history is this magnificence that Tomas Croft thinks he must be going mad. But presently another splendid sail, leaning, rounds the south headland and enters the channel and sweeps along the shore and before his eyes. Tomas Croft reads: *Golden Hind*. Next come *Swallow*, then *Squirrel*, finally *Delight*. Prow to stern the stately vessels take a turn round the cove, then follow the *Mathew* to the north.

His heart thunders. Tomas Croft clambers up the ridge and mounts the lookout boulder. Already, in the next har-bour, wider but more exposed to the sea than his own snug cove, the magnificent fleet rides at anchor.

Tomas Croft watches a rowboat come ashore. Sailors step onto the strand. A brightly dressed man marches forward and runs his fingers through the grass and drinks the dew, then pulls out a piece of turf which he surrenders to a min-ion for safekeeping. On that spot he raises a banner. Tomas Croft steals down the far side of the ridge until he is close enough to catch the voices on the wind.

He remembers enough Latin from the monastery and enough English from his *Trinitie* mates to make sense of the things he hears. The man declares solemnly that he is the First Admiral of this *prima terra vista*. The land will be called Avalon. The waters, because they contain such inex-haustible stores, are hereby named Conception. This settle-ment they are to build will be called Golden. Furthermore, because he and his men are the first Christians to set foot upon this soil, the territory will reside for ever in the pos-session and authority of the English Crown.

On the banner Tomas Croft reads: *Quid non?*

The admiral bids a flagman make a signal. The flagman does, and presently a flotilla of rowboats embarks from the vessels and commences transferring cargo to the beach.

The first items unladen are guns. The sailors install a deadly arsenal of falcons and culverins and cannon in a wide battery threatening all quarters. Then they bring to shore barrels and hogsheads and drums and crates and chests and casks and buckets and puncheons, and vast measures of lumber, and set all this within the circle of weaponry. Next, as though from an ark, come caged beasts of every species: sheep and goats and swine and rabbits and pigeons and poultry and cats and dogs, even heifers and a bull, and finally two noble white horses that leap from the deck of the *Golden Hind* and swim majestically to shore. The day happens to be the longest of the year, and the Englishmen take advantage of the generous light and work well into the evening, unpacking the stores and corralling the beasts and raising temporary shelters.

In the falling dusk, Tomas Croft hears voices like birdsong. From the hold of the *Delight* emerge creatures of a variety unfamiliar to him. Whole flocks are put ashore, until each of these beasts is matched with an Englishman. The men behave with the curious tenderness Tomas Croft witnessed so many years in the past, on the part of his *Trinitie* mates, and he realizes that these creatures must be women.

At nightfall the company gather driftwood and build a fire. They uncork casks of rum and they sing and dance around the flames until they collapse from drunkenness and exhaustion.

Tomas Croft abandons his hideout and slips past the unattended guns into the enclosure. The animals stir in their cages but he whispers to them and they are silenced. Stealthily he explores the camp.

In the fire-glow he is able to make out all sorts of wonderful objects, things he has never seen before, or has long forgotten: butter, bread and cheese, biscuits, barley, lard, beef, bacon, malmsey, sack, cider, a stove, candles, lanterns, pots and pans, bowls, cauldrons, ladles, a still, beds with linen, shirts, waistcoats, breeches, stockings, boots, cross-bows, fowling-pieces, mattocks, adzes, pickaxes, spades, scythes, mortars and pestles, grindstones, bellows, pitch, tar, hooks, lines, rhodes, nets, seines, canvas, killicks, even a Holy Bible.

At sight of such wealth Tomas Croft is amazed. He prowls the encampment and beholds these riches, and he is dazed to intoxication.

He stumbles across a figure lying upon the sod, asleep and breathing deeply. It does not stir. A mound of white glows in the shadow. Tomas Croft kneels beside the figure and reaches forth his hand and cups it just above the glowing form.

It is the bared breast of a young woman.

The naked pale knoll of flesh and its dark crowning nipple hypnotize Tomas Croft. He brings his palm as close as possible without touching, and feels the pleasure of a rising warmth.

The woman shivers and stirs and covers herself. Tomas Croft slips away and retreats to the fire.

For a long time he stands close before the flames, trembling, and gazes into the embers. In the incandescent cinders he imagines the shape of the woman's breast. He becomes suddenly delirious. He plucks out of the fire a branch still smouldering, and he bolts from the camp and runs to the crest of the ridge. In the reverent manner of an altar boy lighting a candle, he touches the torch to a clump of blasty boughs. He laughs hysterically when the shrubbery bursts into flames. Up-country he runs, firing the trees here and there just for the sheer joy of it. He swings round towards the northern cape, then back again to the south, and so on throughout the night, all of it in a mad frenzy, until the hills surrounding the encampment are crowned with light.

When the sun appears and the English begin to stir, the morning mist tastes of smoke and ash.

With animal stealth Tomas Croft lurks and eavesdrops. He overhears the English argue about the source of the fires. The admiral declares that, because yesterday was the Feast of Saint John the Baptist, the fires surely are the work of Christians like themselves—but possibly Frenchmen or Spaniards or Biscaynes or some other such bead-mumbling papists, maybe even priests. With the command: Go and hunt the priests, he bids a company of musketeers sally forth to seek after these Romish interlopers and make plain the authority of the English Crown.

Tomas Croft withdraws to the camouflage of his tilt. The English roam over ridge and bog and meadow, but all they find are frightened beasts sniffing wild-eyed at the acres of charred brier.

Henceforth, the English do little except work. Inland they fell tall trees and drag them down to the shore and hammer together a proper stockade. To house the admiral and his wife, they quarry slate and erect a flagstone mansion with a door on each of its four sides. This mansion they name Sea-Forest House. For the commoners they build cottages of stout dealboard. They construct sheds and a saltworks and a forge and coopers' shops and a sail loft and a brew-house and a sawmill and a kitchen and stables and henhouses and a hayloft and outhouses, and a jail. Soon the level ground is fully occupied, and new buildings climb the slopes, or else cling to the cliffs like seagulls. The English build their wharfs and stages and fish-drying flakes astraddle the land-wash, hindlegs on dry beach and forelegs in the wet water. They sink a well deep in the rock. In leather bags the people transport topsoil and make land and start plots of carrots and cabbage and potatoes and turnips. And they set aside a field for a cemetery.

Within the span of a mere fortnight they fabricate out of the raw wilderness a fishing plantation, neat and orderly.

Tomas Croft gives over his usual routine of hunting and

fishing and berry-picking, and instead he spends every waking hour observing the newcomers. At night he vaults the palisade and creeps into the very cottages in order to study the sleeping women, in order to wonder at the warmth rising from their bodies. With the dawn light he flees, pilfering food and drink and clothing and cookware and tools and fishing gear and whatever else he fancies. He overhears the admiral swear furiously that it is not Christians at all who torment the countryside, but a tribe of thieving savages. He posts sentinels, but the sentinels sleep, and Tomas Croft is able to come and go unmolested.

One sunny morning, Tomas Croft steps round the great boulder atop the ridge and comes face to face with a young woman. She is alone.

The woman's hair falls to her waist and it is thick and red. In order to cradle the fat blueberries she has picked, she has gathered up her skirts, exposing her bare legs to the full gaze of his eyes. The woman does not flee but smiles at Tomas Croft. She smiles up at his red hair, and merrily she speaks:

Sláinte!

That night, Tomas Croft lies wide awake and listens to the sound of the sea yielding to the sea. He gets up from his pallet and in the dark he crosses the ridge to the English plantation. He listens to the voice shouting within the stockade.

A masterless man! the admiral rants. An evil, lecherous masterless man who craves the flesh of the plantation's Christian women and schemes to kidnap them one by one!

At first light the admiral dispatches a pair of cavalry to search for his missing wife. But even before the morning fogs have burned off, the great white horses return riderless. The bodies of the soldiers are discovered atop the ridge. Their skulls are beaten to jelly. Of the admiral's wife, no sign is found but a scattering of blueberries.

Terrified now, the English whisper that it is not a mere masterless man but the genuine Boo Darby himself who haunts the interior of this godforsaken island. From that day forward they regard the hinterland as the realm of evil and danger, the domain of mystery and sin. They fear that the bogs and trees and boulders will spring to life and swallow them up. They surrender their plan to survey and map the countryside, to search for gold and silver and spices and sassafras. Henceforth they keep close to their pale and rarely venture more than a gunshot's distance from the sea. The entire plantation falls into a deep melancholy and lethargy. Out of sheer despair, many of the people become ill and die.

The woman tells Tomas Croft that her name is Sheila nGira, that she is an Irish princess, from the islands of Mayo, and that she has been kidnapped by the English. Once she has instructed Tomas Croft in the proper manner of making love, she is perfectly happy with him, and faithfully she stays by his side.

The life of Tomas Croft and Sheila nGira is filled with love. He steals from the plantation such small items as ribbons and chimes and tin whistles, and presents these as gifts to her. She gathers him great baskets of the berries he devours with such relish. The years pass and they give birth to ten russet daughters. They name the girls with words that are beautiful when spoken out loud, names like Innismara, and Clare, and Kilronan. Tomas Croft and Sheila nGira love the children every one. As each is born he adds chambers to his hut until it becomes a warren of plank and bush and sod.

Meanwhile, in Europe, the royal courts one by one get wind of the bounty of cod swimming in the western seas. Companies of adventurers dispatch fleets and plant flags and declare claims. After some pushing and shoving over the lucrative berths, fishing stations appear on every sheltered beach in every one of the thousands of nooks and harbours. As well, accidental settlements are founded, by the infrequent survivors of the numerous wrecks, upon the wild headlands and bleak unprofitable coasts. Practically every square foot of shingle and cliff and ledge is barnacled with a fishflake or a stage or a jetty or a house.

Before long, so many western adventurers under such a motley assortment of flags ply the island's waters so busily that no one takes notice of the red-headed bog-Irish squatting in destitution in the cove. Any barrelman who happens to catch sight of the mean clutch of tilts and huts and shanties decides the place is too ragged to bother about. Tomas Croft no longer bothers to conceal himself. He even begins to consort with the newcomers.

As his daughters one by one sprout breasts—in some cases, even before—Tomas Croft marries them off. The husbands he finds for his girls are feral men, scoundrels and knaves and reprobates all: a naval deserter, a defeated mutineer, an absconded fisherman, a general scofflaw, a mad religious dissenter, a freebooter, an escaped convict, a stowaway, a son of a whore, and a man, called Nameless, about whom absolutely nothing is known. All these men are expert in the seven deadly sins.

Since nobody else will tolerate such people, the newlyweds settle alongside Tomas Croft and Sheila nGira. They erect crude shelters out of materials stolen from the plantations or salvaged from wrecks. The structures resemble a fleet of dilapidated hulks that have abandoned the waves for the security of the high and dry. Chickens, ducks, pigs, cats, and dogs occupy the premises in company with the people. The husbands confound the Gaelic spoken on the beach by adding so many other languages of Europe that the family develops a pidgin Irish all its own. Grandchildren arrive and the family becomes a clan, united by blood, by speech, and by the sheer physical authority of Tomas Croft.

Now a powerful man in his prime, Tomas Croft subjects all to his stern command. His deadly cudgel he wields with lightning fury, especially upon the bones of his wild sons-in-law. He is quick to flog anyone who refuses to bow down before him. He compels all hands to address him as "My Lord", for he styles himself now the First Admiral of the cove.

And thus it comes to pass that Tomas Croft, the orphaned castaway who for so many years lived in such hopeless solitude on the edge of nowhere, reigns with absolute dominion over a society born of his own loins.

The monarchical houses of Europe settle their squabbles by way of the spilled blood and broken bones of their poorest and remotest subjects. When the fishermen are not fishing, they are kept busy harassing and killing one another. Biscayne ships prowl the coast and shell Spanish stations. The Spanish clamp hooks and cables to the spindly legs of Basque stores and pull them tumbling into the sea. Basque brigs ram French pinnaces. French infantry drag cannon overland and surprise the English with bombardments from the heights.

After years of this, one by one the flags fall away until it is the English who prevail. Meanwhile, during the same period, shoals of destitute Irish wash up on the beaches or crawl across the sea ice to the shore. The population gradually takes the form of English masters and Irish servants.

The English accoutre the island with the trappings of state. A flag of vertical bars — orange and green separated by a band of white — indicates, for the benefit of the illiterate, the respectful distance that bog-papists are expected to keep from women of the established church. A coat of arms bears lions and unicorns passant, supported by "two savages of the clime and apparelled according to their guise when they go to war" — the existence of which savages is mere rumour.

Its motto reads *Quaerite prime regnum Dei.* A dreary dirge to
the contrary climate of the "smiling land" and its "blinding
storm gusts", "wild waves", and "spindrift swirl and tempest
roar" becomes the national ode. The Gregorian calendar is
adopted. By decree, the word "fish" refers exclusively to the
species cod, thereby fixing in law a usage already common.
By statute, five days out of seven are to be "fish days" when
cod, not meat, must be eaten. Because merchants accept
cured codfish, on which they set the value, for gear and sup-
plies, for which they set the price, dried cod becomes legal
tender in the territory. The government's main source of
revenue is the auction of licences for the distillation and sale
of liquor. The English even institute a court and appoint a
bewigged magistrate who regularly hangs urchins, usually
for petty theft, from the yardarms of the governor's flagship.

Despite the new law and order, Tomas Croft and his crowd
survive by freelance brigandage.

　　With ever more tempting fat plantations, ever more hungry babes to feed, and ever more youngsters to help with the
stealing, thievery becomes the natural occupation of the
Irish. Under cover of night Tomas Croft himself guides ex-
peditions that range overland, far up and down the coast, to
raid the well-provisioned stations. After an ancient tradition,
the Irish light false beacons to lure fully laden merchantmen
to wreckage and plunder on the cliffs. Soon the family seizes
a formidable magazine of small arms: maces, pikes, halberds,
pole-axes, dirks, cutlasses, sabres, scimitars, crossbows, pis-
tols, blunderbusses, muzzle-loaders, matchlocks, and flint-
locks. Bristling so, they venture in mere shallops into the
broad sea, where they prey upon the traffic. They stand and
await the inevitable fog and then row down openly, in re-
gatta, upon the becalmed and helpless prize. In such an easy
manner they commandeer a fleet of brigs and frigates and
carracks and war galleys and cutters and gunboats. With

this armada, a navy more threatening than that of certain realms, the Irish are able to embark at last upon serious piracy. Sallying forth into every harbour around the island, they demand tribute of each watercraft and station they discover. They menace the vast fishing fleets, the floating plantations that harvest the offshore banks. Roving even beyond the horizon, they prowl the balmy stream and sack treasure-laden merchantmen homeward bound from the gold and silver troves of the new El Dorado.

Tomas Croft caches, far inland, bushels of the nuggets and bullion and coin and precious gemstones that are pirated by his clan. This task he performs always on moonless nights, and always alone.

The Irish are not satisfied with raw New World wealth. They loot as well all manner of crafted riches in transit westward to colonial mansions—tasselled silk curtains, velvets and brocades, fancy inlaid furniture, white pottery, masterworks of oil painting, flower-patterned wallpaper, brass candlesticks, prisms, chandeliers, marbled stained glass—and with such finery they embellish their rude shacks. Although he knows not how to tell time, Tomas Croft installs a bird-clock inside their tilt. At the creature's appearance the pirate imitates its song, for he hopes to converse with the beast. The bird only mocks him, so he bashes it to pieces with his stick. And one day, before a gilt mirror, he giggles at the back-foremost image of Sheila nGira therein, but he is enraged at the sight of the dirty red-bearded monster standing by her side, and instantly muckles the glass to shards.

The booty the pirates prize most—and, providentially, the one they capture in richest volume—is drink. They extort rivers of liquor in tribute from plantations that wish only to be left in peace, lakes of it from the offshore fleets, oceans of it from intercontinental shipping. In this way, in the vicinity of the cove, rum rather than fish becomes the medium of commercial exchange. The people possess

so much alcohol and consume it so greedily that they all become semi-lunatics. Within their circle, sobriety brings a
person under suspicion. Every dwelling in the cove is a public house, every vessel a floating tavern. Well-nigh impossible it is to traverse on foot the span of the beach and yet
remain trim. Tomas Croft himself invents a mad concoction
of rum, spruce beer, gin, blueberry wine, Madeira, and gunpowder, and of this vile stew all hands, including the children, drink, from the barrel of a blunderbuss, until they fall
to brawling among themselves. This sort of bottled thunder
the people consume with such determination that whenever
the cove runs short of liquor and they are compelled to turn
to pure spring water, the water acts upon them like a poison,
loosening their bowels and making them vomit hideously.

Under this onslaught the authority of the local governor
breaks down. The English court buzzes with tales of terror
and disorder in the New World, with breathless reports of a
deranged Irishman, a red Merlin living in polygamous union
with red witches, haunting bestial caves wherein they carry
out human sacrifices in a notch known as Rogues' Roost,
from which vantage they govern the winds and the waves
and the fogs. The well-born victims of this monster complain
to the Crown, and, after the usual protocols of flattery and
bribery, a man-o'-war charged with dispatching this bog-
nuisance sets sail across the sea.

Irish lookouts are posted on the bolder capes. When they
signal the approach of the royal warship, the pirate fleet
runs out its shotted guns and conceals itself behind headlands and islets. Under a full spread of canvas the man-o'-
war breezes up the roadstead. The brigands burst forth and
encircle the startled vessel. Without firing a shot they board
and capture the prize.

Tomas Croft, wild-eyed, his hair knotted into red horns,
his beard into red braids, candles blazing from his tri-
corn, presents himself jauntily. And now, declares the arch-

pirate, let us inhale the stench of hades. At pistol-point he forces a dozen captured seamen into the hold. He climbs down the ladder and joins them, and orders the hatches battened. Tomas Croft ignites brimstone.

When the hatches of hell are reopened, it is only Tomas Croft himself, cackling with glee, who steps forth alive.

Sláinte! he howls with laughter.

Then he invites the English commander to join with him in piracy. Politely the captain declines. Tomas Croft, no longer laughing but furious, does the blood eagle to the English captain: he slices open the man's back, pulls out his lungs, spreads them like wings, and kicks him into the sea. Still breathing, the Englishman bobs away like a bloated fish into the stream.

No more warships broach the horizon. After his victory over the Crown, Tomas Croft begins to style himself king. He accepts tribute. He issues proclamations. He lays hands upon the diseased and tells them that their sicknesses are cured.

Tomas Croft accordingly drifts to his old age in a kind of royal splendour. His grandchildren marry and in their turn beget a gaggle of infants. The clan becomes a vast tribe. All the while, nonetheless, the everyday order remains an unremitting squalor of anarchy, chaos, and riot. There is drunkenness and gluttony, and debauchery and promiscuity, and of course, looting, robbery, kidnapping, extortion, brutality, torture, and murder. The realm of Tomas Croft is a place where anything may happen.

Each Midsummer's Night Tomas Croft steals away. Alone he climbs the ridge above the cove and sparks the hilltops ablaze. And each Midsummer's Night the glowing sky serves to stir, within the plantations below, all the simple primitive terrors about the Masterless Man, all the ancient fears of the Boo Darby. Even though not a single Christian soul has ever come face to face with this ghost, every station has its own name for it, and its own idea of the form of the creature. On the eastern shore it is the Hairy Buggy, or else it is the Black Man or the Headless Man, or maybe the Hockshaw. On the western coast it is Jack O'Lantern, or Bloody-Bones, or the Mog-Daw, or the Uni-Ped. In the south it might be the Big Rat, or the Cat-Man, or the Giant, or one of the little people. In the north, the Hobgoblin, the Gollywog, the Wriggler, the Yahoo. Anywhere, it might be the Mummer or one of the Janneys. Even the Irish of Tomas Croft's clan, every bit as green as the rest, tremble under the weird flickering lights of which they know not the origin. Hoping to ward off the evil, they gather on the beach and light their own giant fire. The entire village huddles within the safety of its glow. Other stations do the same, until the coastline is illuminated by a necklace of fearful lanterns.

Far away in Europe, the legend gains currency that this is no mere buccaneer or common sorcerer but the Evil One himself, on the loose and haunting the western world.

Arising late one spring morning after a night of drinking and fighting, Tomas Croft is startled to witness the approach of a strange vessel — not a mighty man-o'-war, but a mere pinnace. Insolently it drops anchor within the shelter of the pirate's lair.

The craft bears the name *Ariel*.

Although no guns show on the little ship, Tomas Croft bellows to his people to arise and stand and repel these trespassers upon his kingdom. They gather and advance to the beach, at the ready with their arsenal of ordnance and daggers and spears and axes and bludgeons.

A flat-bottomed rowboat pulls away from the *Ariel*.

Women propel the skiff. Blackness clads them top to toe. High on the bow stands a man, also in black. In both hands the man bears aloft a crucifix that glints in the sun.

At sight of the cross, Tomas Croft starts back in fear. He drops his weapons and retreats a few paces. Quaking, he makes the sign of the cross. He comes forward again, stares a moment, and then wades, defenceless, into the surf.

His people are dumbfounded. They halt in bewilderment. Tomas Croft bids them lay down their arms and follow behind him. This they obey, uneasily.

Just before the skiff touches the shingle, Tomas Croft grasps it by the gunnels. He orders his family to do likewise and to shoulder the boat high out of the water. Together they bear it and its passengers across the landwash to shore.

Tomas Croft falls to his knees before the invaders and bows his head.

The priest and the nuns alight and kiss the sand. With the manner of one accustomed to being obeyed, the priest directs the skiff be turned bottom-up. The nuns unfold a white linen cloth and drape it over the hull. Upon this crude altar the priest there and then celebrates the sacrifice of the Mass. The liturgy is delivered both in Latin and in Irish.

Apparently mesmerized, Tomas Croft himself comes forward and takes the role of acolyte. The service lacks sacramental wine so he provides Jamaica rum, bread so he provides hardtack, a proper bell to mark the Consecration so he fires off his pistol. His tribe, utter pagans for the most part, and mystified by the entire spectacle, neither kneel nor pray but only stand at a distance and stare agape. At one point Tomas Croft notices that a member of his flock shows insufficient respect for the rite. Without offending the progress of the liturgy, and as deftly as one might slice the fins from a codfish, Tomas Croft carves off both the smirker's ears.

Under the direction of the priest, and on the command of Tomas Croft, the family during the days that follow dismantles the *Ariel* piece by piece. Ashore they reassemble the same materials into a chapel. The gunnels form the altar rail, the lantern the sanctuary lamp, a slab of ballast the altar stone, the mainmast the spire, the yardarm hung with the wheel the Celtic cross, and the mizzenmast the campanile. The people decorate the church with their booty of fine linen and candlesticks and coloured glass. They moor the structure firmly to the earth by way of a sturdy hawser bound to the anchor planted deep in the soil. The chapel sits upon a knoll and dominates the cove.

On Midsummer's Day the ship's bell is hoisted to the peak of the campanile, and rung joyously. The chapel is finished. The priest consecrates it in honour of Saint John the Baptist and deposits the Blessed Sacrament in the tabernacle. He delivers a long sermon full of the horrors of hellfire, condemning, as sins against God, drunkenness and debauchery and piracy and all the other evils that are the stuff of daily life in the kingdom of Tomas Croft. His words terrify Tomas Croft far more than real burning brimstone ever has done.

The congregation moves to the beach, where the priest sprinkles holy water across the landwash. With Tomas Croft assisting, he baptizes the assembled multitude as a body by launching bucketfuls of seawater over their heads. Upon the lame and the sick the priest lays hands, and he tells them that by the grace of the Lord they are healed of their afflictions.

The priest declares: The waters are stilled. And now God smiles upon his people.

Finally, he commands the people to confess their sins. Tomas Croft must go first.

The last time the old man told his sins, decades before, the confessor was his own father. Now, one by one, in the order he committed them, he yields up the transgressions of his life. Only he and the priest and God Himself know the penance that is assigned, but from that day forward Tomas

Croft rings the chapel bell whenever the task is required of him. He brutalizes his people no more, and in all things he surrenders to the will of the cloth.

Strangely, that Midsummer's Night, the Darby fires fail to appear atop the hills. In great alarm the people of the cove gather on the beach with their own stack of wood and debris. The priest appears with Tomas Croft by his side. The people stand back. The priest makes the sign of the cross and recites a prayer, and then he himself ignites the pile. He stays with the crowd until the bonfire has burned to cinders.

So it is that the priest becomes the master of the cove.

Soon, everyday life in the cove is timed to the rhythms of prayer—of Mass each dawn and twice Sundays, confession Saturdays, benediction during Lent and Advent, Stations of the Cross round the clock in Holy Week, plus endless fasts, retreats, vigils, sermons, churchings, christenings, confirmations, weddings, blessings, consecrations, anointings, and funerals. In the pews the nuns hold a grammar school where they lead the children in worship first thing each morning, then at recess, again before the midday break, on their return from dinner with the recitation of the Rosary and the Litany of the Blessed Virgin Mary, and at day's end. At all hours the faithful may stop in at the altar. On bypassing the chapel—or the rectory, or the convent, or even the graveyard—parishioners make the sign of the cross. At the tolling of the Angelus, each whispers a prayer. And always, on meeting the priest, each of the faithful bows the head in homage.

When the people are not praying they are working.

The men and the boys sea-work. They jig squid and trap lobsters and seine capelin and herd whales. In spring they take up gaffs and venture leagues oceanward on the pack-ice and club seals. In summer they launch forth in open boats and shoot bullbirds. The women and the girls shore-work. They keep the gardens and the chickens and sheep and goats and pigs and cows and even the horses. On rare sunny days, all hands mow the meadows and make hay. Up the country—where no one dares go without a companion or a gun—the men shoot partridge and trap fox and arctic hare and cast for trout and salmon, and the women and children pick chuckleypears and partridgeberries and whorts and blueberries. In the darkness of winter there is woodcutting and cooperage and fencing and boat-building and sail-making and net-mending and ironmongering and masonry and quarrying, and woolcarding and spinning and knitting. The people rest on Sundays.

During the other six days of the week, work and worship enlace so harmoniously that labour itself comes to be sanctified. And no labour is more pious than the special business of fishing for the cod.

The whole back-breaking routine of handlining and pronging up to the stagehead and splitting and gutting and boning and heading and rinsing and salting and stacking and spreading and turning thousands of fish, one at a time, becomes an ardent prayer, a kind of litany.

The priest with his own hand carves in relief on the reredos of the chapel an icon of the cod. He preaches that this lowly fish embodies the Blessed Trinity itself. The cod, he says, is the spirit of fertility, like the Almighty Father the seed of generations, the very root of life. He explains that the Greek initials for "Jesus Christ Son of God Saviour" spell the word FISH. Such an abundance blesses the sea that surely the Paraclete, the greatest of egg-layers, has overflown these waters. The cove comes to embrace a cult of the cod, and its people, fishers like the disciples of Christ, see their calling as a blessed and glorious one.

Thus the ragged band of castaways and outlaws is transformed into a civilization. Violence and debauchery and heathenism give way to order and piety and work.

As his red hair turns grey, so Tomas Croft in temperament turns quiet and soft. No longer the tyrannical overlord of the cove, he is its benevolent patriarch. His comfort rests merely with the pleasing echo of the chapel bell that he rings faithfully. His delight runs to a simple meal of cod tongues. His blackthorn serves him no longer as a cudgel, but as a cane.

One warm summer evening, Tomas Croft knocks at the sacristy door. It happens that he has certain questions to ask of the priest. The two men go to the nave and sit in a pew. Tomas Croft asks about Ireland and about the kingdom of God. His mind seems to confuse the two realms. In long silences he dwells upon the answers the priest gives. Then, to the priest's ear, the old man whispers not sins but images of fabulous troves, of hoards of gold and silver and precious stones, in numbers beyond tallying, in shine and dazzle beyond belief. Were such trimmings to emblazon this little chapel, promises Tomas Croft, they would render it the most resplendent basilica in the sight of man and God. As best he can, for his memory is hazy, the old man surrenders the landmarks pointing to his buried treasures.

The sky reddens in the west. Tomas Croft asks for the priest's blessing. Forgetting his blackthorn behind him in the pew, the old man departs the chapel and hobbles down to the beach and seeks out his beloved skiff, grey and worn like himself. He takes up the oars and he rows across the calm and out the mouth of the cove and eastward into the open sea, into the darkest part of the sky.

Tomas Croft is never seen again.

Every morning for a fortnight, the priest, bearing a shovel and waving a large crucifix, walks alone up the country. Every evening he returns to the church covered in mud, weary and defeated. Finally he climbs atop the boulder at the crest of the ridge and there, bellowing to all quarters of God's universe, he damns the soul of Tomas Croft to the fire and brimstone of hell.

Sheila nGira enters the convent and lives out in madness the few years left to her.

The sprawling labyrinth of a shanty wherein she shared so much love with Tomas Croft and produced so much life is pulled apart and tossed into one of the midsummer bonfires that, for reasons nobody can remember, it remains the custom to light on the peaks and headlands.

Tomas Croft's name disappears with him. After a generation the man is forgotten.

Centuries pass.

Lord Baltimore abducts a harem. Captain William Jackman rescues twenty-seven people from drowning. Fishermen catch monsters in their nets. The *Great Eastern* unrolls a telegraph cable across the bed of the ocean to surface at a place called Heart's Content. The Reids blast railroad tracks out of the barrens. Marconi's kite transmits the letter 'S' by wireless to England. Dosco mineshafts web the red rock for miles under the sea. The *Titanic* hits an iceberg and sinks at 41° 46′ N, 50° 14′ W. A doctor with the White Fleet constructs a model cathedral from the extracted teeth of sailors. An arctic blizzard swallows the *Southern Cross* and its crew without trace. The same storm sweeps dozens of seal fishermen to oblivion on whirlpooling icepans. Alcock and Brown taxi down a bumpy field and fly to Ireland, where they crash into a bog. An earthquake causes a tidal wave, and the wave drowns villages, deposits fish flapping in the branches of trees, and poisons the gardens and meadows and marshes. The number nineteen becomes taboo. Church bells ring, announcing the election, weeks earlier, of a pope. Wars happen. Enemy submarines probe the bays and sink a ferry called the *Caribou*. Across the ocean, near a French village, with shoulders turned and chins tucked to chests as though braving a stiff north wind, a regiment of eight hundred boy-fishermen, whose motto is "Not Found Lying Down", launch the July Drive by walking into machine-gun fire that slices up their bodies as blades might slice codfish. A lunatic asylum is founded and promptly filled.

In the modern century, the descendants of Tomas Croft hardly notice that any of these things have happened—that any time has passed.

If the people of the womb-cove should hear the drone of an airplane behind the clouds, or the horn of a steamer passing through the fog, or, in the calm of night, the moan of a locomotive sounding down the corridors of the land, they might take any of these sounds to be the lament of the Boo Darby, suffering in beastly solitude somewhere in the wilderness.

Although it is now the age of science and reason, the people of the cove still fear the Masterless Man, who carries off to the barrens any children he can catch. From time to time they still sight Old Black Scratch, the dark figure who wanders the ridge, digging until doomsday the graves of those about to die. After storms, they spot mermaids upon the sea. They still dream the dreams they did in the forgotten days of Tomas Croft. Their tongues speak the same polyglot of English and Irish and thieves' Latin. Ashore, their scythes mow the meadows with the same sway and swing as did the scythes of their forebears. Afloat, their oars ply the waters with the same steady stroke. In the modern century, all these rhythms echo the pattern that they echoed in the time of Tomas Croft—the touch of the sea upon the land.

In the middle of the new century, the swell advances up the shingle with the same surge and hiss that the monks heard, that the northmen heard, that Tomas Croft himself dreamed of, that he heard from the barrel of the *Trinitie*, that finally he saw in all its luminance. For the children of Tomas Croft, the sound of the landwash is so constant and so hypnotic that it goes unheard. Just as the breath of the sleeping mother comforts the infant, so the rise and fall of the sea soothes these people. They suffer no memory of the horrors of history, no sense of past or future, no terror of time. They live every day a kind of earthly immortality.

The waves are petrified in the rock, and here the testament of the patriarch himself is etched for all eyes to see. The steady come and go of the tidewater speaks the pledge of Tomas Croft to his children: eternal constancy. The dream-breath of the landwash, the sigh of the sea upon the shore, proclaims the easeful sound of warm snug love — the plain silent sound of home.

VIII

Harmonicas

Johnny the Light extends his arms and takes hold of the latticework and angrily he rattles the trellis.

The old man curses the padlock. He limps round to the front window. Although he does not realize it, the glass is stencilled:

MESSRS. CASEY & SON
Grocery & Confectionery
Post Office
Tavern
Undertaker

Johnny cups his hands over his brows and squints into the dim shop. From the rafters hangs a clutter of oilclothes, long rubbers, pots and kettles, platters, ladles, spades, saws, pickaxes, scythes, stakemauls, lanterns and candles, cordage, and fish-hooks. Johnny notices none of these things. It is the four-faced clock he searches out. The clock tells his hazy vision that the time is half-past nine.

He bangs on the glass and damns the storekeeper to hell.

Johnny's good ear registers a raucous sound. He turns

and looks up, and perceives a dark splotch that might be a crow, perched on the spar of the church cross. He searches the road left and right. A large dog, black and bear-like and vaguely familiar, snuffles in the drains, eating grass. As near as Johnny's eyes can make out, the landscape is empty of children. For that, at least, he is grateful. But there is still no sign of that fat merchant Casey. Please God the storekeeper shows up before his shopgirls do, for those witches will turn him away.

Johnny draws the rum from his overcoat and upends the bottle above his mouth and drains it dry. He regards it with disdain, then furiously heaves it smashing into the ditch.

The dog hears the noise and comes up and sniffs at the shards of glass. The beast itself stinks, of the sea, yet when it sniffs at Johnny's boots it cringes back on its haunches and growls at the old man.

"H-H-Hushta!" Johnny rasps. At the sound of the voice the dog ceases its snarling. It wags its tail and comes forward, and grovels. Unbidden it raises a big webbed paw. The old man takes the paw into his two hands and shelters it a moment and looks deep into the aninmal's eyes. When Johnny lets go the paw, the beast snuffles off placidly round the corner of the octagon.

Johnny clasps his hands behind his back and paces before the window. From time to time he peers in at the clock, but it seems to have stopped.

Painfully he sits his body down on the landing. He searches his pockets and brings forth a ragged homemade which he fixes upon his lower lip. He fishes about in his garments until he finds matches. Tightly he grips a match and leans forward to ignite it against the sole of his boot. The match breaks. He curses, digs out another, lists as though uncooping a fart, and whips the match along his buttock. The brimstone blazes. Johnny's shivering hands, however, snuff the flame before he can apply it to the cigarette. He pauses, collects himself, ignites a third match, succeeds. Deeply he inhales, and like a dragon he sighs long slow cones from his nostrils. His eyes stare torpidly into the flame until the fire sears the stumps of his fingers.

Johnny leans forward between his knees and hawks and spews a stringy mass in the direction of the ditch. He shakes his head against the cloud of flies tormenting him like children. The flies have migrated from a pancake of fresh horseshit, nearby, that it just beginning to crust. Ash gathers on the sleeve of his old coat. Vacantly he inspects his dilapidated logans. In the cuff of his trousers he discovers a loose thread, and he tries to tie this into a crude knot, but his fumbling fingers cannot manage the job. A bundle of newspapers is strewn beside him on the step. Although Johnny can fathom none of the lines and circles printed on them, he pulls one from the bundle and stuffs it slyly under his coat.

The breeze brings to his nose a sharp voltaic smell. At this, suddenly, the old man's expression brightens. His smoke, douted anyway by the spittle that drools along its length and dribbles from the end, falls unnoticed to the ground.

Tenderly he pulls himself to his feet. He supports himself against the clapboard and stumbles to the end of the wall and looks round the corner of the stores. The dog is there, rooting about in the kelp that is exposed by the low tide. Johnny pays no heed to the animal. His eye is riveted instead upon the blazing white iceberg that sits fabulously triangular upon the sea.

Johnny's hands shake. His tongue quivers. His face breaks out in a dazzling smile. The old man shouts to the sky.

"H-H-Here's our boat, boys. Yes by J-J-Jesus. She's fetching us home!"

"Children. To your knees."

The stragglers scurry in from the yard. The nun pulls shut the door after them. The classroom's high ceiling absorbs the stir, so that the chamber fills with its own bustle, unheard. It is like the hum of blood coursing through veins. The Superior makes the sign of the cross firmly—a gesture of command.

"In the name of the Father, and of the Son, and of the Holy Ghost."

Instantly the room is sanctified.

Little Kevin Barron, front row, clutches his prayerbeads in his priestly fingers and he crosses himself. The gaunt figure of the nun soars above his bowed head like a steeple. The child is pleased: he is with the holy nun, and they are in a holy time.

"The Sorrowful Mysteries."

Hand over hand the Superior gathers up the black beads that cause her belt to sag. The beads are majestic, each one as big as a castnet ball, and drily they clack one against another. The heavy crucifix is jammed dagger-fashion inside the belt. A stiff length of leather dangles at her hip. Fingers have been sliced in the end of the leather to give it the shape of an elongated hand. The boy observes this item as though it speaks to him, for words are poker-burnt into it:

HA
NG
ME
UP

"On this day, children, on this, the Feast of the Nativity of Saint John the Baptist, I want each and every one of you to dwell on the Sorrowful Mysteries. Today—and every day of your summer holidays—I want you to fix these Mysteries in your hearts and in your souls. I want them to be a blessed example to you. Our Holy Mother the Church teaches us that Saint John the Baptist prepared the way for the coming of Jesus. God Almighty sent His only Son to this world, to suffer and die a terrible death so that our sins might be forgiven. And now, thousands of years after that glorious event, we remember the pain and the sufferings of Jesus. We re-live the pain that Jesus suffered through the Sorrowful Mysteries of the Rosary.

"As you know, children, these mysteries are: the Agony in the Garden, the Scourging at the Pillar, the Crowning with Thorns, the Carrying of the Cross, and the Crucifixion. Christ Our Lord suffered these horrible and ignominious punishments to save us from eternal damnation. He died to redeem our immortal souls. He sacrificed Himself so that we might enjoy the forgiveness of our sins and sit one day at the right hand of His Father, at the right hand of God the Almighty in all His honour and glory and majesty in the kingdom of heaven."

Kevin Barron can smell the cool dry odour of chalk that always lingers on the Superior. Once upon a time he believed that this was the odour of goodness — only the nuns, after all, gave off such a smell. With her fingers so clean and white against the dark habit, the nun seems joined together from sticks of chalk. The child cannot imagine her possessing an ordinary body of flesh and blood. He cannot imagine that her hands ever got so dirty she had to wash them or even that she needed to eat or sleep. Jennie Moores said to him once that nuns never even went to the toilet. He fancies now before him a white skeleton giving shape to the soot-black shrouds. In his mind the nun already straddles the dirty world of the living and the pure world of the spirit.

"The Passion and death of Our Lord had a special purpose: Jesus died for our sins. The pains and discomforts that you yourselves will suffer during your lives will never be as cruel or as agonizing as those that Jesus in His infinite mercy endured for all of us. But your sufferings too have a special purpose. You can offer your sufferings for the forgiveness of sins. You can offer them up for the forgiveness of your own sins and for the redemption of the millions of poor souls in purgatory. So remember, every hour and every day during the summer, to dwell upon the terrible pains and sufferings of Jesus, so that your souls—and your bodies—will remain pure and clean and holy in the sight of God."

The Superior's face, shaded by the veil, shines with a paleness that seems to glow from a candle deep within. The cowl draws the flesh taut across the bones of the skull and presses the forehead to a frown. Yet her eyes gleam in the way they always do when she prays. The nun surveys the files of children and her glance galls upon little Kevin Barron. The child glimpses a smile—a smile that can only be for him.

Of course, he says to himself, pleased. She knows.

"Morning, Johnny, my son."

The voice addresses him with casual familiarity. It comes from a portly man with florid cheeks who is perhaps half Johnny's age. The man wears a jacket and a waistcoat and tie, and on his feet shiny wellingtons. He is a foot taller than Johnny's stooped figure, and when he speaks he levels his eyes at a point some inches above the crown of the old man's cap. "How are you getting on?"

The portly man advances confidently and mounts the step. Johnny shuffles aside to let him pass, at the same time removing his cap. Johnny's mouth forces a smile, but his bloodshot eyes bulge. "Number one, Mr. Casey, sir. Hundred p-p-percent."

"Fine day."

"Yes, Mr. Casey, sir. A g-g-grand one we're having."

Cursing the tardy shopgirls, Mr. Casey becomes preoccupied with unhitching from his belt an enormous ring of keys. "Well, Johnny," he says, "what's strange and startling." The remark is put offhandedly, a reply not wanted.

"Eh, w-w-what?" Johnny cocks his head to bring round his good ear. He presses close.

With fat pink fingers Mr. Casey searches among the keys. Irritated that he cannot find the one he wants, he roars down upon the old man's uncovered head, "What's new in the world this morning?"

Johnny lurches backwards. Like a guilty child trying to conceal his dirty fingers, he twists his cap compulsively. He smiles. "Oh, seen nothing worse than m-m-meself, Mr. Casey."

Mr. Casey is not listening and he says nothing more. While he unlocks first the trellised gate and then the oaken door, he is forced to tighten his nostrils against the ammoniac smell of urine.

The door swings inward. The cowbell clanks and startles Johnny. He croaks, and gapes overhead. Mr. Casey picks up the newspapers and briskly enters the shop. He exhales with relief. Devouring the familiar cool aroma of oranges and sawdust, he retreats behind the counter.

The shop, its wood floor naked and bordered by casks of every size, smells of these things and more: squat brin bags bursting with potatoes and turnips and onions, barrels of McIntoshes and pickles and salt beef, flitches of bacon, bins of mash and oats and barley and teas, pipe tobaccos and chaw and makings, bread and hardtack, butter by the firkin, flour and sharp cheddar, tierces of molasses, white sugar and syrup, marmalade and jam in mason jars, raisins and currants, bright crates of blueberries and strawberries and oranges, and low shelves with chocolate and caramels and candies of every hue.

Johnny puts his cap back on his head and follows in. His

nose sniffs and wrinkles. Cutting through the heavy air comes the tang of the sea. It stings his sinuses. Behind him in the corner are rows of poor-john—cod sliced and gutted and stacked like slabs of dry wood—and briny puncheons wherein lobsters scratch and clamber grotesquely over one another, and, most alarming, fishheads, tongueless, each one bug-eyed like a dead man.

Mr. Casey visits a barrel filled with rotting cod livers and takes a mussel shell and dips up a measure of the oil and drinks it down. He then commences to make his way around the perimeter, switching on lights, raising blinds, unlocking a variety of drawers, safes, cupboards, and doors. All the while he keeps one eye fastened on Johnny. He unbolts the post office, which is an alcove elevated like an altar, and within this room the gun-rack.

On the floor of the post office, besides a large kneehole desk, sits a hundredweight tub overflowing with torn envelopes. The envelopes bear postage stamps from every colony in the Empire. Johnny limps across and gazes slack-jawed upon this sight, which always astounds him with its implications. The telegraph barks and makes him quail. Through a door slightly ajar he observes an array of brown caskets, varnished and gleaming and metallic, like gigantic harmonicas.

Johnny retreats to the vicinity of the pool table, which commands the middle of the shop floor. Against the backdrop of the green canvas the cue ball looks to him like a moon in a big emerald sky. He grips the simple perfect ball in his maimed hand, and marvels at the thing.

Muttering that he ought to find himself a wife to take charge of all this, Mr. Casey continues to busy himself. Johnny rotates like a lighthouse beam and follows the shopkeeper as he moves round his circuit. Mr. Casey passes, but fails to open, one particular door.

TAVERN

Open 7–10pm   *Closed Sundays*

NO MINERS ALLOWED - BY ORDER BD LIQR CNTL

Johnny starts to sway. He lumbers side to side, like a schooner broadside to a heavy lop.

Mr. Casey takes a broom from a fresh shipment stacked against the wall and upends it and pokes the handle deep among the lobsters. He speaks absently, dreamily, as if to the monsters in the barrel. "So. Johnny, my son. What have we got to report?"

Johnny does not hear. He has placed one foot in front of the other and he lurches back and forth. He is like a man who longs to leap to safety but judges the span too great.

Mr. Casey steps outside to sweep the landing. He takes care to leave the door open so that he can observe the other man. When he comes back inside he stows the broom and escapes again behind the counter. He drops the keys into the till and shuts the drawer. From the bundle of newspapers he takes one and unwraps it on the countertop and becomes engrossed in the sporting headlines.

FIRST ROUND KNOCKOUT PREDICTED
WORLD HEAVYWEIGHT TITLE AT STAKE

Johnny removes his cap again and twists it in his hands. He pitches to and fro. The floor creaks under his logans. Mr. Casey, annoyed, looks up from his newspaper. He glares at Johnny's feet.

"That's one goddamned sad pair of boots you got clapped on your dogs there, Johnny, my son."

"Yes, Mr. Casey, sir. Them boots, they is on their last l-l-legs."

The trick works: Johnny stops rocking and he stands

stock-still. Now the only sound is the ticking of the four-faced clock.

Mr. Casey reads in peace.

Suddenly Johnny cries out, in anguish: "Is there any w-w-war?"

Mr. Casey doesn't bother to look up. He only mutters, "What?"

"How goes the w-w-war?"

The storekeeper grunts, shakes his head, smiles faintly within himself, and returns to his news. Carelessly, to change the subject, he remarks, "So, Johnny, what's what at the light, eh?"

"First-rate, sir. N-N-Number one. Shining on brightly."

"Any nice wrecks for us today?" Mr. Casey reads as he speaks.

Johnny inhales deeply and announces, "Our steamer, sir, she's in."

At this news Mr. Casey raises his eyes. He fixes on a point above Johnny's bald head.

"And the whole fleet behind her. The *Beothic* and the *Nascopie* and the *Bonaventure*. Come for m-m-me and the lads. Yes, sir."

Mr. Casey blinks.

Johnny's eyes bulge. He speaks excitedly. "Come to take us h-h-home." In a grand gesture he raises his arm and extends a stump of a forefinger towards the shop's rear window, beyond which lies the ocean. Mr. Casey can see that the hand is twitching.

The shopkeeper straightens and stands at his full height. Casually, to signal that he is merely amused, that he doesn't take seriously such a report, he strolls to the window. On the sill next to a big conch shell rests an ancient spyglass. Mr. Casey extends it and jams the small end into his eye and looks towards the daylight. He swings the glass in narrow arcs, then, firmly with the palm of his fist, he shuts the glass and sets it down next to the shell. He clasps his hands behind his back and chews on nothing while he returns to the counter. He chuckles and shakes his head and goes back to his paper, as if nothing had happened.

"Johnny, my son. All I can see is that goddamned block of ice."

Johnny takes his breaths in great gulps. Furiously his body pitches. "I'm after s-s-seeing her. Our steamer. With my t-t-two eyes. And the *Diana* and the *Eagle* and the *Kite* behind her. They come for us. For m-m-me and the boys."

Mr. Casey tries to find the place where he left off reading. " 'Tis t-t-true."

Mr. Casey speaks without looking up.

"Johnny. Listen to me. I was on the cove this morning myself. I set my trap in back of the ice — the cod, you know, they likes the cold. You needs to watch for the tide shifting and the ice breaking up and taking out your nets, so I'm after having my glass on the water all the morning. Listen to me: there's no steamer, let alone a fleet."

Johnny swallows. His Adam's apple bobs. He looks wildly about. He fixes on the door to the tavern. His mouth smiles but his eyes are savage.

Mr. Casey speaks quietly: "Johnny, my son. Why don't you go home."

Johnny's smile withers. He stops rocking.

The four-faced clock ticks.

Mr. Casey tries to read, but his mind is unable to hold the words that dance in front of his eyes. He gives up. With a flourish he folds the paper and slaps it back on top of the pile. He fidgets. He goes to the till, rings it open, looks inside, and shuts it without adding or subtracting a thing.

The clock ticks.

Mr. Casey sighs. He leans his hands on the counter. He looks down upon the old man. This time he stares him straight in the eye.

"Well, Johnny. Tell us then. Come on. What is it you're after?"

The Superior smiles towards little Kevin Barron because she knows: she knows that he dwells in the state of grace. She saw him take Communion this morning.

"The First Mystery: the Agony in the Garden. *And His sweat was as it were great drops of blood falling down to the ground.*"

The nun closes her eyes in a way that suggests she is enraptured by some secret pleasure. In the space where her words were, a silence hangs, audibly. When she speaks again it is in the ageless cadences of prayer. Her voice comes into the room like a disembodied spirit, joined with the dead, joined with the souls of all eternity.

"*Our Father, Who art in heaven, hallowed be Thy Name; Thy kingdom come; Thy will be done on earth as it is in heaven.*"

As usual, Kevin Barron takes up the response ahead of the other children. He is eager to jump into the rhythms of the Rosary, into the holiness of the holy time. He is eager for the prayers to become mere sounds, sounds drained of all sense, sounds as hypnotic as the Litany—that most exquisite of all observances.

"*Give us this day our daily bread. And forgive us our trespasses . . .*" The other children follow his lead and blend into a chant, a harmony that rises and sweeps up each of the voices, one by one. "*. . . as we forgive those who trespass against us. And lead us not into temptation. But deliver us from evil. Amen.*"

Under the plainsong a scrim settles before Kevin Barron's eyes. His imagination fills with seagulls. One by one the birds lift from the face of the water, take to the air in trim formation and wing across the sea-spaces in his mind. So entrancing are the gulls within his brain he does not notice that the Superior has opened her eyes. She stares, fixedly, above and beyond him, towards the grade sixes at the back of the room. He does not see it when she makes the rising tilt of her head, the inverted nod that commands: Kneel up, child, kneel up straight.

"*Hail Mary, full of grace* . . ." In the middle of the prayer, in the middle of the holy time, abruptly the nun stops. The birds in Kevin Barron's brain tumble crashing into the sea.

All heads twist round to look.

Kevin Barron thought it would surely be one of the bad boys—the boys with snotty noses and scabs and cold sores and warts. But no, it is Kitt Hughes. The girl's mouth hangs open and her eyes are unfocused. Having failed a couple of grades, she is thirteen, years older than the other sixes. She has even started wearing the kind of stockings that women wear, with the black seam running up the back. Her body has the blunt shape of the Dixie stove that squats in the middle of the room. Her thighs are tightly clenched, but her calves, thick like loaves of bologna, are splayed across the floor. The girl is back on her heels, doing the Protestant kneel.

The nun glares. In her iciest tone she resumes the Hail Mary.

"*. . . the Lord is with thee. Blessed art thou amongst women, and blessed is the Fruit of thy womb, Jesus.*"

Raggedly the children gather themselves.

"*Holy Mary, Mother of God, pray for us sinners* . . ."

"Kneel up," the Superior speaks aloud. The prayer sputters like a match. A cloud of puzzlement passes before her eyes. Then the eyes go hard. Her mouth becomes fixed in a tight smile of decision. In measured, clipped syllables, like the click of scissors, she pronounces the girl's name.

Kitt Hughes gawks stupidly. The classroom bustle is hushed. It is a long empty moment, like the swelling up of the seconds that precede the discharge of a gun.

A shiver runs up Kevin Barron's spine. He thrills at the thought of what will surely happen. Shamed by his own tremor, he turns front and lowers his eyes and fixes them upon his hands wrapped with the rosary, fingertips joined in the priestly style.

He fixes his eyes upon his own hands, but the gently arched shape that they form vexes him with a strange fear. He is reminded of the kaleidoscopic image of Saint John the Baptist, colours bolting through the sanctuary dust to ignite the tabernacle veil and fall like the eye of God upon Kevin Barron himself. The dread he feels now in the classroom is the same that struck him this morning, in the church. Before this day he has never known such anxiety, and he makes no sense of it. To calm himself he shuts his eyes against the sight of his own hands. He dwells upon the holy time that was the Mass: he recalls the peal of the tower bell, he watches the candle-smoke curl in the vault of the apse and bear prayers aloft to heaven.

Kevin Barron hears the nun drop her beads with a rattle and sweep down the aisle. Her shoes thunder the planks. The breeze that her passing makes lifts the pages of his copybook. He opens his eyes and raises his head to see the Superior pinching the girl's earlobe and dragging her to the front of the room. Kitt Hughes actually smirks — clearly the girl does not understand what is about to happen to her. The nun shakes her by both shoulders and fixes her in position. She unholsters the strap and says matter-of-factly: "The hand."

Kevin Barron leans forward to get a better look. His senses jangle. An acidic nausea stirs in his gullet. He can taste the buttered toutons that Mother fried for his breakfast, but he imagines instead that it is some slippery slimy creature he has swallowed, a jellyfish perhaps, that now squirms to escape from his stomach.

The nun grips the leather tight and raises it above her shoulder. It hangs there a moment like a long glove that she has peeled from her forearm. The Superior's eyes squint and shrink from the sight of the girl's callused fingers. Smartly the nun brings down the strap, and the stillness breaks with a sharp report. Kevin Barron blinks involuntarily. It is the kind of blink that happens to him in the forge, when Mr. Fewer smashes the big hammer down onto the anvil and makes the sparks fly up.

Kevin studies the girl with a scientific interest—will she bawl? or crumple up her hands like leaves? or wet her drawers the way Annie Slaney did one time? Kevin Barron himself has never been strapped, not once in all his five grades.

He studies the face and observes the vacant expression of shock: eyes distant, cheeks whitened, blood surging back in a flush. It reminds him of the faraway face of the Jesus in the Stations: Jesus Is Scourged. A real strapping, he reckons, must feel like an electric current shooting up the elbows. His hands tingle at the idea.

The girl's arms are starting to shake and flinch, and the nun must hold the fingers in place. Kevin Barron marvels at how she can bear to touch the warts and the dirt. There comes another smash, another, and more. Absent-mindedly he has been telling his beads, and he finds that he has counted off a decade of blows for each hand. By now the girl's mouth is twisted, he eyes wide, her breathing heavy. The Superior draws back and delivers a final cut across the cheek—the signal that she is finished.

The nun sends the girl to kneel at the front, facing the class. Kitt Hughes's cheek is swollen and red with the mark of the strap. Her bulging eyes are bloodshot, and they stare blankly like the eyes of old May Penney, who went blind the year before she died. To look at Kitt Hughes right now, you would swear she was not really here in this crowded classroom—not at all. She is somewhere far away. And she is all by herself.

When the Superior is satisfied that the girl is kneeling bolt upright, she carries on with the Rosary. Like gulls rising from the surface of the sea, the prayers of the children, led by little Kevin Barron, lift again in chorus.

"Hail Mary, full of grace, the Lord is with thee . . ."

"I was w-w-wondering, Mr. Casey, sir, I was wondering about . . . about a drop of the Dock. Just a m-m-mickey. . . ."

Mr. Casey sets both fists on the countertop. He adopts a sober face and uses it to glare down on the low bent form of Johnny the Light. It is the expression of a parent about to scold a child. The shopkeeper shakes his head in a vague manner that might mean: No. Or it might mean only: I'm *very* disappointed in you. With the bearing of one in command, the shopkeeper turns his back on Johnny and strolls to the rear window. He chews his gums with a smacking noise and gazes upon the out-of-doors. Johnny twists his cap in his hands and wraps one leg around the other, like a child impatient to go to the toilet.

"I don't know, Johnny, my son. I don't know." Mr. Casey speaks in a liturgical tone. The parties are falling into a routine, a mouthing of words, a form to be observed, like the listless Latin of an aged priest. "I'm not supposed to, you know. The controllers will get on me." Forgetting that Johnny cannot read them, he nods over his shoulder towards the words printed on the tavern door.

"Just a m-m-mickey, sir," said Johnny brightly, detecting from the timbre of Mr. Casey's voice that he has already surrendered. "No t-t-tick." He jingles coins in his pocket.

Mr. Casey squints out the window. He shifts his angle of vision—his attention is drawn by something on the water. He picks up the spyglass and opens it, and stands looking a long time towards the iceberg.

Johnny jingles the coins, softly.

Mr. Casey starts, irritated. He sighs in a manner that

clearly means: You naughty child, you've been bad again, but I'll forgive you one last time. Impatiently he sets down the glass and he comes back to the counter and bangs open the cash register and picks up the keys.

The cowbell clanks.

"What did you say? Dock, was it? . . ."

The cowbell clanks again and the door slams. A bloated mousy woman in a red bandanna bustles into the shop. From her fingers a rosary dangles.

". . . Well, good morning, Mrs. Pelly. And how are you getting on."

Mr. Casey, smiling, drops the keys with a rattle atop the counter. He clicks his heels in welcome, then he and the woman fall to exchanging pleasantries.

He inquires about her health: she is very well . . . considering. They are brain to brain on the weather: a grand day. He wonders if the capelin will spraug tonight at long last: she hopes so, as she suffers this wonderful craving. And the two of them agree on the matter of the new parish priest: a queer stick indeed. So thoroughly do they ignore Johnny the Light that the old man might be one among the squat sacks of meal lining the aisles.

Johnny's eyes study the keys. Suddenly he smiles and blurts, "Our steamer!"

Mrs. Pelly turns and glares. She sniffs and coughs and wraps her arms over her abdomen, and moves aside a step.

"S-S-She's in, you know."

Mr. Casey and Mrs. Pelly exchange a knowing shake of the head.

Mrs. Pelly gets down to business. She wants a candy for each of her youngsters. Two hotknobs and three jawbreakers, please, and a stick of licorice and four bubble gum. How much is a five-cent scribbler? Eight cents. And Radway's Ready Relief too, for the mister, who is feeling off, and a few kippers for herself. By the each? or by the pound?

By the each, please. And the paper please. Yesterday's or today's? Today's please. Well, I'm afraid Mrs. Pelly you'll have
to drop back tomorrow.

"Come to take us h-h-home."

And, and, and . . . there was something else. It has been
distracted clear out of her head. She glares at Johnny. Oh,
dear! She can't remember! Sacred Heart of Jesus, she just
can't put her mind onto it. She closes her eyes and thinks
hard.

Mr. Casey tries to help by darting about the store and
pointing. Carrots? Chops? Onions? No, no. It's useless, she
just cannot call it back up. Baker's bread? No, no, no. Ah
well, she's completely addled this morning.

"M-M-Me and the lads."

Mr. Casey rings up her purchases and he speaks towards
Mrs. Pelly in a certain tone, "Now, then."

Mrs. Pelly blinks rapidly while her fingers probe the
depths of her purse. She counts out the coins one by one,
replacing some in the purse before pulling out others, as
though she does not want to reveal the fullness of her means.
Suddenly she shouts.

Ah yes! She remembers it now! She will take one airmail
stamp please. On the tip of her tongue for sure, ha-ha. She
wants to write Nina in the Boston States. She counts out the
seven cents before Mr. Casey's eyes. He takes them up,
counting again, and goes to the alcove to fetch the stamp.

Mrs. Pelly glances down at Johnny's maimed fingers. The
old man catches her looking and whispers to the woman,
rasping: "F-F-Freak of nature."

In the end, all wrapped, Mrs. Pelly waves a cheery good-
day to Mr. Casey. She gives a sidelong look at Johnny and
waddles out the door. The bell clanks after she has gone.

"Hushta!" Johnny mutters. "Divil haul ye!"

Mr. Casey turns to him and catches his attention. "Yes,
yes, Johnny. What was it now? Four Star?"

Johnny is confused by the question and it takes him a moment to answer. "Oh, right, Mr. Casey. Right. A mickey. If you p-p-please."

Mr. Casey gathers up the keys. He clicks the big padlock, swings open the door, and, after peeking back at the old man, who stands near the apples, he disappears into the blackness. A large tawny cat bounds out of the tavern and slips under the counter.

Johnny is sweating hard. His pate gleams.

Laden bottles clink from a cabinet within. Directly Mr. Casey emerges, shuts the tavern door and takes care to secure it, and resumes his station behind the counter. He snaps open a paper bag and slides the bottle down. The package thumps solidly on the counter. Like a chick sheltered under a hen's wing, it huddles closer to Mr. Casey than to Johnny.

"Now, then."

Johnny digs into his overcoat and removes in several stages coppers, nickels, dimes, and the scattered shilling. With quaking, stumpy fingers he counts out the usual amount.

The storekeeper proceeds to tally the coins himself, with full, dexterous fingers, two by two as if scratching the countertop, in the manner of one much practised. When this is done the package slides across.

In cupped hands, Mr. Casey carries the coins carefully, as one might a robin's nest, to the register, where he reckons them yet again, one by one this time, into the appropriate compartments of the till.

The cowbell clanks, twice, and the door slams.

Like a trace of a ghost, there lingers the smell of urine, and on the counter the torn bag and the cap of the bottle.

An odd structure, this—a little wooden platform under a trapper shelter. Father MacMurrough takes a moment to work out that it is a crude lych-gate. A narrow lane ascends at right angles from the road. At the top of this path, perhaps a hundred yards distant, a wrought-iron fence glowers.

The wind tumbles out of the west and whips his cassock billowing like a spinnaker, as though pulling him back to the bottom of the grade. With one hand he claps his hat to his head, with the other he pushes himself forward with the cane. The copse on either side of the path is dense and dark, a barbican of heather and dwarf-spruce and bramble bushes. Although the wind is tinted with the perfume of blueberries, although they hang fat all around him, the priest pays no notice.

He is only halfway up the slope when he halts. It is because of the bramble. He remembers: he has been to this place once before.

From the spectacular pass known as the Vee, the southern slopes roll gently downhill in the direction of Cappoquin. The village itself is not in sight, but the young man can spy, at last, the massive block basking on the distant lower ridges. It looks to him like an angular sphinx sunning itself in the meadow.

Melleray, he speaks out loud. A daughter's name.

From this point on, the tower will guide his course.

After his day-long climb up the northern face of the mountain, picking his way through hard bramble, the young man is exhausted. But here on the upper barren the wind is dry and hot. It sweeps the ground bare and turns brittle the thick low shrubbery. The heather gives way soon to a calcified bog, and the going becomes easier. The young man comes to a dark curtain of wood. In a stride, he leaves the wild mountain air and enters the peace of the grove. The tower is lost to his sight.

Within the wood the air is cathedral-calm. The light slants down through a maze of branches and speckles the undergrowth so colourfully it might have been filtered through stained glass. He hears far above his head the wind tearing at the roof of the trees.

His way is directed by a network of aisles worn deep into the earth. At regular intervals on the paths, he finds low boulders placed about ornamentally, like Stations of the Cross. In this region the air is wet and cool. The young man can hear the trickle of water running under the ground. Close by, southward, a heavy bell rings out with relentless energy. The sound flutters against the wind like a flag.

The paths bring him to a system of little canals, a miniature waterworks. He bridges the canals by way of oaken planks that serve as rudimentary bridges. When he emerges from the shade of the wood, his eyes are blinded by the sharp sunlight.

The tower that guided him stands tall and near against the blue sky. The block beneath it is no longer a sphinx but is a grey stone jumble. From all directions in the fields, white figures converge and disappear into the buildings.

The young man steps into the field before him and finds that it is newly ploughed. He crosses in a straight line by following the moist furrows. He bypasses milk-full cows, lowing, and tractors with motors idling, and bursting silos, and barns tended by well-fed cats, and everywhere the lovely smell of warm damp manure.

He vaults a fence and passes down a lane. His footsteps echo back to his eardrums from stone walls at either hand. Rounding a corner, he is startled to find himself standing in the sweep of a broad empty square.

The wind rakes the square so hard that the pavement, although it is dustless, appears to ripple.

A sundial is stranded in the middle. The shadow falls on three o'clock. Wearily the young man sits at the base. On his left, a little graveyard nestles beside a leafy grove. On his right soars the great church.

Fragments of male voice, ghostly in plainsong, escape from the windows. Before they reach his station the sounds are captured and torn to pieces and scattered by the breeze, and the words are lost to him.

The voices stop. The heavy door clanks open. The young man struggles to his feet. It is half-past three. One by one, a dozen white-clad figures issue from the church.

Each figure is hooded and shrouded. Silently they file past the sundial, where the young man is waiting. They do not greet him. They give no sign they are even aware of him. He might as well be invisible.

He can see under the cowls the faces of gaunt old men. Their skin is sunbaked and weatherbeaten, and bears the shrivelled dusty aspect of mummies. Firmly and with purpose, they cross the square and head straight for the barns and the fields. The young man leans upon the sundial and watches them disappear from him, one by one. . . .

The young man sits in the public stalls. He is the only person in the church. His body aches from his long walk, and he is dizzy with hunger.

He takes from his pocket a piece of paper. His eye moves down the hours of the timetable until he reads:

Vespers 6:00

Supper 6:30

When he returns the paper to his pocket he feels there the key that the guestmaster gave him. He grips it and thinks of the comfortable bed that awaits him in his cell.

His hand caresses the wood of the pew. The wood is warm and alive to his touch. He rests his head against the back of the stall, and his eye travels aloft.

The nave is long and narrow and vaulted. The walls are whitened ashlar. From the west windows the late sunshine slants low into the chamber. It paints little patches of light, like fallen leaves, upon the masonry of the east wall. The ceiling is arched and beamed with plain dark wood, and in the approaching dusk the young man can barely make out, dimly in the high shadows, its skeletal ribs.

The sanctuary lamp flickers wine-red above the tabernacle. He *fixes his vision on the candle. The flame hypnotizes him, and his eyes close. His head fills with the blood-rich smell of wine. His ears hear the dying wind sliding over the rooftop. He senses the rustling of coarse garments: shapes are moving through the silence.*

The tower bell thunders and rousts him full awake.

Again and yet again the big sound rebounds down the core of the tower. It fills the sanctuary, again and again, until finally the sound echoes and fades, and slowly dies away.

One by one the monks appear, uncowled now. The young man can see that every crown is grey.

The monks take their places in stalls that run on both sides of the aisle, lengthwise in the nave. Curtly they bow to one another, then turn towards the sanctuary and bow long and slow. They take no notice of the young man.

After a hushed silence of anticipation, the organ sustains a single granite note. The monks make the sign of the cross and again bow towards the tabernacle, then raise their voices in plainsong.

The young man starts to join them in their prayer, but he finds that he cannot make out the words they are chanting. He shifts his place in the pew, but still his ears cannot hold onto the words as they echo in the nave. He gives up trying to understand. Instead, he listens to the chanting as though he is listening to soft music.

The monks come to a point where, as one, they lift their eyes to the heavens.

The young man too looks up. The evening light is fading now, and where the roof was visible he sees only darkness. He imagines it is the yawning black sky.

The young man sits with his back against the cold slab of marble and thinks of the old monk's eyes.

Thin films of western cloud draw a curtain on the tabernacle of the day. From that direction, a breath chills the grove. The wind dislodges a leaf. It flutters down and falls upon a gravesite nearby. There is no noise in this evening.

Across the supper table the old man's face had been ashen, but his eyes, like those of the young man himself, shone a moist green, exactly the colour of a meadow after a sunshower. The monk had knotted his fist at his breast and whispered fiercely: Thank God his failing heart soon will grant him his glorious moment. During those few seconds it will take, his soul will span earth and heaven. And in that blessed instant, at last, he will know.

The cowled shapes are drifting in from the fields. At the square they fall into file. The young man cannot tell which is the green-eyed monk — the figures move with a uniform weariness. They take no notice of the young man sitting alone among the gravestones.

One by one they enter the church. The door is shut behind them.

Soon the young man can hear their voices. They chant the Salve Regina. *Through the windows of the church the sounds come to him as though from some other world.*

The twilight dims. Only the light from the church windows defines the square and its sundial.

The bell tolls for compline, solemnly and slowly.

In a blink, the lights go out. The windows are black and vacant and staring. The young man sits and waits, but the monks do not appear.

The silhouette of the church darkens the night sky. Other than the sanctuary lamp that glimmers through a window, there is no signal of warmth. Against the chill the young man crosses his arms in front of his body, and he marvels.

It is all so plain and simple.

Now then, Alexander Pindikowski. After dinner is done and that pack of savages, God love them, is gone out the door and gets lost in their summer and we got some peace to ourselves, I'm going to sit down and order a Christmas box from the wishbook and write a few lines to Ciss in the Boston States, and then you and me the two of us we'll haul on our coats and dodge on down to that rogue's roost for a money order and stamps and a bar of Sunlight and maybe a block of butterine and Cream of the West and molasses and currants so I can bake up the marvel cake, and salt beef, and soap to clean your smelly drawers—for God's sake don't let me forget that—and some Minard's, God help me, for my rheumatiz. Please the Lord give Casey the charity to put the lot of it against the capelin. If he got the cash to put up a new house, he's good for it. Maybe after that we'll drop in for a visit and say a Hail Mary to the Baby Jesus.

On the way home then we'll pick a feed of dandelions over in the meadow. A plate of greens, now that would go tasty with a meal of capelin, wouldn't it? Good for the heartbeat too. Please God the skipper gets back in time to cast us a few tubs—if ever them narrow-faces makes up their minds to spraug. A meal of fresh, that wouldn't go astray. It's them gulls you got to study, my honey. Them gulls will spy the capelin before anybody. I can see them now, over on Admiral's Beach. That's the spot the capelin will spurt, my love. Sooner or later every bloody creature in the sea brings up on that strand.

Them capelins, they are not the only ones belated. And don't you and me know it? I swear to Jesus, a contrary wind is after blowing him over the horizon, all the way to the Flemish Cap. Anyhow, when he drags his face in the door I don't want him carrying on with his jinking nonsense—not so much as my dirty grey shadow ever fell near to his old tub, never the once, and he knows it. Isn't that so? Yes, you'll stand up for me, won't you, my love.

Meanwhile, my darling, I got your handsome face to see me through the long day.

Yes, you're the berries, you are. You can keep me company down on the flake—I wants to turn the yaffle while the weather is balmy. Then we'll chop some sticks and hot up the oven and bake the loafs quick for dinner before them sleveens comes home with their racket. And won't they be making a racket this day! We'll stuff their faces with pork beans and 'lassy bread and tea, nice and morish, and send them off to play in the summertime. God bless them all.

And what you think? Your sister will have a surprise for us? This will be her red-letter day? That dumbledore that blundered into the kitchen, now there's a first-class token — the only time of the year I'm glad to see that stinger. And we bought a lucky new broom in May, just like everyone else. Between you and me and the cat, I know one thing: if that girl don't get herself claimed this of all dates of the calendar, may the Lord have mercy on you and me. The saucy gawmone doesn't do a tap. Isn't that the truth, my love? If she don't get claimed we'll have twelve months of her sloth to try our patience. But if ever she do manage to tell out her man, by all that's good and holy I don't know how she'll keep house for the poor bugger — the youngster couldn't boil water without scalding it. Hasn't got a clue. Do you know what her notion of chicken soup is? I'll tell you: she takes the hen by the throat and pours a gallon of boiling water through it.

My sweet, isn't it lovely having the windows wide again after the long winter. The smell of lilacs airing through the house — right there you have more proof of summer than ever Dr. Dodd can prophet you. The wind is picking up grand. Grand for the fish on the flake. Grand for the sheets on the line.

Look at that: a wolf among the tuckamores. Let me hoist you to the window where you can take a gander. There he goes, hauling his arse up to visit the graves — God forgive me but I never gives them a thought myself. Do you know, the man is just starved for company. That's all it is. Even for the company of the dead. There you have the first and last of it. Any fool can see that. Poor devil.

Yes, it takes all kinds. Isn't that so? Such a gob on him —

face like a hard winter. And who is he fooling with his rambling over the hills? Day after day leaving his dog conveniently unhitched, then pretending he's beating the paths hunting for the ugly beast. You and me knows what the man is up to. And it's not watching for treasure lying on the ground.

Well, look here. It don't rain but it pours. We're maggoty with bleak sights. With barren men. Just you take a gawp at that: the royal magistrate. His honour himself. Nine parts gone. Three sheets to the wind. This spring, why, he got the jag on practically every morning. Swaying in the breeze. The poor fish would keep a bond store going. Casey, that beady-eyed barnacle, bad enough he's bootlegging at all, but bootlegging to a cripple. He should be strung up, I'll tell him that for free. Yes, a tinker is one rogue, a merchant is many.

It must be his thoughts. What horrible thoughts he must be harbouring! A miracle he don't just crack: I know I would. A ward for dear Saint Dympna. Such a sorry sight it is, the fall of man. Thank God we still got the church bells, because by the Lord Almighty these nights I wouldn't put much stock in that beacon. And you know something: he don't mean to swipe things—sure, he couldn't tell you where he is half the time. And not the blade of hair on his head. And I bet you this day he smells. A feist to sicken a horse. Worse than you smells, no doubt. Yes, I mean you. This day Johnny the Light, he smells of death itself.

IX

Ogive

The iron fenceposts shoot a chill through Father Mac-Murrough's hands. Wild grasses choke the crosses that decorate the grillework. The path is steeper than it looks, and after the climb he wheezes and coughs. His noise startles a goat sleeping in the shade of a stone. The creature, yokeless, bolts away through a gap in the fence.

South, somewhere far off, a muffled rumble rolls dully, like cartwheels under a heavy load. The sound recalls to him the tremors of Mount Hagen, mild poltergeists that would rattle the teacups and put a tingle in the chair and give the world a pleasing vertigo — and fail to do a scarp of damage. They were nothing like the big quakes that he has read periodically shake China. Afterwards, people stand in the street, naked and oblivious to the fact, dazedly telling strangers, over and over, the peculiar events that have just happened.

But earthquakes never bother this northern place, surely. This land is rooted and solid.

It is the iceberg that makes the rumble.

They come in from Skellig and the young woman waits on the jetty while the young man moors the boat. He walks beside her up the slope to the little square at Cahirciveen.

There she takes his hand and, at last, she speaks to him. After the

heavy silence of the voyage, her voice startles him. It issues from un-
der the brim of her hat, and he cannot see her eyes. She says some-
thing or other that is meant to be consoling, but he is too numb to
register the actual words.

It is the last time the young man will hear the voice. He knows that
this is true even as he watches the ponytrap disappear round the cor-
ner, bearing away the light.

Father MacMurrough swings open the gate. The rusty
hinges scrape. He steps inside the cemetery.

Cemetery. He thinks of it in the pidgin. *Matmat.*

The grave-makers are bare bones, raw and pale and cold.
North Atlantic blizzards have washed away inscriptions and
left the stones teetering, or else they are already fallen and
smothered under weed and scrub.

The priest makes the sign of the cross, but he has not the
will to pray. Against the wind he buttons his cloak. He takes
a moment to study the layout. Then, picking his way carefully, the blackthorn poking the ground before his feet, he
sets out on his search.

EDMUND LANDRIGAN
Planter
1851 1910

In the Cahirciveen hostel the young man cannot sleep. He feels
numbed, emptied, as though he has had the air let out of him.

He rises with the sun and he hikes aimlessly, mile upon mile
across the barrens. By noon he looks down on a cluster of cottages
hidden snug in a valley. The scene is splendid and peaceful.

But the chimneys are cold. No children play. No wash hangs to
dry. He comes along the ridge a ways farther and he can see more
clearly: the place is a ruin. Likely it was abandoned during the
Famine. The thatch is long rotted and the stone walls are naked.

He walks down to the dead village and sits on a doorstep, and lis-

tens. For hours he listens, to the ghosts passing to and fro in the brilliant sunny lanes. It frightens him to realize that the place leaves him feeling less hollow, less alone.

ALOYSIUS LYNCH
Beloved child of Davey and Nin
1922–1924

Now, here he stands on another rise of land looking down on another village, but his own parish breathes warm and vital before his eyes. Smoke bolts gaily from every chimney. Lines of bright wash snap signal-fashion. Standing here and there on the road or in the green meadows, or resting on the fishflakes or the wharf, people cluster in twos and threes, speaking together, arms waving cheerfully.

SAMUEL BLANDFORD
1872–1914

It would please him now to sit quietly, round a kitchen table perhaps, and pass the time of day. He would be happy simply to warm to the special light that enters through kitchen windows, to share a cup of tea and listen to the voice of another. No doubt in every one of those houses, at this moment, such a plain event is happening. Maybe someone is baking bread, with a cat purring on the sill. Maybe someone else is making dinner, or suckling an infant, or telling a story to a child. Maybe, even this late in the morning, a husband and wife are making love. The priest's eye travels from house to house, wondering.

RIP
JEREMY FORTUNE
Adventurer
1905–1945

He himself has never made love. Since his ordination, he has not even danced. In fact, from that day to this no one has laid hands on his body. Other than churching that woman, since he came to this parish he for his part has laid hands on no one. He has not even anointed a corpse. His own family are long gone to their Wexford rest, and he is sure that not a soul on the planet gives a thought to him. He is sure that no one shares his troubles, for he no longer bothers to confess. Even the trees seem to shy away from his advance. . . .

Aloud he laughs at his own pompous, piteous woe.

UNKNOWN SEAMAN
Merchant Navy
Killed in Action
2nd Nov. 1942

After Skellig, he did not return direct to the seminary. Instead he wandered the countryside alone, on foot or by bicycle, visiting the ruins of monasteries. He was driven by the notion that at one or another of them he might find some goddess, some sort of Sheila nGira, who would rescue him.

Abbeylara, Mellifont, Graiguenamanagh — the monks claimed for their houses the most melodic names. Whenever the young man gives voice to these words he hears himself singing. He reads in his book how the mother abbeys fostered daughters. The monasteries decorated Ireland like daisies, people say, but he comes to think of their remnants as something else: as lovely, sleeping women. Every approach is the prelude to a kiss.

Each morning, he sits on a tomb-slab somewhere and reads the history of the particular place. Beneath the slab, he knows, rest the unconfined bones of some nameless monk, arms folded solemnly in

*front of the body in the Cistercian style. Sometimes, the thought of
this human form, at peace and so near him, gives him a degree of
comfort.*

*He explores, peering under arches, searching out passages and
chambers and vaults, gazing from the outlook of gaunt towers. He
strolls through the spaces where living monks once did their eating
and sleeping and working, and where they prayed. Other than crows
perched on the windy battlements, or rats swimming in the drains
that run from the graves, he meets nothing that moves.*

In the end it was the exalted, hardened certainty in the
faces of the living monks of Melleray that persuaded him,
not towards the monastery, but back to Maynooth. He con-
soled himself by insisting that he had lost nothing, because
love and loneliness are only different degrees of the same
want—love is the aching for a particular other, loneliness
the aching for a generalized other. He recognized that the
solitude of the collar offers a certain beauty, a purity and
clarity that are impossible to achieve in the complicated
world. Most of all he foresaw the occasion for continuing
atonement—everyday penance for the sin that he knew his
entire life would surely become.

For no reason other than to get away from Ireland, to
eliminate any chance of an accidental meeting with her, he
put his name down for the missions. He had been struck by
the story of Matteo Ricci, the Jesuit who by lighting every
candle in his church had frightened off its pagan attackers,
and so he had asked for China. Instead, they sent him to the
New Guinea highlands.

Here. Here is a fresh grave.

Neither fringe nor stone marks the plot, only a rough
cross assembled of lengths of an old dory paddle. The in-
scription has been poker-burnt into the wood, crudely, as if
by a child:

L U K E
D W Y E R
Drowned   1947

Gone
But
Not
Forgotten

The priest speculates as to whether a hollow casket is buried under his feet. The sea makes for a roomy grave. During a lull in the wind his ears catch the sound of young voices.

Halpim mi. Halpim mi.

With alarm his eye searches the salt water. He can see on the yawning emptiness, besides black dots of seabirds, only the iceberg and a straggle of pans drawn leeward into the open sea.

Ricci's friend Li Zhi wrote of good ways to die: for a noble cause, in war, as a martyr, and so on. But merely to float away on a pan of ice — how horrible, how pointless a death! Father MacMurrough has heard such stories of the seal hunt, of men making one small mistake, choosing to place a foot here instead of there, and consequently being separated from their mates.

And as the end approached, what moment would be the most painful? The final slide into the deceivingly warm waters of the Stream? By the time that came about, death might even be welcomed. Or earlier, when hope was lost, when dusk fell on a barely floating pan, when you yearned for an axe to hack away your limbs that you might float a little longer, when you knew you would not again see the sun? That too might be a relief, a shift from aching doubt to tranquil certainty. No, the hardest part, it would come at the beginning. It would be watching your mates drift off, float away from you, each one isolated on his solitary block of ice, each one, like yourself, already a ghost, each within sight and sound of the others yet infinitely distant, all together drifting to their solitary deaths.

If such a fate ever should threaten him, he wonders, would he wait for its slow conclusion? Or would he step?

What can it feel like, to drown. *Luʃ long wara*, the old Goroka men would say. Dead from water. He himself nearly drowned once, up there, in a roaring mountain stream, all of it a panic of boulders and rapids and foam and pain. But in still waters like these it can happen with such ease — a splash, perhaps, a cry, a few mild thrashings, then a soft floating descent into the sheltering womb of the sea, and peace for ever. Just a step. . . .

Dai. Die.

The shouting is only the schoolchildren. Recess is out. The youngsters pour from the door like rainbows from a spigot.

BERNICE WHALEN
In Loving Memory
1937–1947

The family names on the tombstones appear again and again. It is a kind of litany: Murphy, Kelly, Sullivan, Walsh, Smith, O'Brien, Byrne, Ryan, Conor, O'Neill, Reilly, Doyle. Entire clans are buried here. Father MacMurrough pictures their seed flowing down the generations, in pyramid, from the loins of the cove's Adam and Eve, whoever they were. He reads the names on the stones and once more he hears voices. But this time the voices are inside his head. They come from over the water, from out of his childhood: he hears the dip and roll of the Wexford tongue. The tongue speaks of faeries and of spells, of hexes and herbs and charms. It warns of banshees and the evil eye and the touch. It tells of places with musical names, like Lisdoonvarna, and Skibbereen and Ireland's Eye, and Dingle, and Muff. It blathers commonplaces about the weather.

It strikes the priest then that he has not yet seen his own, the Irishest name of them all. But just at that moment he happens upon the grave he came here to find.

When he arrived in this parish, all he knew of his predecessor was a few tangible things the man had left behind, such as his mongrel, a basement lined with emptied bottles, the dilapidated condition of the rectory, the cane which might or might not have been his, and that which, when the sun lifts high and the air warms, makes itself known down the pit of the outhouse.

RT REV FRANCIS CONROY, PD
1880–1948
Son of the Parish
Requiescat in Pace

A low fence of white pickets, neatly painted, encloses the plot. Despite the raw cold spring, the grass by some miracle already comes up green and lush. The stone glows a pale pink. Its glassy polish answers back the sun.

Father MacMurrough surveys the forest of memorials. Quickly he reckons up the corpses that Conroy must have interred during his long ministry. Now the man himself lies here among them. One would think that after conducting so many requiems he might have gained some command over mortality. Perhaps the opposite is true and instead, Conroy accumulated during his lifetime a little residue of death from each funeral that he administered, and eventually they collected like a poison to kill him.

But of course everyone knows what was the poison that really killed him. Among the holy trinity of cures, Father Fran made a clear choice.

Silently Father MacMurrough cackles down upon the grave: *Yu longlong long wiski.* And instantly he regrets having done so.

He turns away and gazes about the field and wonders: As for himself, where?

Nearby in one corner lie the nuns. The religious are cloistered even in death — but where are the earlier priests?

Like an intruder in a convent he tiptoes down the tidy row of stones.

SR MARY ALOYSIUS NOLAN
1877–1940

ST MARY STANISLAUS MALONEY
1860–1896

SR MARY TIMOTHY CLEARY
1873–1922

Reading their maiden names the priests feels a lewd thrill — he is peeping into the bedrooms of their youth. He has stripped away their nunhood and they are girls again, virgins. But reading the religious part of their names, he sees a different vision, the same virgins but this time lying warm and full-blooded here in their coffins, each one embracing her martyred lover.

He steps on a vine and he jumps, startled — he thought it was a snake.

The wind shivers his flesh. He moves on.

He arrives at the limit of the cemetery. It is the limit of the parish too, for beyond the fence lies an unblessed landscape of rock and marsh and barren. On the point of land at the bottom of the wilderness the lighthouse waits.

The priest considers whether he should try to pray. A crow clatters out of a thicket. It climbs into the sky and circles and glares down at him, and flies off. In the place where the bird came from, outside the fence, he is surprised to see still more graves.

Hand over hand, in the method of a sailor negotiating a rolling deck, the priest makes his way along the fence. Thorns like fingernails reach from the undergrowth and clutch at the hem of his cassock.

In unconsecrated ground lies a clutch of mean wooden crosses. The graves have been dug haphazardly, and they are untended and desolate. He can make out a few of the inscriptions. Most of the dead are women, and they lie alone.

The saints' corner.

Here. Here then is my place.

He threads his way back to the drowned Dwyer. He sets his blackthorn leaning against the blade of the paddle. To warm himself he buries his hands in his pockets, and he finds there the rounded pebble that he picked up on the beach.

A Gaelic legend explains the mounds of stones strewn about the Irish countryside. Before going into battle, each warrior would throw down a pebble. Afterwards, each survivor would pick up a pebble. The pile that remained both recorded the number of the slain, and memorialized them.

Father MacMurrough does not throw down this pebble — not just yet. His fingers grip it, and he marvels again at the hardness, the clarity of the thing. He grins, foolishly, without knowing exactly why.

On a fallen headstone nearby he takes a seat, and he imagines that he is relaxing at a kitchen table, over a cup of tea perhaps. He lights up a cigarette and he waits. He waits for the Irish voice to speak to him out of the ground. He waits to hear what the dead man has to tell him about the lovely peaceful business of drowning.

Little Kevin Barron presses his forehead against the glass. He is watching the Superior make her way to the convent. The nun's black silhouette parts the youngsters just the way the prow of a steamer parts the sea. She stops a pair of grade twos who are playing ring-around-the-rosy and she bends over them and wags her finger under their downcast faces.

Meanwhile, at the convent, the lay nun, laughing gaily, ushers a clutch of grade ones through the back door. Maybe, since it is the last day of school, the nuns are giving out candies to the young ones.

Here in the yard the girls are playing hopscotch and hide-and-seek and Goosey Goosey Gander and skin-the-cat and Little Sally Saucer and Here We Go Round the Mulberry Bush. They sing:

> *Don't treat the poor papists*
> *With scorns and with jeers,*
> *Just remember what happened*
> *To Winton's two ears.*

The young boys are playing catch and leap-frog and Pussy and It. A crowd of the older boys, the bad ones with warty hands and dirty faces and smells, have started a game of Just Thread on the Tail of My Coat. Already Billy Doherty and Tommy Doyle have had a round, and the two of them wrestle in the ditch, howling. White smoke curls around the corner of the building: the grade-eleven girls are sneaking a cigarette. Kitt Hughes stands among them. A voice swears, the bad word cutting sharply through the noise. The voice belongs to Billy Doherty. Imagine! Billy Doherty—and he an altar boy like Kevin Barron himself.

Through the shamble of legs a rubber ball comes bouncing. It weaves and darts like a frightened animal trying to escape. It's just as well Kevin Barron did not go outside. He would only be standing here beneath the window, his back pressed against the wall of the school. He would only be trying to shrink, to dodge the notice of the others—the ones with the dirt and the smells and the badness.

Last week, Kevin Barron did go out. A ball squirted from the crowd and along the ground and across the yard. Without thinking, he abandoned the safety of the wall and ran to catch it. Instantly he was seized. His arm was twisted up behind him while a hand came round to his front and clamped him in vise. The pain jolted up his shoulder-blade. He smelled the stale dirty clothes, the foul breath. He felt against his wrist the diseased warts. He smiled his feeble smile and pretended that nothing was happening. The hands steered him towards three grade-eleven girls chattering in the shade of the porch. The hand at the front came down to his fly and undid it and pulled out his dickeybird and held it up to the girls, and the voice said bad things to them. He looked deep into the clouds and pretended nothing was happening. Tears welled in his eyes. He retreated into the daydream he relied upon at such moments: he fancied he was coming down with TB. He thought how nice it would be to go away and rest in the san, as Bernice Whalen had done. How nice it would be if he could just lie down in a coffin and be dead, as she was. But the tears kept coming until he saw only watery streaks where the clouds were. One of the girls cried: Oh, leave him be, the poor child. Afterwards he stood for a moment, dazed, like a lamb separated from its flock, his direction lost. The girls watched him with idle curiosity, then turned back to their gossip.

Yes, he is glad to stay inside, here where it is safe and good.

Just before recess, in the middle of the prayer, Kevin Barron felt one of his nosebleeds coming on. He raised his hand and the Superior came and looked at his face and she sighed. From the supply she keeps in her desk she gave him a rag to

stanch the flow, and she excused him from play. As soon as
the class was all gone and Kevin Barron was left alone, the
bleeding stopped.

The child quits the window and turns back to the room.
Although he would have been happier if the Superior had
stayed with him, he enjoys being in this place by himself.
The classroom is always more alive when it is empty. The
crucifix that hangs above the board, and the pewlike desks,
the smell of Dustbane, all give the space a mood of sanctity, the air of a chapel. He can feel the presence of other
beings. One of them, of course, is God Almighty, but his
own guardian angel too is here beside him, watching over
his soul.

Kevin Barron wanders across to the grade-six side of the
room. It gives him a small tingle of excitement to explore the
foreign aisles. Since this is the last day, the nuns let them put
away their workbooks and go round to Sister Donatilla's
room, to the shelf at the back there, and take down anything they want. He is curious about the encyclopaedias and
storybooks that the bigger children have left open. He forbids his eye to glance beyond the pages and to look at the
woodwork of the desktops — some of the boys, even some of
the girls, have scratched bad words in the varnish.

He finds wonderful things in the books. He sees diagrams
of fish and plankton. He learns to pronounce *ogee* and *ogive*
and *ogival,* and he discovers words, like *phosphorescence* and
bioluminescence, that are so big they are unpronounceable. He
finds sketches of the great auk and of the Beothic that exist
no more, not even one. He learns about the bowerbird of
New Guinea, and about the carnivorous pitcher plant, and
about the action of the moon on tides, and about Joseph of
Arimathea arriving at Glastonbury with his hawthorn. He
reads about Osiris and Mithra, and about the sexton beetle,
and about the magical chemical that is called visual purple.

A mediaeval map shows the island where he lives to be a cluster of smaller rocks. It surprises him to learn that his country was once broken up, like a cracked egg, or like a big icepan split apart. The image gives the boy the notion that the floor is moving under his feet, that he is drifting off into the Stream. He goes over to the map of the world that hangs like a windowblind above the blackboard. In this map his island is reassembled, a solid mass. Its triangular shape is that of a hand, index finger extended, pointing vaguely northward.

The floor resettles firmly under his feet.

Kevin Barron presses his face close to the map and finds the stretch of coast where the cove is. The distance between the big capes is hardly the thickness of his fingernail. The distance from here to Ireland is that short distance strung end to end more times than he could ever count. The child stands back from the map and stares flabbergasted at the real size of the world. This is the way God must see it, gazing down from heaven, measuring the magnitude of His creation.

Something rustles in the corridor: someone whispers there. The child peeps round the door to see who it is.

But the hall is empty. The walls and the pine floor are bare. No coats hang on the hooks. No gaiters line up. You would think the school were already barred for the summer.

Still, someone, something, was there. Kevin Barron heard it clearly. His soul is disturbed by the same anxiety he felt earlier, in the church, he felt again at the Rosary. There is no denying it: something peculiar torments him today.

The child retreats, tiptoeing to the sanctuary of the classroom, to the asylum of the Superior's desk.

The class register sits in the middle of the desk. Across the broad cover the nun has inscribed in flowing script: St. Joseph's Convent School. Beneath the words she has sketched a bearded man in a long flowing garment. He holds a saw and a hammer. That is the saint himself: the patron of carpenters.

Kevin Barron knows exactly what is beyond the cover of the book. So often has he heard the nun call out the register that he can recite the names unprompted, just the way he knows the Litany by heart—he is the only one of the altar boys who can say it through to the end without looking at the missal. He is proud that he has also memorized the Ten Commandments and the Six Precepts of the Church and the Stations of the Cross and the Rosary and all the Latin of the Mass. He knows too what he will find at his own name:

Barron, Kevin √√√√√√√√√√√√√√√√√√√√√√√√√√√√√√√

Nonetheless, idly he lifts the cover. He is so startled that he jumps back a step. The nun's strap lies across the page. Like an accusing hand its forefinger points at his chest.

He stares at the thing. He extends his own finger and gingerly touches the leather. The coarseness of the article makes his pulse race.

Kevin Barron runs to the window and presses his eye to the glass. The Superior is nowhere in sight. He hurries back to the desk. His heart thunders. His right hand picks up the strap by the handle. He allows the leather to dangle, stirring and alive.

HA
NG
ME
UP

The child can feel the blood flowing hot in his veins. He unfolds his left hand well before him, beggar-fashion. He lifts the strap and brings it down lightly on his outstretched fingers. The report echoes loud in the big empty room.

Frightened, the boy drops the strap onto the page and shuts the register. He scurries to the Dixie and pretends to sort the chunks of wood piled behind. His face is flushed. The blow has left a delicious warm buzz in his palm.

No one comes in. His heart pushes against his ribs. He goes back to the desk and picks up the strap. This time he swings it hard against his delicate fingers. Just as he imagined it would, the blow jolts his forearm with an electric current and leaves it tingling, pleasurably.

Without setting down the strap he checks at the window: still no sign of the nun.

Kevin Barron no longer cares if anyone can hear. Once more he swings the big piece of leather. With as much force as his little body can manage he brings it whistling down into the soft flesh of his palm. The shock shoots the length of his arm and across his shoulder and explodes inside his skull. His anxiety, his fear of the whispers in the hall, are gone.

It is good, he assures himself. It is good.

His nose starts to bleed. The boy doesn't bother to stanch the flow. He allows the blood to run like a river into his mouth. The blood is heavy and thick, and it tastes sweet.

It is no sin, he says to himself. It is good.

Mary's fingers twist the scarf. If anyone saw her, they would think she was trying to wring water out of the cloth.

She wanders to the window and flattens her nose to the glass. Over next to the bolts of linen and duck, Moira and Alice and Casey share a joke. Mary makes a face at her chums, but they ignore her. She wishes they would hurry on out of there: she wants to know.

Herself, she would rather stay clear of the place. Casey's premises are such a maze of murky stores tacked on to one another, the shop and the funeral parlour and the tavern and the coal-bin and the seed-room and the gearloft and the berry barn and God knows what else, that as a child she feared going astray inside the octagon, going astray in the puzzle and never being heard from again. Them women he has got hired on, how they can stand to work in that gloom, day after day, for the life of her she can't make out. She favours the sun and the breeze and the space.

Mary stands back from the glass so that she can see her reflection. Her brows, thick and black against the whiteness of her face, run together above her nose and shade the eyes naturally. The eyes seem always to be searching in the distance: even now, people tell her that she has her father's eyes. The light brings up the shine of her dress so that in the glass she sees, no more a witch in a dark bandanna, but a princess. She does a hopscotch spin and she watches herself pirouette and her dress fly high and her lean thighs, her best thing, flash in the sun.

She drifts along the shop front towards the corner of the building. She bends to pick a stone out of her shoe—the shoe that still wears its coat of orange-brown dust. For a game, she shuts her eyes and lets the smooth straight clapboard guide her way.

Mary loves the plain courage of clapboard. She wants the woman to rip the blue shingles off the house and put on white panels instead. It is the simple neatness of the lines she loves. None of that snaggletooth look that shingles give to a place. Bad enough that the whole frame is asquint from the storms, bad enough that to hide it the woman is after doing every room up in flowered wallpaper. Sometimes, when the sun beats down hard against clapboard, Mary will stand for half an hour and gaze at the side of a wall. She will stare at the parallel lines until they bend and throb and hypnotize her—until she sees things that are not there at all.

The boards draw her towards the corner, to the edge. Beyond the edge wait things that she knows truly are there, such as the sea, and storms, and distances and danger, and over the horizon somewhere, Ireland, and—she is sure of this now—her new husband, whoever he may be.

Yes, this is the day it will happen.

Her hand reaches the corner and she opens her eyes. She peeps hide and seek round the edge.

A man sits at the landwash. A cushion of newspaper protects him from the wet sand. His back is turned to her. He bellows in the direction of the iceberg something or other that Mary loses in the wind. She cannot imagine why he shouts—no boats are to be seen on the water. Maybe he is talking to the echo-cliff under the Brow. With both hands he raises a flask of liquor and upturns it above his mouth. The drink runs down his throat as freely as spring water.

Mary knows perfectly well who it is, but still she imagines he is a pirate. He has come ashore to tally his booty of gold and jewels. Any second now, he will turn and he will see her, glorious in her dazzling white dress, with her legs golden in the sun. He will rise up from the beach and he will take her and sweep her up in his arms and kidnap her away in his white sailing-ship, to his kingdom far across the sea. And she will be his princess for ever. . . .

The cowbell clanks.

Alice bursts out of the shop clutching a bottle of pop, uncapped. Moira follows behind bearing an unlit cigarette and a Popsicle. With the heel of her shoe Moira kicks the door slammed shut after her. Like Mary the two of them sport coloured dresses today, but both theirs are a dark purple. They plop themselves onto the doorstep. Mary comes along from the corner and squeezes down between them.

"Oh my bones," Mary sighs. "First time I sat down since the last time."

"Here, suck on this," Moira hands her the Popsicle.

Alice says, "A grand whore's breakfast."

Moira spits something between her feet. "Well, Mary, you should have come in and heard that dirty pig for yourself."

"He came out of his office and served us himself. He says to us, 'You girls shouldn't be puffing.' So I says, 'Bless me, Father, for I have sinned.'"

"'Stunt your growth,' he says. Meanwhile giving the both of our rear ends the horny eyeball. Brigit and Frances, the poor things, they must be poisoned with his tormenting. God help me if I ever has to take a job in that place."

"But he scooped the coins up quick enough. Did you notice him do that?"

"How do you find Casey when he's lost? Answer: Roll a copper down the road."

"And he was sizing up Moira's tits something fierce. Moira, darling, think of it. I do believe you're after finding your honey. He's a bachelor, after all. And he's putting up a frame. It's an advertisement. You know what they says: You got to build the cage before you catches the bird. Yes, by the Christ, Moira, you lucky girl, I allow this is your red-letter day."

"Mister Extreme Unction? No damned fear. He's too fat and oily for me."

"And a bit long in the molar for your virgin titties anyway. Grand as they are. If they're not falsies."

"I might as well go chasing after Johnny the Light. Besides, I couldn't stand him clicking his heels at me all the time."

"And telling his war stories."

"Not to mention the thought of all them caskets in my back room. The empty ones is the worst. You're always wondering which one is for you."

Alice makes a face at the bottle of pop and displays it at arm's length. "Warm as goat's piss." She offers the bottle to Mary. In one motion Mary takes it and hands it straight on to Moira.

Moira wipes the mouth of the bottle and drinks, smacking her lips. "Give to the poor, lend to the Lord." She passes the bottle back to Mary, and again Mary turns it down.

"Well, aren't *we* the miserable ingrate this morning." Moira leans forward and pointedly speaks around Mary to Alice.

"What's the matter with this long-legged bitch?" Alice takes the cue. "Tomato boat in port?"

"Mary, my duck," says Moira. "Are you in a snit? If so, be a good girl and crawl straight up out of it. Immediately if not sooner."

Alice looks Mary up and down. "By the way, my dear. It's one dandy get-up you got hanging on your branches this morning. Not the usual rag-moll. If I didn't know better, I'd say you was dolled out for your First Communion."

"The Virgin Mary!" Moira guffaws and slaps her thigh.

"Marry in white," says Alice smugly, "you'll always be right."

"By the way. Did you ever hear about the virgin who always said no?"

"Shut up, you walrus."

"I allow it's hardly virginity on this one's mind. Certainly not today." In a husky, mannish, lecherous voice Moira sings:

> *Forrrr . . . the wind was in her quarter,*
> *her engines running free. . . .*

"Speaking of which," Mary speaks crossly, interrupting their nonsense, "how about it?"

Moira brings matches from the pocket of her dress and expertly lights the cigarette. She offers it to Mary. Mary sighs and takes the cigarette between thumb and forefinger. She ponders the smoke that curls from the flame.

"Shove it in," says Moira. "You'll feel a damned sight finer."

Mary places the cigarette daintily between her lips, inhales, coughs, then thrusts it towards Alice.

Moira responds to Mary's question. "Nope. Nothing. Not the stain."

"Nor me." Alice takes a long drag on the cigarette. "Not even a visit from the auld hag."

"Well," declares Mary firmly, "*I* had a dream. I remember that much. But whatever in God's name was in the dream, it's all gone out of my head for good."

In the schoolyard across the square, the heads of the children float disembodied above the points of the picket fence. A rubber ball with a mind of its own flies to and fro in lazy arcs. Mary shuts her eyes, then opens and shuts them in a blink—she is playing her camera game. The woman won't ever let her try the real camera, the black box. She keeps it barred away in the parlour, along with all the snaps. Mary makes the ball stop in mid-air. It holds its place magically, like a gull sitting on the wind. Once already today she had that very same notion, of flying or soaring or gliding. Or maybe it was yesterday. She can't be sure.

She aims the lens of her play-camera at the children's faces. It freezes their shouts and smiles and colour, and turns them straightaway serious. Her camera makes the youngsters different entirely—it turns them into the sort of people you see in real snapshots. The faces are made grey and distant and long ago, their eyes fixed with sadness. Her play-camera halts the boys and girls in the middle of their hopscotch or tag or baseball and, regardless of what their eyes are showing, it sends them to some place that is very far away.

"There you are then," says Alice.

"There it is," says Moira.

"There you have it." Mary wrings the scarf. "That's that."

The sanctuary lamp is visible through the stained glass. Mary moves her head this way and that, trying to make the pinpoint change colour among the tinted panes, change to pink or green or some other shade. How lovely and quiet it must be this moment, inside that place.

When she was around four, Father would light a red vigil and set it on top of her dresser. He said it worked like the lamp in the church: it meant that God was with her, watching over her while she slept. The candle made the room glow purple and warm and sanctified. But one night she woke up to find that the candle had burned out. The room was black and cold, and filled with a strange, evil smell. Some creature was lurking there in the dark. She screamed and screamed for Father to come and protect her.

Moira bursts into song:

> *A great big sea hove in Long Beach*
> *Graaaaanny . . . Snooks she lost her speech. . . .*

"Well!" Decisively Alice sets her empty bottle on the step. "We certainly got us a fine frigging water-haul, didn't we then?"

"Listen," says Mary. "Do you remember what the woman said? She said the dumb-cake wasn't a guaranteed thing. Anyhow, we was going to try other ways too. Remember?"

"A little bit of this and a little bit of that," Moira sings.

Says Alice, "True enough. For a start, me and Moira, I'll have you know, we made a visit this morning. We said a Hail Mary to Saint Margaret."

"For all the good that will do us," Moira mutters. "We might as well pray to Saint Jude."

"And by the way, Mary my duck, where in Christ was you, marleying in the school door at the end of the fourth Mystery?"

"Never you mind where I was at. So what about all those other ways she said for us to try?"

Moira raises her hand the way she might in the classroom. "But first you got to cross your hearts and hope to die."

The other two, grumbling, draw index fingers in a big X across their chests.

"Now then. When I got home from the hen party I went direct into the back garden and scattered the seeds abroad in the dark, like she said, and I sang out:

> *My seed I set,*
> *My seed I sow.*
> *Whoever is my sweetheart,*
> *Come after me and mow.*

Believe me, I felt a proper Jesus fool, talking to myself in the dark. But now this morning I went out and had a gander in the garden, and what were them seeds after doing but falling on the ground in the shape of a . . ."

The other two wait.

"*. . . fish.*"

Although it is a plain everyday word, this day it bears a special new meaning. As if she had overheard a bad word spoken in the church, Mary pretends she hasn't heard it at all. She looks down the road, hoping to find something that might reasonably consume her attention. She fixes her eye upon the Pothole Man and his nag and dray. They are near the forge, and they trundle in this direction.

Alice snickers.

"What's so funny, shitarse?" Moira reaches round and punches Alice in the ribs. "A fish means a fisherman. What else does it mean? That's something to know. If you're so smart, you red-headed cow, what wonderful news did you discover?"

Alice hoots. "Shut your fat face and listen to me: last night on my way home I picked a cliffy flower, like she said to do, and I planted it up above, where it can see every door in the parish. Now this morning what way does the stalk lean but towards . . . the water!"

Moira and Alice together shriek laughing. But Mary's head sinks, into the sort of vague buzz you hear in the river when your head goes under, noise but no sounds. With intense interest she watches the Pothole Man pick up his little cup and spit a gob into it.

Moira rubs her hands lasciviously. "Well, whoever the scaly bastard is, I got first claims on his trout."

Alice elbows Mary. "What about you, duck? What did you find floating in your famous tumbler?"

Mary gazes at the church tower, at the crucifix tall in the sky. She feels the sun hot against her brow and she thinks again how grand it would be if she could pull her skirt up and let the light warm her thighs. She speaks quietly. "There was a schooner."

Alice and Moira fall into hysterics. They roll on their backs and kick their feet in the air, like dogs. Their skirts fly up and their drawers show.

"So let's see. What have we got?" Alice rights herself and wipes the tears from her eyes. "A blessed trinity? Or the one true spirit?"

"If it's the one," shrieks Moira, "I guess we'll have to go three-share partners!"

"He better have lots of wind in his sails!"

"And a fine stiff mast!"

"Three stiff masts!"

Moira and Alice howl and roll and kick. The cowbell clanks. Casey is standing in the open doorway. Grinning his grin, he clicks his heels.

Moira sobers. She speaks precisely, to no one in particular. "Can you feel a draft?"

Casey retreats and the bell clanks and the door closes.

"What a Nosy Parker. That man has got such an ear for
the dirt," says Alice.

"He's just a pain in the hole," says Moira. "That's all there
is to say."

"Enough of this malarky. Let's get back to business," says
Alice. "If this telling is reliable, then who do you suppose
they are?"

Mary throws up her hands. "What frigging telling are you
talking about? Devil's the use of this sort of telling. It's like
the signs saying to you: Your man, he's got a dickeybird between his legs. Answer me: what man in this place is not at
the fish? Or was once? Or will be?"

Alice is cowed by this outburst. "The priest?" she offers
meekly.

The three sit in gloom. Angrily Mary snaps her Popsicle
stick into small pieces. Alice blows across the mouth of the
bottle and makes the mournful sound of a foghorn. Moira
tosses the butt of her smoke into the ditch. She tries to cheer
the others by singing:

> *Ohhhhhh . . . I the boy who builds the boat,*
> *I the boy who sails her,*
> *I the boy who catches the fish. . . ."*

Mary is glum. "Look: if we had a couple of names to
start, then at least we could do the apple. That would be
something."

"Do the apple?"

"You remember what the woman said? You takes seeds
out of an apple and you gives them names of fellows and lays
them on the scalding damper. The first one that hops, why,
he's your lad."

"That's all very fine and good," says Moira, "but which ones should I stick onto my stove?"

"Well," says Alice, "there's Billy the Cluck . . ."

"No thank you. I'll leave him to his hens."

"All right then, I'm after noticing Fernic Furey pinching your bum."

"That gawmone. He wouldn't say boo to a sheep."

"He's just a touch shy, is all."

"Shy like the cheeks of my arse. It's plain stuck-up he is. Anyway, he's my cousin. That's the trouble: I'm the cousin of every bird along the whole length of the shore. All but for this one here."

The Pothole Man and his nag pass through Church Square and in front of the stores. The horse steps square into the paddy it dropped on its downward journey. Now the box-cart is empty, but a smell of damp clay fills the breeze. The man turns his face away from the girls. The horse stales in a great yellow splash that leaves a snake in the gravel. The air stings of ammonia. Slack-jawed, the girls watch the man and the clopping horse and the dray retreat up the road.

"All right then," Alice presses on, "there's Billy Nolan. He's not shy, is he? I saw him grab your tit—don't deny it!—I saw him lay his paw on top of your hope chest, right there on the church steps, one night after Benediction—may God forgive him. Anyhow that's a sure sign of affection."

"Tub of lard. He's got a back end on him big as that horse."

"Listen to this: the pot calling the kettle black!"

"And something else: the men in this place, they is all broke out in warts, my dear. Tell me, would you want a pair of warty hands laid on your pure flesh?"

"Warts is easy to get rid of. You just go out the night of a full moon and you say: Moon, moon, take my warts away. That's all there is to it."

"Get out. All that is pagan superstition. That's all that is."

"Christ, girl, you're contrary. Satisfying you is like catching an eel in a barrel of snot. Let's start over: how about Gus Gallant?"

Moira makes a leering smile. "Now you're talking. That's a piece of breeding stock. Yes, by God, that buck can stick his seed into my hot oven, any day of any week."

Alice sniggers. "We're getting our wind up. It's time we had a proper try." She takes two matchsticks and pinches them together. "This one is Gus, and this one is our Moira." She lights a third match and ignites the two. The girls hold their breath and watch the matches burn and expire.

The cinders bend in opposite directions.

"Too bad," says Alice. "But what odds. You know what some people says about him. But tell me this: what do you make of his shadow?"

"Aloysius Butt?" Moira rolls her eyes in false passion and lets her head fall between her knees. She inhales her skirt and pants like a dog and moans obscenely. "Aloysius Butt!" she mocks. "God, I'm hot. Aloysius Butt! Oh, my bowels are melting with animal lust."

Alice and Mary laugh so hard they make no sound.

But when they have stopped laughing and wiped their eyes dry and settled down, nobody speaks for a long while.

Mary sniffs at her fingertips. She smells her woman's smell.

Moira stretches her fat calves before her and curls her feet back. She whispers, "It's all right to laugh joke and carry on, but you know — I would do it. Not ever with that lobster Wish Butt, not with him, no I wouldn't. But with just about any other I would. Warty hands and all. Yes."

"So would I," says Alice solemnly. "In two seconds."

Another long silence, and to lift the heavy mood Alice and Moira recite.

"Have you ever?"

"No I never."

"Would you like to?"

"Would I ever!"

The three stare at the ground and dwell on their own thoughts.

"What a trinity of nuns we are," says Moira. "Three cherries."

"I suppose we could always join the convent," says Mary plaintively. "That's better than being unclaimed . . . isn't it?"

"Which reminds me," says Alice. "I forgot to tell you. Mother Beef dragged me into her office this morning."

"What did that wharf-grump want you for?"

"You weren't doing the Protestant kneel, were you?"

"Wasn't that a sin!" says Alice. "Mary, you came late and missed that. You could hear it through the wall. It's plain badness to take the strap to such a simple one as Kitt Hughes. Half the time that one doesn't know if she's asleep or awake."

"At least she never got the class of trimming that Martin Mullowney got," says Moira. "Don't you remember?"

"The time he was picking his nose?"

"Yes. You know the way he picks his nose: he roots away until it bleeds. This time—I swear this is the God's truth—he had his pointer finger right up to the second knuckle. So she calls out to him: Martin, my boy, let us all know when you manage to find it. And he just up and said to her . . ."

"Mother Nilus, go fuck yourself!"

"Wasn't it a mortification! Well, you knows what she did: she thinks it over a minute, then she kneels him down in front of her and she grabs his tongue in her fingers and makes him say the Act of Contrition. And when he was done that, she gives him her usual vicious lacing with the strap."

"I swear to God, if she had a slab of cod handy, she would of clubbed him across the chops with it."

"Anyhow, what did she have you in for?" says Mary.

"She does it on someone every year. She tries to find out if you wants to be a nun."

"I'll be no black widow," Moira vows. "I'll tell you that for nothing."

"She sits you down and she proceeds to make a sermon. She says thousands of women is after devoting their lives to God. Wedded to Jesus, she says, the greatest husband you can want. She asks if ever you heard the voice of the Lord, or saw signs, or felt the call to a vocation. Then she invites you to join their 'community'."

"And so you said: Where do I enlist?"

"I told her I would listen carefully for the call."

"If ever she has me into her office," says Moira, "I'll say to her face: No thank you, Sister, the fact of the matter is, I wants to get married, I wants a white wedding, I wants a real husband with flesh on his bones and blood in his veins and a horse's dick between his gams, but no warts. And I wants a houseful of babies."

"Don't she ever have the lads in?" says Mary. "It's not fair."

"Don't be foolish, girl. What sermon could she make to them? 'Marry the Virgin Mary, the best wife you can hope to have'?"

Up behind Domilly's henhouse, out of sight of the men, supposedly, a line of women's underwear flaps in the breeze. "New-fangled ladies' drawers," the lads shout, every time they see such a sight. Dreamily, for no particular reason, Mary remarks. "Theresa Kilbride says you can pick out virgins by the way they walks."

"Of course." Moira grins. "Didn't you know that? Why, one glance at your chaste wiggle, Mary my dear, and I can tell for a fact that you never ever once in your life laid eyes on a proper trout, let alone had your paws clapped onto one—unless, of course, it was your little brother's."

Mary attacks Moira, tickling her under the arms, and she says, "You streel. I suppose you did have your paws on one?"

"Well, at least I saw one. I mean a grown-up one. And it was grown up, let me guarantee you!"

"Where? Where?" Alice and Mary cry as one.

"Where? It was hanging from under his chin. Where did you think?" Moira looks at the clouds and hums a tune.

"God damn you to hell," says Alice. She reaches over and twists Moira's arm. "We'll have your guts for garters. Here and now."

Moira hisses, "Are you any good to keep a secret?"

The other two cross their hearts. Together they recite, "And hope to die."

Moira takes a deep breath and declares: "I saw it."

"It?" says Alice, rolling her eyes. "It?"

"You know. It. Everything."

Alice and Mary stare.

"Well?" says Alice. "Do we have to prise the story out of your mouth?"

Moira glances behind to make sure no one is listening from the door of the shop.

"I never told anyone this before. Last summer, I was over back, picking blueberries. Graping—no, it's not what you think. I wasn't dogging. I was minding my own business."

"What?"

"Well, I heard noises and I saw something white and I looked through the bushes and ... there they were, stretched out in the clearing."

"Who?" Alice and Mary demand with one voice.

"Cross your hearts?"

Alice and Mary groan. Breathless, they cross their hearts again.

"Victor Thomey and Bridey Fitzgerald."

"But . . . they're married!"

"Of course they're married. *Now.*"

"So what happened?"

"Well, it happened."

"What happened? Look: if you're going to tell us, tell us."

"And if you're not going to tell us, don't tell us."

"Well . . . they did it. All right: they screwed. I saw the whole thing, start to finish. When it was over, I cleared to Jesus out of there. If you saw me you would think I had the scootberry quicktrots. Dropped my empter in the path—it's probably up there yet. And wasn't I the bothered one. The steam was spewing out from under my drawers. In heat just like the cat. Right crazy. I figured I was going to set fire to the berry hills, I tell you . . ."

"So: what was it like?"

"It's sort of like . . . I don't know. What can you say about it? It just is."

Mary says, "I think you're making this up, just to tantalize us."

"Yep, that's a goddamn big shark, Phonse," says Alice in a mock baritone.

"You never saw nothing at all," says Mary. "You're wetting us just for badness."

"You're sure about that shark, Phonse?" Alice won't let up.

"All right then—didn't Bridey launch a baby this spring?"

"Jesus." Alice, astonished suddenly, speaks in her natural voice.

The girls consider.

"I was present at the creation, I guess." Moira smiles inwardly. "Constantine, they named it."

"No, Constance."

"Whatever."

"When the child is old enough to know the facts of life,

Moira, you ought to stop it on the road one morning after Mass, and tell the story."

A voice shouts from in back of the store, from Admiral's Beach. Alice is rising to go see but Mary says, "Never mind. It's only Johnny, hiding from the youngsters."

"Hushta!" Alice mocks.

"That's a sin for you," says Moira. "That poor man, he's so ugly. Did you ever see his fingers? They're not even there."

"My aunt told me Johnny even got the cloven hoof," says Alice. "That's why he has such a gimp. But she said something else: she said Johnny got a medal from the king, once upon a time. She said Johnny the Light is the greatest man ever to walk these roads. Can you believe that?"

"Speaking of walking the roads," says Mary, "which one of you scallywags went flying by me in the pitch dark last night? Whoever it was, you was too stuck-up to say hello."

"I went up the road, my dear. I told you already. Beeline out your door. Never say a living soul on the way."

"Likewise, duck. Fell snug into my bed. Alone, I regret to say."

"And what were you at anyway, beating the paths that hour of the night?"

"She sent me out to do the scarf."

"You devil yourself! You never let on about that."

"So that's how come you were so belated. Tell us then: what did the scarf have to report?"

"Not the stain. The sun was after burning it off." Mary unrolls the very scarf and holds it up so that Alice and Moira can see for themselves. "After you lot went home, I ran down to the Brow. I swear to God I couldn't see the hand in front of my face—but I know some nightwalker passed me by. I said to myself, if it isn't one of you streels it surely is the Darby. Frightened me half to death, you know."

"Maybe it was the Amadahn," says Alice brightly. "Or a giant leprechaun."

"It might have been the Headless Man," says Moira.

"Or a pirate."

"Maybe it was a stranger."

"Oh, probably it was only Johnny."

"It wasn't Johnny. I would have heard him talking to himself."

"Hushta!"

"And you would have sniffed him too. You can smell Johnny before you see him. If you're so misfortunate as to be downwind."

"Maybe it was Martha," says Moira.

"Of course! That's who it was, Mary, my dear. The old woman, she was roaming the roads, looking for someone to die. Or else, she was busy casting a jink on Sweetheart's Day."

Mary's gaze swings round towards Martha's shack. White smoke appears at the mouth of the stovepipe and whisks off straightaway into the wind.

"By God, Mary, yes," says Moira excitedly. "That's who it was. As sure as there's shit in a dead goat. That old woman, she knows the day and the hour for proper divining. I bet she's after putting the curse on all of us. Make no wonder all our tries is useless. We ought to boil the witch's piss."

"Mary, you're lucky she didn't spit in your face. One time, she came up to Walter Halleran on the bridge and spewed right into his eyes. No reason. He was blinded, practically. Had the next day off school."

Mary remembers her fourth birthday. She was over in the lane, trying out the red tricycle that was her present. Old Martha appeared from behind the fence and pushed her aside and snatched the bike—just grabbed it like she owned it. Her gums were dry and champing, but the woman spoke not a word. Martha straddled the toy with her sticks of legs. She sat in the saddle and her knees stuck up high and she wheeled circles around the child, like some grotesque grasshopper. At first, Mary was too surprised to cry. But when she saw the thing raw and red between the old woman's legs the child ran screeching to Father. But she was never able to tell him what it was that had frightened her.

Wide-eyed in her own thoughts, Mary whispers, "Do you think we're really jinxed? Do you think we're never going to be claimed? Not one of us three?"

Alice and Moira together give her a long-drawn look.

"Oh, cheer up," says Alice. "On the contrary. Look here: thanks to the tries we're after having already, now we got our pick of every bachelor in the parish."

"Yes, Mary my love," says Moira. "Buck up. Besides, there's several fine specimens got their beady eyes fixed on your arse . . . or haven't you noticed?"

"Tell me a single one." Mary speaks petulantly. "Where's he at then? Point him out to me. This instant."

"Well, . . ." Moira thinks.

Alice blurts, "Michael Barron, for a start. I spotted him admiring your hat at Easter Mass. Now there's one smart lad."

"Four Eyes!" Moira bursts into giggles. "The Professor. But . . ."

"But so what?" says Alice. "Besides, he's not the professor he looks. He shaves already. He even dodged school today. Mooching, the three of them, they said they were staying on the water all night. Up to some devilment. No, he's not the professor you would think."

"Robbing traps, no doubt," says Moira. "Mary, my darling, maybe he'll put you in his book. In fact, he won't be much use to you if he don't."

"Now there's one book I don't ever want to read," says Alice.

"Would be a sacrilege if you did," says Moira.

"You know, we should abscond too," Alice dreams. "It is such a grand sunny day. We could be playing hopscotch."

"Or up the mash, sunning."

"Wading in the pools."

"Catching warts off the frogs."

"Michael Barron?" Mary breaks in.

"Oh, my duck," says Alice, exasperated. "It might be that one, it might be another one. Have faith. We got the whole day ahead of us yet."

Faith: Mary remembers the instant she lost her faith. Even before her tongue had worried the tooth out of her jaw, she had made up her mind to do a test. So that they would not know, she had swallowed the blood, and she had left the tooth under her pillow. In the morning it was still there, dry and grotesque. She had cried then, not for the loss of a few coppers, but for the loss of something she couldn't even name. Only years later, when she began to take catechism, did she learn what it was called.

"Are you going to drop your egg in the road, like the mother said?"

Mary shrugs: Probably.

"There you are then! There's hope for us old maids. Oceans of it."

"Just my luck," Mary mutters, "Johnny the Light is the one that staggers along and sticks his cloven hoof into it."

"As for me," says Moira, "I'm pedalling up the line. To Father Duffy's Well. Have a gaze into the barrel and see what there is to see."

"And," says Alice, "I'm going to pick a dozen apples and heat up the stove hot as it gets, and make every bachelor in the place pop."

The girls watch the nun stride outward from the school door and make a wide circle, billowing. The children swirl about her, a schooner surrounded by a clutch of dories. The nun wields the handbell by the clapper, holding its tongue. Then she grips the handle and raises the bell high over her head. Recess is done.

"There it is, boys," says Alice.

"There you are."

"There you have it."

The three stand and stretch.

"Maybe," says Moira, "jigging a man is like jigging a fish. A bad beginning makes a good ending."

"So we pray," says Alice. "But maybe we should not pray. As for this love nonsense, they says it's thunderbolts. I says: thunderbolts my arse. I allow it's one of the Lord's dirty jokes."

Alice and Moira go back inside the shop. Mary wanders again to the corner of the building.

Johnny is gone. Only the priest's black dog roots in the kelp. Waves gallop outward to the horizon. Even against the breeze Mary's nostrils pick up the briny smell of seaweed. Tonight, for sure, the capelin will roll up in this place. She makes play-binoculars with her fingers and scours the water. She passes across the horizon again and again. But she sees no sign of the red punt.

The top of the lighthouse is visible in the notch in the road. It looks like a gunsight. This day, Mary makes a promise to herself, I will go there. I will go to that place where I have never been.

Yawning, she returns to the front step. Moira has dropped her matchbox. Idly Mary picks it up. She peeps through the pane in the shop door. Alice and Moira and Casey together are grinning. He has taken the empty bottle and now he slides a coin across the countertop.

In the doorway Mary stands close, out of the wind. Quickly, before her friends return, she pulls three matches from the box.

———

Such a lovely clatter. Clean white sheets slatting in the wind. Like sails on a wedding schooner. Sometimes I wants to leave them spread on the line all week, just to hear them.

Now, Cornelius Quirk, my sweet. We'll set you up here atop the woodhorse, clear the blade of the hatchet. Else you'll get beheaded. At the very least befingered, you and Johnny the Light together. The chooks will have your tiny toes in their mash. You'll be one of the faeries, one of the fallen angels with the cloven hoof. We'll put you up safe where you can catch the sun and the breeze. Tuck you snug into your paisley bonnet. You can lie here and be a good boy and let the rest of the world go completely mad. I'll just be a minute chopping us a few splits.

Well there goes your sister and her pards, back through the gate for their final hour. Think of that now. Just think of that. I wonder if she knows anything yet. Thank God she has got the angels on her side—the moon is out with the sun. Like I says to her, every piece of chance is a help. It all adds up. That rooster that crowed, she must have heard it. And I pray she happened upon that button I hid in her chest: of course, she never said a thing about it. She wouldn't anyway. This morning, not a civil word did I get out of her mouth. Only sulk. Wouldn't eat nary the morsel. And I swear to God, I nearly lost my patience over that sundress. Just about took the belt to her arse. And what does she do but run off and leave the mirror stuck up there in the garden, thank you very much. Be damned if I'm going to carry it in for her. Well she better not spoil her fortune with badness—she just might catch herself an ugly sculpin.

But I suppose I should knock off talking her down. Her mind is full of thoughts. After all, my dear, this might be the day of her life.

My love, some fine sunny morning like this I should buy

them seeds and get out the mattock and make up that park
and be done with yawping about it. Put some order in the
world. The ground is thick and damp and mungy enough,
the buds would sprag by the Feast of Saint Bonaventure.
Only thing you got to watch for is the seals coming out of
the water and robbing the gardens. Them lilacs is lovely but
a few blossoms would be grand. So nice it will be to stand
here in the sun and breathe them in.

Here's Sol and his chariot. Isn't it sad, my love? Here we
are now smack in the middle of Sweetheart's Day, and nothing is beating the paths but lonesome men and dirty animals.

Yes, he's up there yet. Still brooding in the boneyard.
Father Longshanks. Daddy-long-legs. The northern ranger
himself. Putting the rest of us pagans to shame with his
piety. Either he's got a woman in purgatory we don't know
about, or he's saying a prayer for every stone. You and me,
my love, we knows what it is, don't we: the poor man, he
hates to go back to that hollow old house. Maybe he's looking for a bed up there on the hillside. He'll be granted that
soon enough. Won't we all? I hope he brought his cross with
him: it's his own soul he's likely to meet. The demons and the
angels up in that place is fighting over him this minute. I can
almost see them myself.

Well, Sir Percival Willoughby, my duck, the cat is calling
us from the windowsill. We must haul the sheets off the line
and go in for our sit-down. Get dinner on the stove. Start
our day of creation. Hot the sad-iron on the damper. Then
we'll have our mug-up: tea and raisin buns and partridgeberry jam, and a Purity biscuit and a slice of that fresh
bread—it smells so good just out of the oven—and hardtack
for your little gums to chew on. Just the two of us, cozy together. What do you think of that?

X

The Blue Drop

"Gone . . ."

The bow shatters the wafers of slob ice. In shape, the barbed inlet echoes the thousands that rupture real granite cliffs up and down the infinite coast. These vertical walls here however are pale and ghostly. They pulse with gauzy tones of green and blue, crimson and gold, their pigments bleached away, leaving only traces, diaphanous tints that are reminiscent of the subtlest of stained glass.

From his left comes the sound of canvas ripping. An entire mural peels from the face of the berg and collapses into a ravine. The icefall bares a black scar—a vein of coal dust. A musty smell passes before Michael Barron's nostrils, then a death chill. He shivers.

In 1914, Pop told him, waves washed over the bodies and laminated them in layers of ice. Most of the pans drifted into the Stream and melted, and the bodies were lost. But one block washed up on the Fogo, its kernel the body of a young man, a boy no older than Michael himself. A fisherman towed the pan to the jetty in the casual way he might have retrieved a jolly-boat.

Michael marvels at the size of this mountain that embraces him. He marvels at its age, at the distance it surely has travelled, and he wonders how many young bodies are entombed within.

". . . but not forgotten," says Wish. Wish towers astride the cuddy. The shotgun rests close and handy between his feet. He grips the gaff and he poles the nose of the boat gondolier-fashion and searches for leads. Gus at the thole-pins dips the sweeps with deliberation, one following the other, wherever he can find water.

"Haul off!" Wish warns, pushing aside a big pan. "Haul off!"

Michael shovels the widowed oar in the soupy wash astern. Like pond scum the slush smothers the surface of the ice-cove so thoroughly that it dampens to mere swells the offshore chop that veers around the corner. The progress of the boat is snarled by the brash and pancake and growlers. The hull bumps against the bergy bits and the thuds echo back from the walls. A cold static drones.

"Haul yourself off," Gus grunts.

Michael is fed up with this chase: they have been at it for hours. His bones are infected with the cold. His stomach aches from hunger.

"Gallant," Wish drawls. "I have to say this: that was a smart move, making a present of our one and only fish. All it done was, it give them the strength to keep on. I allow the pair of them archangels is under our keel this instant, smacking their lips and having a grand laugh at us. Now we got no crop of fish at all to bring home to our poor starving children. Nothing. Zero."

"Shut up, Butt. What the fuck does it matter? Small difference bringing in none as one. It was rubbish anyway. Now shut up."

Wish howls, "REPENT, REPENT, REPENT, YOU SINNER. FOR YOU SHALL ONLY FIND SALVATION . . . IN THE LORD . . . JESUS . . . CHRIST." His words echo back repeatedly, in diminishing volume.

"I said: Shut your gob. They is inside this gut some place. The bastards is cornered. They got to breathe. You'll send them off again, you stupid arse."

Wish dismisses Gus by hooking his thumb obscenely upward. With studied bravado, as though merely ambling out the door of his outhouse, Wish steps off the boat and onto the edge of a tippy pan. The pan sinks under his weight. He shouts with glee, "I got my Jesus boots on!" Just before the water tops his wellingtons, he steps casually onto a bigger, steadier piece of pancake. He braces his feet against the frozen ridge and poles with the gaff and challeys ahead of the punt to the head of the inlet. He sings:

> *Oh, we'll rant*
> *and we'll roar. . . .*

Soon the rowboat bumps the continent of ice. Gus drops the paddles. Nimbly he climbs atop the cuddy, and picks up the grapelin and rocks it at arm's length, as though soothing an infant. Muttering, "Get out and walk," he heaves the grapelin high up the ice and leaps after it, splashing. He retrieves the anchor one-handed, as if it were a suitcase, and carries it above the tideline, where he impales the flukes hard and deep into the base of a hummock.

At the stern Michael draws on the rhode. The boat skids uphill so easily he fancies that ghosts are helping push. When half the keel is high and dry the vessel slumps on its side and comes to rest leaning on its clinker-boards.

Michael wraps the stem and eases himself over the gunnel. When he sets his feet down on the milky blue berm his knees wobble, and he waits while his body adjusts to the strange solidity: this one is aground, no mistake. The brackish sea-wash leaves the ice sticky and gives him a measure of footing.

Already the berg suffers the withering corrosion of the salt sea. The water—rising now—has already etched a tideline undermining the entire girth and producing the mushroom-signature of age. But the eerily polished berm bears none of the debris of a natural landwash—no kelp, or dry sticks, starfish, mussels, seashells, periwinkles, sand, pebbles, or beachrock.

Wish comes up and impales the gaff as he might a flagpole, and chants, "In the name of His Majesty King George the Sixth, I hereby takes possession of this new . . ."

Gus hisses, "Shut the fuck."

The boys stand in a patch of shade. Gus nods curtly towards the glaring light across the inlet. Without a word he skids to the boat and lifts out the gun. He rests the barrel handily between the tholepins and cocks the hammer and aims.

Michael too sees the black tail. It peeps from behind a knoll.

After a long breath of expectation, the gun blasts. Ice explodes and settles in a silvery mist. The report ricochets thunderously. Michael is sure he can feel the berg shudder under his feet. When the noise has died, the boys hear the piteous squeal of an infant. A circular red blotch stains the ice-cliff.

"And," Gus intones solemnly, "may the Lord have mercy on your soul." With a boastful gesture he clicks open the breech and points the barrel skyward so that a smoking blue shell slides into his palm. He perches the broken gun on his shoulder like a parrot. Michael enjoys the lovely smell of gunpowder.

The bull flops into view from behind the knoll. In the style of a child on a funfair chute the animal glides face-first down a natural channel in the ice. One eye is shot away. The graceful curve of its path is traced by the streak of rusty blood it leaves behind. The creature plops into the slush and sinks out of sight.

Seals, Pop says, they are the souls of sailors drowned at sea.

"Well, God damn you to hell," says Gus. He pushes a fresh shell into the gun and clicks it shut. Wish has already scrambled with his gaff round to the rusty circle in the slush. Gus unties the gunline and runs after him. Side by side the two wait for the animal to surface.

Michael stays in the shadows. His breath steams. He jams his fists deep into his oilskins and shivers without rest. The cold is primal and it penetrates his boots. Like sluggish electricity it travels up his legs and settles at his groin. From there it chills his body through.

Framed by the blanched, spectral fiord, the bright red punt in which he has just spent so many hours appears curiously distant. The boat is somewhere back there, left behind in the real world, among the hard things—among the colours. He fears that he has fallen into some peculiar parallel realm, detached and remote, and cold. He yearns for simple kitchen warmth.

Swelling light draws his eye up. The crown of the berg glows in the sun. He turns his back on the boat and on his mates, and makes his way round the corner. As soon as he finds a likely path, he starts his climb up the face of the pyramid.

The sun was swallowed by the goddess Nut as it sank in the west, was reborn from her thighs in the morning.

The clock on the wall says half-past eleven. Any moment now, a knock will thunder on the door. It happens every year.

Light pours in through the high windows. To warm her face Mary raises it to the sun. She squints her eyes nearly shut. When the sun passes behind a cloud she is able to look straight into the black disk. She tries to imagine what it feels like to give birth. Could it feel like heat, like fire? Or, with all that water pouring down, cool and wet?

Any moment, a knock will thunder on the door. Mary can almost hear it. She is in one of those in-between times where you know that something is just about to happen. In fact the whole day has been like that. Sometimes, if you think on the future hard enough, you can make it happen even quicker.

Yes, the knock will thunder and the nun will flutter over and swing the door ajar and a dark pillar of a man will be framed in the portal. At first he will step back slightly, as though surprised. The children will leap from their seats and stand at attention. In harmony they will sing out, "Good morning, Father."

Mary has chosen the letter M—her name letter. Whenever the nun lets them read whatever they want, she pulls this particular book down from the encyclopaedia set. And today she will finish it, on this the last day of all her schooling, for she has got as far as "Mythology". Already she has learned about Ganymede, and Ahura Mazda, and Balder, and the Colossus of Rhodes, and Cheops and Teotihuacan and Stonehenge, and the cult of Mithra, and Venus the goddess of love, and how a cock crowed when Apollo was born, and about all the other gods of the sun and the moon and the stars, and the source of the calendars, and many wonderful things.

She likes to read most when there is no test. But today her mind cannot stay with the words. She is distracted by the clock—the woman warned her: Noon sharp, my child, else forget the whole affair.

She is distracted too by the empty desk, by the ruler and pencils and books scattered upon it. They make it appear that he has only this moment stepped out. Mary slips her hand into the shelf under her own desk and touches the charred matchsticks. She strains to form his image in her head. Although he has been in her class since the two of them were five years old, she cannot bring his face to her mind.

Twenty-five minutes to twelve.

Dazed by the sudden sea of smiling faces, the priest will advance slowly into the classroom. He will wave his arm in a semicircle like a wand. Magically the children will fall back into their seats. And he will smile his priest's smile.

Moira has taken down a fat storybook. That is all she ever wants, that and comics. She fans the pages — looking for the romantic bits, probably.

Alice is reading about the sea. She rips a page from her scribbler and, leering, scrawls a note for Moira. Mary reads the note as she slips it along.

ANY BADNESS INTO IT?

Moira answers.

IT'S HOT! IT'S ABOUT FIRES. THE ONE YOU GOT?

FISH, FISHERMEN.

OOO! NAMES, LOVE, NAMES!

Grinning slyly, Alice spends a long time copying, her forefinger pressed into the book.

GADUS MORHUA, AURELIA AURITA, HIPPO-GLOSSUS HIPPOGLOSSUS, NOCTILUCA SCIN-TILLANS, MALLOTUS VILLOSUS — FANCY ANY OF THEM HANDSOME LADS?

The three snort and giggle. The nun glares and purses her lips.

Twenty to.

Although the priest will stand before them beaming, the room will bustle louder and louder. The youngsters will chatter and gather up scribblers and exercise books and pencils and pens.

Mary's fingers fidget with the encyclopaedia. It falls open on a sketch of a fish. But it is not a fish at all—it is a mermaid.

The creature reclines on a boulder by the shore. The lower part of its body is finned and scaled. Its tail dangles languidly in the sea. The upper part is a lovely woman draped in a shawl of thick dark hair. The mermaid's breasts are bare but they have no nipples—to Mary's mind a stranger thing even than the fins and scales.

Flustered, she is about to slam the book shut when her eye happens upon the facing page. It bears a painting of a huge black centaur. A nun's voice inside her head tells her that she should look away, she should close the book.

The monster is powerful and sleek. Its chest is darkly matted, and its head is crowned with thick black hair and a tight curly beard. The arm of the beast is muscular and wields a long spear. Is it an animal at all? If it is not an animal, then it can only be a man.

The fire that she felt from the sun has become a cool dampness that spreads all over her body. It is like the feeling the marsh stream gives her on a hot summer day. She looks frankly at the two creatures side by side in the book, and the notion strikes her that they are man and wife.

The clock says quarter to twelve.

The priest will stand there and the children will chatter and the nun in her nun's voice will command: Silence. The commotion will fade. The children will groan. The nun will say: Before I let you go, children, the Reverend Father has a few words to say to you.

The nun will retreat behind the big desk. She will knit her fingers in half-prayer. She will look expectantly at the priest. He will come to the front centre of the room and he will glance at the clock. He will make the sign of the cross, and the nun and the children will do the same. The priest will clasp his hands behind his back and adopt a speaking attitude. Then he will take a deep breath and he will begin.

Any moment, a knock will thunder on the door. It happens every year.

Michael is surprised at the ease of his ascent. The slope is carpeted with crusty snow so that his footfall fashions his own stair as he goes. The snow persuades him, conveniently, up clever gaps and glens and lanes, along handy ridges and through charming columnar temples. He imagines an invisible hand, warm and inviting, drawing him ever higher.

Silhouetted against the blue the peak is sharp, like the blade of an axe. Michael can see that the summit will be just wide enough for him to stand on.

With each step the air grows milder. The ice at either hand is translucent with crystalline razor wedges, prisms that mirror the sunshine and magnify it and drench even the deepest crevasses in kaleidoscopic patterns. Michael expects to turn a corner and stumble upon a bed of strawberries, or a patch of bluebells, or a lilac bush.

A high-pitched shout causes him to halt and turn and look below.

Wish and Gus have gaffed the bull seal by the tail. They drag the animal clear of the water. The creature squirms and thrashes pathetically. It makes pigsqueals of terror. The boys shriek with malice — they are like demons torturing the damned.

They wrestle the seal above the berm. Wish sits on top of the beast and grips its flippers to steady it. Gus bludgeons the animal about the eyes with the stock of the gun. Blood explodes from the skull and splashes over both boys and stains the ice in a dark circle. The seal twitches once or twice, then lies still, suddenly nothing more than a bag of gore and fat.

Wish spots Michael on high and makes his yodel. Gus waves triumphantly an arm glistening dark red in the sun.

In disgust Michael turns and carries on towards the top. About halfway to his goal he comes to a wide level area.

The space seems to have been carved for the benefit of boys. The area is wide enough to make a camp, even to throw three-cornered catch. Veins of meltwater cascade from a frozen cataract, dramatic overhead, and collect in a series of lovely terraced pools. Ultimately the pools outflow into a hole scoured in the floor of the plateau. The water sloshes down a vertical pipeline and disappears into the core of the ice.

An eggshell-thin membrane of ice trims the borders of the bottommost pool. Michael kneels and breaks off a piece of the membrane and places it on his tongue. It melts like the Eucharist. He bends and drinks of the water. The water is sparkling fresh, purer than anything he has ever tasted, and so cold it makes his teeth burn. He wishes that he could bring someone here, to this special place, to drink from this miracle well.

The berg trembles. Ripples dart across the surface of the pool. The ice, of course, is busy melting. Before the week is out, the entire mountain will exist only in memory.

Something tugs at his elbow.

He turns around. Faint clouds of vapour twirl spiralling from the peak. A thin rainbow appears, dreamily floating within the mist, and disappears.

He can see that the path ascending is clear and straight and easy.

"In the name of the Father and of the Son and of the Holy Ghost.

"My children:

Thank you for welcoming me to your classroom. I know that you are looking forward to your holidays. It is a grand day and you will want to get out into the sunshine and enjoy it — just as I do. So I will not keep you for long.

"Congratulations to you who have passed your exams and will advance a grade. Congratulations especially to you who are about to seek your fortunes in the world. My best wishes to you for every success and happiness.

"Now, can anyone tell me what special day this is — aside from the last day of school?

"Indeed it is, my boy. Today is the Feast of Saint John the Baptist. His birthday, if you like. Saint John as you know was privileged among the saints. Normally, the feast day of a saint is the day of martyrdom — the day the saint died for the faith. But the Feast of Saint John is the day he was born. Does anyone know why our Holy Mother the Church has given Saint John such special treatment?

"Yes, my child, that is it. He made way for the coming of Jesus. Saint John prepared the path of the Lord. The Bible says that he was the chosen arrow of God, the prophet of the Highest. He announced the advent of Christ. He bore witness to the Light.

"It was Saint John who taught the most important lesson we need to know: that the light of our souls is God Himself. This morning, my children, as you prepare to enjoy your summer, I want to remind you of that plain lesson. I want you to keep fast to the basic truth of your faith. Remember what the light is: the light is Almighty God — Christ Himself — in all His wisdom and majesty and goodness.

"Indeed, my children, this day is the Feast of Saint John. But this day is something else, yet again. What could that something else be?

"Yes, my child. Correct. Today is the start of summer. Today is the solstice. At this time every twelve months the sun ascends to its highest point in the sky. At this time every year the hours of brightness are many, the hours of darkness are few. The solstice is a time of radiance, a time of freshness, rebirth. It is a day when we look ahead, to the future. It is a day when we look outward, beyond ourselves, beyond our own small concerns.

"The light of our souls is God, my dear children. It is Christ Almighty. Saint John taught us that. That we believe. But the light of our souls is also . . . something else. What could it be, this something else?

"Does no one have an answer?

"Not even a guess?

"The light that I speak of is also . . . people. It is our fellow human beings. It is our brothers and sisters. That means not just our family, not just our blood brothers and sisters, but our friends too. And our classmates. It means even, my dear children, even our most bitter enemies.

"It is people who brighten the darkness of the soul. It is human contact. It is the link with others, the bond with another soul, the touch, the touch of someone outside ourselves.

"My children: this morning I paid a visit to the cemetery. It was my first call to that holy place since taking up the mission to this parish.

"And what do you think I learned up on that hill?

"I learned that the names on the tombstones are the names that you carry. The people resting there in the ground are your grandparents and your great-grandparents. Not so many years ago, all of those people were . . . what? They were children, just as you are now. In fact, not so many years ago, those children were here in this very room. They warmed the same desks that you fill now. Perhaps they carved their initials in the wood of that desk you sit in this minute. They wrote on this same blackboard. Just like you, they looked forward to their summer freedom. They looked forward to playing in the sunshine. But today, on this lovely summer morning, all those people are in the ground. All those people are in God's eternity.

"The highest form of contact, my children, is love. You yourselves may be too young to know it, but it is the greatest of all truths. Soon—if you are fortunate—you will learn this fabulous truth. You will learn this: love can be the holiest, the most glorious experience you will know in the span of your life. Love can be the most majestic and splendid, the most hallowed and sacred of God's blessed sacraments.

"But love can be overwhelming—even frightening. Many who come face to face with it will run from it. They will fly in panic, as though from some terrible monster. Many will retreat. Many will vow upon their souls never to approach this monster again. That, my children, is what you must have the courage to avoid.

"If the light of love should visit you, you must not fly in shyness and fear. No matter how frightening is your love, whatever you do, you must embrace it. It is the most exalted of God's spiritual joys. It is nothing less than the way, the road, to your soul's salvation, and you must reach out and grip it firmly—and never never let it go.

"My children, my dear children. My message to you as you set out upon your glorious summer—upon your glorious lives—is this: I want you to say yes to the gift of light. It is the way to redemption. It is the way to salvation. I want you to reach out to your brothers and sisters. I want you to step forward into the shining brightness of love. Promise me that you will do that. Promise me . . ."

The priest steps back from the mirror. A bead of perspiration trickles across his brow.

He raises his hand to his dampened forehead.

"In the name of the Father, and of the Son . . ."

———

Michael Barron is close to the sun.

He has reached the summit of the berg. Every molecule of the fearsome pedestal is given over to supporting his weight: clearly, the ice was put here just for his benefit. He was meant to arrive here.

No doubt, once upon a time in the history of the world, a gull or a crow or maybe even a butterfly flew through this same window in the air, or perhaps it was a seaman who happened to occupy the barrel the moment his vessel found the refuge of the cove. Michael fancies the iceberg is no longer grounded and fixed, but a tall white schooner leaning against the breeze. A moment ago he was dizzy, from having run the final yards to the top, and now this notion gives him another touch of vertigo.

Warm winds spill off the slope of the land. They banish the chill that the ice radiates. The boy inhales the earth-smells of hay and pine and roof tar.

From this apex he can take in at once the whole of the ice. The part visible above the skin of the sea is immense enough, but the boy's eye penetrates the water and deciphers the hidden mass too, the deep draft of the mountain, the bulk that surges below the surface in deadly ridges and trenches, all in cathedral shades of blue. This is what God sees: this is the topography of love.

His mates distant at the waterline are tiny figures. Head to head they bend over the seal carcass. They have unwrapped the corpse like a butcher's parcel and spread it open. Dark blotches stain the ice. Knives flash clinking in the sunlight. The boys move with a liturgical solemnity, as might a priest and his acolyte celebrating the Mass.

The parallelogram of Casey's trap bobs just here within the lee calm. The leader runs out from the Foot, from the Naked Man there, in such a way that it appears to Michael Barron that the cairn is flying a gigantic kite.

In the other direction, miles north—well beyond Gelden, beyond even Distress and Isle aux Morts and the other bleak outharbours lining the shore towards the Fogo—a motorboat tows a house inch by inch to some new berth. Pencil-thin smoke issues from the chimney, so that you might think it is the house pushing the boat.

The sight brings to mind Pop's tale of the big sea of 1929. One day, around dinnertime, the stove dampers started to dance. Gran said to him: Noah, goddamnit, I'm dying! And he heard the rattle and he said: Goddamnit, woman, I'm dying too! But neither one of them died, not just then. In fact they only sat down and ate their meal of salt beef. They were washing the plates when the ocean decided to come ashore.

The water lifted the houses sweetly from their moorings and bore them seaward in flotilla. People waved to their friends likewise afloat, and carried on with their card-playing and kitchen rackets and singsongs. When the waters settled, the people installed tholepins in sashes and paddled their homes back to Admiral's Beach, to the precincts of the church—itself firmly anchored—and replanted them precisely where they had always been. The next morning, vessels were found perched in trees, trees in vessels. It wasn't a disaster, Pop said. It was a romance.

Well off, a dozen blackfish breach one after another, spouting hot steam, tumbling. Michael imagines each whale an arc on the rim of a gigantic wheel rolling across the sea bottom, rolling towards the bank they call the Flemish Cap, towards Ireland. The wind fans outwards like horses before chariots, racing for the blue drop. Michael thinks of the winter when the cove froze over and all the lads strapped on their blades and spread their overcoats into spinnakers and the wind whipped the boys, racing each other mad as fools, towards the deadly edge that sooner or later was bound to appear.

But now the wind is warm. It brushes his face pleasantly. It cools the perspiration glistening on his brow. He wipes away the steam forming on his eyeglasses. Through his head passes a whisper of colour, a mere touch, so light it might be nothing but a memory. Before it slips away, the touch sparks visions of bloom, hallucinations of dandelions and yellow buttercups and luxuriant bluebells, cherry trees and cool green pine and blueberries by the mouthful.

He turns and at long last looks towards the parish. The lilac trees leap to his eyes. Their blossoms halo the saltbox. Above the pale blue house the purples appear as red as fire. Towards the house, along the road, something hurries—a pillar of white light.

Michael Barron feels a trace of vertigo as the treacherous ice shifts under his feet.

XI

Cartwheel

The sun halts in the sky.

The boy, privileged to leave school early, runs across Church Square and up to the shop window. Making a frame with his hands, he shades his eyes and flattens his nose against the glass. But a dangle of kerosene lamps obscures the four-faced clock, and he cannot tell what time it is.

He decides to pretend. He pretends that it is sixty seconds to noon. He turns from the window and races — counting: one, two, three — across the sunny square and up the steps and underneath the rose window into the belfry.

Precisely at the score of sixty, the church bell rings out.

Gulls hear the sound and alight on the rocks. They cock their beaks and listen. The convent cat yawns out of her sphinx-nap and blinks and draws back her ears. The dog on the beach raises his black skull dripping from the waves, shakes the salt water out of his ears, sniffs at the air.

On the summit of the ridge, cruel vertical light drowns the boulder. Momentarily, the huge rock casts no shadow.

The fat shopkeeper breaks off tallying his coin. He holds a particular digit in his head while, without bothering to actually look at it, he congratulates himself on the accuracy of his four-faced clock. He smiles and resumes his counting.

Halfway down the slope of the avenue, a breeze sparkles

the birch leaves like shards of glass. The parish priest suddenly plants his cane in the road. He bends and leans heavily with both hands upon the stick. He stares at the hordes of schoolchildren heading home. Inside his midsection, the knife resumes its work.

At hearing the bell the gaily sun-drenched youngsters, as one, bless themselves.

Six Marys gather laughing round a crib. A seventh, within the solitude of her cell, falls upon her prie-dieu and fervently beseeches God that before this day is done she may, following her lifelong quest, find Him.

The lightkeeper sits on the rim of the Brow. His boots dangle over the edge. The sound of the bell bypasses his bad ear. He drinks the last of his rum.

The forgeman, his hammer striking the anvil with precisely the cadence with which the clapper strikes the bell, also fails to hear.

Even while his priestly hands pull the rough rope, the altar boy recites the Hail Mary. He is happy, for it is a holy place and a holy time, and he is safe.

The dirty white stallion draws up of its own accord. The spokes of the cartwheel materialize, magically, out of the whirling red disk.

The priest leans on his cane and shakes his watch and holds it to his ear. He replaces the watch in his cassock, and makes the sign of the cross and allows his eyes to close. Softly he recites the three Hail Marys. For the first time today he truly prays. He prays for his own deliverance.

Crowning the iceberg, steam rising from his back, his eyeglasses fogging, the boy watches a white flash issue from a distant field of robin's-egg blue.

The girl in the pearly dress runs panting from the back door of her house and down the sloping ground and across to the middle of the gravel road. She digs with her heel a depression in the fresh-filled pothole. She spreads her long legs far apart in order to place her feet on either side of the clay.

Above and behind, out of the girl's sight, the mother pulls the infant boy from her nipple and covers her own breast. With both hands she raises the naked child high towards the sun.

On the lee shore of the berg, in the shade of a fearsome overhang, the boy with the pitted face winds up like a baseball pitcher and throws the heart of the eviscerated seal. "Here," he shouts to the walleyed boy, "suck on this."

The fat girl picks a golden dandelion from the green meadow and holds it under the chin of the girl with the red hair. The fat girl makes the sign of the cross and chants in a whisper:

> *Are you a witch, or are you a faery*
> *Or are you the wife of Timothy Cleary?*

The walleyed boy wields the widowed oar like a baseball bat. He swings and drives the seal's heart over and beyond the rowboat and he roars,

> *In the name of the Father,*
> *And of the Son.*
> *Over the fence*
> *Is a home run.*

The man with the gyral spectacles hears the bell and looks aside from the book he is half through reading, but he refuses to pray.

Puffing, the woman with the bloated abdomen postpones her progress up an incline in the roadway. Her fingers leave the loop of her rosary and move down to the tail of the beads, and count off three Hail Marys.

The battered old fisherman huddled on the settle behind

the stove sets aside the toy punt he is carving and feebly stirs the cinders.

The man perched on the gunnel of the box-cart raises his hand to his forehead. He grips the bill of his salt-and-pepper cap and tilts the cap slightly back so the sun can warm his eyes.

The empty flask slips from the lightkeeper's grip. He watches it plummet vertically, one hundred feet, more or less, and splash against the tide that rises to meet it. Afterwards, a waning gurgle bubbles to the surface.

The boy atop the iceberg crosses himself absently, but he is too distracted just now to think about such an everyday business as prayer.

The mother holds the child naked on high and speaks to him lovingly. She tells him about the hearth fire of the universe, and about sharp-horned moons, and falling soot, and mackerel skies, and mares' tails.

The daughter tries to push the mother's voice from her mind. She carries a glass tumbler bearing a cloudy liquid. She is about to upturn the tumbler onto the road when she happens to glance towards the mouth of the cove.

The clutch of people in the hay meadow abandon the windrows and lean on their rakehandles and bow their heads in rapt devotion.

The lightkeeper sees these people and hears in their bearing the ring of chimes. He turns about his good ear and it confirms his vision. His head fills with the wine smell of the church.

The young couple, exhausted from love-making, are stirred awake by the bell. Startled at the lateness of the hour, they laugh hysterically. Their infant burbles at a butterfly that wanders through the open window.

The schoolgirl in grown-up stockings steps out her porch door to toss slops to the chickens. The sun reveals the ugly welt swelling on her cheek. While she listens to the bell she stares vaguely at nothing.

The lightkeeper yells across the sea: "Aha, me b-b-boys. I hears our steamer's signal. And I sees all the rest of them now too: *Stephano* and *Florizel* and the *Bell* and *Beothic* . . ."

The acolyte gives the rope one last draw. He wants the voice of the holy bell Maria to vanquish all other sounds, to sanctify the church, the school, the parish of all evil, all danger, for ever and ever.

The boy atop the berg fixes his eye savagely on the white dress. He is certain that all is about to collapse, that the ice sustaining him will this instant disintegrate into a million shards. When it happens, he will walk upon the water. He will walk all the way to the shore.

The girl in the white dress crosses the road to the railing. The tumbler slips from her grip and shatters on the landwash below. She does not bother even to glance down. Instead, she blinks and makes a mental photograph of the sight she sees in the distance and she stops time.

". . . and *Nascopie* and *Bonaventure* and *Diana* and *Eagle* and *Kite*. We'll be off home now, lads. T-T-Thanks be to God!"

The altar boy abandons the rope, yet the bell thunders on, unattended, ghost-fashion, and rings three times more. With satisfaction the child tallies his ten-year indulgence.

In the mounting silence, the gulls one by one take flight towards the burning sun. The cat, disturbed from her sleep, falls to licking her kittens. The dog wanders down the beach, bladder-wrack tangled in his webbed paws. The priest fondles the precious pebble he carries in his pocket. The man on the box-cart flicks the traces and the stallion snorts and stumbles, its iron shoes ring against the gravel, and the red rims rotate and the red spokes rumble to a blur.

The wind falls. Sea urchins clutch stones. Black smoke swirls from the chimney of the tumbledown tilt.

A shadow appears on the eastern flank of the boulder. The sun begins its journey down the afternoon sky.

XII

Sparks

"You can drown as fast from a punt as from a dory."

Michael Barron observes the white figure distant across the water as if through the focus of a telescope: all else is swept away. Statue-like at the rail, the shape aligns itself towards the sea, but its attention appears to be fixed on something local—perhaps the road underfoot, or the tide advancing up the landwash, or the gulls roosting on the sinkers.

"Bull-fucking-shit. No, by the Jesus, give me a punt any day. Give me a keel under my arse."

Or perhaps its attention is turned inward. Maybe the eyes are fallen shut. Maybe it sees nothing. . . .

Until this spring of his life, Michael Barron himself had seen nothing. Even last summer, when so much happened, when he might have noticed, he did not (he was a child without thoughts). But on the eighth of May—the date is burned in his mind, like December twenty-fifth or March seventeenth, his birthday—for the first time he saw. Since then the world has grown ever more perilous.

On the eighth of May the eyes were downcast, half closed, like those on the statue of the Virgin. Michael Barron saw the eyes, and he felt an urge to leave his own pew and to kneel, as though before a shrine, and pray. Within his soul he was forced to fight against this strange longing. He wondered if this was the sort of serious thought that grown men think—if he was condemned to suffer this for the balance of his life.

Whereas in all the years leading up to then he had noticed nothing, during the weeks since that day he has absorbed every detail: the colours it wears, the way the long fingers grip a pencil, the curves and whorls of the script, even the birth date, which he skimmed from the register: All Saints' Eve. He knows the face it puts on when it laughs, when it is mad. He pockets from the roadway discarded candy wrappers or pop bottles or cigarette ends which he hoards secretly in his room. If it is one in a crowd, he sees none of the others, only the head towering like a spire, or the coltlike gait, or the gestures of the long slender fingers. In a jabber of voices only that voice rings clear.

In jangling sunlight he fixes his eye on any place the figure is likely to show. He plans his movements so that he may simply pass by, in the corridor, the playground, the aisle, the road. The faith that his vigil is shortening with each heartbeat sustains him. Meanwhile, everything becomes that which he awaits. Waves, trees, clouds—all these are merely some proxy image, some reflection.

When finally it crashes into view, he scarcely dares inhale. Whatever act he observes—turning the pages of a book, telling beads, skipping rope, playing squares, paddling the marsh, picking berries—he venerates, as if what he really sees is the figure tiptoeing from the altar rail, eyes fallen. Host dissolving on the tongue. Never has flesh touched. Never has so much as the hair on the forearms brushed (but once, by way of passing within the distance of a breath, Michael Barron smelled what he thought was the hot dark odour of blood). Never has he dared make any gesture, any signal.

Finally, each evening, after watching from his unlit room

the patch of windowshine up the road vanish in a blink, come the hours when he can no longer hope to see, the hours of blindness, when all he can do is imagine: it is then that he pictures the swelling muscle of calf meeting skirt, the moist back of the knee, the glimpse of rounded underthigh. It is then that his memories take command and devour his mind, as in dreams.

"Depends. Depends whether the boat is jinked . . ."

Gus and Wish are climbing the eastern face. They pass just under Michael's station. He hears their voices with growing fury. He does not want them up here. Not yet.

". . . and if so, it doesn't matter a good goddamn there's a keel or no. So a punt can be jinked as easy as a dory."

In a rage Michael tears his eyes from the figure across the cove and turns and looks down. Wish swings the hatchet one-handed and lodges the blade deep in the ice and so drags himself forward. He totes the dipnet slung over his shoulder the way a hobo totes a bindle. In its hammock three bottles relax. Each contains a dark fluid. And there is something else, a black fleshy mass, half alive. Behind Wish, Gus carries the shotgun under his arm, and he hoists himself using the widowed oar as a crook.

Michael does not want them here because they might see. He must go down, meet them, stop them. He is furious, for he is losing a chance: no matter how long it lingers there on the road he would stand in this place and watch it. Happily he would, even if the whole of the ice melted beneath him.

An arm has come up against the sun. The eyes examine something distant—a curious cloud, or the herd of blackfish, or simply the horizon.

Or the ice.

Michael Barron holds his breath. Surrounding him sprawls the fullness of land and ocean and sky and tumbling cloud—half the universe, in fact, a grand sunspace to vanish in. Yet the tiny spark of the dress across the way swells and fills his head with light. How much more of a magnet, then, how much more visible, is the great pedestal upon which he is standing? He must be as obvious as that statue in the book—what was it?—the Colossus of Rhodes. Michael Barron crowns the brilliant pyramid that points skyward, like a big arrow, to himself, that commands: Look here.

The hand sweeps down—was that a wave?

If it was, then nothing on this earth can be certain. All the truths Michael Barron believes in are groundless, are mirages.

Drops of sweat chill the small of his back. He turns and flees. He runs away from the vision he sees across the water. He bolts down the snow-ladder that he himself fashioned. He hurries back to the security of his familiar mates. Thank God he can still hear their voices.

"Yes, by the Christ. There's loads of ways to drown. I guarantee you."

Gus and Wish have already arrived at the level area. Here, the bulk of the ice obstructs the view of the parish. For that blessing Michael is grateful.

Gus gazes down into the hole in the floor that is the outflow of the terraced pools. A yellow spray joins with the meltwater pouring into the heart of the ice. Michael pictures the entire crystal mountain discolouring to become a stinking mass of electrum. Meanwhile Wish, upstream, thrusts his arms to the elbows in the crackling spray of the cataract and rinses the seal flippers. He shouts at Gus, "That mental case Davey Lynch. You remember him? He thought he was Abraham? Well, they says it was out of a dory and nothing else he hove his brat. . . ."

The glass pools are stained with strands of fur and splotches of black blood and grease. The dipnet bearing the bottles lies submerged, the delicate ice shattered by stomping wellingtons.

". . . And don't forget Lukey Dwyer and what he fell out of. The Professor remembers that day, don't you? If you asks me, them goddamned dories even looks like coffins."

Gus has set down the shotgun nearby. The backstock is encrusted with clots of blood and hair. Michael walks across and picks it up. He always enjoys holding the weapon. The gun gives him extension — it gives him voice. It was only last Christmas Day that Pop, after a few rums, confessed to Michael that he had used this very item to compel Michael's father to marry Michael's mother. At first Michael thought the old man was making one of his sly jokes, until he reckoned up when the war was, and the July Drive, and when Pop must have come back and married Granny Ray, and what year Joan would have been born: 1917. So she was only fifteen! He saw then the reason his father came home from the Labrador so seldom that Michael can hardly picture the man's face. He saw why it was he had but one brother, and no sisters. "Look at Sean Rideout," the man joked once, after Joan tormented him about it, "he comes home every year and every year his wife lays a baby. Damned if I'm coming home every month."

With clumps of snow he cleans the gun, tenderly, the way he might console an injured child.

"Maybe the dory was jinked," says Gus. He has taken the axe and moved off a ways, and he hacks at the floor. He chops a pile of chips and scoops them away with his toe, and chops again — he is carving a firepit. "Maybe Lukey was foolish enough to have a pig aboard of her once upon a time. Or a woman. Or a dead corpse. I don't know. Who the fuck knows?"

Michael opens the breech and tilts the barrel and slides the shell out into his palm. He aims at the sun and squints up the chamber. He hopes to see spirals of colour corkscrewing the gleaming steel. Instead, the bore is flecked with gunpowder soot. The stains leave long sinister shadows, the way lone trees do at sunset. Michael is disappointed. He replaces the shell and clicks shut the breech and sets the gun back where he found it.

"Any kind of boat can be jinked. Punts. Dories. Skiffs. Dinghies. Motorboats. Jackboats. Western boats. Capeboats. Look at the *Southern Cross*, for Christ's sake. A great goddamned three-master, swallowed up like a brick. Look at the *Titanic*. Look at . . ."

". . . Barron's punt." Wish waddles up from the pool. "Now there is one that will never be jinked. Although by Christ, I tell you, for a while there this morning I thought for sure the three of us was stuck on a calamity. But no," Wish drawls. He waves the raw seal meat under Michael's nose, teasing him. "For now we got us one fine fat fucking swile. What do you say, Barron?"

Against the blood-stink Michael's nostrils gag. He turns his face away.

"Smells like fish," Wish chortles. "Tastes like chicken."

Michael's bowels churn. He goes over to the edge, to where he can look down upon his boat. He sits on a bank of snow and cleans his eyeglasses.

"You moron, Butt," says Gus. "We had scarce luck with the seals when we was on the water. We never caught up with one till we got clear of the punt. For all we know, that boat is a calamity from here to kingdom come."

Michael loves the sight of the clapboards. His punt is the only clinkered hull left in the parish. Pop built it inside the barn, one long hard winter, helped only by a dog pedalling a lathe. He used to say it was warm inside there because he moulded the frame in the contours of a woman. All of that happened long before Michael was thought about, yet even now, of the word Pop painted on the bow—Ray, his pet name for Gran—only the 'y' has faded. And even now, the keel floats true. In solitude the vessel waits, straddling the ice-berm. It looks forlorn, as though it longs to slip into the sea and float away to some milder place.

If that were to happen, Michael thinks, if the boat decided to leave them, whatever would the boys do? Perhaps they would try to swim for it—but not one of them swims well enough to make shore, let alone as well as, say, Captain William Jackman, who rescued all those people drowning in the Labrador Sea, in October month too.

Perhaps, of course, the boys would not be saved at all. But that notion makes no sense to Michael's mind, and he doesn't bother dwelling on it.

"But what does it matter?" Gus lobs the seal's heart up and down casually, like a baseball. Michael thinks of the Aztecs, who cut the hearts from their human sacrifices and offered them to God the sun. "No one can say we're jinked. We're not just fishermen any more. We're swilers!" He wipes the blood like war-paint across his pitted face and he throws back his head and bawls up at the sky. "Goddamn swilers! Goddamn MEN! That's us!"

His bray echoes among the ice crevasses.

Gus looks to Michael and nods towards the peak, "So, navigator, what have you got to report? What did we spy from the airy topsails?"

Michael shrugs: nothing worth telling.

Gus grunts and busies himself carving the finishing touches on his crater. When he is satisfied he barks at Wish, "Time for the blasty boughs. Scurry along now, Butt, and pick us a yaffle. And be nimble about it."

Michael gives himself over to studying the waves. Half-heartedly they canter, like tired ponies. The breeze is falling. By teatime the water may well be calm. Perhaps then an easterly will appear and bring the boys home, nice and smooth.

Gus positions the steering oar lengthwise across the pit. With vicious strokes he chops the oar into short blocks. The axe makes a noise that Michael can almost taste, for it sickens him slightly. Exactly the same sound fractured his leg. While he lay sprawled across home plate, his calf splayed weirdly, during those in-between seconds when the crowd was still cheering the run he had scored and he had not yet retched, his face wore a ridiculous grin, for he knew in that instant that his body was made of sticks of wood, was nothing more than a complicated frame, like one of those cat's-cradles assembled out of Popsicle sticks, and the idea seemed hilarious to him.

The wood slips on the ice, dangerously.

"Watch out, my son. Watch you don't slice yourself ajar." Wish speaks with the whiny voice of a hectoring mother. "Do yourself to a stub. Like Johnny the Light. You just watch out, my son."

"Barron, tell Butt this for me. Tell him: Be an angel, and fly to Jesus." Expertly Gus whittles the oar-blade into flammable chips and shavings.

"Captain Jackman—did you know?—whenever one of his crew got a finger going septic from a sculping knife, he used to take along an axe and lop the whole thing straight off. Better than dying, he used to say. But in the end no one wanted to ticket with that man, for fear of coming home stumped. And that's the truth."

Gus arranges the chips in the base of the hollow. Above these he sets the sticks in a tepee.

"There you are." Gus stands back and speaks formally.

"There it is," says Wish.

"There you have it," the two recite in harmony. They face one another and bow, with perfect timing, like solemn acolytes.

"Well, lads," says Gus. "That's our spare. Break a paddle now and we are on the way to being royally fucked. Barron, you lazy arsehole, make yourself halfways useful and produce a spark."

Gus roots under his oilskins and brings out the rags of a newspaper. Michael scratches a match against his boot and soon the fire roars mightily. The boys spread their oilskins and sit round the blaze.

Gus mutters, "Jesus, we'll freeze our nuts off." He arranges the seal parts on the fire. With the nose of the gun he pokes the meat to and fro. The flames char the dark flesh. They singe the remnants of the fur and blister the blood. The ice-pit melts with a steady hiss.

"Yes, it's a jink or it isn't a jink," Wish muses drowsily. "Good luck or bad luck. That's all there is to say about it."

"Well, I'm not so sure. One certified thing you can say about the codfish: he is unreliable."

Michael joins his mates in staring mesmerized into the flames. Since yesterday morning when they left their beds they have hardly slept. Since last evening when their mothers gave them supper they have eaten practically nothing. The sheer excitement of their adventure has sustained them. They yawn and nod.

"And the certified way to find the cod, you tries one place, and if the bugger is not there you ups your anchor and tries some place else. And you does that till you do find him."

"The fish they has no bells," Gus declaims.

A faggot of sticks collapses steaming into the basin of meltwater, and rousts Gus.

"Mug-up time, lads." Bravely bare-handed he plucks the seal paws out of the fire. "Sorry, Barron, but the fact is, Butt and me, since we did the actual killing, we gets the actual flippers."

Wish says straight-faced, "To the victors goes the swiles."

Gus roots about and retrieves the heart. The meat is

hot, and he tosses it directly into Michael's crotch. In a panic Michael brushes it away. The smoking lump sizzles on the ice.

"Well, cook, where's our dumplings . . . ?"

"Barron, will you tell Butt to shag off."

"Our flat-arsed kettle, our pinnacle tea, our table rag?"

All three make the sign of the cross matter-of-factly. Wish joins his hands and prays:

> *For this meal of chaw-and-glutch*
> *We thank Thee Lord so very much.*

Straightaway Wish and Gus fall to gnawing at the greasy scorched meat. Michael picks up the seal's heart and squeezes it gingerly, as though testing an apple for ripeness. He is as ravenous as his mates are, but he cannot face the blood that oozes from the arteries and drips and stains the ice between his legs.

"I'll tell you the lad what knows where the fish is to," Gus mumbles with his mouth full. "That fat robber Casey. Why, he even got the icebergs faery-led to run themselves aground handy to his trapberth. I wouldn't put it past the tight bastard."

"Tight as bark to a tree."

"Tight as a muskrat's arsehole."

"Which is . . ."

". . . water-tight."

Wish and Gus nod to one another.

"This minute he probably got his spyglass stuck to his beady eye. Twirling his knobs. Wondering what in Christ's name is making the smoke. Don't you know: he spends his spare time prowling the blueberry hills, skimming for grassers."

"What's the matter, Barron? No stomach?" Gus smirks and winks at Wish.

"Speaking of clever fish-killers. Noah, The Wade, now there's a one."

Wish speaks the truth. Pop's eye can see deeper than the ordinary eye. Michael wishes that the old man was with them now. Even though Pop sits in the kitchen wrapped in his blanket, he can look out the window and survey the water and point directly to the best nobs and shoals and ledges of the bottom. On good days he's just an old codger—he works at his models and plays checkers with Kevin. On his bad days he is not much more than a stick of furniture, propped up on the settle in back of the stove. Then the eyes that know so much bulge with fear, too terrified even to blink. Nothing in particular befell him. He never slipped and fell, or took a seizure, or anything sudden. It just happened that after Christmas was over he started to shrivel up, like a tomcod left dead in the sun. That was all. Joan reckons he is starting to remember Beaumont Hamel, at long last, and that's what it is.

"Barron!" Gus snaps his fingers at Michael's eyes. "Are you with us, my lad?"

"You made the mistake of mentioning the berry hills. That's the first thing comes into this lad's dirty mind: skin. He's only scheming what certain juicy herring he's going to get his hooks into tonight."

"No!" Gus mocks. "Is that true, Mikey?"

"Planning a little bottom-jigging, are we?"

The two of them leer and cackle. Michael makes no sign that he even hears.

"Yes, by the Christ," hisses Wish with sudden vigour, rubbing his crotch. "This is the night for it."

"If you can't get your tail this night of all nights, you're never going to get your tail. Period."

"It's all luck. It's like the fish. The way you does it is this: if you don't find your tail in one place, you ups your anchor and . . ."

With a malicious smirk Gus breaks in. "Barron, tell Butt to inform us: since he is such a famous skinhound, precisely what piece of stock is he going after?"

"I'm hardly going to tell you whoremongers, am I?" Wish tries to suppress a grin, tries to speaks indifferently. "Gallant has got to cough up first. But I'll tell you who it is: it's Rosie Cleary."

"The face that launched a thousand shits? That one the two of you can have. If you got a bridle wide enough to haul over her snout."

Wish and Gus gnaw on the bones and gristle and nail. Michael fingers the seal's heart guardedly. He pretends the meat is too hot to eat. Gus slips Wish a nudge.

Wish says, "Did you know that seals has harems? Some of them do anyway. Wifes by the dozens. The life of a swile, it's not so bad. They comes to a nasty end, often enough, but until then they has a grand time of it. Alice Keating then?"

"Face like a hard winter. Besides, foxy hair is bad luck."

"Jesus, you're a contrary lad. What about her shadow?"

"The wide one? Face like the back of an axe."

"A boiled boot."

"A can of worms.

"But still, a comfortable armful."

"So much for the wide one. Now the long flat one, on the other hand, that one is starting to bud, and nicely. Or did you fail to notice, you queer?"

An eel churns in Michael's gut. He feels the way he did when Father Conroy stumbled during Midnight Mass. The usual church bustle went silent. Michael wanted only one thing: to run out the door and get far far away. For once he was glad he had quit the altar. Otherwise he would have been there in the sanctuary and he would have been unable to pretend that his eyes had not seen it happen, that he did not know the reason.

To settle his stomach Michael surveys the gently curving

horizon. When his eye comes round to the Fogo, it catches sight of the stern of a coastal steamer disappearing under the cape. That's the *Northern Ranger*, carrying the mail round the island. Michael makes his daily promise to himself: one morning he will do it, he will get out of bed before anyone else, and carry the paddles down to the wharf, and climb into his red punt, and paddle out the cove, and bear north, and carry on until he paddles the full circuit of the island. He will do it for the simple reason that everyone would surely say it could never be done.

"Now you're talking there," says Wish with energy.

"That one is so long in the leg, why, you stand up to the front of it, and your nose gets stuck between them tits." Gus makes a smacking noise with his lips. "But sure, you'd never hear me complain."

Liquid heat stings the back of Michael's eyes. He pulls his face from the water, now empty of steamers and blackfish and houses under tow, and fixes instead on the lump of black meat that his fingers clutch. Intently he examines it, turning it this way and that, as might a scientist or a detective who hopes to find the solution to a problem. The meat is cooled now, and starting to go rigid and crusty. Michael brings it to his face and holds it just under his nose. The stench makes the eel in his gut twist and coil.

"Did you hear what Martin Mullowney did one night? He crashed into Theresa Kilbride in the middle of the road. It was so pitch-dark neither one of them saw the other one coming." Wish spits a nugget of gristle into the fire. "But wait. Let me tell you what you wants to do if you ever bumps into that long-legged one. First you says, like a gentleman: Excuse *me*. Then you ups with the skirt and down with the bloomers and out with the lad and shove it up the box right there in the middle of the road, quick before it has a chance to consider the issue."

Michael presses the seal's heart against his upper lip. He

smells the blubber and grease and blood and soot. He extends the tip of his tongue and he licks at the black lump.
Meanwhile he cannot but hear.

"No, no, my son, them gams is too long for that . . ."

"A perfect pair. When they gets together, they makes a
perfect arse of themselves."

". . . A wee tomcod like yours won't reach. No. Listen.
Here's what you does: first, you has yourself a good long
squeeze of them tits, and your lad, of course he wants out.
And what does he do? Well, he whips open the fly, scurries
down the leg of your pants, hops along the ground, then
shinnies up them gams and under the skirt and inside the
bloomers till he finds the cunt, and in he slides! Head first!
Squish! To the hilt!"

Even though Michael's vision is filmy, he an see that they
no longer elbow or nudge. In fact they pay no attention to
him. He is alone.

"Butt, my son, that's the only way a wee dickeybird like
you got is ever going to screw that long-legged one."

Michael shuts his eyes screaming tight and the tears
squeeze out. He sinks his teeth into the meat. The meat is
slippery and half raw. Savagely he rips off a chunk that
comes away soft like jelly in his mouth. The oily flesh slides
about against his cheeks. His tongue cannot hold it down in
order to chew, so he makes a desperate gulp and swallows
the piece whole. He can feel it slithering down his gullet and
lodging in the cavity of his stomach. To keep from bringing
the meat back up, he pushes the heart against his mouth and
sucks the blood out of it and drinks it deep. The blood tastes
rich and sweet, and for that Michael Barron is grateful.

*Bless us, O Lord, and these Thy gifts which of Thy bounty we are
about to receive, through Christ our Lord.*

Amen.

Here we are: all one body we.

Gathered together. And what a marvel is placed in front of us. Sister Mary Irene, my dear child, you've outdone yourself.

Again.

A wonderful grand feast you've laid on.

Aroma like heaven. Isn't it the truth, Sisters?

Our Irene, she is the gift from the Lord.

Peter himself will throw wide the gates when he spots this one tramping up the pearly lane.

Yes, such a treat of a scoff. And so long after the hunt, too.

Thank God for the icebox, sisters.

Thank God for *you*, Sister Mary Irene.

Now then, Sisters. Raise your glasses. Here's to the summer sun.

God bless the sun.

And what a glorious Midsummer's Day it is.

Indeed. A wonder the truants was so scarce.

Unscarce, you mean.

Yes, I'm surprised any one of them children showed a face this day.

Bless me, Father, I must confess a sinful notion: I myself had half a mind not to show.

Right you are, Sister Mary Donatilla. I don't know why we bothered with lessons at all.

Such a gorgeous afternoon. Wouldn't it be a fine job to get a lend of a boat and take a paddle across the cove?

Scull over to Freshwater Room, yes. Enjoy a picnic on the beach.

Under the cascade. What a splendid notion.

Sit in the toasty sun.

Feel the mild breezes.

Wouldn't that make the day a treasure.

Sisters, I remind you: the greater the desire, the greater the sacrifice, the more the merit.

Yes, Superior.

It was only a notion, Superior.

Speaking of treasures. All present have seen our own little treasures?

Our miracle? Indeed we have, Sister Mary Valentine. One and all.

That rogue Joseph, weren't we well and truly mistaken about *him*.

And we so worried about *his* intentions on the neighbourhood.

Valentine, rumour has it you made the dramatic discovery?

Indeed, I was scurrying through the kitchen on my way to catechism when I heard this scuttle in the pantry. I whispered to Irene: Now there's a rat, do you suppose? Having his breakfast. We picked up the broom and opened the door and switched on the bulb and, I sweat upon Our Lord, the two of us nearly had a conniption. Isn't that the truth, Irene?

The words I declared was thus: In the name of the Father and of the *Son*.

And I says: May all the saints in heaven pre*serve* us.

And then, when my wits finally returned to my head, I says to him: Joseph, you devil, that's what reward you get for venturing beyond the safety of the pale.

Next thing you know, Maxima and Secunda and Donatilla are passing through, and they says to us two: Hello, what mischief are you reprobates at, huddled here in the pantry?

And so I says: Sisters, have you ever in your holy lives witnessed a true miracle? Come here and have a gander then.

After that, of course, we had to go roust Mother Zebrinas down from her bed. God save her, I'm not sure she took it in. And only just now we presented them to Superior, at last. So our little annunciation is completed.

May I remind you, my dear sisters: we are a community of God.

. . .

So . . . Irene, in the end, did you manage a head count?

Seven. One for each of us.

We could name them so.

Maybe we should wait and see how they behave. Perhaps we'll want to name them after the deadly sins.

And we gave every man jack the lay baptism.

That Joseph, he just about clawed my fingers off.

May I remind you again: we are not a secular family.

. . .

I'll have another taste of that wine, if you please, Sister.

Irene, bless you, my child. It's a gorgeous crib you're after making. The darlings, they're all settled in, snug and cozy.

A poor creation, Secunda. Sure, it's only an apple crate and tissue.

The ribbons on the edge is a pretty touch.

I tell you, there was ructions getting him to shift over.

Don't be talking.

The darlings. They're done their breakfast and curled up for a nap. Not a peep out of them.

Poor Joseph, he must be knackered. Nursing a brood like that.

It's a holy gift, isn't it. Giving children the breast.

The milk of the mother. One of God's wonders.

I pray, dear sisters, you understand what I am saying to you.

. . .

Father MacMurrough lifts the beans from the bowl with a wide spoon. He regards a slice of the baker's bread, plain and buttered, and bites into the crust and chews slowly. He sips his mug of lukewarm tea.

Suddenly he half-turns in the chair and cocks his ear. He sets aside his spoon and his cup.

What was that? A sound?

From within?

He holds his breath and listens.

His eye falls upon the small collection of stones lined up on the sill, waiting. The pebble he found on the beach this morning waits too, hard and sure, but in the pocket of his cassock. An odd smile takes hold of his face.

Although he sits for a long time, he hears nothing more.

His tea grows cold. Thankful that nobody witnessed his foolishness, he turns back to the table and takes up his spoon and cup, and carries on with his lunch.

We must get busy.

Make a corner of the garden for a playpen.

Yes, with bluebells and tansies and sweet rocket.

A proper little house to ward off the drizzle.

And a heater for the wintertime.

Each of them a warm bed.

And a supper dish.

With the name on it.

And we'll give them treats.

Cod tongues and such.

Flipper pie.

Capelin, as soon as they fetch in.

Bless me, Father, but I've got a craving myself.

Fresh cream.

Playtoys.

And we'll read them stories.

Sing lullabies.

Rock them to sleep.

So tiny they are.

So delicate.

So feeble-looking.

Little eyes still shut.
Sweet little things.
Aren't they just the darlings!
Isn't it all so wonderful!
Gifts from heaven.
Yes, treasures. Treasures from God.

Colours paint the old man's face and leave it delirious
with joy.

One following another they cool his scarred cheek, warm
it, cool it. If he wanted to do so, he might close his eyes and
guess which particular hue touches him at each moment. He
brings his face close to the window and perceives the hazy
mottle of the variegated pigments, oxides of manganese and
cobalt, iron and copper. He observes the coarse bubbles and
abrasion—flaws—that somehow enhance the splendour of
the glass. Each pane imposes its complexion upon the world
outside, so that he thrills not only to the white berg that is
on the water, but to a whole spectrum of bergs in sequence,
each one brilliant and fantastic. From behind the ice, smoke
plumes eastward on the wind, the way it would from the
funnel of a coasting vessel. Johnny beams and hoarsely he
whispers: "There you are, l-l-lads! I told you. 'Tis our
steamer!" His words hang in the empty spaces of the nave,
among the motes that linger on the still air like stars in the
heavens.

On the wall beside the window, where the light is dim, an
image hangs framed. Johnny straightens his bent spine and
cranes up at the picture. Even if he were able to decipher the
caption he would not need to, for the image itself tells the
plain story: Jesus Is Nailed to the Cross. The cross lies upon
the ground, and the soldiers have strewn nearby the robes,
pliers, nails, and rasp. They pin Jesus against the wood
frame. One of them grips the spike poised to puncture the
wrist, another the hammer raised to strike the blow. Johnny

feels pain in his hands and he pushes them deep into his pockets.

From the belly of his coat he brings forth an apple. His trembling palms turn it round and round like a fat red jewel. He ponders how he came by such a thing. He sniffs at the fruit, then sits in a pew and eats it ravenously, core and all, the seeds dribbling down his chin.

Muttering, Johnny carries on up the Epistle-side aisle. He braces himself between the pew backs and the wall, hand over hand, like a mariner negotiating a slippery deck in rough seas. His cap falls askew on his head. He makes a right turn into the east transept. He passes beneath the gallery and comes up before the shrine.

The eyes of the Virgin are downcast, the face exquisitely serene. The Infant nestled in her arms reaches with broken plaster fingers to touch the Mother's face. A votive light dances inside a saffron crystal. Johnny stares at this candle until it swells in his head to a blinding flame, until the light makes the old man dizzy. The pale blue veil shading the Virgin face appears to rustle, as though the cowl were stirred by some divine draft.

"Hushta!" Johnny hisses. The floor shifts under his feet, and he swings his arm violently. His hand topples the mite-box from its cradle and it crashes to the floor. The tin cover flies open and coppers roll about willy-nilly on the bare pine. The noise clatters around the church.

Johnny's eyes bulge. He holds his breath and tilts his good ear towards the door. Natural silence holds the chamber. Painfully he climbs down on all fours to find the coins and return them to the box. His fingers fumble at the simple task. Eventually he slams shut the lid and lifts himself to his feet and returns the box to its cradle.

He makes his way towards the centre aisle. His hand slides along the marble top of the rail, feeling the tokens chiselled there in the stone. He deciphers only the number —

1916—but he knows that the letters form the names of his boyhood mates. He recalls seeing from his sickbed a line of shadows marching up the dirt road, mock wooden rifles over their shoulders, every face disfigured by his fevered hallucination.

Johnny's nose detects among the fragrances of incense and Dustbane and varnish and the leather in which missals are bound a thick, sweet smell. He hurries towards it. He does not bother going round by the gate. Instead he hoists himself over the rail and brings his logans crashing down onto the sanctuary floor. He lands wincing from the pain in his feet. He stands a moment and absorbs the space.

The texture of the carpet is softer than any meadow he has trod. Upon its green sod rests a cluster of bells. The handle is cast in the useful shape of a cross. Johnny lifts it up by the spars. The chimes reflect his fingers fourfold and distorted. Against his flesh the metal is ice-cold. The instrument clangles loudly, like a small animal rudely awakened. Johnny releases his grip and the bell clangles to the carpet and is silenced.

He fears the noise may draw somebody. Quickly he limps up the three steps to the tabernacle and pulls aside the veil shading the gold doors. While he rattles the doors, which are locked, he senses that someone has already arrived here, and even now stands behind him, has been watching him all along. With a guilty aspect he turns and scans the nave.

The pews undulate, row upon row, fuzzily, like waves oncoming in a blizzard. The sight makes the old man reel again. To steady himself he grips the ledge of the altar.

His nose sniffs the sweet odour. Johnny hobbles down the steps and around the side to the little table that is there. A tray sits on a linen cloth, and upon this tray, like tiny ice sculptures, rest two crystal cruets.

Johnny wheezes. He sits on the acolyte's bench and reaches out and picks up the crystal that contains the tawny liquid. He pulls at the stopper, but it is stuck. His hands shake too much to be of use, so he grips the stopper in his bare gums and it comes free with a sucking sound. He spits the stopper to the carpet and without ceremony upends the cruet and gulps down the liquid. The drink is honeyed and heavy.

The alcohol surges through his bloodstream. His lungs heave. He throws back his head and his Adam's apple writhes like a small trapped rodent. He raises the cruet to his mouth again and empties it.

Overhead flickers the red pinpoint of the sanctuary lamp. The facets and grooves and tiny mirrors etched within the walls of the cruet serve to magnify the candle a thousand-fold. The light swells into a ball of flame. Johnny cradles this flame like a bonfire in his bare hands.

Discovery Day

My Dear Ciss, I letter thee,

Darling Ciss, I do wish you was home to enjoy the pleasures of the mild clear sky the Lord is blessing down on us. Just now I am after giving the youngsters their dinner and pushing them out onto the beaches, and so lonesome it is now I says to myself, this minute before I does another item I must sit down by the light of the window and scribble you a few lines of the news.

Well, the youngsters says to me every day, When is Aunt Ciss coming down? My big one, now you would hardly know her, she's sprouting like a weed. This very morning she finished her matric. This being the day it is, she is doing her divinings, and so tight she is about it I will bet you any money she is after striking. Do you remember that sundress you sent down? She put it on when she got up and she will not take it off to save her soul. Anyway, Ciss, the girl is lost to me now.

As for the rest, I do not know what in God's name I am going to do with them all summer, under my foot every day of the week. Mind you, I do not moan, for they helps foil the dismals as you knows your-self. The little lad, God love him, he's getting to be the ticket. He's my redemption. As for himself, he still goes at the fish night and day and day and night. Here it is now half past the Angelus and he is on the water yet.

News is scarce. Nobody is dead. Con Fitzgerald's girl presented Jack Thomey's lad with a bouncing boy, and Anastasia is going around shouting at the top of her lungs, she isn't the first and she won't be the last. And you remember Frankie Hughes, that amadahn, he ran a hayfork through his foot and now they are call-ing him the Christ. The fresh priest is a queer stick. Spends his days rambling the roads, looking for lost souls. He's a lost soul himself. Nothing at all like Father Fran, GBH.

Tonight is torch night and we got the usual rigmarole on the Brow. I must remember to lift off my gate and hide it in the hennery. Do you remember when we used to be up to such badness, bucking barrels for the fire? If you was here now the two of us we would go out in the fools and find us a nice piece of devilment, for sure.

And how is your own crew? It must be wonderful up where you're at, with all them motor cars and skyscrapers, all them people around you all the time. I can hardly imagine it. Send us snaps.

Well dear, I got to go now and put on the stove something for their supper. Please the Lord the capelin shows up tonight. Maybe I will turn a few fish while the sun favours us. When you comes down, Ciss, we will go pull ourselves a grand feed of dandelions—I notice the buttercups is alive in the meadows today. The fields is yellow with them. Do you remember we used to put them under our chins? I can remember like it was yesterday. Oh my dear, I do not know where the time goes. It rushes by like the blizzard.

I am,

Your loving sister, Hestia

Mary will not step inside. Not today. She might stain her dress on the soot. From the threshold she breathes the savoury dark aromas of coal-dust and sizzling metal and steam and woodchips and horse.

More than once the woman has warned Mary: a blacksmith, he can do you harm, if he wants to. Not only does the iron all around him resist the power of the faeries, but it gives him a power of his own. He can turn his anvil upside down and utter spiteful things—things that will come true. Or he can sprinkle you with water from his trough and curse you with the warts. But Mary ignores such lies and nonsense and babble. She herself has no fear of Mr. Fewer. The forgeman tolerates the company of youngsters, so long as they stay clear of his way.

Quickly her eyes sort out the shadows. The ceiling is low, the forge close and sweltering. Fire flares in its niche in the wall. Mr. Fewer is naked to the waist. His fat body, scarred here and there with burn welts, glistens with sooty sweat. He pumps the bellows slowly—huff, huff, huff—and the canvas lung inhales, as if he is drawing air out of the bedrock. The bellows blows at the hearth, and the heat swells and the cinders glow weirdly, and the sparks roar up the flue in fierce blasts.

With his other hand Mr. Fewer stirs a long poker among the coals. He lifts the poker clear of the cinders and the point is frosty white. Mary daydreams that the forgeman is a centaur, and that with his spear he slays the fire-breathing dragon.

He pumps the bellows faster—huff-huff-huff—and the fire thunders and the sparks bolt. From behind the stall comes a snort that startles the girl—a live horse is standing there. Its rump is visible around the partition. The white coat shines in the light. The animal's hoofs prance nervously: the beast is frightened. And with good reason. On the floor Mr. Fewer has scattered haphazardly his rasp and pliers and hammer and nails.

Sight of these instruments puts into Mary's head the tortures inflicted on the Christian martyrs, such torments as flaying and mutilation and crucifixion. She cannot imagine the suffering of those saints. Even though faith gave them the strength to bear the pain—sometimes even the will to embrace it—the agonies must have been terrible. She ponders these things and she is surprised that no shiver of fear troubles her. Instead, a curious pleasure, almost sinful, agitates her. She reckons the pleasure comes from pride, pride at the hardness that is now forming inside her.

She does not yet own a watch (maybe she will get one for a graduation prize) but she reckons that no more than an hour has passed since the Angelus, since she saw—or rather, since it was announced to her—no more than an hour since her soft outer layers dropped away like discarded shells, leaving only the solid kernel, the seed. Mary herself is the core, the hard true faith. Not only is she now strong enough to endure any pain, she reckons the torment will make her all the stronger. The more she suffers, the more certain she will be. She looks down on the implements of torture and she professes, without shame: gladly I would.

Such a strange thought! This is the first time in her life Mary has had such a notion. It must be, she reckons, a grown-up kind of idea—a woman's thought.

Mr. Fewer grips the iron tongs and roots among the cinders until he brings forth a horseshoe. It glows white. Smartly he sets it atop the anvil. He raises the sledge-hammer and slams the head of the hammer hard against the iron. Sparks cascade across the floor, splendidly, like fireworks.

With each ringing hammer-smash Mary blinks. Adroitly Mr. Fewer flips the shoe and pounds the other side. Now the iron glows a mere red. The forgeman plunges the shoe into the trough. In a spectral hiss and bubble and sputter, his head is lost within a cloud of steam. He pulls out the shoe and it is dripping, now neither white nor red but a stern grey. He wields the tongs in both hands and raises the horse-shoe to a point just above his head. Against his blackened cheeks his eyes shine like candles. He gazes up at the thing. He brings to Mary's mind the priest lifting the monstrance, elevating the Blessed Sacrament in Benediction.

The metal that he raises—that he elevates for her adoration—is pure and hard and certain.

The same queer notion troubles little Kevin Barron, the same one that tormented him in the school: some whispering creature lurks after him.

The child squints up into the blue. Sure enough, eyes are watching.

But it is only a seagull.

The bird hovers on the breeze. Ritually it moves. It edges a forward a few inches, then allows the wind to draw it back to the starting-point. Forward again it shifts, and back, a taut to and fro, always returning to the same spot. Kevin wonders whether the gull may be napping.

Abruptly it executes a sweeping turn, then a loop, and dives to within a hair's breadth of the calm behind the wharf. Its passage leaves a razor-thin ripple quivering on the glass.

Why, the bird is playing.

When it is done capering it gathers itself and soars back to its original elevation. Solemnly, like a great vessel edging alongside a familiar dock, the bird resumes precisely the position it held at the start.

The bird relaxes on the wind. Clearly it understands that Kevin Barron will do it no injury. Other boys would throw rocks. Some would even fire off a gun. Kevin and the bird will be mates. The two of them will fish together.

With the point of the hook the boy punctures the head of a worm and he pushes its fat body, still squirming, down the length of the shaft. He flicks the bamboo and the bait splashes on the calm and slowly sinks into the murk. Tomcods approach and taste the worm. None bites. It is the tomcods Kevin Barron is after. Already he has caught a neat stack of them—a gift to the priest, for his dog. It is a good hour to be at it, for a three-rung tide is rising. The bait slides all the way to the bottom. Kevin Barron hates sculpins, so he draws the hook a fathom higher.

With their fat bellies and huge sticky mouths and horns like the Devil, sculpins make the child sick to his gut. They are the rats of the sea. He suspects they eat dead bodies. He imagines all the sluggish bottom-feeders, the repulsive monsters that slither and crawl—not only sculpins, but flatfish and lobsters and crabs and eels too, and slimy jellyfish and squid—gnawing away at human corpses until only bones are left. Sometimes it seems to Kevin Barron that he can smell the putrescence rising up from the sea floor. He would not want to die by drowning. Even to go out in a boat makes his belly twist, for nothing separates you from the sea grave but a few planks of pine. You pass directly over things horrible beyond imagination. He is glad he wasn't along with Mikey and Pop last summer when they brought in poor old Mr. Dwyer. Even though he is a pagan, Johnny the Light sticks to the right plan: stay off the water.

The rod is suddenly heavy.

A fat connor has swallowed the bait.

Kevin Barron is displeased: the connor is another ugly, useless fish. The child vows he will make the beast do penance for the sin of getting caught. He pulls the connor to the surface and bobs it up and down, in and out of the water. When he reckons its brain is well addled, he relaxes the line and lets the creature swim about awhile and regain its bearings. Then he drags it back to the surface where he splashes it about some more. Dizzily, half-conscious now, the fish swims in circles. The boy tortures the beast until it goes inert and turns bottom-up.

Kevin hoists the connor out of the water and flips it onto the wharf. Scrunching his nose distastefully, he steadies the fish with his boot and rips the hook from the scummy mouth. The tail flaps. He grips the tail and whacks the brain against the grump so that the creature is dead. Then the child kicks the corpse back into the water. It sinks to the bottom. He watches tomcods and sculpins and flatfish, even other connors, converge and quickly rip the carcass to shreds.

The seagull hovers, balanced perfectly on the air. It fixes its porcelain eye mischievously on Kevin Barron. It wants to play.

The child rebaits and casts in a long arc. The instant the bait slaps the surface, a whine tickles his ear faintly.

The tarred hull of an outboard rounds the lighthouse. The motor lifts the bow so high out of the water that half the keel is dry. The prow seems to have a pair of eyes. Wings of wash flare from both sides of them. The vessel bears down in a single-minded straight line and it seems not to move at all, only to swell ferociously.

While he is distracted by the boat, the bamboo, oddly, feels light in his hands.

It is the gull. The bird has swooped and swallowed the hook, and now it retreats to its station in the sky. Kevin Barron needs a moment to understand what is happening, but once he does so, out loud he laughs at the very notion. Yes, the bird is determined to play.

The creature flaps excitedly and flies this way and that. The child clings to the rod and chases the bird the length of the wharf, then back, then to and fro across the head, around the splitting shed and back again. He can't be sure whether he is leading the gull, or it is leading him, and as far as he is concerned the two are one, tethered—mates, playing together. His soft fingers fray against the rod. He becomes so absorbed that he nearly steps over the wide of the wharf and into the sea.

Abruptly the gull shoots vertically up. The line stretches taut. The child becomes enraged—the bird is trying to fly away with his bamboo. It is not playing fair. He yanks violently on the line.

The bird rolls in mid-air. It hovers precisely where earlier it sat so placidly, and stares down the length of the rigid wire connecting it with the boy. Its eye—pityingly, it seems—observes the child. Then, beak first, spinning, the gull tumbles and splashes into the water.

Kevin Barron has watched bad boys hurl sick hens off the head of the wharf and then howl laughing while the helpless beasts drift squawking to sea, their unwebbed claws useless to save them. He expects to see the gull mock the pathetic chickens and behave in this way. But instead the gull only floats atop the surface, inert, a piece of garbage.

Kevin Barron pulls the bird to the wharf. A light chop captures the carcass and tosses it among the pilings. The wings splay awkwardly and feathers tangle in the line. A vein of red seeps from the beak, and the porcelain eye, still open, is blind.

With the heel of her shoe Mary drags a rut in the dirt. If people happened to be watching, they might think she was laying out squares for hopscotch. In fact she is making just one line, but it runs full the width of the road.

Taking care to stay west of her mark, she crosses to the wooden platform. From here the path, barely wide enough for three abreast, runs perpendicular to the road and ascends the slope northwards. At the top of the path awaits the fence with its wrought-iron gate. In Mary's head appears again the image of the woman, hysterical, refusing to climb, and Monsignor Conroy advancing up the lane, solemnly, swinging slowly the dreadful censer, and. . . .

Mary pinches herself: this is Sweetheart's Day, and this day for once she will not let the glooms take root. To clear them from her head she breathes deep of the cheerful smell of the blueberries swelling like grapes on the slope. This path, she tells herself, today is not what it was. Today it is a faery lane. Today it leads to the faeryland beyond the gate. And today this little platform is something else: it is her playhouse.

Mary brushes away the dust that coats the bed of the platform. When she is satisfied she will not dirty her dress, she grips the edge with the heels of her palms and hops her bum up and sits cozily underneath the low felt roof. She sizes up the place.

Already she has travelled beyond the last house, which shows her its unpainted grey back. She has no idea who lives in it—maybe no one. Instead of the usual five-point star or crescent moon or sun, its barn doors are painted with cat's eyes, and they are watching her. Westward over the horizon the telegraph poles march resolutely away. It frightens the girl to find herself past the border of such everyday things. To her left, east, the lighthouse gleams against the backdrop of blue-green sea. Never has she seen the pillar so close, so clear and sharp.

In the region between here and the lighthouse stretches an expanse of barren, with no tilts or huts or even fences, few trees, just rocky knolls and scrub glens. The road narrows to a cart track, then to a mere path, and disappears altogether into a bog. The only sign of life is a goat, yokeless and sinister, observing her from the height of an outcrop.

On the shore south of the barren, Mary has heard, is Gallows Beach, where the mad nun was hanged, where the mermaids take the sun. Mary has never seen the place. At this hour, Gallows Beach is in her future. The scratch she made in the dirt is the farthest point she has ever been. The line is the border of her life—on this side she has, on that side she has never. Soon, the beach will be in her present.

Mary's mind is getting muddled with cobwebs. She yawns. She lies back under the shade of the roof and closes her eyes. Her calves dangle over the edge and enjoy the touch of the light. Anyone who came along might see the breeze lift the hem of her dress, see the sun warm her long thighs. But she doesn't care. . . .

Mary dreams of black centaurs. A herd of them gallop after her down a narrow lane. She escapes by stretching her long legs and flying through the air. She dreams then that she lolls on a huge bed where the wind blows through a wide-open window. At one time or another, many others have slept on this same bed, and now, in the dream, all together every one of them lies beside her.

An insistent buzz stirs the girl half awake. Part of her mind is still inside the dream. She feels a sinful urge—to slide her hand under her skirt and down into her bloomers. But she remembers the eyes watching her from the barn door.

At first she reckons the buzz is a horsestinger droning among the berries. She sits upright and in her sleepiness it takes her ears a moment to fathom that the noise is an outboard motor. She hops down from the platform and crosses the road and stands at the rim of the slope. Green meadows roll steeply downhill to the water. When she rubs her eyes awake, she sees a punt with a tar-black hull. The boat has eyes like those on the barn. The hull rides high and sets down a foamy wake. It heads towards the wharf. An old man sits at the motor.

The smoke still curls from behind the ice. Mary spotted it first when she stepped out of the forge. All the way down the road she scarcely took her eyes from the sight. She can guess where the smoke comes from, but still she imagines, around the back end of the berg, a roaring furnace, and a centaur swinging a big hammer, forging his own set of shoes upon an anvil of ice.

The wind is falling. From this elevation Mary can make out clearly the Naked Man piled up on the south headland. Moira says it even has a long stone for a dick — but that's just her dirty mind. Beyond the Foot, down the shore towards Brimstone, other headlands claw at the sea. The only other time she was here she never noticed those places. But she recognizes them well enough: they are on the big map of the island, the map on the classroom wall.

Right now, the girl is surprised to see that the map's lines and colours are not just some fabulous comic book, that the names are not just musical words but real places. Here they are lined up before her down the coast as plain as the sun: Brickhouse and Deadman's Cove and Ireland's Eye and Cappahayden and Bay Despair and Hogueras and a half-dozen others, each one precisely where the map says it should be.

What's more, if she can believe the rest of the map, then the salt water in this cove joins with the salt water washing the shore of the Boston States, and England, and Ireland, and New Guinea, and even China. This means that, had she a mind to do so, she could climb into a rowboat and paddle around the Head and past the ledge and into the Stream, and sooner or later she would bring up at all the great places of the world. Mary feels like one of those Roman goddesses she has read about, who stare down from the heavens and see all things.

Her eye imagines the promise that the world holds. All she does not yet know waits beyond this line scratched here across the road.

The lighthouse beckons to her, draws her, as if she were a sailor in peril on the sea.

Mary sets the toe of her shoe against the line. Ahead, in the middle of the wilderness, the sinister goat watches her, waits. Behind, the parish, the Brow, the spires of the church where she was baptized and made her First Communion and her Confirmation, her school where she became everything she is, the blue house where she was born, call her back. Cabot must have felt like this when his ship passed over the horizon, when he looked sternward and saw his land, his home, sinking into the sea. To carry on at that moment must have taken an iron-hard faith.

Mary's long legs straddle the line. She plants one foot firmly in the old, one in the new. The breeze rustles her skirt and blows her hair into her eyes. She smells in her hair the lingering odour of coal from the forge. She shuts her eyes, and she runs.

Sniffing like a bloodhound, Johnny the Light makes straight for the press. It is unlocked, so he removes one bottle of the sacramental wine, arranges the others to hide the theft, straightaway unscrews the cap, and shuts his eyes and drinks.

When he opens his eyes and catches his breath, he observes that the sacristy is lined with dark-varnished cabinets. He pockets the bottle and explores them.

The old man finds tapers and candles and candlesticks and snufters, a thurible and an incense boat, a pyx, altar linen, white lace surplices and red soutanes, fabulously coloured vestments in rich fabrics, several chalices, even a monstrance. None of these things interests him much. In one cupboard, however, he discovers a silver ciborium. The lid is crowned by a tiny cross. He raises the lid and uncovers hundreds, perhaps thousands, of Communion hosts. They lie strewn like the postage stamps he saw in Casey's barrel. He claps a handful into his mouth. Like candy they melt on his tongue.

Johnny shuffles around the chamber and his feet make the beams creak in the floor. His ear does not recognize that the sounds are of his own making. He rasps, "H-H-Hushta!" and he stands still and listens. Softly he whispers, "Aha, me boys."

A large volume bound in black leather rests on the counter-top. The cover yields to his clumsy hands. The leaves are delicate, filmy, almost transparent, and his fumbling thumbs fail to separate them neatly. He presses his face close and tries to make sense of the letters, but they are thin and fragile, and some, printed in red ink, shift about on the page before his eyes. He is disappointed that the book has no pictures.

Johnny finds a crude door hiding what appears to be a closet. He unfastens the hasp. The door opens onto blackness. A rising surge of stale air chills him. At his feet a ladder falls away steeply.

He hisses, "Lads, h-h-hurry along now. Here's our vessel, come to carry us home."

With the style of an experienced boathand, he pivots and steps backwards and climbs down the dozen or so rungs. At the bottom of the ladder his feet register the raw packed earth. The air smells richly of mould. Its texture is thick, like the smoke of incense: the old man can almost taste it. The space has no windows, so he must rely on the meagre light that falls down the stair.

While he waits for his poor eyes to adjust, he pulls the bottle from his coat and drinks. He sets the bottle safely against the bottom of the ladder. He removes his big coat and folds it across a rung. He undoes the rope binding his trousers and drops them to his feet. His legs shiver at the chill. He squats and urinates in the dirt. Some sort of small creature, a beetle perhaps, scuttles up his leg and across his knee and he brushes it away. Gradually the old man becomes aware of the row of icy white rectangles rising out of the dark.

"Barron, tell me: isn't that a revolting sight? Don't it make you sick to your gut?" Gus cups his hands like horse-blinkers around his eyes. He is pretending to bar Wish from his view. "Eating is the first step in the job of shitting. I can no more watch Butt chew than I can watch him shit."

Wish's face as usual is blank, but his walleye rolls about, an animal with a mind of its own. "Barron, you tell Gallant this for me: tell him, crawl up and branch off. Or he'll be looking for his teeth all over the ground." Wish slurps dis-gustingly at his hack of seal meat. "Yum. Nice and morish." When he is satisfied that he has sucked the bone clean of its last morsel of fat and gristle, nonchalantly he flips the bone over his shoulder. He plugs one nostril with a forefinger and exhales violently a stream of mucus, then repeats the process with the other nostril.

Michael turns away from his mates. He tries to think of land, of rolling hills covered in greenery, like a mattress spread with down quilts. He imagines how nice it would be to rest there, warm in the soft bed of the earth. But he finds it is impossible to disregard the ice under his thighs, for it in-jects up his spine a deathly chill. He cannot ignore the stench of the gore and bones and soot and filth strewn about. This place is a purgatory. Across his tired mind trails the line from the catechism: *where some souls suffer for a time before they can go to heaven. . . .* His throat is sticky with the greasy tex-ture from the seal's heart. He coughs and spits, but there is no ridding his mouth of the foul taste of the blood.

"Barron, my son, it was only a joke, for Christ's sake."

"Honest to God, Barron, we never thought you were really going to eat it."

"Actually, we thought you was going to stick it up your arse. Isn't that right, Butt?"

Michael forces a smile.

"Well, that's where it's going to pitch, in the fullness of time."

The two of them guffaw.

Licks of flame dart from the collapse of half-burnt pine. They are like souls trying to speak, trying to be heard out of the ruin of ash and decay. The warmed air brushes Michael's face on its way to the clouds. He wishes he were floating up there too, up there in the billowing sky.

The sun bears down hard on the ice. No shadows darken the peak. If Michael were to climb there again and look across to the parish, would he still see the white dress standing? Would it still be waiting?

Gus roots under his oilskins. He uncoils forth the chicken wire and the cod tongue skewered upon it. Triumphantly he raises these on high. "My due," he gloats. "It was me hauled the fish." He lowers the grey flesh into the flame and straightaway the tongue sizzles. Gus pops the blob down his throat in a swallow, and then, like a child who has just eaten a candy, he blinks with immense satisfaction.

Wish sings a dirge:

> *Oh, we fished in the summer, we fished in the fall,*
> *And when it was over, we had nothing a-tall . . .*

Robustly Gus joins in the chorus:

> *And it's hard, hard times. . . .*

Now Wish pulls from under his clothes a soggy paper bag. "The loafs and the fishes," he says. He tosses each of his mates a baseball-size lump of hardtack. "Dig your hardy grinders into that, why don't you."

He climbs to his feet and slithers down to the pool. He lifts out of the water the dipnet that bears the three bottles. All the while he sings lewdly:

Forrrr . . . the wind was in her quarter
Her engines running free . . .

"That useless knob." Gus speaks loudly, for Wish's benefit. "Finally caught something decent."

The fire founders hissing into its basin. The last of the
smouldering embers sputter and drown. Meltwater, blackened with ash and soot, overflows the rim of the basin
and runs in an inky stream staining the slope. Gus squeals
with false alarm, "Barron! We're sinking! Help! Get your
spudgell and bail out this leaky old tub!"

Wish advances with the dipnet, the bottles resting in
the netting. "Barron, tell him he's as stunned as my hole.
Now, lads, it's time for our ration." In the style of an alms-
taker Wish holds the hoop under Gus's chin.

Gus lifts out the dripping bottles. He brings forth his
knife and opens the corkscrew, jams one of the bottles between his knees, and wrestles. He grunts. "Tight . . . as a
muskrat's arsehole."

Pok!

While Gus opens the other bottles and passes them round,
Wish labours his wellingtons from his feet. His feet are sockless and covered with a kind of black mud. Gus makes a
sour face. "Jesus, I sniffed them before I spied them."

"What's the matter? Does Gallant think gumboots are for
keeping out the water? No, by God, they're for keeping in
the stink."

Gus tucks his bottle between his legs and takes a bite of
the hardtack. He chews a long time before swallowing. He
furrows his brow and says, "Barron, tell Butt something for
me: tell him his mother's hardtack tastes like a fart."

"The cook will please bite my balls." Wish holds his piece
of bread up to the light. "Surely no worse than somebody's
half-baked flipper."

"Barron, you and me, we saw him licking them bones,

didn't we? He never complained then. As for this flint biscuit, by rights we should be after having it last night, in the
pitch black. That way we wouldn't have the misfortune to
see what's inside of it."

"The cook will please nibble my nuts."

"Barron, let me tell you a story. A true story—cross my
heart and hope to die. One day I was sitting in Butt's kitchen
and his mother, she gives me a piece of hardtack. So I takes
a chomp out of it, and I swear by the living Jesus but didn't
I bite into something *soft* . . ."

Wearily, Michael's head drifts again landward, yearning.
He thinks of the illusion, familiar to sailors approaching
home, of the houses marching down to meet them at the
landwash. He reckons up the distances, and decides that if
he were to be cast ashore anywhere between the two great
capes, at most he would need a day's hike to bring himself
safely to the back door of his house. If only his feet stood on
the concrete earth, he would not feel so dislocated, so remote
as he does now.

". . . and of course I says to myself: A worm . . ."

Michael struggles to keep his eyes open. If he were
dropped into some distant empire, China even, he would not
feel so very far away. He would not feel that he floats in the
dim reaches of outer space.

". . . but no! Only a finishing nail it was." Gus raises his
wine against the sun. The light bolts through the glass and
dances a purple blotch across the pits that scar his cheek. He
sniffs at the mouth of the bottle.

"The cook will kindly chew me up and down," says Wish.

Gus swallows a mouthful. "Number-one horsepiss," he
declares firmly. "This is the sort of piss that Johnny the
Light drinks, I am sure."

"Johnny the *Lit*. And well lit he generally is."

Gus jabs Michael awake. "Butternuts! Have a glutch of
your poison."

Suspiciously Michael sniffs at the bottle. In the middle of the Easter dance, Gus took an empty flask out in back of Academy Hall and pissed into it. Johnny the Light was hanging about, half drunk. Gus offered him the flask and Johnny downed it in one swallow. The way Gus, collapsed in hysterics, told it afterwards inside the hall, Johnny only smiled and smacked his lips and staggered on down the road. But neither Michael nor Wish thought it was funny, tormenting an old man like that. A hero, too.

His nose detects in the bottle only the ripe blueberry, the true item. The fragrance carries his head from the ice-mountain and bears it off to a real land, a natural terrain of honest soil, and lichened rock, and trees that breathe. Within this bottle the earth itself is condensed. Michael drinks fervently. The wine is thick and sweet, and yeasty still, but to his palate as holy as a sacrament. He allows his eyes to fall shut the way they do after Communion.

"Tell Butt to be a useful child, and build us a round of smokes."

"Will the cook please lick my dick," Wish says. Nonetheless, dutifully he busies himself with the papers and tobacco. He cocks up his leg, and in the dainty manner of a dowager at tea he manufactures three cigarettes upon the tabletop of his bent knee. The boys gnaw on the hardtack. They smoke and they drink.

"This dreck, it's not so bad the second taste," says Gus. "But the next batch, we wants to bury it a winter or two in the cellar. Give it character."

"Well, it was on the waves overnight, after all. Wine cures faster crossing water."

Gus glares at Wish with exaggerated scorn. "This Butt, I swear to Jesus, he's so full of it his eyeballs are brown."

Wish spits a tatter of tobacco. "Didn't you know? The White Fleet uses port barrels for ballast. To this day. Full to the brim. That way, the barrels crosses the ocean twice."

Michael's sleepy mind glimpses, curving over the horizon, bow to stern, all canvas flying, the hundreds of vessels that are the Portuguese White Fleet. The lovely image blends into lilypads on a pond, uplifted by the breeze so that their undersides show pale. But he blinks himself awake and the water is dead empty again.

The wind falls. Far off, where the boys were anchored earlier, a foamy lop brushes the surface, but close under the land only thin ripples survive.

"It's true," insists Wish. "Anyway, sometime we must try making spruce beer."

"Spruce beer?"

"Johnny told me how. And there's no shortage of the makings, Christ knows. We could earn our living at it."

Gus waves derisively. "All Butt thinks about is making his living. He's going to wind up like old Jeremy Fortune. Jeremy gets took with the decline but no, by God, do you think he gives up the fishing? He's dying on his deathbed and he wants to get up and he says to the wife, 'Well, goddamnit, woman, I got to make my living!' "

"It's easy. You chops the branches into little sticks and drops them into a few gallons of water, then you lets it boil down to a half a pint. Essence, Johnny calls that."

Michael has never tasted spruce beer. Still, he loves the smell of the oxygen that exists nowhere but in the tight stand of spruce down the far slope of the ridge. The air is so green and thick and cool you can almost roll it over your tongue.

"*Essence?*" Gus looks to Michael and snorts, "Barron, did you ever hear such arseholery? 'Hello Father Mac-Murrough, Your Essence, how are you this fine morning?' "

"Then you mixes your essence with thirty gallons of water, and twelve pounds of molasses, and a pound of sugar. Something like that. It doesn't have to be exact. You heats the lot and you bottles it off, and there you are. And if you wants the prime callabogus, you adds a snort of rum."

"Will you inform Phonse here: that is one goddamn big shark."

With his index finger Wish probes his back teeth. He extracts something black. He holds it up and considers it before replacing it in his mouth. Gus drinks, wipes dribble from his chin, belches, draws on his cigarette absentmindedly. Michael sips the wine and sniffs the aroma of the hills that are inside the bottle. The iceberg sways so slightly that his mates fail to notice, but a mild vertigo makes his head reel.

Wish scratches at his crotch. Lustfully he sings:

And it's hard, hard *times . . .*

Gus keeps one eye cocked shut against the smoke rising from his cigarette, so that it appears he is lining Wish up in his sights. "Listen to my advice, child: leave it alone and let it grow."

"Gallant, up your hole with a knotty pole."

"Up *your* bum with a rubber thumb."

"Barron, did you ever hear tell if Gallant's mother had any children that lived?"

"Is it true what they say, Barron, that when Butt was born they made a mistake? They hove away the child and they baptized the afterbirth?"

Gus reaches deep into his own trousers and now it is he who rubs himself. He sighs, "Oh, give me a land of milk and cunny." He projects his tongue and lays it, flaccid, upon his lower lip, like a communicant. Suddenly the tongue jumps erect and wiggles obscenely. At this Wish falls into a fit of giggling, spewing flecks of hardtack over himself.

Gus turns with baleful wide-eyed wonderment to Michael. "I swear, this lad is cracked."

Wish stifles his laughter long enough to blurt with false petulance, "Kiss my royal Irish." But at hearing his own voice speak these words he howls all the harder.

In a fake English accent Gus declaims soberly. "Mister Barron, I do believe this poor child is mental. But let us make certain." He holds up an index finger as though testing the direction of the wind. He regards his finger with intense seriousness. "Master Butt, will you be so kind as to tell us, please: of this, what is your opinion?"

Askance, Wish peeks at the finger held up — he dares not look directly. The sight sends him rolling about on the ice, like a dog trying to rid itself of fleas, and laughing so deeply, so profoundly, that he makes no noise at all.

"No, Master Butt was never the same since the horse stepped on his head."

Michael climbs to his feet. He goes down to the outlet in the plateau, where the meltwater flows into the iceberg, and, the way Gus did before him, he pisses into the hole. Gus calls, "Watch out, Mister Barron, Master Butt here is licking his lips."

Michael takes his time rejoining his mates.

"Mister Barron, a queer thing indeed, isn't it, the way Master Butt laughs?" Here Gus imitates precisely the sound of Wish's girlish giggle. This makes Wish snort dangerously. It seems he is on the verge of choking.

"All right then, Master Butt, now will you be so kind as to inform us: what do you think of this?" Gus unbuttons his oilcoat and lifts his shirt and bares his midriff. He places his hands on either side of his navel and pushes the folds of flesh together so that they form a hairy dark slit.

Abruptly Wish stops. He stares slack-jawed at the other boy's flesh. His walleye bulges and roams. His face breaks into a smile and he makes as if to speak, but he checks himself, closes his mouth, swallows. In the end, red-faced, inhaling deeply, he only looks down at his feet.

Gus adopts the voice of a scolding nun. He shrills, "Aha, me child! I knows all your sins! I even knows your girlfriend's name! It's Mary. Isn't it?" He winks at Michael.

Michael can feel the blood drain from his cheeks.

"Mary Five-Fingers! Confess now! You can't escape us! Confess your sins!"

Wish only stares at his naked filthy toes.

For a long uncomfortable period no one speaks.

The boys drain the dregs of their wine. "Feeling no pain," Gus swaggers. "Aye!" says Wish, recovered from his fit. Michael reckons they are lying, because the drink has had no effect whatsoever on himself.

Wish holds his empty bottle on high. "Wasn't it dry flasks gave Father Fran his visions and predictions and cures and all the rest?"

"Undoubtedly it was."

Gus draws hard on the last of his ready-made. His face puckers against his cheekbones. He flicks the cigarette and it lands with a *phttt* in the pool, where it floats like a miniature corpse. The last of the smoke empties from his nostrils and is borne off on the breeze. In a serious tone he speaks.

"There was this pair, you know, screwing up behind the palace. The priest goes out for his evening stroll. He's walking along, his nose in his prayerbook, when he happens to step on a fat arse. The priest hears a female voice: 'Bless you, Father,' and he reckons it's the voice of the angels, come to bear him off to heaven."

Wish glances skyward. He nods knowingly. "Grand day, this, for a spot of grassing."

"Grassing! Am I dreaming? Is Wish Butt telling us about grassing? I bet you a whole dollar, Barron, this lad never in his life laid eyes on a set of tits. He wouldn't know what to do with them. Wouldn't know where to stick his wee prick. Soon as a piece of gear comes along and lifts up her skirt and says to him, 'Here it is,' he'd be after taking off, tail between his legs. In fact, do you know the reason Butt has a prick at all?"

Wish pays no heed. He recites sepulchrally, "Have you ever?"

In the same tone Gus responds, "No I never."

"Would you like to?"

"Would I ever!"

Gus and Wish raise right hands to brows and smartly, simultaneously, they snap salutes.

"It is so he can count to eleven. As for myself, Jesus, right now I can hardly blink my eyes."

"You know something, Barron? I do believe this ramcat was born with a bone."

"What we needs is an addition to the Corporal Works of Mercy: Pulling Off the Stiff. I think I will send a telegram to the His Essence the Pope."

"Did you hear about the man walking down the road with a hen and a rooster tucked under his arm? The two birds got clear of him and took off. The man runs after them yelling . . ."

Gus ignores Wish. "If only all the waves were tits . . ."

". . . 'Catch my cock and pullet.' "

". . . God knows I would surely drown."

Out of his exhaustion and revulsion Michael lets loose a sigh. Gus eyeballs him sharply. "What's this now? Did I hear a moan? Confess, Barron, my child: what are you poisoned about? What's on your snivelling mind?"

"I think Barron wants to go in out of this. Isn't it so, Mikey my lad? That was one whore's breakfast, you got to admit. And if he wants to get up to any mischief tonight, we got to find some sleep sometime."

"Mischief! Gates and shithouses and barn doors and such? Is that what you calls mischief? All that nonsense is for youngsters. We're done school now. We're men. And tonight we're going after what men goes after: first, a proper bottle. None of this syrup. And second, a proper piece of skin. Punch and Judy. Isn't that so, Barron?"

Michael will not give them the satisfaction of an answer. He is busy observing the ice-blocks. As the breeze falls some of them drift loose into the sea, single file, bow to stern. Michael envies their stealthy escape.

"Gallant, you're such a bullshitter. You can no more find skin that you can find fish."

Gus kicks at Michael's foot. "Tell us, Barron. Tell us the truth: are you ever after picking a cherry?"

"Yes," Wish joins in. "We wants to know, the two of us."

Michael blinks, but it is enough to betray that he is listening. He cannot help it. He cannot help the colour draining again from his face.

"Had yourself a tit-squeeze?"

"A jolly in the berry banks?"

"Over hill and dale, to get a piece of. . . ."

"Tell us, Barron, we wants the story."

"What's the name?"

"Is she shy?"

"How was the wuss?"

"Smell like fish, taste like chicken?"

"Is she a monkey? . . ."

"Give her a pole, does she climb?"

"Tell us about the tickle."

"The grunt."

"The spasm."

"The squirt."

"Did you start at the toes?"

"Lap your way up both sides of the road?"

"And did you find the man in the boat?"

"The treasure under the bush?"

Gus breaks off. "Speaking of: you knows, don't you know, there's gold buried up beyond the bogs? Privateer's prizes, all of it cursed and jinked and hexed. You don't believe me? It's true. Yes, if you wants to get lots of skin, that's what you needs, a treasure. . . ."

Michael relaxes.

"Gallant, you're a goddamned madman. Don't you think he is, Barron?"

"Listen to this, Butt. You're Henry Mainwaring, I'm Peter Easton, this lazy codbanger down here is Blackbeard, and the pack of us together, we is the Masterless Men. And as soon as we goes in out of this, we marleys over back with a pick and shovel, and we has ourselves a serious inspection of the ground. What do you say?"

Wish looks to Michael and shakes his head with feigned disgust.

"You don't believe in treasure? Well, they found that bloody great war axe buried in the beach. Where do you suppose that came from?"

"Leif the Lucky. Eric the Red. Billy the Cluck. Johnny the Light. I don't know. Who the fuck knows?"

Wish takes the shotgun in one hand and the hatchet in the other. In his bare feet he stands and adopts a belligerent pose, staggering, waving the weapons. He shouts at the sky, "We is the friends of God and the enemies of the world!" He does a prancing step and he sings:

For we was born upon the bright, blue sea . . .

"Listen!" Gus hisses. He cuffs Wish. "Stop! Shut up!"

From a distance, from somewhere in the far side of the ice, comes the faint drone of an outboard motor.

"Mike Landrigan," whispers Gus. "That's his engine. Come to fetch out the padre. I bet you a god damn."

"That old woman, she'll get it one more time before they puts her in the boneyard." Wish drops the weapons and gathers the three bottles, upturns them one by one above his extended tongue and drains the last drops. Then he hurls the bottles one by one down the cliffside to smash and tinkle against the ice below. "She got to be screwed in her coffin."

Wish dances and sings:

A great big sea hove in Long Beach
Granny Snooks she lost her speech.

Two gulls appear, having emerged seemingly from the body of the ice itself. They flail about just above the heads of the boys and greedily scream for the scraps and bones and refuse.

Michael would love to be a plain seagull. He would spread his wings and flee this place. First he would fly high, close to the sun, to warm himself, then he would slide straight down a great imaginary chute to the solid land, to the parish—to home.

The birds get tangled in one another, mid-air, then each in turn crashes against the wall of the ice. Michael becomes alarmed for them. He wishes they would go away, fly to some safer place.

"Alcock and Brown," Wish drawls. "Well, if we wasn't so goddamned hookless. One time, you know, I puts a hook and a worm on the two ends of a fathom of line and I fires the business on the water. By and by down comes these two stupid gulls and they takes in the works. Off they goes, twins for ever. Holding hands, banging into one another, trying to figure it out."

Wish spins out his story in a slow babble. Meanwhile, stealthily he reaches for the gun.

When a gull sees even a waving stick, it will flee. Michael prays that this pair will spot the raised barrel in time to escape. But no, they are too gluttonous. He turns away and waits while the half-second stretches to a small eternity. After the blast, pieces of the ice cliff crash down into the ravine.

"You cockeyed ninny."

"Nonsense. A bull's-eye it was. Tough gulls we got in this country, that's all."

"You fired right between the two of them."

"To tell the truth, I was only gunning after the sun. For luck."

Gus jumps to his feet and grabs the gun out of Wish's hands. He cocks the hammer and aims down upon Wish's good eye. The eye stares balefully up into the smoking barrel. Wish's expression is vacant.

Michael has seen the damage that a 12-gauge can do, to birds like partridge and turrs and crows. Years ago, Pop told him to destroy a chicken that was too sick to live, and Michael decided to execute it. He carried the chicken in a gunnysack down to the Brow, staked it to the sod like it was a condemned prisoner, paced off ten steps, turned and aimed and fired. Feathers exploded in the wind. When he went to examine the carcass, no piece was big enough to pick up in his hand. Michael wonders what would be left of Wish's head if this gun were actually loaded, actually fired.

From behind the hammer Gus hisses, "Butt, did you ever hear about the Harbour Grace gaol? The prisoners there, they was so fed up they drew straws to see who would murder who. And they did it, too. They murdered one another. It wasn't that they hated each other. They just was fed up. They was bored. That's all."

The barrel wavers. Gus grimaces: something is happening inside his guts. In a dull voice he says, "I hope you remembered to bring your coffin."

Wish's walleye rolls farther than Michael has ever seen it travel. Moisture wells at the edges. Despite the lack of real danger, Wish is afraid. The dull voice hisses, "Barron, did you know Butt has blue eyes? . . ."

A low muffled explosion sounds. Michael starts at the sound.

"One blew east and one blew west."

The sound came from the back of Gus's trousers.

"Bless me, Father, for I have sinned." Gus lowers the gun and he makes the sign of the cross. "Fifteen times I broke my wind."

A raw odour passes briefly by Michael's nostrils, a foul presence, a soul on its way to hell.

"Get out and walk," Wish howls with relief. He wipes dry his eyes. He laughs hysterically but strangely, in a way Michael has never before heard.

"Should of lit that toot, shouldn't I, Butt?" Gus laughs too, but in a mocking way.

"Yes. Could of cooked a goddamned whale on the gas of that one."

"Normally I only lights them in the tub, you know."

"Right. Catch the bubbles when they comes up."

"See before you smell."

"That's it. Can't singe your hole that way."

"How does Butt know all this? In your whole life, Butt, whenever was you in a washtub?"

"What's it to you?" Wish speaks this in singsong.

"I'm writing a book."

"Then kiss my arse . . ."

". . . and I'll make it a love story."

The two boys curtsy to one another.

Wish cups his hand behind his ear. "Hark! A bugle." He farts sad, high-pitched squeak, the sort of fluty note that comes from blowing past a reed of grass pressed between the thumbs. He closes his eyes and inhales deeply through his nose. An expression of exquisite rapture cross his face.

"Dog smells his own dirt first. That however, that was no bugle. Butt never heard a bugle in his life, obviously. One thing Butt will never have to worry about: he will never be called up." Gus whispers loudly. "What with his *physical disability,* you know. . . ."

Wish is reaching down and slipping on his wellingtons.

"No guts." Gus waves his hand before his nose. "Thank the Lord. The smell of them feet was starting to sting the eyes. Almost as bad as the toilet in Butt's house."

Wish peers around. "Speaking of, where is the jakes on this tub?"

"Before you." Gus extends his arm in a sweeping gesture. "You filthy pig."

"I used to think I was permanently hardbound. But the company I am forced to keep has give me the jollies. The time has come to pluck me a rose. Lay a dumpling. The hour has arrived. Give me a wad of your newspaper, will you."

"If you wants today's," Gus indicates the ashes, "you'll have to come back tomorrow."

"Well, shag that." Wish shades his eyes and gazes towards the peak. "I do believe the top is a dandy spot. Warm and sunny. Give the nuns something to yammer about over the supper table. Barron, was the parish able to spy you up there?"

Michael stares vacantly. What would be wiser: to nod, or to shake his head? He pretends he didn't hear. Wish chuckles, turns, and weaves towards the summit.

Michael wonders how, when he leaps to his feet and runs after the boy and tackles him to the snow, he will explain what he has done.

"That queer," Gus whispers. "That fruit is just too filthy for the human race." Then Gus bellows at Michael so loud that Wish must hear too, "Hey, Barron. You ever notice the nancy way Butt walks?"

At hearing this Wish halts in his tracks. He cannot take another step. Foolishly he grins. He plugs his forefingers in his ears. Instead of making for the summit, he darts behind a nearby hummock.

Even as Wish squats and organizes himself, the tossel of

his cap is visible above the ice. Gus grins cruelly. He breaks open the gun. He extracts the empty shell and heaves it in a long arc over his shoulder into the sea. He places a live shell in the chamber, and quietly shuts the breech.

"Barron, doesn't the sight of that just make you sick to your gut? That filthy Butt, he's not shitting at all. We know what he's at. He's pulling himself together."

Wish's voice sings over the hummock:

> *Birch wine,*
> *tar twine,*
> *cherry wine,*
> *and turpentine. . . .*

Gush whispers, "Barron, did you ever hear the story of the *Rainbow*? She was stuck fast in a raft of ice. Nothing to do but drift along and wait for the Stream to melt them out. Not a whisker of a harp in sight. The men was just as bored as if they was prisoners in jail. So what do you suppose they did? They took up their rifles and climbed out onto the ice, and squatted down behind hummocks, like real soldiers, and commenced to taking cockshots at one another. Just for fun."

He aims at an icicle above Wish's cap, and he shouts, "Butt, hold up your essence, like a good man, and show it to us."

Michael turns his head and awaits the passage of the long half-second. He looks down towards the rowboat, and he is startled to see the two gulls. No mistake—it is Alcock and Brown. They strut about on the ice, picking at the seal carrion. Michael is sad for them, for he thought that they had flown away to safety and freedom, that by now they were roosting on the public wharf, or gobbling capelin over in Admiral's Beach, or simply flying high within the bright warmth of the sun. But there they scrabble clumsily on the slippery blue ice, looking for all the world like lonely vultures.

To make better time, old Landrigan swings the punt inside the barricade of sinkers and above the shoals skirting the bluffs. The boat weaves among the lobster-pot floats strung in a line like the connecting dots of a picture puzzle. Landrigan, intent, presses his lips white and fixes his eye like a gunsight on the lighthouse that marks the halfway point of their passage. He grips the throttle full ajar and the outboard whines and the bow heaves clear of the water.

The child clings to the roof of the cuddy, facing aft. His hair blows in the wind. Father MacMurrough regards him with contempt. The boy's expression is grave and his flesh is pale and drawn. In Wexford, they would say a youngster with such a face is an old man, an old man left by the faeries in exchange for a child taken. This boy lives up to his name—it was the aged hermit Kevin who took refuge at Glendalough and repulsed the women seeking his ascetic company.

One of his pious little hands clutches the paper bag holding his surplice, the other grips tightly the boat. He looks as though he may heave up. Here in the shelter the skiff runs smoothly, with none of the bronco-bucking they suffered on the lop. Since the boy no longer needs to brace himself against being flung over, the priest wonders scornfully whether it may be the sea from which he cringes.

Father MacMurrough leans across the gunnel to look down, to see for himself.

The sun is aloft, and the sea reflects all the light of the universe. The very breeze is ablaze. The priest shelters his eyes with the brim of his hat as he studies the water. The surface in advance of the hull's wash is undisturbed, and so the sandy bottom, here a mere fathom or so below, is clear. The sea floor hurtles by at an alarming clip, the way a meadow might appear to one flying low on a magic carpet.

Abruptly an unnatural shape darkens the sand. The priest recognizes it straight off—it is the skeleton of a wooden ship. With that, time slows. His thoughts swell to fill the span of the breath that it takes the punt to slide up the spine of the keel.

The remains are half-buried in the sand. So black are the beams that the priest guesses the vessel is centuries old. The structure has survived the pulverizing storms by grace of the protecting rosary of sinkers—the same rocks, probably, that holed the vessel in the first place.

The punt surges forward and the figure of the ship curves with a womanly shape, widening and narrowing, then widening again. The ribs have collapsed in such a way that they spread outwards, expansively. The skeleton offers a generous embrace.

How grand it will be, the priest imagines, how lovely it will be, to slip over the side—unseen, unheard—and swim down to the black shape and fall within its tender loving grip. The punt charges onward, and in the surge of his delirium, without stopping to think, he looks up towards the child and points down into the sea, offering to share with the boy the rapture of his thought.

But just then the child is distracted. He is looking away, to shore, towards clouds of gulls and gannets and puffins that shriek. There, a lovely sandy beach shelters snug between sharp cliffs. The boy's face is drawn and fearful. You would think that he too had seen a corpse.

By the time the priest turns back towards the water, the punt has passed beyond the wreck and the wreck is gone from his sight. In the span of a long breath the moment was started and it was finished.

The priest watches the wake of the punt draw across his vision a foamy white screen, in the way that he himself might draw the veil across the tabernacle. He feels a jealous, covetous anger: it is himself he is furious with, for he very nearly gave the wretched child a share in his dream.

Mr. Landrigan waves a trembling bony finger towards the rear wall of the kitchen. Little Kevin Barron sees a low door, an orifice really. It leads under the linney.

When they were climbing the meadow from the boat, while the nausea of the sea voyage was fading, Mr. Landrigan told them that he had been born in this very house. It is true: the place has a last-century look to it. He said it in such a wounded tone that you would think he felt cheated, as if, on the grounds of his birth therein, the house ought by rights to have kept its promise and for ever spared him any suffering.

Although it is his own home, the old man stands aside timidly, the way a stranger might do, and watches as the priest and the boy unfold their surplices and shake the starch from the linen and pull the vestments over their heads and tug them into shape. Kevin is pleased to see his fear: it gives the boy the fancy that he himself is already a priest. He lights the candle with a touch of vanity. As soon as Father MacMurrough is ready with the oil and the missal and the pyx, the priest nods towards the same door, signaling for Kevin to lead. But suddenly the boy himself is a little afraid, for never before has he done such a thing as this.

The child bends under the lintel and steps into the chamber. Once upon a time the tiny space may have served as a pantry. A square window, about the size of a confessional wicket, thickly curtained, admits a ration of light through the rear wall. The room is cold—Kevin can see his own breath—and the air is infested with a stale brown stench. The foulness infects the boy with a deep anxiety. He reminds himself: we are in God's hands. This is a holy time.

The bed emerges from the gloom. The pillow frames a

round object. The object brings to the child's mind, from a photograph he saw in the encyclopaedia, the shrivelled globe that the New Guinea cannibal clutched so lackadaisically by the topknot, like a coconut. In the way the sink in his kitchen sucks the water spiralling down, the object on the pillow drains all the boy's attention. During the boat journey, his head spun with a vertigo of disgust, revolted by the sea and by images of the ugly creatures that swim in it. The same kind of revulsion torments him here.

The sheet is pulled tight to the throat. The flesh of the face is brown and leathery. Blue veins web the forehead. The cheek is so lichened in moss, the cranium so wispy with smoky white hairs, the head could be mistaken for that of a man. The sunken eyes are half open and the irises are exposed, obscenely, as on corpses. Whether the eyes can see anything Kevin Barron cannot say.

He swells again with his glow of privilege, his pride at being in this place during this holy time, at being assembled with the priest, and with God Himself—the sunburst of the viaticum rests here on the washstand—even with death. Yet Kevin is certain that the room contains still another, a whispering being that is as tangible as the priest, as true as God, more terrible even than death.

He draws his stare away from the woman's head in order to survey the room. The floor bears the low double bed on which she lies, and the washstand, but nothing else. The posts of the birch bed are as thick as oarshafts and are daubed in ochre. The headboard is carved out with a twinned circular pattern, a pair of sunbursts. The washstand bears a backboard designed like Cupid's bow. A large brown crucifix is nailed to the wall.

Father MacMurrough falls to his knees and signals to Kevin that he should follow. The priest begins the prayers.

At the sound of Father MacMurrough's voice, the eyes on the pillow burst open. They grow wide and proceed to take in the whole room. Slowly they pass over the priest and then over the boy. The child must struggle within himself to keep from bolting. The throat bobs on the pillow. The lips part and then close mechanically, like those of a fish, but they make no sound. The eyes blink and focus finally on a point that is midway between the priest and the boy. The old woman sees something—something that they do not.

Although Kevin Barron has been to parlour wakes and gazed upon corpses, even kissed them, this is the first time he has watched a death. His fear subsides and again pride and vanity take its place. The priest intones solemn Latin verses that Kevin does not recognize. In the doorway behind, Mr. Landrigan cowers. Kevin has heard Pop talk about the devils and the angels that descend upon a death-bed and fight over the departing soul, the sounds of great armies marching and of drums beating, the lightning that flashes, even on a cloudless day, above the houses of the sick, the banshees wailing. But nothing pagan like that is happening here.

The woman is Mr. Landrigan's mother. He himself wears the dry withered skin of a man in his seventies, which means that she could well be a hundred years old—she may even have been born during the Famine.

The idea fascinates the boy. He gawks at he leathery face and he marvels, not so much at what she has seen, but at what she is about to know. The old woman is like a window, a pane of glass separating a century's worth of this world and the eternity of the next. If only he could look through the windowpane that she is. If only she would speak, and tell them what she glimpses on the other side of death.

Something stirs under the blanket. The boy is hypnotized: a small animal, a ferret or a muskrat perhaps, moves slowly from the vicinity of her abdomen up towards her neck. But what emerge into the light, above the top of the blanket, are only her hands. The fingers are purple, and twisted into enormous shapes resembling lobster claws. Frantically they push back the cover so that the old woman's chest is naked. Her breasts are shrivelled like empty balloons. They remind the boy of Pop's dickeybird, bared to the kitchen whenever they have to carry him, like a baby, to the enamel pail in the back porch.

The claws lift and reach for the priest's head and grab his face like pincers. Father MacMurrough does not flinch: Kevin is astonished to see this. The priest allows the claws to caress his cheeks. You would think he wanted this to happen. The old woman whispers. Her voice is so thin and rasping it draws the priest down, close to her dry lips. The boy can make no sense of the sandpapery hisses that vent out of her.

Now another sound fills the room, a low moan, muffled, as might issue from a creature that lives in the dungeons of the sea.

The moan is coming from the woman herself. It grows louder and rapidly turns into a cry, then a shriek. In panic her feet kick the blanket from the lapstone. The cover lifts and the horrible foetid stink slices the nostril membranes like a knife blade.

Calmly the priest brings one hand behind his back and gives the boy a shove, ordering him to quit the room.

Kevin Barron stumbles into the kitchen. Uncertain of what he ought to do, he stands in the middle of the floor and picks at a scab on his hand. Mr. Landrigan has already fled there. He moves about the spaces as if the boy were not present. He sweeps the faded canvas—he must do it while he can, for it is unlucky to sweep near a corpse—then shuffles from cupboard to table to woodbin to stove, arranging plates and cups and saucers, stoking the Rover and filling the kettle from the galvanized bucket and measuring tea into the pot, all with a resolve, as though simple tasks will make everything right, will drown the awful shrieks coming from the linney.

Through the open door they can hear the soothing murmur.

"This day, I promise you, I will be with you in . . ."

Gradually the shrieks become mere cries, then fade to moans.

Hissing noises startle the child. Mr. Landrigan has noticed him at last. The old man's eyes bulge like those of a snared rabbit. With a furtive, hooking gesture of his fingers, he beckons the boy to his side. The child obeys and crosses the kitchen. Mr. Landrigan leans above him and grips his wrist and smiles oddly. Kevin sees that he makes the noise by inhaling sharply through his shrivelled gums. When he exhales he breathes upon the boy the smell of stale tobacco. Mr. Landrigan whispers:

"Isn't death wonderful."

The boy has heard this utterance many times, at wakes and at funerals, and he is about to offer some sympathetic response, but abruptly his tongue is stopped. His attention is taken up by the table: the old man is setting only two places.

The child has a notion: why not ask him? The old man is bound to know. He has lived his whole life in this house. Surely he can say what it is that dwells within that tabernacle of a deathroom. What is the creature with claws, hidden from children like himself, the whispering beast more horrible even than death? But the boy does not have the nerve to ask.

The brown curtains flanking the windowpane swell with warm living sunshine. The light tells the boy that the day outside is filled with promise. Through the pane he catches sight of a gull flying past, but it travels so swiftly he cannot be sure that it was real.

Old Landrigan, without glancing up from his tea, jabs his bony forefinger in the direction of the out-of-doors. Through the kitchen window the priest spots the surplice gleaming in the sun.

The boy stands on the roof of a potato cellar. He stares into the earth—a motherless lamb dazed in its orphanage. Father MacMurrough is annoyed at the child for taking such pleasure in his misery. And a wise thing it was I sent him from the room. Had he witnessed what followed, he would have good reason to feel sorry for himself.

In hushed movements, as if he were in church, Father MacMurrough takes up his cane and his hat. He swings open the door and steps out onto the slate slab that serves as the front riser, and draws the door shut quietly behind him. He wonders: how many days or months or years has old Landrigan been doing that—having his tea across the table from an empty setting? And who is that vision opposite, to whom the old man whispers so tenderly? His mother? A wife? A child?

The priest will wait a decent interval until he—until they—have finished. Then he will go back inside and sort out what needs to be done. The old woman may last another day, maybe two.

The wind is falling generally. In the lee of the house the air is stagnant. Father MacMurrough discovers that he has been perspiring. His cassock draws the sun and sweat plasters the shirt against his skin. An icy trickle runs down the small of his back and he shivers in the heat.

Rich hot smells distend his nostrils. Bluebells bedded in an elongated crate bask under the eaves of the south wall. On a dilapidated table nearby a fat cod sprawls gutted. Its entrails spill across the long board like painted jellies. The knifeblade, bloodied and greasy with offal, sticks halfway

out of a sliced gill. The dead eye is cloudy. The old man must
have been at this when she cried out.

Father MacMurrough surveys the hamlet and confirms
what he has been told: Gelden itself is near death. No dogs
bark, no children shout. It would seem that every house but
this one has been jacked clear of its foundation and rolled on
logs down to the bench and floated off to a more sheltered
berth, to a less gaping harbour. People started shifting during the years following the tidal wave, whenever that was.
They even moved the cemetery. Judging by the vestiges of
jetties and flakes and by the rusty stains of mooring rings
pounded into the cliffs, and by the empty base of what appears to have been a stone house, Gelden once upon a time
was a thriving station. Little remains of that grand history
but overgrown lanes and sagging fences and naked concrete
rectangles with crude beachrock steps forlorn in front. The
priest feels that he has walked into a room where he had
hoped to meet friends, only to find, not only that they have
crept away and abandoned him, but that they have left behind their shoes, cruelly, so he will know what they have
done.

In this place you can't hear the Angelus bell. There is no
way to tell time. When his mother dies, Landrigan will be
alone among the vacant foundations, just himself and his
teacups and the wind howling in the nights. The priest shivers at the simple horror of it. The knifeblade, the one he has
carried inside him his life long, slices at his midsection.

The pathetic child has not moved a muscle. The priest
feels an urge to go and stand beside him.

He remembers that the boy is brother to that other lad,
the silent one who pokes the notebook through the grille.
What is his name? Blessed Peter of Luxembourg—that is
what he ought to call himself. Peter was so tormented by his
own sins that he wrote them down, constantly. But imagine,

in this day and age, keeping a shrive-book! It is like keeping an audit of God.

Nonchalantly the priest ambles past the henhouse and the sawhorse and the uncut wood stacked conically like a tepee, across the mud and the wet sawdust of the yard. He spears the tip of his blackthorn into the sod and pushes himself up the slope of the cellar.

When he himself was a child, he often fought his way to the top of knolls like this one to claim king of the castle. As he got older and stronger he loved to fight more and more. In fact, had his uncle not noticed this, not taught him the fists, he might well have fallen in with the Boys.

The mildewed odour of iced turnips wafts out of the cellar, and his child's mind fancies that a troll or a leprechaun or some sort of mad beast lives in the chill under his feet.

In Ferns, before he was old enough for school, he would stay awake in the nights listening to the shanachie, the itinerant who appeared out of the dusk with tales of the Sidhe. He grew up convinced that, behind everything you could see, there lurked something else you could not. It was his aim to give over the everyday life and learn this other world. When he was bad, his mother threatened to call down the faeries on him, but he only answered her back that he wanted to go off with them anyway. He vowed to run away with the travellers—and that, after a fashion, was what he did.

He could hardly have fled farther, and now, after decades of pig-littered chapels and makeshift altars and dark highland faces uplifted at Communion, what he remembers most vividly are words, the names of his village parishes: Dzong, Donggala, Ok Tedi, Susuwora, Wuruf. These were the names of monsters that lived in volcanoes, names echoing the piteous cries that might issue from their throats.

But after he had been in each parish only a short time, the

novelty of the village would fade. His soul would lapse into hollowness, into hunger. He would feel a need that he could never explain. All he knew was: I want. He feared he was turning into one of those pious people who do the Stations of the Cross over and over for no reason they can say. He began to shiver from chills that ran deeper than did even the fevers of malaria, and that were followed by sharp pains under his heart.

One day, he hiked alone into the razor-backed central cordillera. He stopped to rest on a stump. Without warning out of the bush stepped a band of Kukukuku. Squat Stone Age warriors dressed only in grass loin-skirts, with bones through the septum, clutching spears and war axes, they filed past him in silence. They looked clear through him, as if his pallid skin rendered him transparent. Mere seconds after their appearance they were gone. The bush had swallowed them again. Upon the air lingered the oddly pleasing stench of their war-paint of pig grease and soot. The priest shivered uncontrollably. At last he had got his wish—he had joined the other world, the invisible realm, the kingdom of bogymen and darbies.

That night he wrote to his superiors, complaining of the sun and the dengue. Hinting again of China, he asked to be transferred to some northern parish, some cooler post. Instead, they sent him to this country—this echo of Ireland, this reminder of everything he had fled in the first place.

On achieving the crest of the cellar Father MacMurrough enjoys a mild triumph, the tremor of a child's freedom, as when he used to swim naked in the Blackstairs brooks. This elevation provides a grand view of the meadow sweeping down, and at its base, the sea. *Solwara. Bik ʃi.* On three sides the field is bounded by a fence, on the bottom by the broad beach. *Shor.*

Landrigan's outboard rocks there atop the tide, alone, as

though awaiting the final days. It is half in, half out of the water, its nose drawn up on the shingle and its heels dragged just clear of the sea-clutches. The priest feels for the little boat, feels sorry for its in-between state, its wretched indecision. Even the eyes painted on the bow look sad.

The uptilted engine reminds him that they must return by way of that vessel—a pity for the queasy boy. The priest comes up and takes a position alongside the child. The linen of the boy's starched surplice crackles in the slight breeze. The child clenches his fists. Father MacMurrough wonders if he ought to offer some words of comfort, but all he can think to do is point his stick at the east and say, "Ireland."

The child lifts his eyes from the ground and his face forms a tight smile. Why, the boy imagines that I am here for his sake, to comfort him. Doubtless he imagines too that it was for his sake—to spare him a macabre sight—that I ordered him out of the sickroom. And doubtless the old woman herself, if she is sensible of anything, imagines that the simple gesture he made to her was for the consolation of her dying soul. Please God they are deceived, all of them.

The priest is surprised to notice a pair of white horses in the meadow. Earlier they were not there. The animals canter, circling one another, nuzzling. He fears they are about to couple—but no, they are only playing.

The people of the Arans believe that their horses gallop the floor of Galway Bay, to and fro among the islands. The priest pictures himself and the boy capturing these beasts and like gypsies riding them down the slope to the sea. They will hurtle the animals across the landwash and splash them into the water and along the ocean bottom. They will trot among the bleached bones scattered on the seabed—among the skulls and femurs and ribs of sailors shrouded and jettisoned, of drowned fishermen entangled in gear and dangling weirdly overhead, of unlucky sealers carried off by shifting

ice, of women and children who while searching the storm
for their lost men were themselves swept from the headlands
by pitiless waves, of shipwrecked thousands strewn among
the ribcages of their own vessels. The priest pictures himself
and the boy and the white horses passing unscathed through
this valley of death. They will leave it all behind them. They
will canter full across the ocean, and they will ride out of the
sea, joyously, somewhere on the wild coast of Kerry. . . .

He must be tired, to be thinking such notions.

The day is slowing down, the atmosphere getting loomy —
the big capes appear much closer than they really are. The
priest tries to trace the route the boat must take on their return passage. The cove is tucked behind one or another of
those headlands to the south, but the sun has started to fall,
and already the shadows slanting down from the cliffs confound the shoreline. Father MacMurrough cannot distin-
guish one jutting finger from the next. Among a half-dozen
lighthouses he fails to identify the one that he knows. He
sees no sign even of the iceberg — the brightest object in the
universe this day.

He panics: he is lost.

The ice-cellar emits a sharp draft. The chill grips him beneath the cassock. Desperately he searches the world for a
familiar marker, for a single sign that might give him some
bearing.

And there it is. All along it was in front of him, yet at the
farthest point visible. Straight off, eastward, nothing at all is
to be seen — no ship, no land, no ice, only the meeting of sky
and water. Lovingly the priest's eye traces the gently curving line, from cape to cape and all the way back again — the
familiar empty horizon.

Look, here she comes.

Nell, my dear, how are you getting on? I spies yourself

making the Stations, gate to gate to gate, so I says to my little pirate: Here she comes, pell-mell Nell. Tacking the road, herself and her eternal stroller. Storebound on the winds of gossip. By God I says, when she floats by this fence we'll waylay her for a chin-wag. We'll see what news she caught in her net. And if she got none, what odds—we'll get her to make some up.

A grand midsummer, isn't it? Tar-melting day. Puts into my mind the morning me and the mister trod the aisle. I can see that sky like it was yesterday. Yes, our summer is come. I notice the wind is falling off a touch. Plus the gulls is high. I allow we're in for a stroke of weather. Please God we gets an onshore breeze, bring his nibs in safe and sound.

That frigger, so far this day he never showed his face in the light, not the once. He must be gutfoundered by now—he went off without his morning mug-up. But I got no tears for him. Let me tell you, my dear: that man is no great shakes of a husband. Only uses the land for sleeping on. And I'm sure he's doing this for badness. Just trying to get a rise out of me. Pretending he's galooping around with some mink, over in the back of beyond. No, I'll tell you what he's really at: he's hauled up on a beach somewhere round the Head, having a boil-up and a feed of fresh mackerel and a fine laugh.

We're only just after getting back from the shop ourselves, me and this marauder. I was darting in for a stamp, to send off a letter to Ciss. I takes the chance to give Casey junior a small piece of my mind. That bloody snake, you know he's as tight as bark to a tree. If it's the long and hungry month of March and you got nary the stain of butterine left in your pantry and if the coal is down to the dust, still the stingy robber he'll charge you a dollar for a bag of flour that won't feed half your crew for a week. A bad crow from a bad egg, that's what that is. May he be drawn unto the bosom of his fathers. Him and his four-faced liar. But that wasn't what was on my mind. No, it was this. I says to him: Mr. Casey, you know it's a sin, selling drink to that poor old cripple just to make yourself a few measly coppers.

Well, the jellyfish, he pretends he never heard me. Just sticks his nose fast up his barometer. Not a minute before that, Johnny himself just about knocks me to the ground with the smell of rum. Staggering up off the beach and across the road and into the church. Now you tell me, Nell: whenever did you hear of that old pagan setting foot into a Christian place? You can imagine what salvation he's after in there: the redemption of the Mass wine. We was going to go in ourselves and say a Hail Mary, but I didn't want the child to witness. The whole church is stinking of him, I am sure. Isn't it terrible, and him a hero, too. Of course, some-one like me shouldn't be calling down someone like him, af-ter the wonderful thing he done. Such a pitiful creature, always by himself. It wouldn't be so bad if he was a regular tavern rat like the rest of them. They says the closest he ever got to a woman was his mother, and the Spracklins was so poor she kept him on the breast till he was five. You know, Nell, sometimes I think the whole place is full of lonesome souls wandering the roads. Like ghosts, looking for some-thing they don't know what.

Anyway, that ignorant shebeen-keeper, he answers me neither first nor last. Cute as a fox, you know. He only grunts like a toad and dodges on over to the window with his spyglass, like he's trying to change the subject, and he looks out the cove and he says, smile in his voice: By God, there's the Paraclete Himself, out for a stroll on the water. It was a line of smoke he was spying, coming over the top of the iceberg. Of course I says to myself: That must be my man, marooned like Robinson Crusoe, lighting a fire to call for help. But no, Casey says it was only a few of the lads, shagging around, that's all. Can you imagine? Idle buggers, you think they would have sense. Why, they might melt themselves right into the sea.

No doubt you heard Mike Landrigan come round the point fetching the priest. He was in the shop too, picking up his newspaper. He was asking after his dog—you know, that mongrel of Father Fran's. If you wants to know the truth, Father Fran should have took that savage to the grave with him. Now there was a specimen of Holy Orders. All breath and blood. Monsignor Conroy, he shouldn't be dead at all. A saint, God bless him, despite his faults. And such a grand wizard for doing the cures! Anyway, Casey says, straight-faced: Father, not to worry, that's one fine swimmer, that dog, why, that's the saviour of drowning men. And then he winks at me behind the priest's back. It's the truth: that stinky beast, it gobbles fish well enough but it can't paddle a stroke to save its own life. A wonder it never drowned already. Well anyway, all Father MacMurrough needs is to have a gander along the waterline and he'll find his cur quick enough. If that dirty thing wasn't as stunned as my arse I'd allow it was the Devil incarnate, all black and beady-eyed.

I suppose, when you lives in a big empty house and you got no one to talk to, you wants your dog at the very least. I think he was glad enough to chew the rag with us two-legged beasts. He was rattling on something fierce—you know I used to think he was as prune-faced as a bucket of pickles—he was rattling on about Joe This and Joe That. I can't understand such a sport, can you? Sticking two grown men in a cage and paying money to watch them smack each other in the gob. By God, it's all I can do to keep my lot from clawing one another's eyes out. He can come and cheer in my kitchen any time, for free. By the look of that snout of his, I'd say he's after taking a few knocks himself. Face on him like the back of an axe. But Nell, you know something queer: he don't smell like a priest. Priests has a sniff all their own. Father Fran had it. Even Joan Wade's boy smells of it, the one with the old man's face. But this priest, I tell you, he's as odd as the day is long.

Joan's boy it was who called him out of the shop. They grabbed the death kit and off like a shot they went, poor Mike leading the way. The old one must be after taking for the worst. I must remember to get a Mass card. If the grave is the price you pay for life, then that one did well out of the bargain — when my mother was a child, Galena was already tanned and seasoned. I suppose you heard about the day her husband took a stroke and passed away. She spent the afternoon scrubbing out the house, and as soon as she was satisfied it was decent she sent Mike tramping over the winter path to fetch Father Fran. And, my God almighty, wasn't she a sinner in her day! When Mike was a youngster and he backtalked to her, she used to bar him in the cellar for three days and three nights. Like Jesus in the tomb, she said. She put the fear of God into him and it never left him. They says she was a convert, you know. A flat-assed Methodist. But such a spiteful old bitch. Once upon a time people wouldn't think of dying in the summer — everyone was too busy to bury them — so I'm sure she is doing this on purpose. Anyhow, God bless her black soul. I pray she has a good death.

Such a sad journey for any priest. Taking passage to that boneyard of a place to anoint a skeleton of an old woman. So seldom does a priest set foot into a home without having to minister to the sick or the dying or the dead. Without having to deal with someone else's tears. I often says to myself, the next time I catches him coming along the road I must drag him in for a cup of tea.

My wee pirate here, he'll be into the fisticuffs before long, won't you, my sweet Sir Henry Mainwaring. Now, don't you be a trial to me. Have patience while I talks to Mrs. Pelly. Or she'll take you away and feed you to the strangers.

I see this bundle all toddled up in your pram is gone off to the sandman. Not a peep—that's the ticket. Proper place for the lot of them. I see you're swelling fast. When your day comes round, I'll be on my knees for you, Nell, no fear. Thank God you drifted safely past the . . . you know the dire number I mean. In that regard we had a close call with this lad. Yes, my love, your saint's day, it's a national holiday, and when you gets old enough to have sense you'll think every-one is getting drunk and making toasts to you. But Nell, this birthing business, it's only a misery and a torture, isn't it though? If the Lord was a woman we wouldn't have none of this pain. Thank God we're so busy at the fish nowadays we're sleeping back-on. No time for the work of nature. Sometimes I wishes I was a nun, and was all done with this family nonsense. Take my crew for instance. From this day forward no rest for the wicked. No sooner I give them their pork beans and 'lassy bread and tea and I wipe their faces and pick up the switch and lace them out the door like cows but they're back underfoot, demanding grub. Dawn to dusk. Not two hours off of school and into their summer and al-ready they got me poisoned. But you know, with me it's the same it is with you, I'm sure: they aggravates me till I screams, but I pines for them when they're out of sight.

And herself, the big lazy gawmone, no sooner she gets her matric than she's traipsing off on one of her mystery jaunts. Takes after her old man. Where she gets to only the Holy Ghost knows. They says you can't understand someone un-til they lives in the same house with you, but be damned if I can work her out. By rights I should be giving her a feed of my tongue, but today I suppose I will forgive her. All the maids is out trying for the fellow. Crawling over the rocks and hills, divining this way and that. My dear, you're as wise as I am to how she's making out. The sulk, she won't open her gob a word. And when that one shuts up like a clamshell you can be sure she got something she wants to say. Such a face she took with her you would think she was after seeing a vision. The sauce-box. But I suppose I shouldn't complain. She'll be up and gone out of my life before long, and then I'll miss the streel and all of her sloth.

Meantime, my arms is full enough with this privateer — yes, Peter Easton, you little buccaneer. Where did I get you at all? Soon you'll be marching away too, with your school-bag and pencil and scribbler. Then I'll have nobody to torment me. Be a good boy, and stop hiding your face like a crab.

Speaking of, well, last night, you know, I had my regular visit from the hag. Yes but wasn't I hag-rid in a dreadful manner! Let me tell you: something woke me in the middle of a good sleep. There was this big white cat in the room. Filled the whole wall. Then, a red spot starts up on the cat's chest. And a claw comes out of the red spot. And the chest opens up. And a giant crab crawls out and sits on top of me. This is no dream, mind: here I am wide awake, watching it happen in front of my eyes, but be frigged if I can move a muscle. Not a pinkie. So I says the Our Father, the wrong way round of course, and then and there the hag leapt off me and my senses come back. Afterwards, the room had a stink of burnt bacon. I can't imagine what brought it on. I suppose it's the month of June. Such a fright, I sat up in the bed, all a sweat. I had to get up and get out the cards and have a few rounds of two-deck eighteens.

Pardon my mouth, pouring on like a river. I ought to shut my gob: the fewer the words, the fewer the mistakes.

Nell dear, it's time I was off. I wants to turn that yaffle of fish one more time while we still got a patch of sun. And pick a feed of dandelions. They grows so fast nowadays you can hear them with your ears. The buttercups jumps up right in front of your eyes. And maybe we'll run down to the marsh and haul a few stalks of rhubarb. Rhubarb goes nice with a dose of kippers. Kippers will fix anything. Better than a dose of salts. Even better than the Rosary. And, good God, I must remember to hide the gate: the little fellows is roaming tonight. Plus I'll start on knitting some cuffs, and make up a marvel cake. Like I says, if you wants to flourish, you only got to work half a day—don't matter if it's the first twelve hours or the last. Then for their supper I'm putting on a feed of fish and brewis and duff and colcannon. Please God the capelin strikes in. It will be nice to have a few fish to drag down a slice of bread. But before I does anything else now I'll run aloft for a minute or two, have another gander out for my stray. That rogue, I'll scald his arse when he shows. I'll tell you that for free.

Now, Sir Alexander Clutterbuck, be a good lad and wave your bye-bye to aunt Nell. Else I'll give you to the faeries. I will too. Half the world is in with them already, don't you know.

Nell, my dear, get yourself along now and look after your man. After all, that's the only thing that matters in this world: having a man to watch out for. Nothing else is worth a damn.

Thunder-rolls roust Johnny the Light from his nap. The old man sits upright against the big cold slab. The dampness of the earth chills his thighs. A fine white dust falls like snow.

Hoarsely he calls towards the shadowy corners of the chamber: "Lads! You hear that? They're shooting off the g-g-guns for us!" His words echo straight back from walls that are somewhere in the dark.

He scrambles to his feet and locates his bottle and drinks. By now his eyes are awake to the dim, and there is no longer need for matches. Bending under the low ceiling he makes his way back to the ladder and climbs to the sacristy.

Johnny limps across to the Epistle-side door, holds his hand shading his brow, and scans the pews. The nave is empty. He shuffles out into the sanctuary and round to the front of the altar. He is about to step through the gate when abruptly the ranks of vacant pews billow before his eyes with crashing swells of sound, wave upon wave upon wave. From the height of the organ loft the thunder-rolls tumble down upon his head.

Johnny panics and flees. He hobbles to the Gospel side. He stumbles up against the wrought-iron cloister tucked in the corner like a rococo animal pen. He fumbles with the latch and slips inside the cloister and slams the metal door behind him. He clings to the baroque grillework and endures the roaring, suffocating fugue.

Inside the old man's head, fields of ice collide and explode, raftering pans fall back and pile atop one another, the fault line advances closer, louder, and threatens to bury him, to crush and suffocate and drown him, and his mates too, under tons of cold marble.

The music reaches a crescendo and abruptly it stops. The church reverberates to silence. In the new wide space that is there, Johnny can breathe again. Shaking, he takes a seat, gingerly, on the bench that runs the width of the cage.

He runs his hand over his head and discovers that he has lost his cap. He mutters a low curse.

Somewhere in the back of the church, pages are turned impatiently. Even Johnny can hear the snapping sounds. Meanwhile, down some corridor vaguely beyond the sacristy, a bell tinkles. Johnny bellows, the way he might do if he were out-of-doors and his friends were scattered miles afield, "There now, lads! You hear? 'Tis the b-b-bell!"

After his voice fades, the church endures a stern hush, the kind of quiet you might hear at the eye of an awful storm.

The scrape of a chair comes from the choir, then the bang

of a door, the stomp of footsteps down a wooden staircase. At the back of the church, a sullen black form steps into Johnny's field of vision. His eyes see a huge dark bird, a bird taller than he is himself.

With whispering steps, accompanied by a dry clacking sound which Johnny does not recognize, the beast glides up the main aisle.

From time to time the beast pauses. Its beak wrinkles and sniffs at the air. At the head of the aisle it stops a moment, intensely searching, listening, sniffing. It floats up the steps and opens the gate in the altar rail and passes into the sanctuary. It genuflects, then resumes its hunt. Somehow the bird hovers just above the carpet, for it makes no footfall that Johnny can detect. It sniffs its beak towards the very place where he hides.

Just before the creature reaches the cloister, the bell chimes again from behind the sacristy. The bird halts and listens. Johnny sees that the beast is equipped with a claw, and that the claw counts the chimes by way of great black beads—it is these that make the clacking sound. When the bell stops and the counting is done, the beast hisses through its teeth.

Decisively now it floats onward, past the cloister where Johnny hides, and through the Gospel-side door to the sacristy, and from there, through another door evidently, and— he can hear the angry footsteps fading—down a long, long passageway.

Johnny exhales with relief. Grimacing, he bends and removes his decayed boots. He examines his sockless feet, splayed at quarter to three. They are dirty and swollen. Tenderly, scarred fingers knead scarred toes.

He drinks and sets the bottle on the floor, safely out of harm's way. Yawning, he curls up on the little bench and resumes his interrupted sleep.

———

Half-heartedly Wish and Gus mumble:

> *Oh, we'll rant*
> *and we'll roar*
> *like true . . .*

But soon their voices peter away.

The sun slumps. The sea is calm, the air oddly warm. Wish and Gus settle back on their oilskin quilts. They unbutton shirts and expose chests to the light. Steam sizzles from their flesh. Limbs relax. Eyelids droop. Forelocks tumble over brows. Michael thinks: they are children again.

With dismay he watches his mates fade into sleep. He tries to push out of his head the tune they were singing. Longingly he gazes upon the rowboat. Perhaps he ought to climb down and jump aboard and push off and leave them here. But just now he finds that he himself has no energy—not enough even to enjoy the pleasure of the fantasy.

When he is sure they are asleep he pulls from within his clothes his book and the pencil that is moored to it by the string, and he writes. He returns the book to its place and he leans back and props his head against an ice-pillow. The sun grills his cheek like the touch of a heated coin. He remembers reading somewhere that mountain people worship the sun while seaside people worship the moon. Since he is on top of a sea-borne mountain, and since the moon is out with the sun, he is not sure what sort of worshipper he is. From somewhere or other comes the hum of the outboard, but his mind hears the sound of light.

Yellow dogs trail the sun. Pop would surely say that they are a sign of weather—but Michael is too drowsy to recall what sort of weather it might be. Although the winds have died, the high thin clouds continue to drift magically eastward. Against the peak's knife-edge Michael easily measures their hypnotic progress.

The coasting sky gives him the notion that it is not the clouds that travel, but the ice. The tide is at its height just now: perhaps the sea has finally lifted the berg clear off the ledge. Perhaps the berg sails, like a schooner, straight up the cove, straight to Admiral's Beach, where it will run aground again—and where, at long last, he will step ashore.

The black punt with the eyes whirrs round the point. Mary, startled, scurries out of sight behind the rocks.

Even though the vessel travels in the same direction as before, this time, spookily, not one but two men are aboard of it. Avoiding the sinkers it stays well offshore. The big arrowhead that the hull lays upon the calm aims the outboard straight and true for the wharf. When she can no longer hear the engine, when the gulls and gannets and baccalieu birds settle down, Mary reckons it is safe to step from her hiding-place.

Never has she seen a beach like this one: such a wide marsh of blazing sand! She kicks off her shoes and digs her feet deep and she scuffs to and fro, forcing the hot white grains to flow between her toes. If only Alice and Moira were here too, they could all three of them enjoy the pleasure of this.

Zigzagging, she leaves a dragon slinking in the sand after her, all the way down to where the beach is hard-packed and damp and littered with bony starfish. She walks into the sea until the water, which is uncommonly warm, washes her calves.

All her life she has heard stories about Gallows Beach. Aloud she announces: "Here I am at last," as though by saying it she confirms the fact. Before this moment the place was in her future and, what's more, it was only a small part of that future. But now the beach surrounds her—it is here in her present time, and it is not just a small part of her present time either, but the entire thing.

She studies the cliffs to guess where was the gibbet they used to hang the nun. Perhaps it was that gnarled spruce high up there—she pictures them slinging the cord over the trunk and pushing the madwoman into the abyss. She imagines the black form, suspended as by a glass thread from heaven, kicking and squirming in the sunshine.

She scans the waterline then, to guess where it was Johnny the Light spotted the mermaid. At that moment, the wash of the outboard drifts ashore—even, surely, at the same moment its other wing nudges the skirts of the berg—and the swell rises tingling the backs of her knees, and carries on and falls onto the beach, whispering some secret there.

"Here I am, and this is now." Mary speaks aloud.

Her toe treads on something hard. She puts her hand into the water and roots under the sand and pulls up a whore's egg. It is bigger than her fist, and strangely heavy. She turns it over and, sure enough, it grips to its belly a cluster of pebbles. Father used to tell her that when the spiny-skins take on ballast, look out for weather. But the water gives no sign of a groundswell, and the clouds are high and peaceful.

Mary recalls the mermaid in the book. She reaches behind and bunches her skirt and pulls it tight against her legs and watches her reflection in the mirror of the sea. Slowly she draws the skirt higher and bares her long legs to the daylight. Her legs form a kind of arrow: a path, a way.

Why not? she giggles inside her head.

Why not here? Why not now?

On the headland the lighthouse has a vacant look. The parish is a long ways in the other direction. Still, anyone with a spyglass might see. She can hear from somewhere over back the sound of woodsmen slicing logs with a bucksaw. Upon the water, other than the blackfish miles off, wheeling their slippery way across the calm, nothing moves.

Why should she not, here and now? She is a grown-up now, and she can give whatever she wants to give, in whatever way.

Mary wades ashore. Spinning like a ballerina, dusting her sticky feet with sand, she pirouettes giddy up the furnace slope. She travels until the bluffs serve to blinker from sight on either flank the lighthouse and the parish. In a spot well free of creeping shadows she plops herself down on the beach. The sand scalds her underthighs.

The tide is as high as it gets. The ice must be standing on its toes. When the tide falls, tonight, it will slam the full weight of the berg down upon the ledge. The smoke that lifted from behind the back of it, earlier, is no more: the blacksmith's job is finished. By Sunday no doubt the whole ice mountain will be vanished, but at this moment the spectacle before her is the hardest of diamonds, the most certain thing.

Directly facing the ice she sits.

When she reaches behind to undo the buttons she inhales the delicious coal smell that is in her hair. She reclines on the sand and the sand toasts the wings of her bared shoulders. The heat of the beach makes her think of something she read in the book—the masculine sun penetrating the feminine earth. Her two hands reach down together and slowly they draw higher the hem of her skirt. She enjoys the pleasure of the masculine sun warming, gradually, inch by inch, her long slender legs.

With magical quickness she makes it happen. While the last sparks cascade she sees, through half-closed eyes, perched on the summit of the iceberg with hoofs planted, with head high towards the horizon, a black centaur.

Then it is over, and she is pleased, and her eyes fall shut, and she sleeps.

XIII

High Tide

The eight-day grandfather tick-tocks.

The hands say three o'clock.

The gaze of the crucified Christ falls upon the drowsy Waterloo. Cooling, the cast iron pings. Embers snap inside the firebox. The poker rests on the oven door. The nursing rocker is drawn up close to the stove. The teapot and the squat black kettle and the sad-iron, fallen over, nap atop the damper.

The holy gaze falls upon the splits and chunks and the bucket of coal waiting behind the stove, upon the worn canvas, the nodding wellingtons, the new broom, the galvanized gully, the sooty kerosene lamp and the bare lightbulb, the radio tall and brown and snoozing, the whatnot in the corner, the barometer, falling, the stitched "God Bless Our Home", the Doyle's calendar June 1947, the yellow teeth in the yellow mug, the sailcloth couch and the cushions in repose, the Dodd's almanac, the missals and the harmonica on the sideboard, the table leaning against the window, the schoolbooks strewn about on the birch chairs, the checkered oilcloth, the deck of cards on top of it, the molasses bowl and milk jug and biscuit box and butter dish and jamjar, the heel-ends on the bread plate, the raspberry syrup, the dirtied cups and saucers and knives and forks and spoons, on the wall the sunflowers blazing silently, the tomcat sleeping atop the unfinished knitting, its fur flattened against the windowglass.

The Christ gazes down on all of these things, and sanctifies them.

The grandfather tick-tocks.

The tide is high.

It is three o'clock.

XIV

Watch

A litter of gull feathers and tinted petals of smashed glass decorates the scree slope.

Approaching the crown Mary pulls herself hand over hand until, hot-faced, sweat cooling her forehead, she scrambles up the final stretch and achieves the sod platform that tops the Head. She steps warily round stingers that reek of Johnny the Light. Fearful the old man has returned, she tries to hold her hard breath while she brushes the dust from her skirt.

The calm presses on her brain like an iron cap.

She finds that the tower up close is hardly the gleaming pillar she has known all her life from the distance of her bedroom. It is a coarse squat shed, its four windowless, triangular sides tapering to a peak. Storms have ripped away shingles and left the walls bruised, as if the structure had been badly beaten in a scrap.

The lantern stares from the summit and inspects the girl with its baleful eye—the eye of God. Mary feels the mild thrill of exposure. She recalls the pleasure of that childhood afternoon when, alone in the church, she slid over the altar rail and then, under the gaze of the Christ, she stood frozen, a statue, on the soft rug of the chancel, in the sacred place where females are taboo.

Mary follows the path round to the west face of the building. A mean low entrance leads into the body of the lighthouse. Alongside the door, which is shut, a wooden ladder presses against the shingles. The ladder climbs towards the lamp.

Under the blazing sun Mary imagines, fleetingly, not the lamp atop the pillar, not that at all, but instead the shape of the woman—the woman sitting in her chair, on top of the roof, waiting.

The vision alarms the girl. She retreats a step. Whatever may happen, she thinks, I want never to be like that one. Never.

She looks towards the iceberg. But then, then of course—her mind races—this is hardly the same, is it? Although still Mary sees no sign of the punt, she says to herself: At any moment that little vessel might appear. Especially if I can get a little higher, can get a better outlook. The red rowboat may really swing into view. There is hope yet. No, this and that, the two are not the same at all.

Mary grips the ladder and swiftly ascends to the light.

"Aha, me boys."

Johnny the Light opens the door upon a long narrow hallway. The corridor, bare of furniture, is flanked by rows of windows, but the shades are pulled and the light is dim. At the far end of the hall, another door bars the way. Chimes ring somewhere beyond that. Johnny tallies seven bells.

The old man turns towards the vacant sacristy behind him and he smiles and croaks, "Pick it up now. M-M-Move sharp, lads. Go to the bells." He hesitates, as if for others to pass through, then steps into the corridor and draws the door shut after him. He shuffles down the hall. His logans scuff the varnished mahogany.

At the second door he presses his good ear against the wood, but he hears no sounds. Cheerfully he wheezes,

"Keep up, lads. H-H-Hurry on!" He pulls the wine from his pocket and drinks. He doesn't bother replacing the bottle, but clings to the neck of it even while his fingers fumble at the knob and he pushes wide the door.

Before him a large square room takes shape. The space is thickly settled with dark cabinets and dressers and tables. High candles flicker against the walls and ceiling, so that the room whirrs with a pale light. A half-dozen doors lead to other places, and one, facing him, stands ajar. Through this door shines an area bright with real sunshine. Johnny's nostrils flare against the dry smell of chalk.

"Irene! Sister Irene!"

The same gaunt bird-creature that stalked him in the sanctuary floats abruptly across the far gap. It bears on its wing a bundle that might be a brin bag. The creature fails to notice Johnny, but its passage leaves on his retina a fading negative of its image, so that long after it has gone he can still see its shadow against the bright wall.

He steps inside the candlelit room. From somewhere behind the doors came stirrings of prayer. A movement at his left makes him jump and clutch at his chest.

He goes up and strokes the glass. His dirty hand leaves a smudge. His mind is only vaguely sensible that the aged, bent figure, the scarred face, the bald head before him are his own.

The railing and the narrow landing are splattered with gull droppings. The lamp smells of kerosene.

The lantern resembles a block of ice. Its face is sculpted in zigzag tattoo. Mary marvels at the crystal. It is only half the size of herself, yet it is the source of the great shafts of light that carve up the nights for miles around, that touch her entire world and every person who lives in it.

From this station she can spy more of the earth than she

has ever seen. She pinches her thumbs and forefingers together to form her play-binoculars and presses them around her eyes. Slowly she rotates.

The sea devours half the horizon. Anxious clouds hover well offshore. The sky is drained and blue. A gull advances at altitude—all the way from Ireland, she fancies. The bird bypasses the lighthouse and flies straight up the groin of the cove. Mary tracks the creature until it fades to a dot and disappears into the west. It is making for the Gaff Topsails. Gulls heading inland: now there's a token of weather.

Somewhere miles up in that region runs the track. Streak of rust, the woman calls it. Mary reckons that if she waits here long enough she may even spot the train passing through. She has never seen it, although often enough she has heard the sad sound that it makes, in the nights.

Mary brings her binoculars back to the shoreline and finds Gallows Beach. In the past the beach was in her future, but here in the present that bit of her future is in her past—all that thinking addles her mind. She traces in reverse the route she took today, up from the beach to the tail of the path straggling down off the wilderness, to the road skirting the graveyard, to the forge and the church and her home. The buildings look like dollhouses.

Crowning the ridge, the lookout, which is a monstrous boulder when you stand on top of it, appears to be but a grain of sand. The Goat Shore down the north slope of the ridge stretches as wide and empty as the sea itself. It fails to offer so much as a house or a tilt, even a fence. Far up the coast looms Fogo Cape. In the sea between here and there, Mary has heard tell, rest the corpses of so many vessels: *Stella Maris*, and *Rover*, and *Saint Christopher*, and *Waterloo*, and the foreign-going *Hogueras*, and *Maid of Avalon*, and *Comfort*, and two different boats each called *Rainbow*. Around the bend somewhere, hidden in the cliffs near a place called Motion, are the coastal defence batteries from the war, and somewhere beyond those, Heart's Content and the old cable that runs out of it.

Mary remembers when the war was on, the day the American flying boat came down — *Dixie* it was called — and parked on top of the cove. She wishes she could take a ride in an aeroplane. She even wishes she had one of her very own. She would fly away to far-off places, where she would meet all sorts of strangers: brown people and black people and yellow people. She would fly the machine to the ends of the world.

At the base of the slope, just here below the lighthouse, the sea-tongue licks the tip of the land. The beacon's stubby shadow extends northwards across the water. There she is — herself, in silhouette, at the very crown of the shadow. She waves, and her shadow waves back. Her gesture seems to stir the ocean, for mild skitterings dart about the calm.

Mary crosses her arms and grips her own shoulders. The starkness of this headland — that is what brings on the shivers. You would think the sheltering hollow of the cove had been pulled inside out, like the pelt of a skinned rabbit, its nerve endings stripped and raw and bloody. Could that be the way old man Johnny feels every morning when he steps out of his shack, here at the edge of nothing? Today the ocean is so empty that it fails to offer any hint of the day of the week, or of the year, or even of the age that Mary lives in. Imagine it: living on the open sea. Imagine the life of a fisherman.

She remembers why she came up here. She turns full around to face the ice.

On all sides of it she scours the sea, but there is no sign of the rowboat. The berg presents a fresh profile now. Perhaps that is only because of her new bearings, here at the end of the point. But she wonders whether instead the ice may have

shifted on the rising tide, may have spun round, may even
quietly have overturned.

A clock strikes, once. The sound startles the old man. The
sound is close, here within this candlelit room. In the far corner hides a decrepit grandfather. Johnny shuffles across to
the clock. The minute hand is missing, and the hour hand
points to just past three.

He drinks.

When he lowers the bottle he realizes that a tiny old
woman stands at his elbow. She fills an open doorway and
stares at him blankly. She wears a pale nightdress. Her face
is bleached like flour, and her white hair is clipped flat to her
skull. Johnny can see behind her a chair and a bed and, on
the wall above the bed, a crucifix. The curtains are drawn
shut. While the old man, rattled, backs away, the woman
shuts the door firmly and dismissively.

Johnny gropes to the door that stands open and finds himself in a vast kitchen. The light falls so brilliantly through the
windows that he must, like a man emerging from a cave,
bring up his hand to shade his eyes. Pots and saucepans and
kettles bubble merrily on top of a stove so broad it sports
a dozen dampers. The scene is like a ship's galley, only far
roomier. He breathes the warm smells. His stomach twists
with hunger. He adopts a station in the middle of the floor
and places one foot in front of the other and he sways.

Rustling sounds come from in back of the stove. The
crude pine door is latched shut. Johnny lifts the latch. A
large closet, a room really, is stacked with oatmeal and
honey and jam and such things. From underneath a table
comes the rattle of newspaper.

"You must understand what I am saying to you . . ."

The angry voice, drawing near, confusedly mingles with
another's sobbing.

Sitting on its back in a cardboard box, a cat licks between its hind legs. One of the legs is a stump. The creature tries to scratch itself with its missing limb, but the stump waves uselessly in the air. A litter of sightless kittens clutch at the cat's teats. The shadow of Johnny's stooped figure falls upon the animal and the animal stares him straight in the face, then hisses viciously and swipes a claw towards his eyes.

". . . Irene, my child: obedience is the rule."

Despite the spitting cat, Johnny slips into the pantry. He pulls the door almost shut and he watches, through the gap, two bird-figures float briskly across the kitchen and straight for the place where he is.

Mary lifts the latch and opens the door just a crack. The hinge scrapes and the noise makes her pulse race. The interior is pitch-dark. Boldly she pushes the door ajar and straddles the threshold. The heavy smell of Johnny the Light makes her catch her breath. Unmindful of soiling her dress, she steps in.

The floor, sunk deep into the bedrock, and the ceiling of rough planks, so low that the girl must bend, conspire to give the chamber the air of a snug cellar. If only Alice and Moira were along, why, the three of them could play a cozy game of house.

In the corner, outspread on the bare rock, lie a tattered mattress and a scattering of mildewed blankets. Clusters of rum bottles, empty, slump tally-fashion in a ragged line against the baseboard. The light that pours through the open door filters through the bottles dully, and speckles the chamber in shades of brown.

The sunshine highlights a patch of blue. It is a wooden box the size of a cigarette pack, of the sort that wedding rings come in. It rests on a crude shelf seemingly purpose-built. Mary picks up the box and tries to prise it open, but the lid is stuck shut. She shakes the box: something rattles. Clearly, the object inside is heavier than any ring, heavier even than the two-dollar gold coin that Casey once showed off. Even though she is dying of curiosity, Mary returns the box to its place.

Against the south wall slouches a melancholy stove. The grille says Maid of Avalon. A poker, a kettle, and a dirty saucepan crowd close atop its one damper. A huge kerosene lantern swings from the rafter. Near the door rests a galvanized bucket with fresh water at low tide. The dilapidated table is strewn with a half-eaten loaf of baker's bread, Purity jam, sugar, a can of Carnation, teabags, a tin cup but no saucer, a plate, and a twisted pewter spoon. The flour-barrel chair is pushed up to the table. Mary looks about for other seating, but finds none.

The ammoniac air brings forth in Mary's head an image of the old man sitting in the chair, his back to the door. The room contains no mirror, no picture, no book or newspaper. It contains not even a deck of cards to help him pass the time with a game of treasure trove or grandfather's clock or stalactities or watch—but of course, how could Johnny manage cards anyway? Instead, in Mary's vision, painstakingly, using his fingerstump rather than the knife that he does not seem to have, the old man spreads jam on a slice of bread. He fishes the teabag from his mug and pours the milk and spoons in the sugar. Clumsily he stirs. He takes a bite of his bread and a sip of his tea. That is all Mary sees: she cannot imagine more.

Outside, something brushes against the shingles.

It is only the wind, soughing in the grass. The sound is a lazy one: it makes Mary yawn. She would love to lie down here on Johnny's mattress, to rest for just a little while.

But no: it is time for her to leave.

She steps over the threshold and she is about to pull the

door shut when her conscience stops her. She hurries back inside and lifts the blue box from its shelf. She sets it, instead, in the middle of the table, next to the bread. Only then, quietly, as if fearful of disturbing a sleeper, does she latch the door behind her. Shading her eyes against the sudden bright light, she shivers at the chill of the rising breeze.

"Shank's mare, that's the article," the priest declared to Mr. Landrigan. "That's the thing for a lad."

When the priest was himself a lad, in Ireland, he went on to say, in a jovial voice hitherto unknown to little Kevin Barron, he had been a great one for the rambling. Mr. Landrigan gave Kevin two pieces of bread, one for himself and one for the faeries, and poured Kevin a cup of tea—to keep body and soul together until the boy made it safely home. For that, Kevin was thankful. Even though the wind had died and the water was still, he was thankful too for being absolved from another journey across the sea and the monsters that swim in it.

The blazing sun warms the child's brow pleasingly. The land is firm and the going is easy, and soon he leaves behind the last of the gaping foundations. The path cuts diagonally across a high grass garden, and then it follows, on his left, the top of a curving bluff that slopes sharply down to the waterline. The air vibrates with bees and summer crickets. The outboard is long gone down the Goat Shore, and although the V of its wake has faded and the boat itself by now has pulled round the Head, the cry of its engine persists inside the boy's brain.

He stops to look back. The Fogo soars menacingly and gives the illusion of being only a short ways up the coast—a loom like that is a sign of dirt coming. Out at sea the wind is already blowing, for the high clouds present a texture that looks like kneaded dough. An aeroplane with four propellers inches towards the west, but the craft is too high for its engines to make a noise. Already Gelden is out of sight under the curve of the meadow. Other than the old woman who is dying, for miles in every direction the child may be the only soul.

Little Kevin Barron reckons that never in his life has he been this alone. The notion does not alarm him. On the contrary, he thrills at the thought: right now he can do anything he wants to do. He can yell bad words at the top of his lungs, and no one will hear. He can take off his clothes and run through the bushes naked like an Indian, and no one will see. Only, of course—God will hear, and God will see. But God need not worry. Kevin Barron is not one to commit any such sins.

He picks up a flat piece of iron ore and studies it for fossils. The boy imagines that rocks are alive with the prehistoric creatures embedded inside them. He takes a running start to the edge of the bluff and hurls the stone in a tall arc towards the sea. He is trying to make the stone punch down sharp with a deadman's bubble, but it falls short of the water and clatters among the storm-boulders. If Mikey was here, Mikey would have done it, easy.

A black stench brushes the boy's nostrils. Splayed grotesquely across a ledge below, a white sheep, a lamb with a blue mark, lies glassy-eyed. It has been disembowelled in the fall and its entrails hum with bluebottle flies. Dreamily the child gazes down upon the carcass. He wonders how it died. It was not the work of faeries, that's for sure, because faeries have no power over sheep. That is on account of Our Lord, the Lamb of God.

A short ways farther along, the boy finds that the bluff is ideal for foundering rocks. He kicks at the loose shale until he dislodges great lumps of stone, some bigger than himself, and sends them crashing down onto the scree slope, where they kindle avalanches that slide all the way to the shore. The boy loves foundering rocks, and he wishes he were carrying his beloved hammer and chisel. He would stay here in this place for the rest of the day and chip away at the earth, just for the pleasure of it.

The uproar of his mischief startles from the embankment a herd of baccalieu birds. Sometimes baccalieu birds will discourage an intruder with their vomit, but this bunch only flutter scrambling out of their nests and whirr off clumsily and sail downhill and squirt neatly into the sea. Miraculously then, they transmute into fish. They swim, as smart as tomcods, just below the surface, in every direction from the water-rings that they leave like ghosts.

The ripples evaporate and the afternoon fills with space. The sun blazes. Kevin Barron flips his arms and makes a whirring sound with his tongue, and gallops along the sod bluff.

His progress is stopped by a brook. The stream rattles over boulders and flings up a mist that is flavoured of bake-apples, then shoots down the throat of a gully to the beach. Beyond the brook, the path turns right and abandons the shoreline. A good distance inland, Kevin can see, it snakes through a grove of tall spruce that cluster close like a gang, then rises wiggling across the breast of the ridge, elbowing its way among the dwarf trees and the widely spaced starrigens.

The winter path. That is the way Kevin will go.

Never has he walked this end of the famous track. Once last summer, playing Indians by himself, he wandered with his bow and arrow up the parish side of the ridge, and even climbed the lookout. There it is now: the tremendous boulder, silhouetted against the sky. It looks different viewed from this angle—it looks inside out. Once he achieves that rock Kevin Barron will overspy the cove, and he will be as good as home.

Between here and the lookout lies the broad wilderness. The only sign that any human foot ever crossed the wilderness is the winding signature of the path itself. Stay aboard the track and you're safe enough, Pop warned him once, but you leave it, my boy, and you risk bestirring all sorts of evils. Kevin doesn't mind — he prefers by far the vague risks of the winter path to the certain monsters of the sea.

By way of stepping-stones and a tread pole he spraddles a steady patch of the brook. He launches forth up the path. The path follows the stream uphill, past chutes and rattles, until the stream settles and dissolves into a bog. The track makes a wide loop along the firm land that rims the marsh. The sun roars and the child perspires. Mosquitoes and black flies buzz before his eyes.

In the middle of the bog, among the hummocks, a red pointed shape flashes like the tip of a faded candle-flame.

Could it be?

Kevin stares hard at the red barb. Despite the calm, it stirs weirdly: yes, it could be. The child's heart races.

It could be a faery cap.

Kevin Barron's first notion is to flee, to run up the path, up the ridge to the lookout, and from there to home, to safety. Misfortune befalls anyone who violates the terrain of the Boys. Everybody knows that. What's more, this is June, the month when the Amadahn gives the touch. The touch is hardly some old biddy's superstition. It is real — just look at Johnny the Light. Anne Marie Reilly says that when Johnny was a normal youngster the faeries kidnapped him away, and they brought him back in the shape of an ugly man with a stutter. Yes, the faeries are true and they are bad. Pop claims the grass is full of them — who else makes all those little trails? And Pop knows. Once when he was a lad he stumbled upon a band of them playing checkers on a tree stump and, thinking fast, he sat himself right down and joined in, and won, and so saved his soul. That's what he says.

The woods must be alive with them. This minute they

probably have got Kevin Barron surrounded. Clearly, one of them is trying to lure him into the bog, where the rest will beset him and tie him up and bear him off. He makes a circle with his finger and thumb and looks through, but he sees nothing different about the world. If only he was midnight-born and blessed with the second sight! If only he was in mortal sin! — dark souls can see the other world. But as soon as he wishes that, he worries it was a mortal sin to wish such a terrible thing.

Easily he could flee, but his legs fail to run. Instead, against his will he leaves the path. Treading carefully so as not to stop his school boots, he steps into the deadly marsh and crosses to the hummocks.

The barb is only the red tip of a pitcher plant. That's all it is.

Mudsucker is what some people call the pitcher plant. If you are careless where you put your foot, the creature that lives in the soft wet places below will reach up and suck you down. Cautiously, the boy approaches and bends over the bowl and inspects the carcasses of flies and insects and mosquitoes floating in the rainwater and saliva. Not mudsucker, or Indian cup, but *Sarracenia purpurea,* said the big book this morning. Queen Victoria put the plant on the tail of the penny. It lives only in the bleakest soil, and so must be carnivorous to survive.

But up close Kevin can see something that the book did not show: the swollen purplish lips that form the rim of the bowl. The lips curve gently round the chamber and meet delicately at the tip. The boy remembers how a similar curving shape, that of his own hands joined loosely in prayer, so disturbed him during the Rosary.

The sun scorches his neck. Kevin Barron feels uneasy. Eyes are spying on him again. He hears a muttering, scratching sound. No doubt about it: some new creature occupies the world today, and it follows him, watching, whispering, haunting.

He smells a pungent, sticky smell. Here in the middle of this bog Kevin Barron is helpless, just as helpless as he was that time he got stranded on the growler, when, but for Mikey hearing his screams and leaping into the punt and rowing frantically to rescue him, he might have been driven out to sea.

Kevin darts his head around suddenly, and his brain spins and the whole of the marsh swirls with light.

It is only the tree, that big snotty var there beyond the marsh. With all those turpentine bladders, downwind you can smell a snotty var well before you see it. There must be a breeze stirring.

Kevin Barron picks his way back to dry ground and continues up the slope. Mosquitoes and black flies bite. His way is littered maddeningly with dead branches and exposed roots, but then it crosses smooth bedrock where the walking is easier, and after that a region of scrub strewn with alders. The child's tread raises a robin. The bird thrashes out of a bush and flutters under a thicket nearby.

The boy knows that the bird is trying to lure him from its nest. Sure enough, after a probe of the undergrowth he uncovers a rough circular bed of twigs and straw.

The nest shelters snugly six eggs the same pale blue as the Virgin's veil. Each egg is the size and shape of the candies you can buy four a penny at Mr. Casey's, so it looks as though some child has concealed them here. Kevin reaches in and grips one between his forefinger and thumb and lifts it free. It is warm, and feels so fragile he fears he might crush it without even trying. Were he to crack the shell, what would tumble into his palm? Would it be wet and sticky? Or dry and furry? He fights the urge to carry the egg away, the urge to bring it home and hide it under his pillow.

The egg does not belong to him, and anyway he is not one of those bad boys who steal eggs. Some of them even build false nests to trick other people's hens into laying. Carefully, he returns the egg to its home.

Nearby, alders rustle vigorously. Surely it isn't the mother robin making such a racket. Whatever the creature is, it is bigger than a bird. Maybe it is a fox. Kevin squints through the undergrowth. Pop says fox prints are painted, so it's no trouble to tell whether the animal that is tracking you is black or red or white. Occasionally they will show themselves, as robins do, as faeries do too, and try to lead you astray.

Pop was faery-led once, for miles and still more miles. If only Kevin had thought to hang an iron nail round his neck, or to turn his clothes back-foremost, surely that would keep them from steering him abroad. He sets down in the middle of the path the faery bun that Mr. Landrigan gave to him.

The path takes the boy straight into the spruce grove. The air within is cool and fresh, and here and there so cold he actually shivers. The boy thinks: There's the Devil. But he knows it is only a patch of summer snow, an old man's whisker, lingering deep in the undergrowth. He thinks too of glaciers, of how the solid ice can become covered in dust so thick that vegetation, even a forest, might grow. Meanwhile, the ice underneath continues to melt. Sooner or later, the landscape simply collapses. That is the sort of place where anything can happen.

The trail winds crazily, then narrows so that he must place one foot over the other, like a tightrope walker. Kevin turns a corner and is surprised to find his way barred by a wire fence.

The path runs so boldly through the fence that you would think the obstruction was a mirage. From the meadow below he saw no sign of this barrier. In both directions the fence loses itself among the big trees. It seems pointless, for it doesn't appear to enclose anything at all.

The child places his palms on the longer-pole and braces his boot in the wire. He wishes he could jump as cleanly as Mikey—Mikey can hop fences on his fingertips. Kevin is about to give himself a lift and a heave when from somewhere behind him comes a liquid noise, a hiss and a splash and a trickle.

The first thing that comes into the boy's mind is the old witch Martha. One dusk during Lent he was passing her shack, hurrying to serve at Benediction, when he heard the same noise, and there she was: squatting in her doorway—no, actually settling her haunches on the step—her skirts hiked, and a thick horse-like stream flowing from deep in the shadows between her legs and splashing so heavily on the road that it stirred the dust. (He wonders why girls pee the way they do, squatting. He wonders why Johnny the Light squats, even though he isn't a girl. Kevin often wishes he had at least one sister so that he would know these things.) She grinned up at him and showed not a tooth. As usual when he is afraid, Kevin Barron pretended to have seen nothing, and just carried on to the church.

But surely it can't be that old crone, not way out here in the back of beyond. No, it must be the bad boys—the big boys with warts and blackened fingernails and scabs and snotty noses and cold sores and dark smelly breath. That's who it is, for sure, three or four of them at least, peeing all at once, facing one another in a circle. They're playing a game with Kevin Barron. They are off school for the summer, and they would like nothing better than to badger him and tease him, in a place far from the protection of the nuns.

Kevin Barron resolves: he will not turn around. He will not look. He will deny them the satisfaction. He will not play the game they have in mind for him. He will pretend that whoever is there is not there at all. This after all is his refuge whenever the bad boys vex him: he makes out that nothing is happening. Sometimes it works. Sometimes they give up and drift away and hunt for another child to torment.

The trouble is, the watery sounds make him want to pee too.

He hears a throat hawk, a rough spit—that is what the big boys do when they are zipping their flies. Now they are free to come after him.

Trembling loose from his paralysis, he catapults his little body over the fence. His boot tangles in the wire and on the far side he stumbles face-first to the sod. He wrenches himself loose from the wire and scrambles to his feet. Stifling his laboured breathing, he proceeds up the track as casually as he can manage.

The lookout boulder is lost under the curve of the ridge. He prays that he will choose the right path.

In this zone the track is a dry streambed, and although the way is steep his passage is smooth over bare rocks and, here and there, pools of sun-dried sand. The child is drenched in sweat. His hair is damp and his cowlick falls into his eyes. The mosquitoes and flies devour him. He slaps and rubs and scratches fiercely. He takes only a dozen strides before he hears the barking of the fenceposts, then the footfalls.

With relief he detects the sounds of a single pair of feet. They are heavily shod, with logans, or wellingtons, or gaiters, he cannot say which. Although the steps keep pace with his, still the boy offers no sign of being aware of them. If he wants to keep up the show that no one is behind him, that nothing is taking place, he can hardly turn and look. He can hardly break into a run and try to escape.

The streambed withers to another network of rabbit paths. Still nothing has happened, and the child asks himself: Is this one of the malicious boys after all? If it was one of the tormenters he knows so well, surely by this time he would have started in. By this time he would have grabbed Kevin Barron and wrestled him with his dirty hands or pinched him or pulled his hair or punched him between the legs or done something to aggravate him, to make him bawl.

Abruptly the footsteps go silent.

He is playing a trick, whoever he is. He is halted on the trail, staring at the small of Kevin's back, grinning, daring the boy to turn, to look. Without slackening his pace the child sets his sights on the line of the ridge, and he climbs.

The starrigens lean away from his approach as though to give him room. He travels fast. His flesh sweats, his heart races. A hot sweetness wets his lower lip: his nose is bleeding. He sniffles back the flow but his nostril is gorged on the blood. He watches the bushes for cobwebs to stanch it. The blood falls in wide splashes onto the path and, rather than let his pursuer see that, he attempts to collect the drops on his outstretched tongue.

The footfalls start again, and at a faster pace. They hurry to catch him up. Kevin thinks: Perhaps it is Johnny the Light. The old man likes to roam over the ridge just to pass the time of day. Everyone knows that. But then again, Johnny is all crit over, and he walks with a slow gimp.

The path widens across a patch of easy sod. In trying so hard to make his stride look unhurried and natural, the boy stumbles. He prays the other didn't notice. The flies are driving the child half mad. His flesh burns.

It could be a stranger. Other than the new priest, Kevin Barron has never in his life spoken to a stranger. It might even be a stranger with a gun. That afternoon last summer, when he was on his way down the ridge, he spotted a figure standing off at a great distance. It wielded tucked under the elbow a stick that was shaped like an old musket. The next time Kevin looked, the figure had vanished into the trees.

Kevin wishes he had a gun under his arm, Pop's 12-gauge for example. He wouldn't even want shells in it. Over back, a gun doesn't have to be loaded for it to be useful. It's enough that it gives you a reason for being where you are. If Kevin happened to meet someone, he could call out airily, the way Pop used to do: Grand day for a bird! In fact he would be happy just to have his bow and arrow, the set he made all by himself out of the alders and the codline and chicken feathers, and the bottle caps for arrowheads. At least then he could make out he was playing Indians.

A branch tugs at the child's sleeve and he leaps with fright. Desperately he yearns to run, but he forces himself to keep to his pace. If only some hallowed window, some doorway, some sacred portal would materialize before him, he could just march through it and everything beyond would be holy and good and safe.

It is true: the footsteps are catching up. The soles thump against the hard-packed ground. Could it be a pirate? Everyone knows that a society of Masterless Men hides up the country, giants every one of them. Once upon a time they used to be sea-pirates, and for trophies they liked to slice the ears off their enemies. He pictures a fat red-bearded buccaneer balancing a gigantic spade on his shoulder and searching for his lost gold. After all, midsummer is the time of year when treasures lie open on the ground, in remote places, just waiting for someone to happen upon them. If pirates are about, they say, you will hear on the wind the sound of fiddle music. Kevin listens, but he hears only the stomp stomp stomp of the big boots.

Just then, inexplicably, the tread grows lighter. Perhaps his pursuer has kicked off his boots. Kevin tries to remember whether John the Baptist wears anything on his feet. He fancies that the saint himself is here in his company, unshod, clad in animal hides, bearing in his arms a bleating Lamb. Or maybe the figure is buck naked, the last of the Beothics perhaps, all daubed in ochre and war-paint, and carrying a real bow and real arrows. Kevin Barron is sure of one thing: the creature chasing him, whatever else it may be, is no longer a giant. Judging by the faint noise it now makes, the body is as slight as his own.

The taste of Mr. Landrigan's tea rises to Kevin's palate and reminds him that he wants to pee. The tea replaces the taste of the blood that has caked rough and dry on his lips. Thoughts come into his head, and the hair on the back of his neck lifts with the horrible notion that his stalker is the old woman, Mrs. Landrigan, that she has just this minute died, that she carries in her clawlike hands the ferret or the muskrat that lives under her blanket, that her naked sparrow-thin corpse chases after him to whisper something or other that he would rather not hear. Once you view a corpse it cannot haunt you later — Kevin makes now the sinful wish that the old woman had died there in front of his eyes.

He passes a level clearing smouldering with wild strawberries. The child would love to take a spell and pick a mouthful, but he dares not.

A slight breeze brings to his nostrils a strong, choking stink. Could it be that his pursuer is not even human? Some beast is hunting him, a centaur perhaps, with a huge thing hanging down, like the one that dangles from the Pothole Man's stallion. Or a wolf, on the prowl for children to devour. But then, the wolves are as dead and gone from this land as the Beothics. Perhaps it is only the priest's dog — that's it! Jackman is after chasing the noise of the outboard motor across the ridge to Gelden, and now chases it back again. The beast is capable. But centaurs and wolves and dogs walk on all fours. Kevin Barron imagines a bizarre notion: a horned sculpin, as monstrous as a blackfish, slithering over the ground on its two huge scaly fins.

Kevin wishes that he had a dog of his own — a big golden Labrador, say, with a name like Watch. If only a good dog was along to keep him company, to scout ahead for danger, to bark at stalkers and drive them away, he would have no fear.

Or is this stalker not even corporeal? Is it a fetch or a ghost or a spirit, his own guardian angle possibly, somehow fallen from his shoulder and desperately trying to regain it? Or the banshee, summoned to keen over dead Mrs. Landrigan, and lost its direction? Maybe it is the faeries after all. Maybe Kevin is already being faery-led, to God knows what precinct of space and time. It occurs to him that he cannot tell whether minutes or hours have gone by since he departed Gelden.

He entertains a shocking possibility: that, in truth, he does not really want to escape. It may be that his soul craves, instead, to look upon the thing, whatever it may be.

A clacking noise carries over the scrub. Kevin knows well that particular sound. He can picture the black beads, the big balls like castnet sinkers swinging from the belt. He can read in his mind the letters on the strap:

HA
NG
ME
UP

So then, it *is* a ghost. It is the spirit of the mad nun they hanged at Gallows Beach. A length of rope twisted round her neck snakes behind her along the ground. She aims to catch Kevin Barron by the ear and to pinch the lobe of it and to give him a beating on the hands and across the face as penance for all his dirty sins. A twig snaps under the boy's foot, but what he hears is the dreadful strap coming down against his palm. The electric jolt ignites his forearm.

But then of course — why did he not think of this before? — the creature might well be the Boo Darby. Everyone knows the Darby is really the Devil. Kevin smells it: a filthy bearded goat, with sweeping curving horns, the fur of its haunches knotted with clumps of dung, strutting after him on its hind legs, its cloven hoofs, grinning.

He mutters an Ave as the sailors do in moments of peril. He wishes he had held onto his surplice, to give power to his invocations. He wishes he had his missal, to yield up every prayer that might possibly save him. He wonders if he should try to invent a new supplication just for this occasion. From his pocket he pulls the beads that he always carries and he determines to say the Rosary while he hikes. The nuns do that, on days when the weather is fine, strolling in the garden behind the convent. Today is the Sorrowful Mysteries. The first Mystery: The Agony in the Garden. *And His sweat was as it were great drops of blood falling down to the ground.* Silently Kevin Barron mouths the words: *In the name of the Father....*

But he is too distracted to take the Rosary further. Instead, with his thumb he signs crosses over his heart, the miniature kind you make in Mass. During the Holy Sacrifice the priest crosses himself some fifty-two times, Kevin Barron knows, so he tallies his little crucifixes and aims to achieve this number. But soon, in his agitation, even this observance sputters out. He imagines a terrible struggle in the air around him, a fight among these awful beasts and monsters and spirits and demons, the prize in the balance his own immortal soul. He reckons that all he can manage to do is to spit in the path—spit, after all, has magical powers. He tries, but he only dribbles bloody saliva over his shirtfront.

The gap is closing. The creature is at his heels.

Kevin Barron tops the ridge. The breeze comes clean and steady over the crest. It cools his brow and bears away the mosquitoes and the black flies. Here dead in front of him, surprisingly near—a stone's throw, even for a feeble arm such as his—stands the lookout.

Atop the rock a crow struts.

The child decides that at last he will run. He will break for the safety of the boulder.

He fixes his sights on the rock and commands his legs to churn. And they do. But even as he flies across the ground, he is convinced that his legs are not moving. To his horror he has tumbled into one of his nightmares. In every instance of this particular dream—this hag—which troubles him too often nowadays, he lies paralysed, wide awake, his eyes open to the shadows that surge and spiral out of the corners of the room, and he wants to run, he screams to run, to go some place, anywhere, but no matter how fast his legs spin, his soul travels not one inch.

Kevin Barron collapses upon the base of the boulder. His arms outstretch and embrace the whole of the stone. Patches of lichen coat the rock like leprosy. His prayerbeads rattle against the granite. An emmet crawls across his little hand. The sun beats hot upon his brow. His head swirls. His eyes see in the stone a pattern—a corkscrew, a spiral, the shape of water being sucked down the kitchen drain.

The crow flies away. Weakly the boy climbs the boulder.

The iceberg juts out of the bay and puts into his mind those faery islands that are said to ascend, every nine years, from the North Atlantic. If only he could scream loud enough for his voice to reach the water, then Mikey would surely come and rescue him. But the red punt is nowhere visible. The only boat on the water is Mr. Landrigan's black hull, heading eastward into a rising wind on the passage out to Gelden. Kevin can hear on the breeze the whimper of the engine. He even wishes, despite the sea and all its terrors, that this instant he was aboard that vessel.

The vacant schoolyard has a forlorn look. The back ends of the houses are unpainted and grey. Kevin locates his own house, his own gate, the door to his mother's kitchen. A black figure walks the road between the wharf and the church: the priest. Father MacMurrough bears the bag containing Kevin's surplice. Kevin wants to wave, but he cannot bring himself to raise his arm. He watches the priest approach the church and climb the step. The boy opens his mouth, finally, to call out, but no sound issues from his throat.

The door closes and the priest is gone.

Kevin Barron surrenders then. He bows his head submissively, in the manner of a cornered rabbit. He surrenders in the way he so often does in the schoolyard, when the warty hands are about to take him, when flight is impossible, when defiance is futile. What Pop says is true: there are places on the water where drowning happens, and no man can save himself from them. It is the will of God.

He hears the hiss and the trickling sound before he feels the wetness that spreads inside his trousers. He would love to weep but his eyes are dry, and burning hot, as if every drop of his body's fluid had already drained out of him, had already dribbled down his leg. The wind sings in the grass and chills him where he is wet.

He shuts his eyes and vividly he sees the delicate curving folds of the pitcher plant, purple and swollen. And although he will not even glance in the direction he has come from, the strangest urge takes hold of him: he wants more than anything else to return there, to hike all the way back to that miserable bog, and to gaze one more time upon the carnivorous maw.

Something is new in the world today. His body where he is wet stirs and shifts clammily against the cold damp of his underwear. Something is strange, and powerful, and dangerous. And he is afraid.

If only Kevin Barron could turn himself into a bird—a baccalieu bird, say—he would launch himself into the air and glide smoothly down the long gentle slope of the ridge, all the way into his mother's kitchen. He would be home then. He would be safe.

An eunuch, whose testicles are broken or cut away, or yard cut off, shall not enter into the church of the Lord.

Deuteronomy: the book always strikes him as a litany of divine maledictions. He is troubled less by the image of mutilation or by the ghostly pain tugging at his privates than by the meanness and spite of the eviction, the frank exclusion. For comfort, the way he used to do as a child, he flips the pages of the Old Testament and seeks out the solace of his own name.

Gersam they christened him, straight from Exodus. They gave it the soft G, like Gerald, and called him Baby Ger, then later Gerry. Gerry Mack!—that had great sound, great dash. Just the name for the ring.

The ring! He remembers the newspaper in his pocket. He pulls it out and rapidly his eye scans the heads:

MOLOTOV ARRIVES IN . . .
NOMINATION OF DEWEY NOW SEEMS . . .
CANADIAN COMMONS HOLDS
DISCUSSION ON . . .

Raising the paper aloft in both hands, he claws at the page. He ignores the editorials:

ST. JOHN'S DAY

and the classifieds:

GIRLS WANTED

It is the sporting news he searches for:

FIRST ROUND KNOCKOUT PREDICTED
WORLD'S HEAVYWEIGHT TITLE AT STAKE

He snaps the paper into shape and draws it to his eye. The words on the page stir a memory from the alleys of his soul.

The Enniscorthy fair it was. A raucous crowd was on hand for the afternoon match. The sky flooded colour on the grounds under the castle. Such a long time ago, yet he remembers clearly every blow: the crunch of cunning McHugh O'Byrne's fist smashing his nose, the taste of blood in his throat and his roaring anger and then the frenzied battery connecting like dynamite with the temple and then — then! — that beautiful frozen moment, the perfect instant when he knew, by the horizons beyond O'Byrne's eyes, that his rival was about to fall.

Afterwards, girls followed him. Droves chased after him and his victory belt. All the way to Ferns some of them came, right to the gate of his father's house. Gerry Mack! they sang out. The conquering hero!

Gerry Mack. How many decades has it been since he heard it? In all that time, probably the nearest to a real name that anyone has called him has been the *"Prista Wetman, yumi wantok"* that was smiled so generously, so spontaneously, by the Goroka hawker as he accepted the proffered smoke. The sacrifices of the collar are little different from those of the veil: you surrender even your name.

And for giving up your name, what in return? A priest enjoys one pleasure, so-called — that of hearing other people's secrets. But the sacrament of Penance, as Father Mac-Murrough has long known, is God's bitterest joke, for the secrets travel only in the one direction. Nobody hears your own thoughts, and at the end of it, when the footsteps fade and the big door slams and the church falls silent, you're left sitting behind the grille just as alone as you were at the start. Perhaps even more so.

He stuffs the newspaper into his pocket. He shuts the Bible — who was it left the book open there anyway? — and slides it along to its station on the countertop. He returns the pyx to its cupboard and hangs the boy's surplice in the press. He is unfolding his own surplice when his missal falls to the floor.

He picks it up and randomly flips the pages.

The crimson words scattered among the waves of black put before the priest's mind an image: a clutch of small red vessels drifting across a darkening sea. His nostrils draw the smells of the leather and paper and ink, and instantly the missal smoulders with life. A voice comes out of the book, a feeble shout such as a drowning man might sputter, just before the final plunge. The priest brings the page to his ear and he listens to the desperate, whispered shriek.

Ironwork rattles and clanks at the bottom end of the nave. An expectant smile lightens the priest's face. As he pockets the missal he fondles the stone that waits deep in his cassock. He leaves his hat and his cane on the countertop and hurries into the sanctuary.

Although the church is palpably vacant, the priest relishes the idea that the pews actually are full and bustling. The rattle scrapes again: yes, the doorlatch.

Forgetting to genuflect he crosses the sanctuary and passes through the gate, and bustles down the long aisle. He throws open the heavy door expansively, as if welcoming friends to a grand party.

But the landing is empty.

The priest snorts at his own foolish melancholy. He is getting to be like that doleful boy. . . .

He steps out onto the landing. The wind is rising. He lights a cigarette and he daydreams: if only, instead of tobacco to smoke, he had betel nut to chew, he could see the winds in all their colours and textures, the way they do up in Bulolo. If only he had a kaleidoscopic kite to fly on top of this breeze, the way they do, he has read, on the sandy beaches at Tsingtao. . . .

The road is empty. The school playground, just hours ago alive with children, already bears that abandoned, overgrown look. The whole world is hollow.

On the slope of the ridge the priest sees no sign of the boy, and he wonders if he made it back after all. A small, shameful voice inside him takes pleasure in the fancy that the child may have gone astray.

When he finishes his smoke he hooks the church door ajar and steps in. He bears to the right and advances up the Epistle-side aisle. Through the windows he is exhilarated to see, above the eastern horizon, tiers of pewter-coloured clouds swelling dramatically, a canopy looming above the iceberg. Soon the ice will be no more. The priest marvels at how solid, how certain, how positive the berg still appears. The hard shape of Skellig has crossed leagues of ocean, decades of time, to arrive at this precise place and moment, for no purpose other than to harden his own soul.

He feels a terrific yearning: how he wishes there were someone he could tell all of this! If only somebody would come!

He has not felt such an urge since he was a child, since, on the day of his first Confession, he spent hours examining his conscience, so eager was he to tell his sins, and then, that he would not forget them, printed his tally on a piece of paper and memorized it, and practised the recitation over and over, aloud, like school verse.

He stops at the shrine of the Virgin — *Vertjen*, they say on the highlands. Or *Thien Hau*, as she is, he has heard, in seagoing Canton, where Matteo Ricci advanced the faith with court eunuchs by confounding her with the Chinese goddess of sailors. Father MacMurrough lifts from the floor a wayward penny and drops it clanking into the mite-box. He genuflects before the altar — *tebol tambu* — and crosses to

the opposite arm of the church, his travels shaping, he observes, the sign of the cross.

In the west transept he sits in the rank of pews facing
the confessional. He inhales the magnificent smell of varnish
on pine that is peculiar to this alcove. The same smell clings,
it seems, to every confessional in every church, even the
poorest. He imagines that the fragrance is the perfume of
the rose that is carved above the confessor's door, the rose
that smells, splendidly, of admission, of contrition and ab-
solution, of salvation and of salvage, of souls cleansed — of
connection.

He drifts into a half-sleep, and he dreams.

He dreams of moving down a long, widening aisle towards
double doors, varnished doors made of pine. Beyond these
is another set of doors, but smaller. And beyond these is
the entrance to a tunnel. Above the entrance a vested arm
reaches down and offers the viaticum. Just as the priest's
tongue extends to receive . . .

. . . he awakens with a jolt.

He digs the missal from his cassock and flips the pages
and finds the devotions for Confession. The red words
among the black whisper to him, urgently.

*Represent to yourself that this may be the last confession you may
ever have the opportunity of making.*

Father MacMurrough longs, just once, to say the truth.
He yearns to tell the new secret — the possibility, the wonderful opportunity that, as tangible as a stone, he has carried
since this morning on his person.

*O Father of lights, Who enlightenest every man that cometh into
the world, send into my heart a ray of light, of love, and of sorrow,
that I may know, detest, and confess the sins which I have committed
against Thee. I desire to see my sins in all their enormity, and just as
they are in Thy sight; I wish to detest them for the love of Thee, and
to confess them with the same sincerity as I should be glad to do at
the moment of my death.*

The priest is troubled by these words. My secret, he thinks, is hardly a sin.

From the back of the church comes the scuff of a shoe against the threshold, then footfalls on the rough pine floor. Someone advances up the Gospel-side aisle. The sound, more substantial than the rattle of the wind, this time is real.

Father MacMurrough rises and tiptoes the short distance across to the box and opens the confessor's door—but he does not go inside. Instead he slips into the penitent's cubicle. Softly he pulls shut that door after him. He kneels.

The enclosure is cold. Father MacMurrough shivers, but his soul burns with joy. He is in the middle of his sublime moment! He is within his landwash of possibility! He fondles the stone in his pocket. A feeble light sifts through the grille. The priest puts his mouth to the screen and he whispers out loud, as he did before he made his first confession. He rehearses what he is about to say.

"Bless me . . ."

Wind and wave have carved a grotto framing the mouth of the tunnel. The arch reminds the boy of hands joined loosely in prayer. In the same vague manner that he fears the wrath of God, Michael Barron fears this dangerous grotto, this maw. He pulls his face away from the sight of it and turns towards the parish—towards the blue house. He wishes that his mates would give it up, this nonsense. He wishes that they would swing the punt about, right now, and make straight for the wharf.

The surface of the cove is knobbling. The wind is rising. Please God it holds easterly. Please God they won't have to beat their way home.

Lolly barricades the entrance to the tunnel. Easily the prow rends and batters aside the film. The boat slips into the arch, into the murky shaft beyond. Overhead hangs a huge icicle, perhaps a yard in length, and as they pass under, it baptizes with a bracing dribble of meltwater each of the boys in turn.

At the last instant before the fissure swallows them, before the church, the Brow, the blue house disappear from his view, Michael spots the prow of Casey's motorboat, like the sniffing snout of a rat, nosing silently out from in back of the wharf. The wind sweeps the thump of its motor away into the hills so that the vessel moves in ghostly silence.

In the canoe style of Red Indians, Wish and Gus ply the oars kneeling. The hull slides so softly, so neatly down the tunnel, you would swear the cavity had been carved out just to receive it. The walls are sculpted like ribs. Michael allows his hand to reach up and stroke the ceiling. The ice runs with water that is so cold it burns his fingers.

The punt travels a dozen times its own length. Eventually the light dwindles to nothing. The boys are in absolute darkness. Neither Wish nor Gus utters a word. The half-throttle pott pott pott of Casey's motorboat passes by outside. The engine pounds like a pulse, and it gives Michael the notion that he and his mates have penetrated the body of some colossal dinosaur.

The walls recede beyond reach—the tunnel has widened. Globes of water plop down all around them. Judging by the spacious, wooden echoes that the sounds enjoy, the boys have brought up inside a vaulted chamber, a place about the size and shape of a chapel.

Wish and Gus are silent with wonder—perhaps with fear. They boat the paddles and allow the vessel to drift.

The chamber contains, after all, a small measure of light: a glow sifts down from the ceiling. It is the same blue that he saw this morning, filtered then through the membrane of the salt sea. The light seems to come out of the body of the ice itself. It is starlight without stars, like a lone candle burning behind a mural of stained glass. The noctilucence is hardly strong enough to define anything, but serves only to give scope to the blackness.

Michael Barron reclines across the stern. He stares up into the blue ceiling, into the gentle, fearful throb. Here at last, perhaps, he has found his voice—perhaps, at last, he has found the way he can say it.

Look at them clouds, Sister Mary.

    And such a breeze.

    Bound for a blow, I fear.

    The trees, Sister Mary, soon you will see them genuflect.

    Already the gulls they're scattering.

    Every which way.

    The wise creatures, all too well they know.

    They know, yes, what's coming down the chute.

    A pitiless gale.

    One to rip the bark off the birches.

    Peel the shingles from the sheds.

    Strip the feathers off the hens.

    Another Seventh of June gale.

    Time to chain down the houses.

    Pour gravel into the walls.

    This place, it should be somewhere else.

    I daresay we might even enjoy a touch of a blizzard.

    Sheila's Brush.

    Belated however. Months.

    Snows in June.

    A fisherman's holiday.

    Pray the fisherfolk are off the water.

    God save the poor men.

    Pray the youngsters are off the roads.

    They are. The playground is barren.

    I miss them myself, already. Even the stragglers and the reprobates and the troublemakers among them. This morn-

ing I caught a pair of the darlings coming in the gate just as
the last call was after ringing, and I says to them: Oh, my
goodness gracious. Isn't this the grand hour. Your little ears
never heard the bell I suppose? Now, what were you at to
be so late? And they said to me: We was down on the beach,
Sister. And I said: Tell me the mischief you little devils was
after finding there . . .

Hush. Look.

Irene?

Yes. There she goes now.

The poor child. What a miserable errant.

And she with such a kind heart, too.

A motherly heart.

But she doesn't know the rules, does she?

Not yet.

Sister Mary, I don't want to watch this.

Nor I.

Let's come away then.

Come away, yes.

Come away and let's put our minds to happier things.

Please. Lets.

. . .

So.

So. . . .

How is our man getting on?

Well, God bless her kind heart, it was Irene herself sat
him down to the kitchen table and laid a scoff in front of him
big enough to save his soul, and gave him a knife and a fork
to eat it with. I just had a peep in at him through the crack
in the door. Solitary like the Holy Father. Won't take off that
smelly old coat. You'd think he was hiding some treasure inside it.

That Irene is such a Christian. We're blessed to have the
like of her.

It was Irene and . . . herself discovered him. Lurking in the pantry. Such a day we're having for discoveries in the pantry. He was like a child playing hide-and-seek.

Sniffing for a bottle, no doubt.

No doubt. But judging by the way he is lashing into his spuds, hungry is all he was. He's wolfing them into his gob like it was his last supper. Won't even glance at the fish however. Or the flippers.

I am surprised herself allows an unbelled man within the walls.

Oh, she doesn't mind Johnny. He wouldn't say boo to a goose.

And I suppose, what need for a bell with the pong he left hanging in the air? And anyway, as you know . . .

. . . Yes, I know. The poor benighted creature.

Tell me. Does he ever pick up a bar of soap, I wonder.

It's a miracle he can pick up anything at all, what with those relics of fingers.

Nothing but the stumps.

An unnatural leper.

God save him, he puts into my mind the martyrs.

Isaac Jogues himself.

But a fat bottle now, that he can grip tight enough. With his two hands clapped together like he's saying his prayers.

I know it. Every year, when the ice comes down, there he is, praying.

Set your calendar by him.

A case for good Saint Jude.

What was the name of that boat? Was it the *Southern Cross*?

No, it was the . . . I forget. Mind, that happened at the start of the war.

The war before the war.

That's the one.

A long road from yesterday.

But what an ordeal he suffered.

Think of it. Ice-blinded and all.

The wind and the cold.

Not a stain of shelter.

Not so much as a miserable tilt.

Such emptiness.

That's the worst.

Ice to all horizons.

No landmarks.

Nor a compass.

Not so much as a clod of dirt underfoot.

A heaving ocean of growlers to all quarters.

I can tell you, I would not last fifteen minutes in such a limbo.

The agony and the terror.

So lucky we are to be here.

Aren't we though.

Dry land.

Warm walls to keep us snug.

Safe in God's pocket.

Us and our . . . community.

Indeed, Sister Mary. Our community.

And don't forget another thing: this pitiful man, he was the salvation of others.

I know it.

That poor wreck got a medal from the king.

Think of that now. And all he knows is his numbers.

A hero.

A saviour.

Hard to credit, by the state of him now.

And do you know, a fine-looking specimen he was in his youth.

Would you believe it.

Sure, all the girls were mad after him. He was on the Banks.

Now just look at him.

What's going to become of the poor man, I wonder.

He must be a lonesome soul.

Nobody to talk to.

No one but himself.

Indeed, he does prattle.

Always a slate loose.

Him and Zebrinas, God save the pair of them.

A fine match they would make.

Two buttocks of one bum.

Sister Mary, the queer things that go on in this world.

You hardly catch the tail of it.

So much happens is never known.

So many secrets.

Yes.

Sometimes, you know, in the evenings, just when it's getting dark, I will look out the window upon them houses. And my mind floats, and I have a kind of wide-awake dream.

Yes.

And in the dream, there's just been a calamity. A big wave or a storm or a pestilence or something awful. And all the people are after fleeing their houses and leaving them behind, empty. I come out of the cloister and I go up the road, and the road is full of wild animals wandering out of the woods. Deer and hare and fox, all so tame you can walk right up to them. I feel like Saint Francis himself. And I go into one door, and I explore the house, every room, top to bottom. When I'm done with the one house, I go on to the next, and so on, until I'm after seeing the secrets of the whole parish. Oh, the things I do learn. . . .

Listen. Did you hear that?

The windows are rattling.
The waves must be high, down at the Brow.
Yes, they're crashing up against the cliff there.
God save us, Sister.
God save us.

Here. Step across the road. Come over here to where your
ears can pick up the sound of me.

I said: It's them leprechauns. They undresses you just for
badness. They plucks your hat off your head and rolls it
up the road, and before you knows what's after happening
they tumbles it back straight into your paws. They're re-
hearsing, that's all it is. Tonight's the night the faeries ride.
After dark, them bold laddybucks, they gets real brazen, and
they swipes everything you forgot to make fast. When the
sun goes down, ships will fly, I guarantee you, Father.

Look: come in, why don't you. Right now, yes.

Yes, come in out of the lashing elements. That wind is a
real barber. Enjoy a sit-down and a nice hot cup of tea.
Warm your bones. It's no trouble, no trouble at all.

Well I knew I was going to have a visitor. The cat was just
after washing her face. The only thing that matters in this
world is company, isn't it? Anytime you fancies a cup of tea,
Father, you just march right on in. Don't you ever knock on
my door—it's only strangers bothers with that nonsense.
You just march straight in. This minute my pot is full to the
brim, steeping on the stove, just waiting for the two of us.

Me and my little love, the Reverend Erasmus Stourton
here, we was just after darting out to hoist our gate off the
hinges. We got it hid away nice and snug. The chickens is
keeping watch over it. Yes, this night you wants to chain
your outhouse fast to the corner of the palace. Elsewise tomorrow morning when you looks out your breakfast window you'll see it's after rearing up on its stilts and traipsing

off down the avenue. For that matter you better chain your old dog too — God knows but it isn't one of them itself. Did you find the wandering creature in the end? No doubt it's up along the landwash some place. Hind legs in the sand and snout in the kelp. Never you worry your heart about the welfare of that beast. That can look after itself. It done well enough scavenging on its own for all them weeks before you showed up to claim it. Eating seaweed, scooping eels out of the water, half the time like a bear up to its hips, chewing the finny things.

Here we are. A rare blessing indeed to have the comfort of a cozy quiet kitchen. My brood is done slurping their tea and stogging their faces, and thank God I dispatched them off to gallivant on the rocks. Most of the time in this place you can't hear yourself talk for all the racket. Can't hear your ears. I'm forever shouting at them to behave their manners and keep their gobs shut. If their daddy was home there would be no skylarking, I guarantee you. Father, you are one lucky man to be spared all that torment. Believe you me.

Now, hand me over your hat and haul off your rig. We'll string them up here in back of the stove, draw the chill out of them. And we'll prop your stick here in the corner. You settle yourself there on the daybed. A nice snug nook. Melt the ice out of you . . .

Puss! Skit out of that! I swear by the Almighty, if it wasn't for the politicians, I'd slam the stove hatch and bake that vexation. A wonderful thing to have at election time. The politicians, they praises up your handsome tom and they pulls out a five-dollar bill and buys the beast off of you then and there, but they winks: I'll come back for the animal later. I hope you don't mind sitting in the kitchen, Father. The parlour is barred up, going on a year now. If you finds it too warm I'll open the glass. I suppose you're after hearing the joke why it is the air in this country is so pure and healthful and wholesome — the people, they never raises up their windows! Anyway I reckon you must be taking this poor shack for a shambles, next to that grand mansion you got to live in. I'll shut my gob for a minute now while I fetches the good china down out of the press.

As a matter of fact, Father, I set my foot inside the palace only the once the whole length of my life. Monsignor Conroy, God bless him — Father Fran he said we had to call him — last Christmas he had the Auxiliary in for tea and biscuits. Mind you, it was us ladies had to bring the tea and the biscuits. I notice you this morning hunting out his bed. I'm ashamed to say it, but myself, I haven't made a visit to the graves in donkey's years. At any rate, Father Fran, he had his faults, I'm sure you know that by now, but by God wasn't he the man for the fun! A far cry from the one before him — look at that, I can't even remember the name. That fellow had nothing better to do nights but prowl the lanes dogging the courting couples with a switch.

Father Fran, on the other hand, now he used to sing and dance and spin the yarns. This winter past he showed up at a bingo and scuff in the Academy Hall. Feast of the Purification it was. For once the windows was wide open letting the cold in, and you could count the nails in the floor from the frost shining off of them. In no time at all he had the women up, swinging them round in the lancers. Such a sight. He could wallop her down. No Methodist toes on that man. The time went on till the sun come up. The skipper was grinding away at his mouth organ — that one resting there: you'll hear the glorious strains of it this night, God willing — and he was just about falling over beat, but Father Fran, he was going strong. Steam rising off his neck. Of course, it was not many days after that the good man was called to his eternal reward. At the wake everyone declared it was the lancers swung him into heaven. The truth is, one morning while he was in his outhouse the Lord came for his soul. God rest him. A queer hand, he was. Always good for a laugh. Not like a priest at all.

Here we are, Father. A steaming hot cup. Let me get down the molasses and the Carnation. I was afraid them ravenous youngsters is after glutching the last crumb of this morning's bread, but here's a pair of heels the greedy buggers missed—we'll finish them, me and you together. It would be grand to have a stick of fresh capelin to offer. They makes grand tea fish. When the skipper casts them up we'll send along a bucketful to the palace, that's a promise. Since you takes it bare-legged, I hope the steep is not too strong for your taste. The skipper complains that whenever I makes it the spoon stands up straight and you got to chew.

You carry on and enjoy your tea, Father. I'm just going to sit here in the window and keep an eye out. Last I saw of my oldest, she was gumbooting it into the barrens beyond the graveyard. Making a beeline for the lighthouse. Putting miles between herself and me, no doubt—she's snarly today. Right snappish. But I shouldn't be calling her down. She's got enough on her mind. This is the day the maids goes prowling after their man. Well I told her she won't find no herd of fellows in that place, in that godforsaken desert, where the nights are long. One or two stinky goats maybe. Pray to God she don't come to any mischief. At least thank heavens I can make out the spot with my two eyes. Around here they says: If you can see the lighthouse, it's going to rain, and if you can't see the lighthouse, it's raining already.

But Father, isn't it a wonderful strange day full of weather this is turning into? I foresaw it—the spiders is lively. This morning was so mild and sunny I says to myself: Here is the chance to put in that garden at last. It would be lovely to have a few flowers and a bit of colour, take the edge off this wilderness. Sure, you saw with your own eyes what miracles the nuns is after doing with that little plot they got. Anyway, Father, what with the offshore breeze this morning, butterflies and the smell of lilacs everywhere, it put into my mind our wedding day. The spring snow was just about melted, and the bells was ringing, and off we sailed into a fine westerly, off for the Labrador and a summer of good fishing. The best of it was, we was saluted around the point by clouds of seagulls blowing about in the sunshine. Yes, as I says to my Mary: marry in white, girl, you'll always be right.

But now the wind is turning so cold and hard. Have you ever seen such a day for boisterous air? If this easterly brings any filth, sure there'll be no faeries abroad this night. Light a bonfire in an onshore gale and you might well singe the whole parish to the ground. Like scorching the hairs off a pig. I remembers one midsummer when I was little, Maurice Duggan—you knows Moe—he nipped a flanker out of the pile and hove it over his roof. For good luck. It's supposed to keep your house safe for the year. But he was nine parts on, and he stumbled and the flanker landed on the felt and set the roof ablaze and burned the place to the foundations. Nothing left standing but the naked chimney. We had two bonfires that summer. The next year, Moe brought out his old gun and he was so blind drunk he shot the wires off the poles. Even though he's never been to either Front, after that night they started calling him The Gunner.

The fact is, Father, judging by the rattle in the windows, I venture we might even see a touch of the white stuff before the sun sets. I can fairly smell it. And will you just take a look at the ice. The waves is splashing up past the knees of her. She won't be long for this world, I guarantee you. And them foolish boys is still out gallivanting aboard of her. . . .

Have a gander at that, will you now. What do you suppose that one is at up there, loose out of her kennel? If she don't watch herself, the wind will pick her up off the ledge like a big black kite.

In case you're wondering where my skipper is to, Father, he's still on the waves, God save him. That's his chompers there in the glass, as you can see. Two years ago he hooked a big ray and he was bent over the side of his boat gawking down, and his jaw fell ajar when he saw the size of it. He said he thought the creature had a hold of him and not the other way around. In the middle of it all his brand-new plate popped out of his gob and sunk like a rock. No doubt some ugly sculpin has got it clamped to his gums and he's very pleased with himself, grinning away at his friends the lobsters. Well, the skipper got another plate but now he's afraid to bring it beyond the doorstep. Takes all kinds, doesn't it? At any rate now that the wind's turned he'll soon be making his grand entrance. He'll wink at you behind my back and he'll be moaning it was all my fault for putting the jink on him.

Hark! A trumpet! Was that you, Obediah Morash? Oh, you dirty pig. Pooping in front of the holy priest. You smelly goat. Father, did you ever see the like? If Father MacMurrough gets vexed with you and your bad manners he'll turn you into a real nanny-goat: think of that.

Well I'm sorry the rest of our brood is not here for you to get a proper sniff of them too. I complains about them dawn to dusk, but I loves them all. The biggest is sixteen and after her there's a string of God knows how many. The twins give us the spars of the crucifix. And this little Irish fellow finally, still waddling in his nappies. Yes, it's you I'm talking about, you stinker. You are as Irish as Father himself—would you believe, Father, you are the first foreigner ever to cross the doorstep of this house? Here, have a raisin bun.

Oh, my child, don't start in getting cranky on me. Most of the time he's as good as gold, but he wants his tea—I calls it tea. He's a trial to me this day, Father. Yes, you are, my love. It's all a trial this day. I was hag-rid last night and now I've got a load of work before the evening is done. I got to haul some water, and clean the dandelions we picked over in the meadow—dandelions is good for the heartbeat—and make dough for rising overnight, and put on their supper. And ahead of all that I got to take the fish in off the flake before the sky opens up on top of it. Fish-splitting and all that goes along with it, around here that's a woman's job, you know, Father. My Ciss—I'm just after writing to her today—she moved up to the Boston States fifteen year ago to look for work and, let me tell you, when they asked her what was her job experience she said: Cutting throats, ma'am . . .

Puss! Father, hand me across that poker, quick. That tom is as big an aggravation as them youngsters. This morning the creature was staring me straight in the face, and I don't have to tell you what that means. Sure enough, I heard you going round the point in Mike Landrigan's outboard and I says to myself: That's old Galena, for sure. You must of had a hard time getting a proper confession out of that flinter. A hard case, that one. They says she is after uttering hardly a civilized word all the years since the mister passed away. You knows the famous story of that, I suppose. When Ed took a stroke and they was waking him, his mates, they dragged his corpse out of the coffin and carried it off in the punt—for one last jig of fish they said. Of course they was all so drunk it fell overboard and they never found it after. A good suit of clothes on it too. Well, Galena, she wasn't going to let that expensive box go to waste: she just set it out on the landing and filled it with dirt and planted bluebells into it. Meanwhile, she told Mike to use the lid for a splitting table.

At any rate, since Ed died it was little else but oaths upon the head of her poor boy. Yes, the youngsters of Gelden was forever terrified of that biddy. The evil of a widow's curse, they said. But I suppose you don't always need sensible words to hear a person's sins, do you? Some people confesses what's troubling them just by the cut of their jib. Anyway, I will say a Hail Mary she has a good death. God is just, isn't He, Father? That's what I was telling Nell. No sooner he takes one away when he puts a new one on earth to replace it. I suppose dying is like being in the womb: either way, you're taking passage to a new world. If so it must be a relief to old Galena, after her life's misery.

Well, I notice Mike took you down the inshore channel. He must of run you right over the top of the *Pegasus*, black as night there on the sandy bottom. An old whaler, that one was. Came up on the rocks there in the year . . . 1777. That was before they put in the light. They used to call that stretch the graveyard of lost ships. Every kitchen in the parish has got odds and ends off of some old wreck that brought up there. For instance, now, the big chair I got up aloft nailed fast to my roof: that's my *Pegasus* chair.

You know, Father, I often wonders if I am sinning, every day perched up there in that maggoty old thing. It has got such a comfortable sit. It never gets time to cool off, I'm into it so much. If it was only salvaged, well, that would be all right. There's no harm in that. But they says the survivors was raided when they swam shore—and some of them was killed. So every time I sits down in my old chair, I wonders if someone was murdered over it. I wonders if it is a sin for me to sit, just to sit and wait for my husband to come home—even if the crime happened before my granny's granny was ever even dreamt about.

To tell you the truth, Father, sometimes I even wonders what is a sin at all. For instance now, you take Johnny the Light—you knows old Johnny. People around here treats that man like the living dirt, but the fact is, he is a hero. Not everyone in this parish knows it, but he saved a watch of sealers. He even got a medal from the king for it. But it was a trophy for lying. He gave his mates nothing but deceit.

And no matter what nonsense he said to them, they believed every word.

The blizzard catches them straight out of a mild day—just like this one was. All of them in their shirt-sleeves. Not one with a proper warm coat. They gets lost from their ship, and for two days the storm blatters away. Horizontal sleet. But Johnny, he sings out: There's our ship, lads. And he sets off across the ice, hopping the pans, and his men, they follows behind him. And when they went along, miles and miles across the ice, there's no ship nowhere. So he sings out: No, lads, she's over this way. And they walks along again, another two or three miles through the gale, back to where they were in the first place. Johnny never lets them stop, even when they were near froze to death. And in the end, that's what kept them alive.

They found their vessel after all. Spotted the St. Elmo's lights blazing in the gaff topsails. They said it was like a crucifix on fire. So Johnny and his own little band was saved, while all the rest of the crew perished, standing up dead in their tracks or kneeling at their last prayers. Froze like statues.

Well, by the time they hauls Johnny on board, he can't eat nor drink nor talk. All he wants to do is lie on the floor, under the bunk, in the dark. He just curls up inside there like a baby, crying and shivering, breaking off his ears and his fingers and his toes. Like sticks of wood—you never thought he was a natural cripple, did you? When they finally thawed him out, he screamed for every minute of the three days it took the vessel to beat back to port. And he never straightened his bent frame to this day.

But the thing is, Father, it was by the lies he told them. The lights and bells and crosses. The salvation was by deceit. You know, Father, the catechism has a question in it, and I learned it off by heart: *Is it lawful to tell a lie for a good purpose?* You knows the answer yourself: *No purpose, however good, can excuse a lie, because a lie is always sinful and bad in itself.* Father, that makes no sense to me. I don't see how Johnny the Light can be a sinner in the eyes of God, after the wonderful good thing that he done.

That's what I thinks, Father, if you wants to know.

Now, here's a few Purity crackers, and the last of the partridgeberry jam. Eat up.

Lie on top of the wind — that's the answer.

The problem is, sometimes the wind gusts, and then of course gravity does what it wants. Mary smiles at the notion: hordes of people all over the parish falling on their faces for no apparent reason.

But she will not witness such comical sights today. Just like the gulls cowering in crannies, beaks buried under wings, the people have all taken shelter. The gardens and meadows and flakes and rooftops are so barren of life you would think every soul was after dying. Even the smelly goat that has been following her along the road has given up and slipped under a hedge. The squall has swept away the summer smells of lilac and roof tar and blueberries. The sea air hints even of snow.

Mary shivers and wraps her arms around her shoulders. She wishes now that when she ran out the door after dinner she had remembered to take the scarf. Her hair blows horizontally before her like a pennant. Her skirt slats like a sail. The wind threatens to lift her clear off her feet.

Even from the stretch of road behind the Brow, where the water is out of sight, Mary can hear the sea booming against the base of the point. The sounds remind her of the biggest storm of her life, the Seventh of June northeaster. That was — imagine! — a dozen years ago.

When the gale was at its worst, Father bundled her up

and took her out of the house, out there, to the top of
the Brow. Just for the delirium of it, he told the woman.
The ocean reared back so deep that the sight of the sea bottom, the writhing kelp and stranded flapping fish, the very
ground raw like a wound, made her stomach churn. She
thought she was looking at something secret, something
sinful and forbidden. But her sickness and fear did not
last long, for Father stood there beside her, holding her
tight, and in the middle of the thunder and saltspray the wet
patch of clifftop where she clung to him became calm and
peaceful. As peaceful as the interior of an empty church at
midday.

That same storm washed away a big mound covered with
sod at the far end of Admiral's Beach, and exposed the hull
of a frigate—*Old Polynia*, the stern said—that had wrecked
there fifty years back, and refloated it, guns and all, and
drove it out the cove, and the vessel was never seen again.
And it was said that after the wind died finally, fishermen
down beyond Brimstone Cape discovered trapped in a gulch
an entire schooner ground to such a slush of matchsticks
that they couldn't even guess at the vessel's name.

Mary is surprised to see a black-robed figure hurry down
from the cliff edge. At first she thinks it is somebody jannied
up for tonight. But no, it is Sister Irene.

Mary has never in her life known a nun to step through
the convent gate. The girl wonders vaguely if the lay sister
is breaching her vows.

Normally, Sister Irene's fat cheeks give her face a dimpled
pear shape. With her merry eyes she always has the appearance of laughing at nothing at all. But now her face is
twisted and flushed, her cheeks wetted.

The nun's feet rip to shreds the dandelion blossoms. She
passes Mary without word or gesture, in the cold blind way
that a stranger might do. The girl turns and watches Sister

Irene hurry away. The wind presses the habit against her body, betraying the womanly shape of her legs, and it occurs to Mary that the nun cannot be much older than she is herself. The gale picks up the dust that is baked dry in the potholes and swirls the dust about the veil. Suddenly the wind, or perhaps it is Sister Irene herself, Mary cannot tell which, rips away the apparatus of veil and cowl, and bares to the sky a brilliant crown of shorn red hair. The flaming head above the black habit strikes Mary as so outlandish that it might as well be a mummer's costume after all.

The nun passes through the convent gate. After she has gone, Mary cannot be sure whether what she saw was real, or was some kind of strange dream.

Wispy grey tendrils skitter from old Martha's chimney. Behind the dirty windowpane lurks a shadow that could be the malevolent face of the crone herself. Claws of smoke reach down and stroke Mary as she hastens by. A mournful drone wavers on the wind, eerie and distant, like the lament of a foghorn—but it is only the gale crossing the mouth of the field gun.

As Mary moves down the slope and into the hollow of the marsh, she turns about and walks back-on to the wind. Before her eyes the church sinks into the land and disappears, like a vessel sinking into the sea: it is a trick that Father showed her. Even in the hollow the telegraph wires strum, the pine branches rattle, the eaves howl—all of it a banshee symphony. Mary devours the churchfront with her eyes and above the noise she recites the words she has memorized:

> *Therefore now they are not two,*
> *but one flesh.*

Walking backwards she crosses the bridge and comes opposite Barrons' place. Although she has bypassed this house

countless times in her life, this is the first she takes any notice of it. The neat fresh-painted fence, the model sailing-
ship in the window, the patch of bluebells in the front
yard—all this looks to Mary like some kind of sacred grotto.

Metallic sounds clank off the cliff-face in back of the
house. On a ledge there, a thin boy crouches. He wields a
hammer and chisel and he chips at the granite.

It is the brother.

As far as Mary can make out, the child chisels at the rock
just to pass the time. Yet he works with such determination
you would think he was trying to hack his way to China. She
halts on the road and waits for him to pause, to look up, to
show the face—the face she has been trying to remember all
day—but the child is intent on his ridiculous task. His tiny
shoulders are bent like those of an old man, and from time
to time they heave sorrowfully. Now she remembers: him
it was, the teacher's pet the lads were tormenting in the
schoolyard.

Mary turns about-face to the wind. Atop the roof of her
own house, the truculent chair confronts the gale. At the
sight of the chair a surge of disgust wells inside her throat.
Furiously she thinks: My vigil, it will have no such lies.
Mine, it will be hard and true.

You would think the woman had heard the girl thinking,
for just then the back door swings open. On a guilty impulse
Mary ducks under the frame of Father's fishflake.

She peeps up through the low ceiling of blasty boughs.
Were she to shut her eyes she would still know precisely
where she is, for she would never mistake the rich tones
of the fallen pine-needles, of the rotted, ragged nets and
tarpaulins, and, strongest of all, of salted fish. The quintal
is mostly gone now—the cats and gulls and crows made
short work of it. What few scraps remain are blackened and
shrivelled.

Mary watches the woman step out onto the gallery. A black-robed figure emerges behind her—it is the parish priest.

The woman and the priest stand side by side at the railing. The woman points at the sea. The priest turns and his eye follows the line of her extended arm. Even against the squall Mary can hear the voice. The woman is telling the priest—even the priest—her crazy stories. Her pack of lies.

To think that he sat in that kitchen. To think that he saw the things she keeps there.

The priest speaks something to the woman. The woman bows the head and the priest gestures the sign of the cross over it. He puts on his hat and leaning on his cane he starts down the sloping ground towards the road. The woman bellows something and he looks back over his shoulder and waves.

He comes down the gravel pressing his hat against his crown. His cassock billows and with effort he fights against the wind. Before he catches sight of her, Mary crawls on hands and knees across the sod and around the barking kettle and hops over the upturned dory. A piece of planking comes off dry and crumbling in her hands. Please God, she thinks, tonight this is ash. Tonight the hag is burned.

The priest passes slowly. His upper body is bent against the blast so that he looks like a very old man. Mary knows that priests can see out of the backs of their heads, and she squats hidden behind a fat strouter. The wind crushes his cassock hard against his body, and she is shocked to see the outline of his legs, of the lump between them—it had never occurred to her to think of priests in that way.

The wind slams the door shut: the woman has gone back inside the house. From behind the screen she stares after the priest. She looks for all the world like an image framed in a painting.

A breaker lumbers up the landwash and bursts into a million drops and douses Mary in saltspray. She shivers. Even though the tide is falling, waves lap the outer pillars of the flake. The breaker carries on up the cove and explodes against the wharf.

Unmindful of her dress, which by now is filthy anyway, Mary climbs on top of the dory's hull and draws her feet under her thighs and sits facing the ice.

Colossal tumbling clouds surge in from the horizon.

If only she might see. If only she can hold her eye fixed on the place where the red punt vanished. Then the bad things that could well happen surely will not: the berg will not split, nor will its halves fall asunder and turn bottomup. Nor will it slide from the reef and smash like a tumbler against the beach, or be ground into slush against the cliffs. If only she can hold her eye fixed, if only she can keep her vigil, with her hard iron faith—the faith with no lies—then surely the simple good thing that she wants to happen will happen: the boat will reappear, whole, and then, after it swings into the clutches of her view, she will pray the vessel up the cove, all the way to the lee of the wharf—to safety. To home.

Mary has overheard the woman mutter litanies and intercessions. For her own watch she chooses, instead, one simple word: fisherman. Over and over she speaks it aloud:

"Fisherman. Fisherman . . ."

The waves have grown so tall they obscure the berg's lower decks. From her own station here so close to the waterline all she can make out are the topsails of the ice. The combers pile and bubble and froth, and just when it appears that one is about to collapse and unveil to her that which she must observe, another, even taller, rises foaming right in back of it, the lot of them mocking and teasing like malicious children.

Mary feels a rising panic: she must see. She must. Des-

perately she searches the world for some higher vantage
point.

Michael Barron wonders idly how much time has passed.

From outside somewhere distant rumbles a ceaseless
thunder. But all that the chamber delivers up to him is a
dreamy floating sensation, the clucks and echoing clicks of
fat waterdrops splashing, imposing melodies on his mind,
and of course the tender blue light that imparts only the
space itself.

A violent crack-sound makes his breath stop. It leaves his
spine awash in sweat. Vibrations buzz the keel. Black meltwater crashes, apparently in solid blocks, and drenches his
oilskins. A volley of bayonets plummet and slice the surface
with gentle razor whispers.

From outside comes a roar, then the full volume of the
water inside the chamber picks itself up and collides ponderously against one wall, like the contents of a huge washtub shaken, and bounces away, plunges weirdly, elevates
the punt, drops the keel thunking against the exposed floor,
recoils off the opposing wall, returns and uplifts the boat
again. Michael grips the thwart. Wish whimpers like a
puppy. Gus curses.

Slowly the water calms. The boat settles.

Michael's pulse pounds in time with the pott-pott-pott-
pott of Casey's engine, audible again. The motorboat hastens
at full throttle. Then that noise too fades and the interior is
dead quiet. Even the waterdrops no longer fall. The silence
reminds Michael of the afternoon, three years ago, when
every hand was jigging and the squid were running madly
and you couldn't hear yourself for all the whooping. An old
woman rowed out in a dinghy to announce to the men that
the war was over, and every sound stopped.

The waterdrops start to tiptoe down again. The salty

stench of the seal carcass, packed in ice in the well of the
midship-room, contaminates the pure smells of fresh water
and prehistoric air.

Gus hisses, "Shut your gob."

"I never said nothing."

"Shut the fuck up. Stop your faces. The two of you."

From perhaps no more than a boat-length distant comes a
moan. The cry is real, from a living throat.

Teeth chatter in rising panic: that must be Wish. Quietly,
Gus takes up the oar and paddles towards the corner where
he reckons the tunnel ought to be. But the stem only bashes
against the wall.

In frustration Gus strikes a match — the tunnel's welcoming maw is right here, directly in front of the boat. During
the few seconds before the flame sputters dead, Michael
feels a small regret that his blue light is extinguished, but he
glimpses in its place the shadows of pillars all around and of
jagged spikes and daggers threatening from above. It could
be the sea bottom turned upside-down. He glimpses too,
across the chamber, the flash of a pair of sad eyes glaring
red, like sanctuary lamps.

Wish mutters an oath and grabs the shotgun and clicks
opens the breech, but Gus screams at him, "You stupid cunt.
You'll bring down the roof."

Gus manoeuvres the boat into the tunnel. The opening
is less roomy than it was earlier. The walls press so close
that the boys have no space to use their paddles. With bare
hands they urge the gunnels inch-wise along the shaft. Here
and there the stem scrapes the ceiling. If the boat jams, Michael reckons, they will surely die: either the berg will collapse upon their heads and crush them, or it will melt slowly
and they will freeze and starve. Inevitably their bodies will
drift up bloated on the shingle at Admiral's Beach.

Light.

The ogive of drenching white light draws the boat, accelerating. Yet as the prow bursts through the arch and into the blinding sun, Michael feels the urge, the longing, to retreat inside, to return to the soft blue light.

The icicle, smaller now, still hangs above the arch. The few patches of sky that survive in the west bolt through its prism. At the moment the boat glides underneath the icicle, Michael takes the axe and stands and reaches up one hand and steadies the point, with the other he prepares to chop. But the icicle comes away easily, as if it wanted to do so all along, and topples into his arms. Tenderly he lays it across the sternsheets.

After the silence and darkness inside the cavern, the noise of the wind, the blazing light, the dizzying volumes of space and freedom have their heads reeling. While they recover their senses they allow the boat to drift in the lee calm.

Legions of whitecaps gallop past at either flank. The waves drag the flotsam of rind and sludge scraped from the rim of the berg and sweep it landward. At the shore, froth marks the landwash—invitingly. Breakers erupt like fireworks against the Brow. No doubt this minute Pop cowers behind the Comfort, fingering his rosary, his blanket wrapped about his head cowl-fashion, and every now and then he will take a pull on his dead pipe and he will declare: The waves they has some mercy, but the rocks, they has no mercy at all.

Michael spots the tail of Casey's motorboat the instant it slips in back of the wharf. The vessel is deep with fish, its driver flying. Michael is chilled clear through, and he prays that his mates, with such a wind to bear them home, will surrender and make for the jetty at last. He yearns for the curious sensation of stepping ashore—the dizzy head, the legs so wobbly you would swear you had actually leapt in the other direction, off the wharf and into an unhandy boat.

The wind has swept the road clear of people. Yet on the roof of the blue house, a figure sits erect in the chair. The boy marvels at the woman: even in such a storm!

To clear his mouth of the taste of brine he licks at the icicle. The ice is hard and dry and it makes his tongue tingle. He presses the ice against his ear. His cheek tickles with a mild hiss—that is the popping of bubbles. It is air that has been trapped since long before Cabot, since before the Vikings and Saint Brendan, even before the Christ. Across the vastness of time and space God has delivered this ice to this moment, this place, just for Michael Barron to drink and to breathe.

"Them widows," says Wish. His nerve is recovered, and he is putting on a brave show. "They jinks you every time. By rights we should of shot the bitch dead."

"Butt, you stupid shit." Gus slings oars into tholepins. "Come on. We got to make one last turn around. Else we're truly jinked. That's what the sailors says. Isn't that right, Barron? And after we done that, we can fly to Christ home out of this."

Wish takes his seat grumbling. He and Gus haul the boat round the corner of the ice and plunge it into the throat of the gale.

The punt pitches and tosses on the long waves coming off the open water. Pop says it is not the number seven that will be the rogue, nor even the number nine, but the number nineteen. Michael starts counting, but with so many waves slamming against the bow, like punches under the chin, he loses track.

Gus and Wish grind the punt slowly past the northern flank. They keep the head up the blast while they nudge round to the windward face. The boat stands on its nose and Michael, from the stern, as if staring down a deep well, looks upon his mates and upon the battered face of the dead seal.

Then the boat rears on its hinders and his mates loom against the angry black wall of cloud that is miles out at sea.

When they reach the patch of water where Casey's trap was set, where only its shade lurks now, they stand the boat, paddling steadily. The galloping foam gives Michael the illusion that the punt thrashes towards the horizon—towards Ireland—but he knows perfectly well that he and his mates are not moving at all.

The boys are drenched in brine. Michael drapes his oil-coat like a cowl over his head and he huddles and watches the Mother Carey's chickens. The little birds flutter about in the troughs, dancing on the water, or else they fly seemingly straight through the crests, the raging sea as nothing to them. Even though the wind and the waves roar mightily all about the boat, for the moment Michael Barron feels an everlasting peace.

Gus points with his chin and spits a curse that is swept away by the wind.

The level area where the lads spent the afternoon, where they ate and slept, has collapsed. Its wreckage, awash, fills the inlet below. The fall of rubble and scree smothers the very berm where the boat waited so patiently. The sight leaves Michael sad and frightened. Waves catapult up the blue haunches of the iceberg and tumble back glass-green. Against the unfavourable wind no sound of this horror reaches the boat: the silence makes it all the more desolate. If Gus and Wish were to stop rowing, Michael thinks, if they were to take no action more dramatic than simply boating their oars, in just minutes all three of them would be shattered against those ice cliffs. That's how little it would take to end their days. He wraps his arms around the big icicle as though it were a child.

The hurricane plucks Wish's cap from his head and sends it flying onto the waves. Wish lunges instinctively, as though to leap after it. The foam bears the cap off towards the iceberg. Gus laughs uproariously. Wish scowls at the back of Gus's neck.

Gus jerks his chin aloft, at the tumbling clouds rapidly gathering, and shouts above the noise: "The Holy Ghost . . . going to dump a white shit . . . on top of us." Easing off slightly on the paddles so that the waves carry them stern-first, he and Wish coax the punt round the southern face. The pinnacle that was Michael's outlook glowers on the port side. Magically flying backwards, mimicking the boat, gulls drift on the wind shoreward even as they appear to make for the sea-horizon.

The boys tuck the punt round again into the calm pocket in the western lee. While they massage life back into their fingers, they drop the paddles and allow the blades to float.

Michael observes again the softly curving arch that frames the tunnel. Involuntarily he lowers his eyes, as he might bow before some holy image. So it is that he notices in advance of his mates the demon hurtling up from the sea.

The sight of the object rising fast towards the hull thrusts into Michael's mind Pop's story about pulling a trap and thinking it heavy, and discovering tangled in the netting neither the drowned whale nor the dead fisherman he expected, but a war mine, horned and sinister. The spectacle left the old man paralysed, and for a long moment, before he bestirred himself to cut the beast loose, all he could do was stare dumbly. He wondered to Michael whether he had behaved that way because, deep within himself, he really wanted the thing to explode and kill him.

The water swells, then bursts like a boil. The white object is an ice-calf, a detached bummock, bloated, a ton in weight. It wedges Wish's paddle against the hull and snaps the oar, then breaches high, in monumental style, rolls and exposes its emerald underbelly, seawater spewing in torrents down its sides, then settles back and wallows. The boat pitches like a rocking-horse. Had the keel been running north-south, the block would have smashed it to splinters the way a sledge-hammer might smash a femur.

Wish has flung one leg over the gunnel and again he looks as if he will leap onto the sea and run after his shattered oar. In two pieces it drifts away on the wash. Gus grabs the good oar just as it is about to slip clear of the tholepins. With the smug face of one who knew all along that this would happen, he paddles calmly clear of the danger.

Cursing from embarrassment, his hair dishevelled, Wish tumbles back into the boat. With theatrical fury he loads the shotgun and cocks it and takes aim at the upper body of the iceberg, and fires. The recoil sends him lurching back on top of the cuddy. Near the summit of the berg, a wide white puff instantly is vaporized by the wind.

Gus snorts, "Fuck this for a game of marbles. Let's batter to Jesus out of here." He pivots the boat and rows—at last—for the wharf.

Clouds swirl in every direction at once. Demented shrilling gulls give up trying to fly into the wind. They turn about and flee, full tilt, towards the land.

The vessel departs the iceberg's shelter and falls again into the full force. The boat plunges and rocks and tilts. Gus paddles air. Cursing, he brings in the oars. He threads a paddle into the sternhold and slides the handle down to where Michael can take hold of it. "Here, Barron, you lazy tit. Make yourself useful."

Gus mounts the thwart and faces forward and braces his feet. He opens his oilcoat wide and so fashions a crude sail. The boat surges, as if drawn by the magnet of the land.

Off to the south, the barrel of Barnaby's Gun detonates. Michael cradles the icicle while he manages the tiller and dodges the scattered trail of bergy bits. Near the cascade at

Freshwater, a serpent of a waterspout spins eerily. If only
the lads had swords, they would beat them against one another in the form of a cross to frighten the demon away.
Michael fancies he is a saintly explorer, like Brendan the
Navigator, bearing down after a long voyage upon the shore
of his Promised Land.

Wish scrambles forward and adopts his gargoyle perch
straddling the stem. Michael imagines that this is a Viking
longship with a splendid square canvas, with a dragon prow,
and that he himself is Leif the Lucky. And then he imagines
simply that he is Cabot, and after a passage fraught with the
perils of ice and monster and storm he is about to discover
his new territory.

Wish bellows in the direction of the parish:

> *Whenever the wind*
> *is in the east . . .*

Gus finishes:

> *. . . 'tis good for neither*
> *man nor beast.*

In harmony the two boys roar:

> *Whenever the wind*
> *is in the east,*
> *'tis good for neither*
> *man nor beast.*

Over and over like fools they scream the same verse, each
one trying to shout louder than the other.

Frost smoke blows steaming off the billows. Michael
spies, half a mile away, a heavy wave smashing against

the Brow. There it is now, probably—number nineteen. The geyser explodes high and the wind scatters the mist so that it appears to bless the blue house, to anoint the figure that sits there waiting, even yet, in the chair. He secures the tiller inside the crook of his elbow and with the tail of his shirt he cleans the salt from his eyeglasses.

He replaces his glasses, and he looks. And he sees.

Just at the moment that he sees, the squall overtakes the rowboat. On all sides fat snowflakes hurtle, tumbling horizontally, melting soft into the water, rampaging onward towards the shore. The cloud drowns the sun. Immediately as the saltbox is swallowed up, is gone from his sight, Michael Barron can see at last, after the perils of iceberg and monster and storm, the shape of the danger that stalks him this day.

XV

Sheila

Wind chills bare flesh.

In a pewter silence the snowsquall devours the lighthouse and the iceberg. For a terrible moment the rowboat wallows just beyond its clutches. But soon the snow devours too the cockleshell and the flock of whitecaps that the boat shepherds from danger.

The squall advances serenely. In its youth it may have been a vicious gale, but now, after wandering the seas for centuries, it has mellowed in its age, and is little more than a great grey net being drawn slowly across the world.

In the space of heartbeats it brings up against the landwash. The snow gathers in the wharf, and behind it, the coffin-shapes bumping their gunnels, waiting for their cargo, and the school and the church and the houses and the fishflakes and everything that is real. All that escapes is this chimney. The chimney is a blurred ghost that floats in a pool of sodden, tarred felt.

The fat cold snowflakes alight melting on bare flesh.

The blast spins and swirls the snow, wave upon wave. The wind is made visible. Yet despite the spiralling light, nothing really happens in the world. All is smothered inside a tranquil limbo. It seems that a minute, or an hour, even a year, may be passing without notice, without effect.

From somewhere near or far, it is impossible to say, a voice calls out, with longing: "Sheila!"

The voice is that of a man.

"Sheila!" the voice calls again.

With that, the parish landmarks reappear as abruptly as they vanished. The snowfall thins. Church and school and wharf step forth out of the murk.

A bright shaft of red—the only patch of colour in the universe—leaps from the slate light bathing the jetty. The punt is already moored, magically, in the lee of the wharf.

On the bed of the wharf three young men stand close. They move unsteadily, as if dazed to find themselves on firm shore.

The clouds break.

The wind falls with each breath. The squall drifts inland like a wedding train. Perhaps the storm will carry on around the world, to reappear in this place half a millennium hence. Or perhaps it will blow itself to nothing, at last, against the bluffs of the Gaff Topsails.

Late sunlight bursts through gaps in the ceiling and descends on slanting pillars. Within the cathedral of light one can see for miles. A rainbow frames the little cascade across the cove at Freshwater Room.

Every surface is glazed. Every surface is rinsed and purified.

The young men collect their gear, and like knights in armour they advance down the sanctified road.

XVI

Summer Dim

A moving shadow.

It boiled out of the sacristy. It slipped along the wall and under the acolytes' bench. It was like a fox flashing through a meadow.

The church is dead quiet. The sanctuary lamp glows brighter as the natural light fades. In such darkening, was it a delusion?

But there again.

The shadow darts from under the bench. It scurries across the chancel floor. The creature, whatever it is, hobbles grotesquely on three legs.

Awkwardly it springs from its single hind paw and bounds to the marble top of the rail and into full view. The thing displays the hideous form of a large maimed rat.

From its perch the creature surveys the ranks of pews. Its skull weaves and swings this way, that, searching, sniffing urgently. Its green eyes flash. Abruptly the beast sits and bends and licks at its distended teats, as if to soothe a burning ache.

The animal glides back to the floor. It hisses at its own reflection warped in the chimes of the handbell. Slinking up the steps, it prowls before the englassed panorama of the

Last Supper. It gauges the elevation of the altar, crouches, and with terrific effort catapults itself and catches at the frontal and by way of its foreclaws pulls itself up the linen and onto the ledge.

From there it vaults easily to the roof of the tabernacle. From the height it explores the nave again. Spying nothing, it emits a mournful, rending howl. Resignedly, the creature slips back to the floor. It limps to the sacristy and is gone.

Father MacMurrough sits at the rear of the chamber. He has observed the beast dazedly, hypnotized. Blood-ruby sunset presses against the rose window. He stirs from his torpor: he must catch what little is left of his day.

He must *see*.

He takes up his blackthorn and hurries out the door.

Although the tail of the snowsquall is still visible above the northern rim of the ridge, already the air hums with a freakish warmth. The roadway is dusty-dry but the grass is still damp and glistening, and it smells anointed. The priest's eye, like that of a Mayan, leaps naturally into the wedge formed by earth and western sky.

The sun is about to drop of the back end of the land. Silhouetted within the half-globe of the sun, a lonely horse and dray crest the road. The vehicle wends towards some interior vale, an unknown place beyond the limits of the parish. The dray sinks into the horizon at precisely the instant the sun does so, and it appears that the dray ferries the star on its journey into the night.

The priest feels bitter towards the drayman: his boxcart bears away the last of the light. He watches the notch in the road, half hoping, half demanding, that the vehicle return with its cargo.

But the sun sinks, and the red sky only bleeds into the earth.

Above the jetty, gulls swarm black and menacing against the last purple edges of the day. Only two other people are visible: the woman in the chair, and the infant she holds to her breast. The priest feels a shaft of envy at the extraordinary peace she has achieved, and at such miserable cost—just a few venial lies.

Miraculously, the sea-waters that such a short time ago roared and tumbled are stilled. The Brow drifts towards night. The evening is becoming duckish. The day has fallen into that enchanted border between light and dark: the summer dim.

All that remains of the sunset is a thin crimson puddle, fast evaporating. The priest drinks with his gasping eyes the last of it—the last.

The darkness swallows up the road and the houses and the picket fences. Rectangles of yellow windowblinds mark the contours of the parish. Luminescent suns and moons hex the barns and privies. In the meadows, over back where no one lives, a match glints and is gone. Incandescent dandelions glow like candles. The village resembles his childhood notion of limbo: tiny, faintly lighted souls isolated one from another, all of them adrift in a void.

On the road, among the houses and the picket fences, shadows flit and scurry and whisper. Whether these figures are animal or human, Christian or pagan, he cannot tell.

The scimitar moon slices thin veils of scud. The half-light it casts down seems to float up out of the earth. It bathes the parish in an edge of nickel-plate, all of it sharp with a peculiar frail glare, like a photo negative, or like the clarity of perception that tortures you waking in the middle of a bad dream. The ethereal light falls upon the iceberg too and the ice throbs, mutely, as if the moon had given it the touch.

The tide is falling. The water retreats, uncovering his landwash—his sublime in-between territory.

In the ditch that runs past Casey's octagon, shards of glass shine like stars. The haunted clapboards stand forth stark and clear. The priest inhales this simple draft of light. The sheer plainness of the planks, the ranks of clean straight horizontal lines, captivates him. He draws his eye along the boards, right to left, and again, pausing at the far edge, at the abrupt outer limit of the wall. To the left of this edge, around the corner, something waits for him—he is sure of this. Something exalted waits for him in this burning night.

Lovingly he fondles the stone in his pocket. He stares beyond the edge of the wall. He stares transfixed by the absolute darkness, the perfect darkness that waits, just for him.

XVII

Shotgun

Sniff sniff. By God, I smells a hole.

Hah! Jug me a fat one. Yes I got a lift right there. Now I'll fix your wagon for you.

Look out then, take this. That's a dandy poke in the eye for you. Put a whoa to your gallop. Leave you damp in the armpits.

And . . . deep . . . into the hole . . . you goes.

Right. Here we are. We're down to it: the who-shall. It's your deal.

Wait! Listen. . . .

Did you hear?

Yes, indeed. It's about *time.* Yes.

Well now. Here's a sight for sore eyes. My child, wake up out of your sleep and come look at the surprise the cat is after dragging in.

Footsteps scuff the corridor.

"Grand of you to come, Father. Grand to see you. But there's no need to confess to me. Every timepiece will give out once in a while. Sure, it was only an act of the Lord, now wasn't it."

The footfalls arrive at the door and the door swings open and a chubby young woman steps into the parlour where they are sitting: it is the lay sister. *Suesta. Vertjen.* She carries a tray bearing tea and biscuits.

"So don't brood about it, Father. The youngsters, they got their parting homily. Yes, I gave them their stirring valedictory in the end."

The lay nun's eyes are swollen, the fat cheeks flushed. You would swear she had been crying. Shockingly, a strand of flaming red hair has slipped from under her cowl. The hair sticks plastered against her dampened brow.

The lay nun arranges the cups and saucers on the table. She takes up the black pot and pours the priest's tea. She offers neither a look nor a word to either of them, nothing to acknowledge any presence in the room. But when she moves around to deal with the Superior's cup, her hands begin to shake.

"Yes, I rained hellfire upon the little monsters. Enough to keep them in the fear of God until the Feast of the Nativity of the Virgin, at least."

The hands shake and tea splashes into the saucer. The Superior sighs. The lay nun sets the pot hard on the tray and without ceremony departs the room. Her footsteps scuff along the corridor, a great distance it seems before the sounds fade.

With the matter-of-fact manner of a celebrant purifying the paten over the chalice, the Superior picks up the saucer and slides the spilled tea back into the cup. She pushes across to Father MacMurrough the sugar and the milk. He declines and pushes them back to her. While she dresses her own tea, she speaks.

"Time? What does any measure of it matter, Father? What's an hour, what's a life, set against the glory of God's eternity?"

What, indeed, is time?

How many years has it been since he approached that other house of women with such urgency as he did this one, this night? —putting the question in this manner makes him almost laugh out loud.

It was his first term up from Wexford. In a pit of loneliness and misery he slipped down to Mary Street one cold wet evening. Outside a particular place he stood among the puddles on the pavement. Through the drizzle he gazed up at the lighted windows. He lingered in that place for an hour, left and walked the quays for a time, returned, smoked a cigarette, finally went away for good.

In the morning he decided it was not courage that he had been wanting, but faith. He had failed to knock because he lacked conviction, the belief that there existed behind those walls comfort sufficient to rescue him. He lacked the trust that salvation in any form waited there for him.

"And Father, no sooner we dismissed the children but we had another juvenile to contend with. You've met our parish hero, yes? Johnny Spracklin. Well, Johnny strayed into the convent today. In the horrors, he was. I discovered him myself, skulking behind the pantry door. The absolute horrors."

But this time, this night, he found it painless to approach, to knock. It was easy, not because at this late hour in his life he suddenly found some measure of faith or expectation or hope, but for the less exalted reason that, unlike before, he could so readily disguise his true purpose. Tonight he did advance, he did knock. The Superior dismissed his false apology and with her cold fingers, like claws clutching at his, drew him within the walls of the convent, and shut the door behind him.

"The treasure he carried, it looked familiar to my eye. Sure enough, the man had poached a fat bottle from the sacristy. Our Dismas. I went down straightaway and slapped a padlock on the press. Remind me to give you the key to it."

The nun shakes her head bemusedly.

"And a hum to pin you to the wall. He hissed at me —you

know the way he does it. Our dear dear Johnny. A trial for Saint Swithin."

And now that her cold fingers have drawn him inside, now that, secure in the protection of his falsehood, he is seated and served tea, he scours the enclosure. He searches it for any deliverance, for any form of salvation.

A huge brown Christ peers over the Superior's shoulder. The face grins: You'll get no help from me, you fool, can't you see I'm crucified! At either hand, candleholders are suspended from the wall like the two thieves. The wicks are white and unblemished and the room is illuminated instead of electric lamps. Their dun shades push the light downwards onto the mahogany floor so that the ceiling is dark.

An ancient yellowed photograph, framed in black, commemorates a rank of nuns—the long-dead founders of this house, no doubt. Five armchairs sit vacant. In the corner, a plaster statue of a saint lurks leprechaun-fashion behind the desiccated foliage. It wears a beard and a long flowing gown, and carries a hammer and a saw. Joseph. The patron of those who work with their hands. Inwardly again the priest smirks.

"Himself and Monsignor Conroy were grand pals. Didn't you know that? Birds of a feather, one might say. Father Fran always forgave Johnny his sins. And vice versa—and may God forgive me for saying it."

Father MacMurrough strokes the arms of his chair. The hardwood is smooth and clean and cold, like marble. The air in the room tingles sharply, of camphor perhaps, or Dustbane, or Sunlight soap, or maybe all of those. He sniffs yet another smell, a soft, sickly odour. A sharp pain passes briefly across his mid-section.

"Poor Johnny. May the Lord help him in his afflictions. I'm not even sure the old man has taken it in that his one true friend in all the world has gone and left him."

They sip their tea. No noise comes from within the convent, no more footfalls, no bells, surprisingly not even the muffled murmur of prayer. Out-of-doors, meanwhile, the distant voice of a young man shouts a greeting. A young woman replies. A clutch of youths raise a raucous cheer.

"There you go now, will you listen to that. This night you inherit one of Father Fran's offices: you must wield the torch."

The Superior pours fresh tea for them both. While she is preoccupied the priest becomes aware of an odd sound. It is a deep-throated moan. At first the cry issues apparently from under the floorboards—but no, it comes from the corridor, from the far side of the parlour door. The moan turns into a horrifying wail. For a moment the priest wonders if it is the lay nun, sobbing. But no, the cry is not human. It is the wail of the creature that was prowling the church.

The Superior speaks brightly, loudly, unnaturally, as if trying to drown out the noise.

"And haven't they got a magnificent night for it? After that blizzard I mean. Sheila's Brush, much belated. The night is so lovely and balmy and calm. That's the ceaseless work of the Lord for you. Here's the sugar and the milk, now—oh, I forgot: you take it bare-legged."

The moan rises in pitch and volume and becomes an angry crescendo, a howl. Then it fades, and retreats, down the hallway and around corners, until abruptly it is gone. The convent is silent again.

When the nun picks up her cup and saucer they rattle in her fingers. The tea spills, and without drinking she sets the chinaware where it was on the table. She leans back in her chair and looks into the foliage.

"Father. Today . . ."

Her voice has changed its timbre. She speaks now in hushed tones, like a penitent. Suddenly the spacious parlour feels to the priest as narrow and confining as the confessional. For the first time since he arrived he observes intently the face of the woman. As she searches for the words in her head, and arranges them, a muscle trembles at the corner of her mouth.

". . . they have to understand, Father. They must obey. It is the rule."

The youths outside deliver another cheer that turns into a generalized hubbub. A crowd is gathering in the night.

The Superior leans forward and gazes so deeply into her cup that he wonders whether she sees something down there, some tiny animal perhaps. Her fingers fidget with the fat beads dangling from her side. The beads rattle like chains upon the mahogany. Her voice cracks.

"I said to them, Father, I said . . ."

She presses her lips and they appear as bloodless as those of a corpse. Were those lips ever alive and full and moist? Have they ever so much as tasted a ripe, fleshy grape? — have they ever been kissed? Her cowl and wimple and her face together form a pool of whiteness within the black landscape of the veil and habit. He stares so intently at the woman that somewhere behind his eyes, on the screen that is in the back of his head, her image undergoes a weird transformation. Light and shade exchange places, as in a photo negative, and before him sits a young girl in a white dress.

". . . I said to them, I said: We are married to Jesus. Every one of us is. To the Lord Christ. And to no one else."

He knows now the source of that sickly odour: it is the woman herself. It is her plain continence. And for a brief moment he imagines that all the living things in the world — not only this nun, but all the fish and animals and plants and people — are as bloodless and dry as plaster statues.

The plaster face of the crucified Jesus leers down and sniggers: Here you have it then, the salvation you came snooping around for. Are you satisfied?

Broadly, ecstatically, the priest beams up at the Christ, for the answer is yes. The priest is grateful, even at this late hour, for the peace of mind he has been afforded. He is satisfied, for he has found the joy that illuminates this clear space, this sublime moment — this ravishing landwash that waits, between the decision and the act.

Yes, I was just having a few hands of auction with the Devil and I hears steps on the landing, and I says to the lad here, that's the faeries dropping in for a game of cards.

I suppose you knows that half the parish is wondering where in God's name you was after getting to today. We was going to send out a searching party.

Here, my duck, come up out of your crib. Your daddy, he's home to us at last. At long last. Safe and dry and in one piece, thanks be to God.

Now then, my mister, get yourself in here out of the black night. Come into the warm kitchen and haul off your fishy old rig. Hand it to me here and I'll string it up in back of the stove. Now, before you does anything else you give your son a squeeze and a big kiss. . . .

Michael Barron picks his way around the dipnets and castnets and barrows and tubs gathered by the side of the road. He weaves among the little girls skipping rope, the boys racing in full tilt circuits of the octagon, the lads huddled against the clapboard and smoking cigarettes and swapping jokes, the shawled women clutching babies and titty bottles and blankets and lanterns and parasols — to ward off bad luck — and the men in cloth caps, relaxed and each one bearing tucked under the arm a cordene or some other musical instrument, or a fifth of rum, or, like himself, a shotgun.

The others — they must be inside. Michael Barron makes straight for the window.

Peeping around the word "Undertaker", he presses his eyeglasses flush against the pane. The interior is blinding bright from a single naked bulb. People clutter the shop. Men bearing mugs of foaming beer squeeze to and fro through the tavern door. Women dealing hands of auction slam the cards down upon the lid of a beef barrel as if beating on a drum. Serious-faced lads shoot pool. Rough youngsters knock about among them, playing tag. The cries of all these people carry outside to join the general din of the night. The clatter of the crowd jangles against Michael's woozy brain. The four-faced clock says half-past nine.

Yes, Gus and Wish are in there. The two of them lurk near the salt fish. Gus, like himself, has put on his long overcoat. Wish wears his fancy smallwood boots, and now that he has lost his cap and his scarlet mop is left bared, you would swear he was in church. His face is beet-red in the glare. Gus's flesh likewise seems darker, more pitted than it does in the sunlight. Michael realizes how very different from one another are his two mates, and what's more, how different he is from each of them. It occurs to him that, even though they were born within weeks of one another, he has grown much older than they have. This day he has travelled a long journey, and he resides now in some remote country, distant from them both.

Gus and Wish eye the tavern door and wear guilty faces.

Casey steps from the tavern. He is in his waistcoat. His cheeks are more florid than usual and he shields under his arm a paper bag. He sidles his big frame through the crowd to where the lads are waiting, and nuzzles close with them awhile. They leave him and make for the out-of-doors. The storekeeper turns his back and pretends to busy himself with the lobster pen.

None of this matters to Michael Barron.

But there.

There he sees, hidden behind a press of others, slouching against the counter, directly under the bare bulb, a white hem dull with dust, a mere edge of cotton, and in its shadow a familiar curve of pale calf-flesh, sweaty and gleaming. No mistake.

Michael feels suddenly conscious of the shiny blue barrel of the gun in his hand. This is the first year he carries it — Pop grinned mysteriously when he gave his permission — and he is proud to be the youngest bearing a weapon this night. As usual there are all kinds: single-barrelled 12-gauges like his, or double-barrelled constructions that resemble portable cannon, or 16-gauges that in such company are mere toys, or, grandest of all, the ancient muzzle-loader that The Gunner brings forth only twice during the year: New Year's Eve and Discovery Day.

"Hello, Four Eyes. How was your beauty nap?" says Wish.

"A waste of time, as any fucking idiot can see," Gus snickers, and tries to punch Michael in the crotch.

Wish draws Michael into the shadows. Giggling, he waves the paper bag under Michael's nose. "Have a sniff, Barron. Look what Casey swapped for the pelt. Bless his greasy black heart. Beats splitting his fish for a half-dozen beers. Hell, don't have a sniff: have a snort. Go on. Cure what ails you."

A sweet molasses smell wafts out of the bag. Michael takes hold of the flask and swallows a thimbleful. The rum constricts his gullet and burns like heated treacle slowly down to his gut.

But Gus rips the flask out of Michael's hand. "Right, Barron. If you wants a flask, run home and fetch back your stick of ice. Casey, he'll trade you that for a mickey of Dock. He's stupid enough." Gus tears away the paper bag, revealing its contents to the eyes of all bystanders. He wipes the mouth of the bottle, raises it high in a toast, and drinks. He surrenders the flask to Wish with a sharp jab under the ribs. "Eh, Butt, what do you say?"

Moira Nolan and Alice Keating hurtle whooping out the shop door. Looking behind their backs even while they run, they skip across the landing and leap to the road. Hair flies from under bandannas, skirts lift, bare legs flash. Casey follows after them in lumbering pursuit. He grins and waves above his head a large red lobster. The people inside the shop spill out hooting.

Gus cups his hands around his mouth and yells, "Watch it, Moira, or you'll catch a dose of the lobsters," and glances about to see if anyone laughs.

Trailing after the mob, but keeping a proud distance clear of it, a tall white dress slowly, with the composure of a schooner, steps forth into the night. Michael Barron marvels: no longer a spark, no longer a candle-flame far across a mile of cold lonely water, but a torch that is so near, so stunningly close, on this same patch of dusty roadway his own feet tread, that he scarcely dares look towards it. A stab of terror rips through him, and unconsciously his forefinger curls round the trigger of the gun.

Moira and Alice skip in circles and taunt the ponderous shopkeeper. Casey soon gives up. Grinning foolishly, wheezing, red-faced, but still threatening with the beast, he retreats inside the shop. The crowd applauds. Someone strikes up a squeeze-box. People join arms and dance in circles.

> *I the boy who catches the fish,*
> *And brings 'em home to Liza.*

Majestically the dress sails through the horde. It moves across the surface of the planet and the land seems to shift under Michael Barron's feet. When the dress arrives at its destination—Alice and Moira—it turns its long, stately back full upon the crowd.

"How's your wuss?" Gus grunts. He grabs his crotch

and leers bluntly at the young women, then seizes the flask from Wish and in one glutch drinks most of what remains in it. Wish, scowling, watches the rum gurgle down Gus's throat. "Butt"—Gus smacks his lips—"go tell your mother she wants you."

More people wander out of the shop or materialize from the darkness. They lean against the window-sash or sit on the step or stand in the path. They drink and smoke and talk, and wait. Michael hears them only vaguely.

". . . she's due to be gone any day now . . ."

". . . such a lovely Sheila, wasn't it? Although belated . . ."

". . . I'm laying my cash on Joe . . ."

". . . *Paddy walks the shores around* . . ."

". . . we'll be saying a Hail Mary for her, no fear . . ."

". . . *and Sheila follows in a long white gown* . . ."

". . . you mean Joe? Or Jersey Joe? . . ."

". . . yes a wonderful balmy batch of snow it was. The finest kind . . ."

". . . the blinds will fall this Sunday, doubtless . . ."

". . . grand blossoms. Fat goosefeathers of snow . . ."

". . . may God rest her soul . . ."

On a patch of sod Billy Nolan is on his back, his fat shiny arse cocked up so that his two cheeks gleam in the moon-light. Fernie Furey holds a lighted cigarette to the crack of Billy's trousers. Billy shouts: "Volley!" and an obscenely lingering tongue of blue flame flashes weirdly, leaving a puff of foul smoke.

The mob cheers. The face, when it turns about to see what is happening, smiles with its eyes.

The assembly hushes. "Good evening, Father," a woman ventures.

The black figure, hands gripping cane behind, passes in the dark. A chorus of voices in harmony greet it. They get no reply.

The figure is gathered by the night.

". . . and a good evening to *you*, Reverend . . ."

". . . what's his problem? Stuck-up, or what? . . ."

". . . suffering the bleeding piles? . . ."

". . . naw, he's just short-taken. Hurrying home to his shithouse . . ."

". . . whilst she stands . . ."

". . . or he just paid a call on the wise virgins . . ."

". . . and the ketchup boat was docked at the wharf . . ."

". . . and now he's feeling deprived and cranky . . ."

". . . heading home to the palace to pull himself together . . ."

". . . well, we pray he will come back and do his duty . . ."

". . . hey, did you hear about the nun that chased the priest around the church? . . ."

Fernie Furey strolls over. Billy Nolan follows him, brushing grass from his jacket, picking at the back of his pants. Slyly Gus hides the flask in his pocket.

"Hello, you shits. Where was you at, all this fine day?" says Billy. He offers round a pack of ready-mades.

"We was outside." Gus speaks in his casual, gloating voice. "Off the ledge." He takes a smoke.

The dress rises on tiptoe, pirouettes. The hem levitates, calves flash, the moist backs of knees show. A wave of rank perspiration pours out of Michael Barron. At the instant white thighs are just about to appear, some idiot of a youngster wheels past, pushing a barrel-hoop with a twisted length of chicken wire. By the time the child moves on, the curtain has come down.

So drenched in sweat is Michael Barron, he is almost grateful to the stupid child, thankful that the youngster prevented him from seeing.

"Off the ledge?" says Billy. In spite of his attempt to appear unimpressed, his eyebrows lift. He lights all the cigarettes.

"That's what I said: Off the ledge. Fishing. And after-

wards we went aboard of the ice. In fact we took possession.
For the king, you know. And we did a spot of swiling."

"Swiling?"

"That's what I said: swiling. You know: seal hunting."

"Go on out of that," says Fernie, spitting in disbelief.
"Great gobs of horseshit."

As if he expected such a reaction, Gus replies with delib-
erate nonchalance. "Ask Casey if you don't believe me. He'll
show you the pelt." At that, he pulls the flask dramatically
from his pocket and with a sneer he drinks.

On the far side of the crowd, Alice tickles Moira's armpit.
Moira shrieks and chases after her. The two young women
detour past the clutch of lads, then make a show of running
off into the dark.

With a husky urgent voice, as gravely as a soldier going
into battle, Fernie says, "Right. What are we waiting for?"

Billy hisses, "There it is. Who's up for it?"

"Just look at the Gibraltar knobs on that." Fernie speaks
in tones of wonder. "My second cousin, you know."

"Them two, they screws like the minks," Billy whispers
fiercely.

But it is Gus who shakes his head. "Naw. They're only
cockteasing. Tantalizing. Fuck them."

Between here and the white dress, which now stands in
exalted solitude, stretches a distance slightly farther than
that Michael Barron can swim underwater. Yet if he decided
not to swim but only to beckon across this space, merely to
wave his hand, it is certain that he could never find sufficient
courage to do so.

Abruptly, even while Fernie and Billy leer at the dark,
Gus lurches into a boastful account of the day's adven-
tures. The rum has loosened him, and he talks with a loud
voice. Behind his back Wish sulks. Wanly Wish strikes
matches, one after the other, and drops them to the ground,

then lets gravity bring down a stringy gob of saliva, douting the fires before they expire naturally.

Under the moon the churchfront throbs. The big cross — the cross that protects sailors from peril — soars among the stars.

A faery-like shadow sits on the church steps. That looks like brother Kevin. In the bad light Michael cannot tell for sure. Joan complained that the child never came in for his supper. Michael is thinking he ought to stroll over and hear what the boy has to say for himself, when Gus brays against his eardrum.

"Isn't that right, Barron? A frigging monster, whatever the fuck it was. Bigger than the goddamned punt. Swallowed hook and line. Nearly pulled us under."

Michael retreats from Gus and looks again towards the church, but the frail figure is gone.

"Yes, I buckshot the goddamned swile myself, from a hundred feet. That cannon right there. Bull's-eye. And then I battered the brains out of it too. Good thing it was me with the gun — that cock-eyed nancy had no guts for it. And as for Barron, why, that useless tit was off strolling in the hills."

Wish stares balefully out of his walleye. A mongrel pup comes within range of his boot. He kicks at the sorry creature but he misses.

Bridey Thomey pushes a pram into the crowd. Alice and Moira point and try to stifle giggles, and skitter about hiding one in back of the other. But at the centre of things the dress holds its place, steady like the sun.

"Yes by Christ but didn't I muckle the brains all over the ice."

The dress revolves again, but so slowly this time that the skirt fails to lift, the calves fail to show. Instead, savage eyes sweep the crowd. At the place where Michael Barron stands with his mates, they pause, and flash, the way the lighthouse beam lingers. The glance is wild and primitive, and blue. Michael Barron has seen the same look—an expression of merciless faith—in pictures of the martyrs.

He lowers his gaze so that the eyes will fail to capture him, so that he can breathe. It angers him that he has been made to look away. His hand slips into his pocket and fumbles at the two shells, hollowed and castrated. His fingers find his comb—a simple, familiar thing, thank God. Nervously his hand brings it out.

Fernie is getting bored with listening to Gus. He jabs Billy. "Holy Jesus, Nolan. Will you look at that."

"Well I'll be tied down and screwed," says Billy with mock amazement.

"When are you ever in your life after seeing Barron with a comb in his hand?"

"Who taught you how to use that, Barron?"

"What's the matter, Michael? Are you sick or something?"

Gus is annoyed at losing his audience. He reaches across and musses Michael's hair. Michael considers slamming him with the backstock of the gun. Instead, he holds his temper and waits until Gus launches again into his story, then sets about remaking his crease.

"And so I lights a fire and cooks a feast of flippers for these two helpless old women. A wonderful grand scoff we had. Right, lads?"

A membrane flies in front of Michael's face, a shadow so flimsy that perhaps it exists only in his mind. But Alice and Moira notice it too. They cower and cover their hair with the full of their forearms.

"Bats!"

The white cotton skirt is gripped tight at the knee, outlining a long muscle of thigh and hard grown-up haunch.

The creature in the air draws all attention from Gus and

his story. Angrily he mutters, "Hey, Alice, I got a bat here if you wants it up your skirt."

"Come on, Gallant. Why don't you then? Pull it out and wave it at her."

The bitter voice belongs to Wish Butt.

Gus is startled. But the rum has made him quick and reckless. "That's all you wants, isn't it, Butt? You queer."

Michael has never heard his mates talk like this.

Billy sees the chance to provoke some fun. "Gallant, you bullshitter. Tell us the God's truth: how many *fish* did you catch?" He winks at the others.

Fernie jumps in. "Not counting tomcods."

Wish chuckles with malice. "If you really wants to know, I'll tell you what Gallant caught. A useless rounder that we hove away. A sculpin. And a rat's tail, because the stupid arsehole lost his jigger."

Billy snorts, "Lost your auld jigger, did you, Gallant. Well, make no wonder you can't show it to the girls!"

"That's a mighty fine dose of fish." Fernie shakes his head in wonder. "Frankly I'm surprised Gallant is able to tally that high."

"The stupid fucker just hooked it in the ground. That's all," Wish is glaring at Gus. "The stupid shit."

Fernie shakes his head in sham dismay, "Gallant, my son, you're after letting us down. The Legion of Mary could of brought in a bigger load, Sunday morning before First Mass."

The veins bulge in Gus Gallant's thick neck.

Alice and Moira link arms with the dress and guide it twisting through the crowd. They shoulder people aside and bear in Michael's direction. The blue eyes flare.

Michael tightens his hold on the shotgun.

Gus collects himself. He decides to pretend that nothing has happened. He takes a drink of rum and bulls on with his story. His slurred voice carries wide across the gathering. "And then we ran the punt up the iceberg. Straight into her. Right up her smelly cunt."

The dress halts a pew's length short of Michael Barron. It casts a terrifying glow. Moira and Alice listen now, and Billy and Fernie too, and others who have drifted over, all of them taken not so much by the details of the story as by the frantic voice that Gus uses to deliver it. You would think he could not afford a moment's pause that might allow anyone else to edge a word in. The ferocious blue eyes are shut, listening, entranced.

"And we thought we was done for. Goddamn icicles falling all around us. Couldn't see the nose in front of me. Figured we was done for. Carved up like chickens."

The eyes open. They devour Gus, or at least the furious words he speaks.

"The whole back end of her was after caving in. Go ask Casey if you don't believe me. He was out there. He saw it too. We come *that* close, that fucking close to being dead."

Children on the fringe of the crowd shout: "Hushta! Hushta!"

"The goddamn block come flying up from the bottom. Goddamned near stove in the keel. Snapped the paddle. I tell you, that Jesus ice was at us from all sides."

Restlessly the head tosses, and for good measure a long slender hand comes up the back and tousles the mane into disarray.

"I thought for sure that blow was going to poop us. But we up our sail and run before the wind. They slapped the right Jesus name onto this cove, didn't they? It's so fucking hard to get into."

"Are you after saying your Rosary, Johnny?"

The children are tormenting Johnny the Light.

The old man is oddly bare-headed. He staggers down the church steps. Beset by the youngsters, he stuffs his hands deep in his pockets, as if protecting from the thieves some jewel that he shelters there. Warily he skirts the crowd. He tries to peer over the heads of the people and into the interior of the shop. The children dog him, pinching their noses.

"Johnny, you're a stinker!"

"Hushta! Hushta! Hushta!"

The old man hisses back: "H-H-Hushta!" The youngsters squeal with delight and run off a distance. He watches bug-eyed while their parents cuff them for their sauce.

Gus is pleased to see the old man. He waves the flask in the air and catches Johnny's attention. As if the two were lifelong buddies, Gus wraps his arm around Johnny's shoulders and says, "My good fellow, will you j-j-join us for a glutch?"

Johnny beams, but presently the smile leaves his face and he observes the bottle with suspicion. Gus grins at the people gathered round.

Gus holds the flask under Johnny's nose. Johnny's mouth falls open and his tongue lolls. With two hands, like a cat, he reaches for the flask. But his maimed fingers fail to seize it, for Gus has pulled it away. Gus upturns the bottle above his own outstretched tongue and drains the last drops.

To Michael's alarm, the white dress takes leave of Moira and Alice and stalks away, alone. It stops at the far corner of the stores. Inexplicably, it stares deep into the blank wall there. It stares as if the clapboard were fitted with a window, a breach through which some romantic kingdom were magically visible. After a moment, the dress disappears round the corner and into the darkness that is Admiral's Beach.

The night is left black and cold.

Michael's frenzied pulse pumps itself to a panic. He can hear it thumping against his eardrums. Like the Andean sun worshippers who sit on mountaintops and pray for the dawn, he watches the corner of the building, the raw edge, and prays for the return of the heat and the brilliance.

Gus waves the empty bottle in front of Johnny's eyes, then hurls it smashing into the ditch.

"H-H-Hushta!" says Gus viciously. Old Johnny, bewildered, fearful, backs away into the shadows.

Wish is indignant. "What the fuck did you do that for?"

"Oh, shut up, Butt. The old man is cracked."

"The old man is a cripple."

"And so are you, Butt. Aim your fucking walleye some place else, will you. I'm sick and tired of the sight of it. It makes me dizzy."

A glow like the dawn warms the fringe of Michael's vision. The dress has returned—but it is not where he prayed he would see it, at the far corner of the stores. Instead its light swells from behind him: it has circumnavigated the octagon, and at his back he feels the heat it delivers.

"Gallant, you're a genuine prick—do you know that?"

"Butt, why don't you run home and cry to your daddy. Whoever the fuck he is."

The light comes up behind Michael Barron. It smells sweet, like berries. His heart rises in his chest. His finger grips the trigger of the shotgun.

Wish speaks quietly, in fact he almost whispers. "Gallant, you're a true cocksucker."

Michael Barron's sweat rolls down his brow. The light is here, at his shoulder. His lungs are paralyzed, and it angers him that this should be so.

A husky voice demands: "Hey. You. Four Eyes. Lend us that comb."

Gus stares at the ground. He makes an odd nervous chuckle, then a ridiculous grin. He shakes his head resignedly, and begins to unbutton his overcoat.

Well, Daddy, fling off them salty boots and shove your teeth into your gob and sit down to the table here and I'll boil up the kettle for you. I made sure them scavenging youngsters left you a plate of dinner. You must be starving, you poor devil. Yes, put yourself here and we'll drop a few more junks into the stove, stir us up a lovely heavy heat now the doors is shut tight, and a few blocks of coal and we'll have the kettle humming right quick. We'll hot up your chowder, get it nice and steaming. Drag the chill out of your bones. And when you're done you better take your mouth-organ and hurry on over to the Brow: I'm after promising your music to half the souls in the cove.

Well, what a long lonely day I'm after having, keeping watch for the likes of you. Dawn to dusk aloft in the sun and the wind. That is, when I wasn't chopping sticks, or carrying water, or washing clothes, or stringing them up, or pressing them, or knitting cuffs, or writing to Ciss—please God she comes down for a visit—or turning fish, or picking dandelions, or hauling rhubarb, or drying kelp, or weeding spuds, or making up the marvel cake, or pounding bread, or cooking breakfast and dinner and supper for them greedy youngsters. Beat to a snot, I am. The brood of them is off raking the roads, scouring for things to burn. A balmy night of weather they got for it. Beware the Darby, I says to them. Yes, they're all gone into the night and left me by myself again. No one to keep his poor mother company but this pirate Francis Bodkin. Already doing a man's job, and doing it well enough.

Aren't you, my sweet?

Well, Daddy, I fear to tell you sad news: our big girl, she is lost to us. No sooner the sun drops in back of the ridge when her two shadows stops in to fetch her. She comes down the stairs and I says: Well then, after all the free advice I'm after giving you lot, did even one of you sleveens manage to tell out your man? And do you think they would drop so much as a broad hint? So I says, sly like: Why don't we all have a cup of tea and a few deals of auction while I wiggles the gossip out of you. But herself, she puts on a

black face and she looks at me with it. That got me poisoned
with all her sulk and I says: Go back upstairs and haul on
another dress, you streel, you're wearing that rag since you
got out of bed, gallivanting all over creation. Sprinkle and
iron it at least. But of course she pays no mind, only makes
for the porch. And I calls out after her: Well, at the very least
take a sweater or you'll catch your death of cold. Before I
knows it, the screen door slams and they're gone. Not a civil
word. So it must be true: she's after divining him out, whoever he is. Yes, Daddy, I can feel it: she's claimed. She's lost.
The next time we sees her, she won't be there. She'll be gone
from us, gone for good.

So after the lot of them deserted me I lets the cat in and I
sits myself down and I turns on the Doyle News. It says that
the big fight in New York is put off because of weather. And
the Belle Isle light is out and a ship named the *Rose* is after
wrecking up against the cliffs there—such a horrible thing,
all those youngsters losing their fathers. And the family mes-
sages come over the wire. A half a dozen women is after having their operation at the General and they're feeling fine,
and a half a dozen men sends their love from the wood
camps. Isn't it a grand invention, the Doyle News. When
poor Father was heading off to the Labrador, Mother, she
would give him envelopes with her address marked on, one
for every mailboat, and off he would go for months at a time,
and he would mark a tick, which was all he could manage,
and send them back to let her know he was all right. Yes, the
Doyle News, it's a wonderful thing.

And then they give out the Steamer Report. So lovely, like
a song, to hear the names of the alphabet fleet, all them romantic places so far away: the *Argyle* and the *Bruce* and the
Clyde and the *Dundee* and the *Ethie* and the *Fife* and the *Glen-
coe* and the *Home*. Home: isn't that a grand name for a place?
And I'm staring at the flowers on the wall and the Barrel-

man and the Big Six program go by on the radio and I says to myself: By God, one of these days soon I will up and do it, I will. I will go into the back garden and lay down that blossom patch that I always wants. A row of sweet rockets, that's all I needs.

But there's too many hours in the nights. Isn't that true? We needs another dose of Anderson time. So I says to myself, to pass them hours I'll kneel now and pray a decade of the Rosary, but then I remembers I was after having the priest in this afternoon, for a cup of tea, and sure that's enough religion for one day. He's a queer hand, that man. Hardly grunted a syllable at me the whole time. I'm after promising him you're going to send over a bucket of tea fish. They're sure to rise this night—that little Sheila was close enough to true capelin weather. They're cute, aren't they? They shows themselves after the gulls is gone to bed. But I couldn't get a spark of a smile out of the man. He wanders the roads all day, maybe all night too, who knows? Some Sunday evening this winter when you're home from the woods we'll drag him in for a scoff and a toddy and a game of cards.

Yes, himself and Johnny the Light, such a sorrowful pair, rambling the roads like homeless ghosts. Poor old Johnny is hitting the bottle something fierce. What in God's name will become of the dear old reprobate I often wonders. Him such a saviour of men, but there's no man walking can save him now.

So what do I do in the end but wind up dealing myself a few hands of Ferris wheel and vanishing cross and Big Ben and whatnot, when I takes a gander out the window and I spies marleying down the road a bunch of men all of them carrying their guns. And the sight of it reminds me, just as sure as if we was there. You remembers the day just as well as I do—of course you do! How could you forget? Such a grand event that was. Yes, the girl is lost to us, Daddy, and before the garden party is come and gone I allow we will see another such joyful day.

Yes, the girl, she'll be in her white dress. The church bells will be ringing out, and the whole parish will promenade the married couple—the married couple! think of that—all the way to the wharf. The men, they'll shoot off the guns. At the head of the jetty the priest will give them his blessing and the two of them, they'll get aboard of the great white schooner, all its fresh clean canvas slatting. Off they will sail on a fine westerly, out the cove, away to some place distant and romantic—maybe to some place called Home. And the gulls will swarm all over them in the wind, like God's confetti.

Is that Mikey across there?

Under the yellow slanting light that the shop window gives out, among the crowd of people, little Kevin Barron catches only scattered glints—eyeglasses, a comb, the gleaming blue barrel of a shotgun.

The crowd thins. Yes it is Mikey. But he is not alone. The tall one from grade eleven—what's her name?—she takes turns walking around him, round and round, in some kind of schoolyard game, combing her long hair all the while. To look at his face you would swear that Mikey does not know she is there. His eyes gaze into space, into some fearful hallucination. It is the same faraway look he puts on whenever he writes in his book—the sacred book that needs no lock, for neither Kevin nor anyone else in this parish, except the priest, of course, would ever dare to read what he writes in it.

The girl cups her hands around Mikey's ear and whispers to him.

The crowd draws together—it looks like some kind of

ructions are starting up—and when the crowd parts again the two of them are gone.

Ad securae taciturnitatis portum me transferre intendo.

Father MacMurrough doesn't bother switching on the bulb. The moonbeams pouring through the kitchen window illuminate his pen well enough. The pen joins with its shadow to form a dark V, so that he cannot be sure whether his hand writes the words, or whether the words guide the movements of his hand.

The moonlight hums. The edge of it purrs against the back of his neck with that magical sensation, seldom enjoyed since childhood, of simple peace of mind.

After the clarity that the convent so blessedly bestowed, he is safe within his splendid borderland, safe now within the glorious moment desired all his lifelong: and he will allow no one to defile that. So it was he refused the crowd's distraction. He refused to submit to that panic he always suffers approaching any throng, especially a happy one. So it was he closed his eyes as he walked. So it was he pretended that his parishioners were not even there. And if they judge him deaf or demented or a snob, what will it matter now?

A hollow noise, wood knocking on wood, sounds from inside or from outside the palace he cannot tell. The pen pauses on the page. While he listens, his tongue probes his mouth and discovers the aftertaste of the convent tea. He thinks a ridiculous thought: Why, this day I have had no supper.

He shrugs away the sound. He signs the note *Prista Wetman* and he sets the paper in the middle of the table. From the sill he gathers up the stones, naming them audibly, rolling the sounds lovingly over his tongue: "Dzong. Donggala. Ok Tedi. Susuwora. Wuruf." He distributes them among the pockets of his cassock, where they join with the other, waiting.

The priest gathers his hat and his cane casually, as if he were about to stroll down to Benediction, and he pushes open the door and steps into the welcoming night.

The ructions are Gus Gallant and Wish Butt. They are playing just-tread-on-the-tail-of-my-coat.

The garment is outspread on the road where Gus is after flinging it down. Wish takes the dare and steps right up and jumps on top of it and wipes his feet. But the strange thing is, instead of grabbing Wish in a headlock and throwing him to the dirt, the way the game is supposed to be played, Gus swings his big lumpy palm and gives Wish a Confirmation smack hard against the cheek.

The sound of the smack echoes off the clapboard like a firecracker. Someone in the crowd sings out: "Racket!" Straightaway all the people who are not there already give over their laughing and talking and music, and hurry over and form a ring round the two lads.

Kevin Barron abandons the fringes of the crowd. He snakes through the throng and squats among the agitated feet at the edge of the clearing. His nose smells a stink—it is no one but himself. His trousers are damp and clammy against his flesh. And he is hungry, too, for he was too ashamed of himself to go in the house and have his supper. He was afraid his mother would smell, would know.

Voices cry good-naturedly.

"Go on then. What are you waiting for? Punch him in the gob."

"Pick the eyes out of his head."

"Use them for alleys."

"Show him the four corners."

"Stick his face where his arse is to."

"All right, all right, all right!" That is the squeaky voice of Mr. Casey. Breathless with excitement, the shopkeeper fills the open doorway with his big frame. He sways and clenches his pink fists.

Wish Butt ought to be mad after taking such a cuff, but the strange thing is, he only grins. Like a mummer's falseface getting knocked askew, the blow to his cheek swats away the vacant look that he was born with. He is turned into a different person—a smiler.

Sure, says Kevin Barron to himself, the lads are only having a bit of fun after all.

Wish backs off a couple of paces, and without taking his eyes from Gus he declaims loudly to the mob, "Listen. I'll tell you a true fact. Gallant here, he wants to suck dicks. I bet you didn't know that."

Wish steps forward and for good measure he wipes his feet in the overcoat again, smirking at Gus all the while.

"Isn't that a fact, Gallant? Come on now: confess. Tell us the truth."

Gus Gallant's dark face is twisted strangely. He hisses, "So help me Christ who was fucking crucified, Butt, I'll beat your Jesus teeth down your throat and out your Jesus hole." His bad words choke through welling tears—you would swear he was about to cry. Gus has turned into a different person too. He has become a sooky-baby.

Wish Butt's warped eye makes it hard to tell which way he is looking or what he aims to do next. In the easy manner of a server presenting the priest with the water and the wine, he strolls straight up to Gus Gallant. Overhand he swings his closed fist and it catches Gus square on the nose. The blow lands with the same soft squish that a connor makes when you bang out its brains against the wharf. Kevin Barron has never seen a real punch in the face, and it makes his stomach gurgle with nausea.

Gus staggers. He looks surprised. Blood bubbles red from both nostrils and runs down his chin. It mingles with the tears already flowing there.

"So help me fucking Jesus, Butt," he bawls in a watery voice. "I'll rip your fucking face off and show it to you."

"Shut up, Gallant. You brags about cunt day and night but you never saw a real one in your life. You pock-faced cocksucker."

Kevin Barron knows all the bad words they spew, but he has heard them only in dirty jokes. He does not understand why they bear such power all of a sudden, why they are not followed by laughter, why they make people so angry.

Gus swings with fury and he misses. In dodging the fist Wish trips in his own big boots and tumbles to the ground. While he is down, Gus lays his heel square against Wish's scruff and grinds his mouth hard into the gravel.

A woman mutters, "Now that ain't proper. That ain't proper at all."

"All right! All right!" cries Mr. Casey, wide-eyed, swaying with excitement. "All right!"

Wish rolls away and regains his feet. His face is streaked in dirt and blood. Small pebbles are embedded in his lips.

"Lay into him now."

"Give him an oiling."

"Shellac him shiny."

Goaded by the crowd, they fall again to a straightforward exchange of vicious blows. Kevin Barron wants to watch, but at the same time he feels an urge to run away. These boys are not playing. What they are doing is real, and he is afraid of that.

Wish and Gus stumble over the castnets and get tangled in each other's arms. They totter to the middle of the road, all the while clutching together in an exhausted embrace. They reel over the horse-paddy lying dried in the gravel. Their feet kick it to shreds. Someone starts up a cordene and grinds out a dance.

Two jinkers in our harbour dwell,
Adventuresome and plucky . . .

The crowd laughs and sings. Thank God, Kevin hopes, maybe now they will only skylark after all.

Gus picks up a shovel and swings it like a baseball bat at Wish's head, but Wish ducks the iron and the weapon slips from Gus's hands and clatters across the road. Wish grabs Gus and twists him into the vice of a headlock. Wish swings his free arm again and again, and pounds his fist, blow upon blow, into the region of Gus's eyes. Unawares, to himself, Kevin Barron tallies the blows on his prayerbeads.

Gus squirms loose and steps back a ways to wipe the blood from his face. His head is a mass of gore. His eyes bulge from their sockets in the odd way that Wish Butt's have always done. Wish grins and spits to the gravel a string of blood and saliva. His mouth hangs slack and shows the gap where a tooth is gone.

They hold up their bloodied fists. Each wheels round the other, both wobbly on the legs. They have become savages, all wild and strange and heathen. Their flesh is swollen, their blood is smeared so much it is hard to tell one face from the other.

Wish connects hard, flush on the temple. Gus's head is flung back heavily. Something hot and wet falls upon Kevin Barron's lips. He licks at it and swallows. It tastes like altar wine.

Wish and Gus trade a mad frenzy of punches. One after the other they rain down without letup on nose and cheek and brow and chin and ear and temple. The crowd howls and claps and stamps.

In the middle of the uproar, Kevin experiences an extraordinary thing—a long moment of quiet, a pause, a splendid peace. Within this moment he hears a whisper. The creature, the whispering sinful monster that has been tormenting him so terribly all day long, that followed him the full length of the winter path, is here, right here in this place. . . .

Kevin Barron turns and flees. Down the road, as fast as he can run, he flees from the fearful peace and quiet.

The moonshadows are sharp. The night is warm. Not a spark of wind stirs.

The noise of the crowd comes over the birchtops. From somewhere deep, apparently from under the ground, the sea-waters murmur. They call to him like old friends: the gentle, cognizant whisper from the landwash, the swift, muffled shout from the wharfhead, the long-drawn scream from the Brow—so many good friends are waiting for him.

He sets off down the yard. A stink, as real in the night as an invisible fence, brings him up sharply.

There by the outhouse. A shape skulks.

Howls rip the dark. The priest is startled. He cringes against the wall of the mansion.

It is only the bloody dog. The beast Jackman crouches on its forepaws and growls with menace. It confronts the privy as if the outhouse were about to kick at him.

The door totters ajar by the thread of a single hinge. A figure steps forth. The figure bends close to the dog and whispers in understanding tones. The dog ceases its baying and stands erect and wags its tail and snuffles its snout happily in the damp grass. Reassured, the animal wanders off into the alders.

The old man Johnny staggers clear of the outhouse. Awkwardly he hitches and belts his trousers, and draws snug around his bowed shoulders a ragged overcoat. He pats gently a pocket of the coat, as if the garment sheltered something fragile and precious. Finally he notices the priest.

"F-F-Father Fran! . . ."

Johnny lurches forward and claps his quaking hand on Father MacMurrough's shoulder. The priest is so surprised he almost brings up his stick in defence.

"How are you getting on?"

The old man's stench sears the priest's nostrils. Father MacMurrough recoils from the face that beams up at him, from the ears and nose scarred by flecks of white, the huge mole luxuriant with a clump of dark hair. Moonlight glistens off the bald head. The mouth smiles, but the eyes are mad.

The waters call. The priest wants the old man simply to go away. He wants Johnny, and all the rest of them, to leave him alone, to leave him to the joy of his perfect moment.

But Johnny grips the priest's forearm. The priest feels the hands shivering. The old man wheezes and sputters, "The s-s-sun, she's after setting. But will she rise in the morning? Will she, Father Fran? What do you say to that now?"

Father MacMurrough disengages himself and stands back and considers Johnny the Light as if he were some kind of physical obstacle.

He sighs and he surrenders. Crossly, the way he might speak to a child, he orders, "Wait here."

He retreats to the mansion, to the pantry. He refuses to switch on the bulb, but he gropes in the press and his hands feel along a range of bottles until they find a likely shape. He lifts it down and carries the bottle to the light of the window and brushes the dust from the label: a fifth of Dock.

Johnny stands precisely where the priest abandoned him. He rolls like a vessel in dangerous seas. The old man mutters, "You know, there's l-l-lots like you and me. Lots." It seems to the priest that Johnny is speaking, not to him, but to some other creature that is invisible in the night and, what's more, that the priest is excluded from their mysterious communion. He recalls one of his nightmares: he is at a party where some malicious injunction forbids the other guests speaking with him, yet the door is barred shut, and he cannot escape the horror of it.

As he unscrews the cap and thrusts the bottle angrily at the old man, sarcastically he singsongs, *"Corpus Domini nostri Jesu Christi custodiat animam tuam in vitam aeternam. Amen."*

Johnny seizes the rum and upturns it above his outstretched tongue. The liquor gurgles down his gullet unimpeded, like a river down a highlands gulch. The priest observes the old man's truncated fingers. His mind wanders and he wonders, how much pain do the bound and deformed feet of Chinese women suffer? He is thinking: I will never see the canals of Soochow, I will never see the Venice of China, when suddenly Johnny doubles over in a coughing fit. He hacks and chokes violently, then just as suddenly stands erect, rigid, his eyes glazed, sleepy, as though he is enjoying some mystical vision. He rasps, "I'm t-t-took, Father Fran. Truly I am. I'm took with the de-cline."

Johnny offers the bottle to the priest. "You want a g-g-glutch?"

The priest waves it away. "Keep it. Keep it, my son."

With the heel of his boot Johnny roots a little depression in the gravel. He bends and expertly secures the bottle in the natural coaster. He probes within his coat until he finds tobacco and papers, and the old man sets about the painstaking task of rolling a cigarette.

Father MacMurrough rattles the stones in his pocket. The sea whispers, shouts, screams. He draws forth his own ready-mades and proffers them under Johnny's nose. Johnny is so slow in sorting his own property, and then in accepting the cigarette, that the priest reckons he may as well have one himself. He lights the match, and the two men stand side by side in the moonlight and smoke.

After a few draws on his cigarette Johnny turns to the priest and declares firmly, "We are two be-nighted."

Father MacMurrough has no idea what the old man means by this. Contemptuously he nods towards the bottle and he grunts, *"Yu longlong long wiski."*

Johnny persists. "In the d-d-darkening, you know, we all of us become the one."

The priest listens to the sea. It thunders in his ears like the sound of drums, like the *kundu* drums that in the highlands, in the nights, go thump-thump-THUMP thump-thump-THUMP round great fires lit in the middle of football fields. He imagines the sea in flames.

Imperno. Hell.

To nobody in particular, certainly not to Johnny, he mutters aloud, *"Solwara shor lait."*

Johnny responds, "The w-w-wind, you know, it do be always in my ears. I tell you, the sound of it, it never stops."

"Bik si, fai ya."

The two cigarettes glow in the night. The priest gazes into the east and he notices that the lighthouse is dark. He remembers that this man before him is its keeper. Meanwhile Johnny gapes at the newspaper peeking from the priest's cassock. He blurts, "Father Fran, how's the w-w-war?"

Father Mac Murrough grinds his cigarette into the gravel. He looks directly into Johnny's eyes: it is time. However far away the old man may be, the priest must reach him.

Quietly, deliberately, he speaks. "I must go. Now."

Johnny appears to have heard something, for abruptly his eyes blaze. He grabs up the bottle and takes a long sucking drink, like a ravenous baby drawing on the nipple. He slobbers and drools a bit, then glares into the dark and cries, "Aye, l-l-lads, there! There's our ship!"

His greatcoat billowing, his body and his shadow com-mingling, Johnny in his dilapidated logans proceeds to limp about the yard, zigzagging, halting from time to time as though to gauge his chances, then leaping this way and that, with a child's range and agility that astonish the priest.

Johnny zigzags back to Father MacMurrough and grips him by the arm. Wild-eyed he drags the priest away. "Come on now, lads, they're bringing t-t-tea!"

The priest draws back. But Johnny takes his hand and holds it in a fierce grip, as a parent might hold a child.

The touch of the roughened, leprous fingers against his own — his own ordained and tender — subdues the priest. He gives over his resistance. He will surrender, for a time at least, to this drunken, demented, stinking old man. What, af-ter all, does it matter?

"That's it, l-l-lads. Come along now. Our salvation, our vessel, she stands!"

Johnny the Light draws Father MacMurrough by the hand and hastens the priest down the avenue, down the tun-nel of birch trees shining white in the moonbeams.

Viewed from such a distance, the light spilling from the shop window reminds Kevin Barron of paintings of the Nativity.

He crouches behind the church fence. Under the moon the pickets make a grille of black shadows across the glis-tening grass. Strange sights appear. Shapes that might be leprechauns push barrel-hoops rolling before them. A mum-mer, headless, glides up the road, floating six inches clear of the gravel. In the upper reaches of an ash tree, its heading fixed on the planet Venus, rests a large object that resembles a trap skiff.

Over back — oddly, since no one lives there — a fiddle starts up a jig. When the music stops the boy becomes aware of the sound of the ocean rolling against the landwash. It rumbles like the distant trundle of a long slow train. At the same time he can see the swell glow in a sweeping curve that pushes in towards Admiral's Beach: the sound has become a sight.

The iceberg that is far off in the night waits upon the moon.

A figure lurches up the slope from the beach. When the shape gets closer the boy sees that the creature has two heads. It pitches across the road and makes for the churchyard—in fact, the creature is not one body but two. The pair clutch each other so desperately that they appear to be wrestling.

They stagger through the gate. It is a man and a woman. They weave across the grass to the niche where the nave joins the transept—where the shadows are darkest. One of the figures bends to feel the grass. A male voice makes a foul curse.

They abandon the niche and return, skirting the moonlit wall. Kevin Barron is puzzled: if they are not wrestling, if they are not playing, why do they cling to one another so savagely? The pair slink through the gate and out of his sight round to the churchfront, to the steps. He hears the big door clank open, and shut.

Kevin sits on the sod with his back pressed to the fence. The grass is damp and it makes him shiver. He stares up at the side of the church. The moon and the stars are mirrored in the tall window. He imagines that it is not a reflection at all, but that the glass is transparent—that he is looking straight into God's heaven. He fancies that paradise is sheltered here inside the sanctuary of this simple parish church.

It strikes him that this hallowed window is the very one, the same, that troubled him this morning. His eye traces the plain shape of the frame. Before this moment he has heeded only its message—Saint John the Baptist, alive with

colour—never its contours: the way the shaft levitates skyward and narrows at the top to a soft gentle point. He remembers his unease during the Rosary, his unease at the
sight of his own joined hands. He recalls finally the contours
of the pitcher plant, the lips curling purple round the gaping
maw to come together, to touch, softly, at the tip.

Here at last he confronts it: the shadow, the silhouette, the
shape, of the monster that has been stalking him, that he so
fears.

You know, when I was a little one, on nights like this, when
the cove was as still as mirrorglass and you could see the
stars in the water, he used to carry me down here, where it's
nice and cozy, and he would tell me to listen to the hump-
backs breaching in the dark. . . .

Pardon my babble. I'm getting to be as bad as that woman
herself. She'll be giving me the blade of her tongue tonight,
for staining my best dress. I swear to God I'm turning out to
be more like that one every minute. Some day no doubt I'll
wind up just the way she is. Jesus save me.

Anyway, thank God we are after dodging that racket
and ructions and nonsense. And now here we are. Didn't I
tell you? Didn't I say I knew a cozy dry spot for a sit-
down, out of the way of the damp grass? There's frig-all else
such a mouldy old wreck is good for. And I know other
places too. . . .

Well, praise be to the Lord for granting us the light of the
moon. Such a spectacle it delivers. The ice, it looks like a
bride cake coming right up out of the water. It was only this
Angelus you yourself was standing on that very spot. Hard
to believe, isn't it? —there you were then, here you are now.

Time, it's such a queer thing, isn't it? The past and the
present and the future, they're supposed to come one after
the other, just like that. But sometimes they don't.

All this day I'm after having the strangest feeling. I am

sure, I know, I just *know*, that something is going to happen. It seems like the future is already in the present.

That must be the way the Lord sees all things. God must have a queer in-between feeling always, don't you think? Say He imagines that next Sunday morning after Mass some girl over in Ireland is going to pick a sunflower. Then of course next Sunday morning after Mass, over there in Ireland, it is going to happen just like that: that girl is going to pick that sunflower, no matter what. Even if she would rather pick a shamrock, or a daisy, or a lilac. Or nothing at all.

This day, ever since I got out of bed, that's the way it is for me. The future is in the present. I know—I just know—that something is going to happen.

. . . And here she is at her First Communion. You'd swear she was born in a white dress, that one. No trouble picking her out from the rest: she has got her daddy's eyes. Them great black brows.

Listen.

Can you hear?

Isn't that a mournful sound—a train going by in the night. They says it's a sign of weather, but all it ever puts into my mind is places far away. Places I never been to.

One fine morning, my child, you and me we'll pack up a picnic lunch and we'll take a walk up the country, over back, all the way to the tracks, and we'll wait for the choo-choo to pass us by. Would you like that? Yes, the big train, and then the comical little handcar scurrying along behind it, like a pony behind a mare. Before the summer is out, we'll do that, you and me together.

Dear Lord, but I'm tired. Pray to God the hag will leave me be, this night for once.

Come, my son. It's time to put away the snaps, get you ready for bed. Time to call the hogs. Here, pull on your shimmy shorts, that's a good lad. We'll leave a couple of potatoes out for the faeries. You never know when they'll want to drop in and warm their furry little toes.

We'll turn out the bulb so them millers can have a rest. You come and sit with me here in the window. You hold onto me and I'll hold onto you, and we'll keep each other warm.

Yes, the only thing that matters is company. Isn't that the truth, my duck? You and me together, we'll sit and look out into the dark and we'll watch for the torch.

Here's another twenty-four hours nearer to the boneyard, me and you together. But every night is followed by a day— and don't you ever forget that.

Oh! There's a big yawn. Off you go then, slip off. Slip off on your journey to the sandman. Soon you'll be dead to this world. Soon, not a queak out of you. Soon we'll put you down in your cradle, into your altar of repose.

God bless, child. God bless all we see and all we don't.

At the bottom of the avenue the two men emerge from the birches into the moonlight. They walk hand in hand.

Johnny stops to drink. Although they are distant from the water, although Johnny's foul smell contaminates the air, still the priest's nostrils suck hungrily at the salty tang of brine.

"Come on now, l-l-lads. Hurry along!"

Johnny's flesh is dry and flaky, but the stubby fingers are those of a child. Limping, muttering nonsense, he draws Father MacMurrough through the concrete gateway and onto the road. The moon highlights the bald skull so that if floats before the priest's eyes like a beacon.

Johnny turns right and heads into the west.

On the left, atop the Brow, shapes like monkeys scramble over the growing mound. Even above the laughter from the people the priest can hear the sea. Out of sight beyond the rise of the land, it breathes against the cliffs. His ear magnifies to crashing breakers the mild swell that rolls up the waterline. He enjoys again the same fearful thrill he felt, decades ago, cycling around Slea Head, along the narrow ledge beetling above the Atlantic, the moment he recognized that surrender to the distraction that is Kerry—the fairest place on God's planet—would send him tumbling to an early death. The weight of the stones sagging in his pockets pulls him down, towards the water that he smells, that he hears, but that he cannot see, and it is only a leprous drunken grip that prevents him going over, that saves him from sliding into the infinite ocean.

Johnny bypasses the Brow. He leads onward, up the road.

The windows of the tarpaper shack are dark, but its chimney spews a whiff of foul smoke. Father MacMurrough feels slightly dizzy, and he remembers again the pointless fact that he has gone without his supper. Opposite the old field gun, hazily he senses shadows darting to and fro in the gravel. Some of these figures appear to be headless, others three-legged. Johnny drags him plunging straight into the dusty air that these creatures stir up.

A voice commands, "Stand and deliver."

Johnny hisses, "Hushta!" and the shadows melt and the two continue unmolested on their way.

On the right, a broad meadow glistens with damp. From behind the fence comes a general murmur that sounds like speech in the Irish tongue, but, as far as the priest can make out, the field contains only a few sheep and goats. The animals converge oddly together. A spruce tree at the far end of the enclosure quakes. One a slight rise of land the frame of a half-built house glows like the bones of a skeleton.

The road slides down the slope and into the pit of the marsh. Above the bridge spanning the brook the air is dead and stale. On the left, between the road and the sea, a house snuggles neatly behind a picket fence. Its window, yellow-blinded as though ablaze with corposants, frames the silhouette of a full-rigged barkentine. The house whispers radio static at the night. A little way westward, the abandoned fishflake waits like a funeral pyre. The frame gives off the odour of decayed pine and rotted fish. The priest stares underneath the flake and he can see it at last, washing calmly against the stout legs of the structure — the North Atlantic, black, grandly moonlit.

He understands now those bands of highland Kukukuku. Armed with spears and longbows and six-foot arrows, they would march for weeks across mountains, swamps, the domains of enemy tribes, for no purpose other than to gaze upon the infinite sea, the Pacific Ocean, about which they had heard so many incredible stories.

The mild swell booms against eardrums.

Abruptly, Johnny swings left. On the roof of the saltbox the chair sits vacant and ghostly. Bats wheel against the moon. The old man draws him down some sort of gravel incline. The universe breathes in and out, visibly, like a blacksmith's bellows. The gravel gives way to a boardwalk that echoes underfoot with the hollow thump-thump-THUMP of *kundu* drums. The stars in the southern sky sort themselves dancing into the constellations that, decades ago, his own fancy invented: Gecko, Cuscus, Boar, Skink, and most splendid of all, Raggiana. The stones sag in his pocket like castnet balls. Together the wonderful creatures that live in the stars make a blast and a roar, as if some celestial storm were gathering inside his head.

His feet stumble. He lowers his eyes from the stars so that he can discover the place where he has been taken. He finds that he is beset, on three sides, by the waters of the infinite Atlantic.

Now don't the lilacs smell lovely and purple? The bush, it's still damp from the snow. Here I'll pick you one for your button. Mind, not that I turns up my nose at the sniff coming off yourself now. Always grand, the smell of a fisherman. And a touch of rum just to make it manly—you're having a taste, I can tell.

God knows why I'm bothering with the whispers. A blind man can see the woman is dead to the world. Now, you lean your gun aside here on the woodhorse. I want to show you something. They say it's seven years' bad luck to look at the moon in a mirror. But I says, what odds about all that old witch's malarky.

See! I told you. It looks so big and close, for sure you could reach into the glass and take hold of it. And the stars in back of it, all so handy too. You would think heaven was after falling down to earth. You might say that Holy God Himself was after coming down to walk among us.

With startling agility the old man leaps atop a wharf-grump. He thrusts his arm into the night and joyfully croaks.

"Our ship! She come to b-b-bring us in! Hurry on now, lads!"

The priest crosses to the side of the wharf. He examines the darkness eastward, in the area where Johnny points. He sees only the fang of the Skellig ice.

"Aye, me boys. Yes, h-h-here she be! 'Tis all over! Come along then. They're brewing tea! Hot tea!"

The sea gurgles around the pilings and ballast underfoot. The swell presses up, on each occasion riding slightly higher on the ladder, reaching up as if to gather and draw down. The stones sag in the priest's pockets like a small gathering of deaths.

" 'Tis true, boys! They come for us! Hurry along!"

Something floats down there among the pillars. The wash draws it in and out of the priest's line of sight.

It is a dead gull.

The corpse is entangled in what looks like a shattered kite—sections of splintered bamboo and lengths of snarled line. The beast is horribly mangled and only the head is recognizable. A single eye stares up so that the creature seems to be winking. It seems to be hinting of what waits below: the bleached bones of the thousands of drowned, and among them, the ghouls that gnawed them clean—the flat-fish and eels and jellyfish, and the crabs and lobsters, and the squid and the slimy horned sculpins.

"Our steamer! I spies the tail of the fleet too, every hull clear as day—*Stephano* and *Florizel* and *Bell*. And *Beothic* and *Nascopie* and *Bonaventure*. And *Diana* and *Eagle* and *Kite*. Warm berths! We'll be home d-d-directly, lads."

The priest tries to look down, and down again, past the oily surface and into the dark deep pool of the cove. He wants to behold the sights that the dead gull promises: is it heaven down there, or is it hell? *Antap,* or *imperno?*

The calm however is impenetrable, for it is a mirror. The Milky Way twinkles. A shooting star tickles the swell. The sky undulates invitingly. No undersea horror waits at his feet, but only the three-dimensional texture of the heavens.

The stars yawn towards him, reach out to embrace him, the way a woman might do. His flesh sweats. He is not sure whether he is looking down into a bottomless pit, or looking up into the sky. He glimpses a line of floating coffins. Noises pound inside his head with the relentless thump-thump-THUMP of *kundu* drums.

The moon spirals down upon his head. . . .

In the rectangle of the mirror Michael Barron studies the further rectangle of the kitchen window.

Behind the glass the woman, her face powdered by the moon, sits upright at the table. She is asleep. The infant is curled in her arms.

The white dress that holds the mirror cannot know the image that Michael Barron sees in the glass, yet it reaches an ivory arm — a tumble of dark hair falling — full across the top of the frame as if to shelter the woman, the child too, from whatever terrors this night may bring.

Sweet fluid rolls down his forehead and into his eyes and trickles into the corner of his mouth. His tongue reaches for it. The liquid tastes like molasses.

He props himself on one hand. He finds that he is sitting on the greasy woodwork of the wharfbed.

Why, he nearly fell into the sea.

His eyeglasses dangle from one ear. He straightens them back on his nose. His hat is missing from his head. It has rolled to settle amid a collection of small desiccated fish neatly stacked over there by the corner of the splitting shed.

Johnny the Light is trying to direct the bottle towards the priest's mouth, but instead, clumsily, he drenches the priest's forehead. Father MacMurrough seizes the rum and drinks.

His breathing relaxes. The world swings back into its correct alignment.

He passes the bottle up to Johnny. With his cane he levers himself to his feet. But just as he bends down to retrieve his hat, he topples over again.

Paralysed, helpless, he rolls on his back and croaks, *"Halpim mi? Yu halmpim mi?"*

Johnny crouches and with his corroded hands he slaps at the priest's cheeks.

"Goddamnit, m-m-man. I knows what you wants: you just wants to walk into the water, don't you? Isn't that the truth? Well by the Jesus, you're not going to do that. Not on my watch you're not. No, b-b-by the Christ. What's your n-n-name, my son?"

"Ger," the priest whispers, wearily. "Gerry Mack."

"Listen here, Gerry Mack. You got to keep walking, my son. You got to keep g-g-going. I'm not going to let you stop. I'm the master of this watch and by God I'm in charge. As far as I'm concerned, you can't even pray. Praying is no use anyway. You try to kneel down and pray, Gerry Mack, and you're f-f-finished. Finished."

In this river of words the only sound that the priest hears clearly, the way dogs are said to do, is that of his own name. It recalls to him vague memories, memories revived with the kind of pleasure one might feel upon discovering, in an old photograph album, a childhood portrait.

Michael Barron halts at the screen door. He listens to the voice that speaks outside on the road. The voice is husky, throaty, so palpable he can almost taste the sound it makes.

The voice instructs a clutch of men and boys. They have set down on the gravel the old cartwheel they were hefting, and respectfully they stand and attend. The words are indistinct. After a subdued exchange, with pointing and nodding and noises of assent, they lift the cartwheel and continue in the direction of the Brow.

As soon as they are gone out of sight, she picks up the shotgun and raises it to her shoulder. She takes aim at something above—a bat perhaps, or the moon, or maybe a shooting star. With his right hand in his pocket Michael rattles the empty shells: one, two.

Although the gift he bears in his left hand burns his fingers, Michael is not yet ready to step outside. Instead, he watches through the screen mesh.

He is distracted by the picket fence.

It is the same fence that has always fronted this house.

The palings are the ones that he himself painted only this spring, white with green points. The posts and longers are white. The posts are sunk into cement foundations, and are decorated with plain beachrocks. He could not imagine a plainer sight, a more ordinary thing.

Yet, this moment, the simple everyday fence appears so strange to his eye that it terrifies him. The more he studies it, the more unsettled he becomes. The palings, the posts and longers, the beachrocks, all have adopted a bizarre, monumental quality, a strange texture, as if they have become harder, somehow more real than real.

He can hear behind him in the darkened kitchen Pop's troubled snore. Bundled in his blankets on the daybed, prayerbeads wrapped around his hands, the old man sleeps fitfully. Michael Barron would like to wake his grandfather and look into his eyes and say to him: Pop, help me, for I am far off. I am beyond the ledge. I am outside, farther from shore than I have ever gone. Help me.

From the barrens over back comes the lonely cry of the locomotive. The train is on its night crossing westward. Michael Barron realizes that he has done it after all: he has stepped into that narrow band of certainty that waits between the iron rails. He stands in that dangerous realm, and now the inevitable train of which he has been so sure, that he has felt rumbling deep in his chest, roars down the track — straight towards him.

He takes a breath and pushes open the door, and steps out into the night.

"No, Gerry Mack, my son. You climb to your two f-f-feet right now. And you turn yourself around, and you walk on out of this place. I won't let you stop here. The Lord Almighty, He'll hold me to account for it, but no by God, I won't let you kneel."

Father MacMurrough like a child sits braced against the wharf-grump. Softly he weeps. Johnny towers. The old man's head falls within the semi-halo of the moon.

Johnny sets the bottle on top of the grump. He reaches inside his overcoat and pulls out his cigarette makings, but instead of launching into the task of rolling a smoke, he only arranges these items ritually on the wharfbed. "For Them," he grunts. "In case they wants a p-p-puff."

He slides off his overcoat and folds it gingerly, as though afraid he might cause the garment some injury, and lays the coat on the wharf beside the other items. He stops in order to drink. He carries out this gesture so reverently that, like the Communion of the Blood, it seems to be the core of his rite. He reaches for his cap, but finding that it is not on his head he curses. Clumsily he pulls off his logan boots, then his shirt, finally his trousers.

Johnny stands naked in the moonlight. His pale flesh glows like a luminescent statue. Revealed, as if Johnny has just made his last confession, had just unburdened himself of his life's secret, is the horrible damage that the cold inflicted upon every part of his being.

"There now, lads, I promised you, didn't I? The s-s-steamer, she's after coming for us. With lashings of tea."

The old man carries the rum across to the leeward bow of the wharf. Carefully he sets the bottle on the wharfbed, close to the edge. He turns about and steps backwards and, facing the ladder, he climbs down, expertly, until his head disappears from view. A pair of disembodied hands reach back over the edge of the wharf and retrieve the bottle, then are gone. It would appear that Johnny the Light has stepped straight into the sea.

For a long time Father MacMurrough remains slumped in a stupor. The empty boots on the wharf make him think of a riderless horse. The smell of Johnny's clothes drifts across to him. Like liturgical vestments they smell vaguely of candied liquor.

Something stirs under the coat. It stirs like a small trapped animal, like a creature in panic. After a short time the movement stops, and the fabric lies still—perhaps in his delirium the priest only imagined it.

A steady noise, hollow and wooden, bounces off the stars. It could be the beat of a *kunðu* drum. A voice sings out.

"C-C-Come along now, lads!"

Round the head of the wharf a red punt staggers. Even in the bad light the word *Ra* is legible on the bow. Johnny wields the oars clumsily. Like a ghost he rows into the night. He bears due east, headed for the mouth of the cove.

Michael Barron pushes the doors and steps out. The night hums.

He crosses the yard and passes through the gate in the fence. The gun rests leaning between the picket-points.

On the road, hands clutched behind her back, she waits.

He comes up and steps inside the cocoon that surrounds her. The two occupy a small echoing place in their own space and time, removed from the remainder of eternity. Blood drums against his ears: his heart roars inside his skull. He thinks of that winter when he was a boy, when he built an igloo and spend a brilliant afternoon curled inside its closeness, hypnotized by the bright sunlight that checkered the ceiling.

Reverently, as if it is a chalice, he elevates the gift of the prehistoric blue ice. Her long slender fingers accept it.

Her fingers take the ice at first gingerly, for it is hot. Gently her hands stroke the shaft, studying its shape and feel, its weight. Her fingers become wetted. Her eyes are fixed unblinking upon the object.

Her hands lift the ice to her ear. Her ear listens. Her eyes smile. Her hands draw the ice across her forehead and cheek. Meltwater glistens and traces the silhouette of her face, the folds of her lips, the curve of her throat. The water forms pools in her perfect flesh and trickles like tears, like blood. Her lips are moistened and slightly parted, as if about to speak.

But they do not speak. Instead, he discovers that a creature is moving inside his palm. It shivers like a small frightened bird.

Her bones are thinner than his own, her skin softer. At first her fingers are wet and cold, but he shifts his own fingers and intertwines them in hers, and before long her flesh has warmed in his.

Her fingers tug at his and draw his hand, his arm, his whole body towards another place. With his free hand he picks up the gun, and they go.

They go towards the east. He has no idea why he is being drawn in that direction. He feels like Cabot, or the Vikings, or Saint Brendan, sailing over the horizon, into the unknown, into mysterious waters where anything might happen. But he has no fear any more of these unknown places, because the simple touch of her hand is his true destination, and he has already arrived.

XVIII

Capelin

Brimstone scrapes flint, and the flame like creation's spark flares from the void.

Disembodied hands cup the match. The fingers blush with the soft crystal transparency of a vigil candle. They uplift the flame in offering.

Father MacMurrough twists his newspaper to a cylinder. He holds it against the tongue of flame until the paper catches. He wields the torch blazing above his head and he circles the pyre. In his other hand he bears his cane, and here and there he pokes at the mound of debris, probing. He finds a roll of tarry felt and he bends and inserts the flare into its core.

For the troubling span of a breath the night is darkened again, primaeval, the flame extinguished. But presently, licks of blue fire dart. Luminous plumes of smoke shoot from the folds and crevices. The felt bubbles and sizzles and pops. The light reddens the pressing crowd that has been, in the priest's mind, only a vague presence, a shadow, but that now presses close. He can feel upon his flesh the hot bolt of ignition. The people cheer and whistle.

The heat mounts and forces Father MacMurrough to retreat. The crowd claps in a second wave, but this time it is for him that they cheer.

His face brightens uneasily. The heat warms the unfamiliar dimples of his smile. The flame betrays the trail of the dried salt tears across his cheeks. As the shouting fades his tears well once more, and to hide them he removes his spectacles and pretends to rub at his eyes.

The fat man who supplied the match — it is the blacksmith — comes up and peers intently into the priest's face. Behind him a wiry friend carries a stone jug. It is the man who repairs the road.

"Here, Father," says the thin man. He is drunk. "Have a swig. Monkey rum. The real shine."

The priest takes hold of the jug. Heartily the two men slap him on the back, then turn aside from the priest to watch the inferno.

Father MacMurrough drinks. The liquor slides down his throat to his hollow stomach and settles there, a little hearth fire warming his midsection pleasantly. He allows himself to be mesmerized like the others, ravished, by the spectacle of the fire.

The flames bound across the surface of the pile. Like the celebrant at Communion, elevating the Host before receiving, the fire illuminates for adoration those holy things it will presently consume: splits and junks and shavings and sawdust plus the woodhorse that produced them, swish barrels, staves from blubber puncheons, barrow-tubs bearing rotted cod traps, aromatic blasty boughs and stanchions fallen off dilapidated fishflakes, raggedy sails, broken paddles, the handle of a shovel, a killick stone with frame and lashings, lobster pots trailing moorings and buoys, ancient castnets, old maps of the world, a shattered length of bamboo, a dead gull and a dead lamb, Jamaica fish, a wet gunnysack containing a brick and six drowned kittens, parched cowpaddies, cigarette butts, horse tackle, articles of ladies' underwear with pegs and lines attached, pickets and fenceposts and longers, a workable gate, shingles and clapboard, a half-gallon of indigo paint, cans of kerosene, a tar-mop, feathers by the pillowcase, seal bones, winter sleds, ice skates, a baseball naked and unravelling, the face of a grand-father clock, a smashed crystal set, scribblers and exercise books and school uniforms, a pair of trigger mitts, leaky wellingtons and gaiters, tattered oilskins, a janney's false-face, spectacles, one small blue box, a kitchen table with oil-cloth and matching chairs, floor canvas, a chesterfield suite, a headboard and mattress, mildewed blankets, window cur-tains, the frame of a mirror, countless brooms, Popsicle sticks assembled into cat's-cradle shapes, candle stubs, apple seeds, a half-eaten loaf of bread, two dogeared decks of play-ing cards, postage stamps, old newspapers, last year's calen-dars and almanacs, a spinning wheel, a child's tooth, bloody rags, bingo cards, nappies, three toilet seats made of pine, wooden prayerbeads, a leatherbound Bible. . . .

Fire wings creep laterally and embrace the pedestal. When the flames meet on the far side, for a time they sit, and wait, and lay siege upon the peak. Then begins the assault.

The drayman and the forgeman and a crowd of their drunken mates wink among themselves and turn and disap-pear into the dark. Father MacMurrough is left alone with the jug.

The flames crackle and hiss, ping and snap. Each sound is small, but together they rumble like a hurricane. The fire erupts in a pandemonium of smells — of tree-sap and stale rum and mackerel and seal fat and tar and manure and bone. Curtains of wild smoke flee the debris and, sucking up the very earth, hurtle vertically, spiralling billowing towards the stars, white and crimson and purple, pursued by flankers of faery-lightning. The scalding fire pushes back the crowd. Under the shifting light every face glows demon-red.

A six-foot fencepost, ablaze its length, topples from the summit and rolls down the pile. It comes to rest in the space between the fire and the crowd. A pair of janneys step forward and run at the burning stick. They wear grand-mother's rags. Their faces are veiled in lengths of lace as dirty as old fishnets. They run and lift their skirts and leap. The flames flash briefly on their grown-up female thighs. The priest feels his body stir.

In the hoopla both veils fall askew and the janneyfaces are stripped—they are the two children who visited the church this morning. The men and the boys clap and whistle.

"Come on, Alice, my darling. Give it to her."

"Higher now, Moira. That's the way."

Other young women in falseface join the circle. Mean-while, a half-dozen lads raise burning sticks, torch-fashion, and gallop on make-believe horses round the rim of the fire, in both directions, all the while screaming like savages. They dare with one another to dodge the fire or else to skirt the cliff edge, the vertical drop to the sea that is somewhere here in the dark, close. The married women cheer and bang upon their pots and pans and buckets. The husbands pass round jars of spruce beer. An old man strikes up a cordene. The old women clap their hands and stomp their feet. A gleeman picks up the tune, and presently all the people bellow at the top of their lungs.

> *There was birch rine, tar twine,*
> *Cherry wine and turpentine . . .*

Father MacMurrough does not know the words, but he pre-tends to sing.

> *Jowls and cavalances, ginger beer and tea,*
> *Pig's feet, cat's meat, dumplings boiled up in a sheet . . .*

At the convent, upstairs, seven faces stare out into the night from seven darkened windows. They try to make sense of the silhouettes they see dancing against the glow of the fire. They try to make sense of the sounds they hear.

The young people start up a kissing train. Growing as new mouths are kissed, the chain weaves among the mob, now and then doing a circuit of the fire, dodging the smouldering tar-barrels and the straw scarecrows that the little boys launch into the flames.

But no sooner does the train come apart from its own sheer size than the youths, complaining of the heat, begin to drift off, to cooler, darker places. Along the way they sort themselves into couples. The married women watch them go, and grin and bang on their pans and their buckets. A few urchins dog them. The grown-ups and the children who remain by the fire carry on with the tune:

> *There was Dan Milley, Joe Lilly,*
> *Tantan and Mrs. Tilley . . .*

On the west side of the parish, a woman raises her head sleepily from the kitchen table. She looks out the window at the big fire burning in the night. To the infant slumbering in her lap softly she hums:

> *There was Bill Mews, Dan Hughes,*
> *Wilson, Taft, and Teddy Roose . . .*

A large coffin-like structure sails high out of the dark. It is borne atop the shoulders of six men. The crowd roars.

The men heave the object end over end into the fire, where it lands with a convulsion of flankers and smoke. The lid falls from its hinges and clatters to the ground. The eerie gloss of a crescent shines in the firelight.

Jim Fling, Tom King,
And Johnson, champion of the ring . . .

The priest hesitates a moment. Then he sets down the jug
and the cane, and he comes forward and lifts the fallen door
and propels it like a caber to the top of the pyre. A cheer
goes up from all voices. The fat man and the thin man and
all their friends slap the priest hard on the back and shout
drunkenly into his face.

"Not to worry, Father. We'll put up a new one for you."

"First thing in the morning."

"In time for your morning roost."

"A two-holer if you wants, Father."

Two large women take him by the arms and swing him
around in the lancers until he is dizzy.

A mile distant, in a place beyond the houses, amid the aroma
of swelling blueberries, and the noise of the crowd floating
gently across the water, and the hollow sound of oars drum-
ming on gunnels, a husky voice hisses into an ear: "Kiss me."

Johnny the Light has forgotten that he fears the sea.

In the beginning, he rows so clumsily that his paddles
stumble even on the calm. Now and then the oarbutts slip
from his maimed hands altogether. But soon his arms recall
the ancient rhythm, and the punt glides smoothly towards
the east.

As he arrives broadside the Brow his good ear picks up,
between the rumblings of the oars, voices singing. His eyes
detect sparkles of light dancing on the waters. Presently the
bonfire itself floats into his gaze.

The great flame, majestic on the height of land, flashes as
brilliantly as the sanctuary lamp. The sight makes his tongue
recall the taste of the sacramental wine. He drops the oars
and reaches for the rum that he stored in the midship-room,

and he drinks. He imagines that the flame warms his naked body. He stares into the fire until it hypnotizes him, until the whole universe spins round the hub that it forms. He hears the voices singing and his mind mixes up the two, so that he fancies the voices are coming out of the fire itself.

Jim Brine, Din Ryan, Flipper Smith and Caroline;
I tell you boys, we had a time . . .

The old man throws back his head and joyfully he howls:

At the Kelligrews soiree.

His nostrils flare at the lovely smell of burning tar. He lines up the stern with the bolt of light on the sea, and paddles directly away from the fire, straight and true towards the mouth of the cove.

As the boat moves offshore the voices fade. Johnny hears instead the mournful call of the night train making its slow journey across the interior barrens. Underneath that sound he hears too, in the swell breathing against the foreshore, a dreadful lament.

The moon threatens over his shoulder. Now he can hear, deep in the sky, the music of the spheres—the cosmic octave. Time comes unhinged for Johnny the Light. As far as he is able to tell, this day could be yesterday. This year could be a million years in the past. For all he can say, his soul already has passed into eternity.

Abreast the graveyard his nose catches a succulent blueberry fragrance wafting off the slopes. It is then that he feels under the hull the sweet lifting and swelling, as if just below the calm some great ponderous creature were passing him by, drawn by eternal instinct to the shore. And his nose catches something else again—a heavy odour, saltier even than the smell of the sea. The old man smiles. From the depths of his memory it returns to him: the smell of his own sperm.

Amid the milky salty taste of something soft flicking against the teeth, then against the tongue, amid the pulse pounding behind the ear and the fragrance of swollen blueberries and the lone voice shouting something somewhere, the ice slips from the grip of the slender fingers. The flaming ice falls against the land and it smashes there into a thousand diamonds.

Kevin Barron feels his way from pew to pew.

He is drawn by a whisper. By a hissing, groaning, creaking. It comes from the east transept. Could someone be praying? At such an hour as this?

Even though this is the same sound, the same murmur that has followed him all day—even though he is afraid—he tiptoes up the Epistle-side aisle, towards the front of the church.

He peeps round the corner and into the east transept.

The light from the bonfire shimmers through the stained-glass windows. Nobody kneels at the shrine. No one sits in the pews. But the groaning persists. The boy searches the dark corners.

Over there.

Under the rickety stair leading to the gallery, two figures lean close against the wall. They could be statues, some timeless scene preserved in plaster. They could be something holy.

But the hands make movements. They tug with small, urgent, frantic gestures. They reach and clutch and hold. Never has the child seen such a thing as the way these hands move. He does not understand what it means. It is no game—that much is clear to him. But what is it they want?

One of the voices—a female's—whispers.

The child has heard the simple phrase often, in the school-yard or on the wharf, even sometimes on the church steps. He does not know what the words mean, only that they are foul. He himself has never dared to pronounce them, even within the privacy of his own soul, and he cannot imagine why they are spoken here in this holy place, and in such a pleading way. The words seem to have a flesh of their own, to be solid, visible, suspended in the air before his eyes, so real that he might reach out his hand and take hold of them.

The bonfire flares. The burst of light shows briefly, like a photo-flash, the thick leg cocked up, the black seam running up the thigh, the downcast eyes, and then the sad, slack-jawed, faraway face that he knows.

Johnny the Light passes beyond the dark place in the night where his lighthouse is.

As he proceeds through the cove's mouth and into open water, his ear picks up the sad call of a steamer. The vessel is rounding the Fogo, on its way north. Up and down the long shore, other fires reveal themselves to him, emerging one by one around the corners in the coast. Although mere pinpoints, the lights swell in his failing eyes. The calm re-flects the flames so that he sees twice as many fires. He imagines that the land from the shoreline all the way back to the interior hills is alight.

He rests the paddles and picks up the bottle and drinks what is left in it. His mind recalls seeing, in his youth on the Banks, on the night of the Feast of Saint John, the White Fleet, every vessel hoisting burning barrels to masthead, and he imagines now that that flotilla is here again, here behind him, that not only the full of the land but the open Atlantic too is a sea of flames, that all the world is embraced by fire.

He drops the bottle overboard and it sinks with a gurgle. He shivers in his nakedness and he takes up the paddles.

Little Kevin Barron, surpliced and soutaned, tiptoes across the carpet on his way back to the sacristy. The child's thin arms quiver under the burden of the candlelighter he bears hoisted before him.

Behind him in the nave linger echoes from the crash of the big door. The candles blazing on the main altar and on the side altars, and the vigils before the shrines, all join with the moonglow and the firespark glimmering through the stained-glass windows, and the sanctuary lamp itself, to light and warm and sanctify every last corner of God's holy church.

A sickening crack like the sound of raftering ice sunders the deep. Johnny the Light lifts the blades from the water and allows the punt to drift. He cocks his good ear.

Above the dribble falling from the blades, there comes from somewhere behind him a lonesome cry—the moan of a widowed mermaid. So near! Yet the old man doesn't bother turning to look, for by now his eyes can see nothing anyway.

He senses underneath the boat something large and cold and sinister, a dark glowing presence stretching wide below, and seeking to enfold him. A shadow chills his spine. He smells a blue voltaic hum.

He rows towards the chill. Before long he feels the bow break through a feeble stretch of mush and lolly.

Soon, very soon, he will have his hot tea.

Brave boys yank flaming sticks from the pyre. They carry the torches to the edge of the cliff and wave them at the water, as though signalling to some lost mariner. They run down the slope to Admiral's Beach and wade out to the limit of their long rubbers and flourish the torches in circles just above the surface. They gather driftwood and ignite satellite fires, like beads on a rosary, up and down the landwash.

Father MacMurrough steps unsteadily to the precipice. He raises his right hand and makes the sign of the cross upon the swelling cove and he speaks: *"Our Lady of Perpetual Help, Star of the Sea, grant thy Son to sanctify these waters and deliver unto us His blessings."*

Instantly from the beach a boy shouts: "The capelin!"

The people on the Brow take up the cry.

"They sprauged!"

"The scull!"

"They struck in!"

Casey sounds his bait horn. All hands abandon the blaze and hurry down to the strand. The men shoot their weapons into the air, reload frantically, shoot again. The Gunner fires off his great belching powder musket.

The calm boils with little fish. From the shoreline all the way to the edge of the dark, millions of silvery smelt churn the water. They heave and surge up onto the beach and ejaculate into the sand and the landwash is wet and sticky and luminescent with their seed.

Time is short and no one bothers with boats.

Men march far out onto the shoals, bearing castnets folded over the left arm and gripped in the teeth. They stop, scan the water, then with the right hand, flick the nets abroad. The nets unfurl, spinning like diaphanous jellyfish, and drift down softly onto the water. The men yank drawstrings, and tuck and gather, and drag out of the sea great dripping sacks of smelt. They dump the fish into boxcarts, wheels immersed to the axles, the horses on dry land, then dash back into the deep for another cast. Meanwhile women and boys and girls charge to their armpits in the congealed sea. Using dipnets, or galvanized buckets with bottoms drilled to form crude sieves, or garden shovels, they launch the fish straight from the wash and heave them into floating tubs and barrows. Even tiny children wade as far as they dare and collect the fish bare-handed and stuff their pockets full.

Father MacMurrough marvels at the scene before him: all this has happened before, he reckons, perhaps a million times during this eternity.

He is left alone with the fire. His eyes spy within the flames all manner of people: the monks of Skellig, Viking marauders with their horrible battle-hatchets, a band of New Guinea Kukukuku, a nun in tears, a laughing red-bearded man swinging a blackthorn muckle, a young woman pirouetting in a billowing white dress, an old madman naked and maimed. . . .

The priest turns from the fire. His eyes remain engorged with light and temporarily he is blinded. Nonetheless, swaying on his feet, he gropes to the edge.

One by one, he retrieves the stones from his pocket and drops them into the calm. As his fingers let each one go, he names it with its own name, all the way to the stone that is named Paradise. He listens for the guttural sound of a deadman's bubble that each stone makes. The priest is sure that he can see, despite the dark, the water circles widen and perish.

Joyously the bells ring from the church.

As if God had clapped His hands, the capelin vanish.

The sea is empty.

The people make their way out of the water. As they leave, one or two dip forefingers into the sea, as if it were a font, and cross themselves. The youngsters scour the beach for tiny flapping shadows. Gradually, drawn by the heat, the parish wanders back to the crown of the Brow, and reassembles round the fading fire.

The people squat close to the flame. They skewer the little fish on lengths of wire. They roast them to a crisp and eat them in one bite, whole.

Once more six men appear out of the dark, shouldering once more a coffin-like object. This time the load they carry is a rotted, buff-coloured dory. A hush subdues the crowd. Solemnly the men lay the boat on its nose and topple it into the fire. One or two people make the sign of the cross, others follow. A drunken little rat-faced man cackles, "Burn yer boats, boys!" but other voices, mortified, order him to silence. The fire scorches the paint from the vessel and turns it black. Rapidly the dry wood catches and burns.

Father MacMurrough notices the young couples. They stagger flushed and groggy from the shadows. Reluctantly, sheepishly, they drift back towards the light. When the priest raises his hand and bestows upon the youths his blessing, he realizes that he is drunk.

From the direction of the church a solitary figure weaves among the couples. It is Kevin Barron. The child looks lost and frightened. He stares in a wide-eyed way at the lovers, as if they terrify him. Perhaps they do, the priest says to himself. Perhaps the boy suspects the existence of that monster, the beast that lies in wait for us all, that will devour even the boy himself, during that long night—which is coming to him soon—when he learns just what it is to be alone.

The priest hears a noise and he turns back to the fire in time to see the dory's skeleton crumble into ashes and smoke.

The stairs groan.

The eight-day grandfather ticks and tocks.

The crucified Christ sanctifies with his gaze the stove, and the splits and chunks and coal behind the firebox, the poker on the damper, the sad-iron, the nursing rocker drawn up to the oven, the wellingtons, the new broom, the galvanized gully, the kerosene lamp and the bare bulb, the brown radio, the Doyle's calendar June 1947, the yellow teeth drowned in the yellow mug, the sailcloth couch, the Dodd's alma- nac, the two decks of cards shuffled together, the pile of snapshots face down, the prayerbeads and missals, the har- monica, the fish and brewis cold on the plate, the butter dish and molasses bowl and milk jug and biscuit box and jamjar, the sunflowers blazing on the wall.

Overhead, the bed creaks restlessly, but soon the house falls silent.

Lads bellow, "Get out from that now!" Nimbly they propel through the mob a cartwheel ablaze with oily rags. They roll it into the pyre, now much levelled, where it topples over and causes an explosion of sparks. The rags bring the fire quickly to crescendo.

Above the roar the people hear a long-drawn thunderroll, followed by the rush of cascading water, like the sound of a dam coming apart. They shade their eyes and try to see into the night.

"The berg! She's turned."

Sure enough, the place in the night where the ice used to glow is black.

Father MacMurrough remembers something. He steps round the curve of the hill and retrieves the bundle he hid there. Solemnly he tosses into the fire the boots and the ragged old coat and all the rest. For a time they do not burn, as though the fire is reluctant to accept them.

A gunshot comes from the vicinity of the graveyard. The people turn in that direction and wait. Soon, a fireburst lights the sky as briefly as might a shooting star, and a few seconds later the blast sounds again. The gunshots together establish the slow measure of a knell.

———

By the time a slight swell creeps up the landwash and retreats, rattling the pebbles slightly, the people on the Brow
are too tired and too sleepy to pay any notice.

Children take fathers by the hand and drag them home.
The young couples with baby carriages, the women about to
give birth, the old men who must be carried, all of these drift
homeward, their way lit by lanterns.

The ragged band that is left cuddles up to the fire.
No more fuel remains to be thrown on, and the flames are
fading.

A voice sings:

> *When sun-rays crown*
> *Thy pine-clad hills,*
> *And summer spreads her hand . . .*

Other voices one by one take up the anthem.

By the time the verse is finished the people crouch close
within the cocoon of light and heat. A chill shivers their
backs. Something cold lurks behind them in the dark, something terrible and dangerous. They know it, and they shift
closer to the dying fire. They watch the white smoke rising
into the sky, rising towards the far reaches of the stars, and
during the short time that is left in this night they will conspire to pretend.

Together they will make believe that the monster is only a
fable, only a fancy, that it is not really there at all.

Epilogue

The grey gives the dawn the texture of aspic.

The old woman pokes among the ashes. Her stick stirs up wisps of smoke. Like ghosts they swirl about her shawl before the wind carries them out to sea.

Soon she loses interest in the remains of the fire. Instead she stares towards the sea. She expects to see something there.

But the horizon is empty.

Abruptly the old woman abandons the pyre and makes her way down to the beach.

The tide is out. The landwash is littered with white bergy bits. Even in the low light they give off a spectral glare. More of them float shoreward, oddly in the face of the wind.

The old woman hobbles along the wetted sand. Three crows feed viciously on the stiffened corpses of the capelin. The birds do not fly away but only step aside, briefly, while she passes.

She stands in the wetted landwash and she looks out to sea. Soon — even in the face of the wind — the thing she waits for will drift ashore. And she will claim it at last.